A Hundred Suns

Also by Karin Tanabe

The Diplomat's Daughter

The Gilded Years

The Price of Inheritance

The List

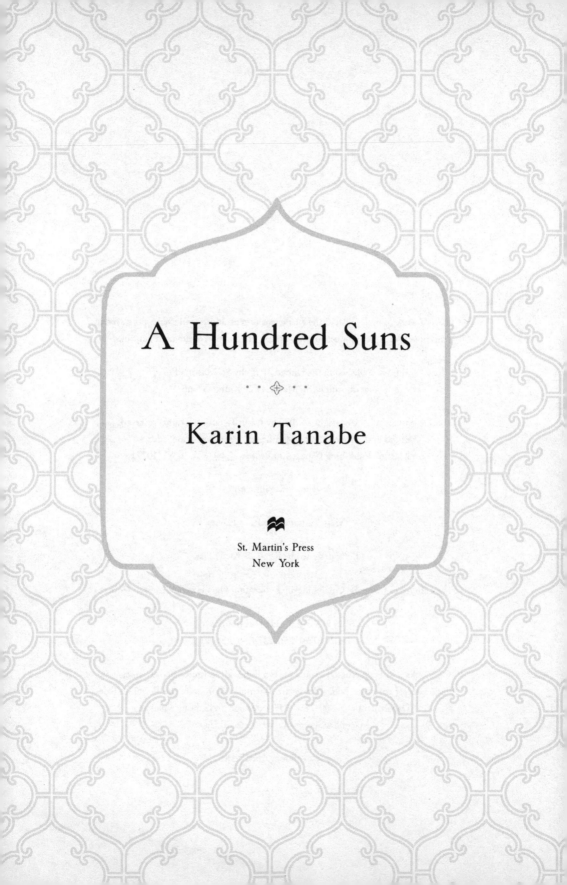

A Hundred Suns

· · ✧ · ·

Karin Tanabe

St. Martin's Press
New York

First published in the United States by St. Martin's Press,
an imprint of St. Martin's Publishing Group

A HUNDRED SUNS. Copyright © 2020 by Karin Tanabe. All rights reserved.
Printed in the United States of America. For information, address
St. Martin's Publishing Group, 120 Broadway, New York, NY 10271.

www.stmartins.com

Map illustration by Rhys Davies

Book designed by Michelle McMillian

The Library of Congress Cataloging-in-Publication Data is available upon request.

ISBN 978-1-250-23147-5 (hardcover)
ISBN 978-1-250-23149-9 (ebook)

Our books may be purchased in bulk for promotional, educational, or business use.
Please contact your local bookseller or the Macmillan Corporate and Premium Sales
Department at 1-800-221-7945, extension 5442, or by email at
MacmillanSpecialMarkets@macmillan.com.

First Edition: April 2020

10 9 8 7 6 5 4 3 2 1

For Daphne. May you always shine
as bright as a hundred suns.

A Hundred Suns

Jessie

November 20, 1933

The house of a hundred suns. That's what my *tai xe* called it. The first time he ferried me to the train station, in a black Delahaye 134 as polished as a gemstone, he slowly circled the building, avoiding the rawboned rickshaw drivers. I craned my neck, watching as the car's exhaust left a trail behind us like a mollusk's track, and tried my best to concentrate on his words, not the quick tempo of my heart.

"When I was young," Lanh explained, moving his white-gloved hands to the top of the large metal steering wheel, "the government posted hand-painted advertisements all over the city boasting that railroad construction was booming and that one day the country would have one hundred train stations. I promised myself that I would visit every single one in my lifetime. There were several versions of the advertisement, with different stations featured, but all of them had a bright, many-rayed sun painted at the top. I used to trace those suns with my hand when I passed the posters on my way to school, as the government was kind enough to put them in the poorer neighborhoods, too."

He turned the car smoothly, his voice quietly laced with enthusiasm. "But as you can see, all roads, even railroads, begin right here. Hanoi.

Even if they build a hundred suns in Indochine, this will always be number one. That's why it gets to be the house, the orb. The rest are simply rays."

"How many have you visited so far?" I asked.

"Thirteen," he replied. "But I'm still quite young."

He cleared his throat and in his pleasant baritone added, "I once told a Frenchman that I called this station the house of a hundred suns, and he laughed in my face. He said, 'Lanh, don't be fooled by appearances. Most of those train stops that the government boasts about are in the middle of nowhere and have a train go through every three days at best. The sun shines on them, but they're also full of malaria and poverty. The rest of Indochine is not like Hanoi.' He called Hanoi 'a city kissed by the French.' He said that the French had brushed their lips against Saigon as well, but that the rest of the country was still waiting to be kissed."

Lanh shifted his grip and said, "I don't see it that way, *madame*." He caught my eye in the rearview mirror and smiled. It was unexpected, since as a good chauffeur, he knew to keep his gaze on the road and not on his employer or, worse, his employer's wife. But Lanh must have sensed that on that particular day I would appreciate the personal connection and wouldn't mind a breach of etiquette.

"Those iron tracks mean freedom. They mean a life away from the one you were born into," he said softly. "You'll see. It will grow in importance to you. The house of a hundred suns. *Nhà Trăm Thái Dương,* as I say in my language."

I had only been in Indochine for thirty-three days, having arrived from Paris on the first Saturday in September 1933, after a month-long endurance test of a trip, including a four-day sandstorm in the Suez Canal and the dark, shark-dotted waters of the vast Indian Ocean. But on that sun-soaked day in Hanoi, alone with Lanh, it was not my arduous journey to the Orient but my new life that was weighing on me.

Since arriving in the bustling colonial city with my husband, Victor, and our little daughter, Lucie, I had barely left the inviting neighborhood where we lived. The streets were wide and welcoming, and all our neighbors were French. But after a month had ticked quickly by, Victor decided that I'd had more than enough time to get used to Indochine—the singsong tones of the language; the rush of the rickshaws, or *les pousse-pousse*, as the French called them, as they zigzagged along the avenues en masse; the tan faces shaded by conical hats; the sea of black eyes when they peeled their hats off; the places where the French went to avoid all of it—and that I should see the country outside Hanoi.

The city of Haiphong, to the east of Hanoi, on the coast, was a fine place to start. It was where our boat had come to port and wasn't entirely foreign to me. The train journey took only six hours, and the first-class cars were touted as luxurious, matching the comfort of any in Europe. French Indochine was our home now, Victor reminded me. It could be for some time—three years, perhaps. Or if he did well in his position, overseeing the vast Michelin rubber plantations in the south in Cochinchina—one of the five French colonies and protectorates that made up Indochine—then perhaps even longer. I couldn't just spend my time in the house, even if it was lovely.

Our house was painted yellow ochre, set off by dark green shutters on every window, and the sun seemed to be drawn to it, turning the walls gold as it sank in the late evenings. Inside, the rooms were painted a vanilla white and the floors were dark gray and white patterned encaustic tiles, each measuring nearly two feet across. The four staircases were marble, with curved iron railings, and there were balconies or terraces on every floor. The imposing architecture was softened by the comforting whispers of servants who seemed to float through the halls like spirits, their black-and-white raw silk and muslin garments billowing slightly as they hurried from room to room.

I had wanted Victor to accompany me on the trip to Haiphong, but in the end, I traveled alone.

"You'll feel the country more that way, anyhow," Victor had said.

Two hours after sunrise, on that October day, Lanh drove me to the Hanoi train station on the route Mandarine. It was an elegant building, constructed from gleaming white limestone and marble, wide and long like a birthday cake, with an elaborate facade. A central clock watched over it all, ticking soundlessly. To Lanh it may have been the house of a hundred suns, but with its French Second Empire style, it felt like a sliver of Paris to me. That feeling of home—as Paris had been my home for eight years—along with the idea of Lanh's suns warming me, had helped me slip out of the car and onto the train with a brief surge of confidence.

Earlier that morning, after a breakfast of fried eggs and rice, I had dressed in the outfit chosen for me by my servant Trieu, and the hat she had topped it off with was a flat-brimmed affair in a cheerful geranium red, with only a thin similarly colored ribbon for adornment. It was a shade that a very confident woman would wear, she said. I felt like an impostor in it.

Of course, my husband was right. That train trip had brought me a changed perspective of Indochine and had helped me understand how I could define my role as the wife of a Michelin in the colony. It also introduced me to the vast countryside, the stretches of verdant land that existed between cities. It was the parts of the country that the French neglected to change that were the most charming, I observed. I devoured the landscape from the half-open train window, losing myself in the hypnotic churn of the heavy iron wheels, taking in the local stations, all curved and molded in the French aesthetic, imagining Lanh ticking them off a list he'd penned as a child. In the weeks following the trip, those images had also helped pacify me when I was exposed to the country's darker elements.

The geranium-colored hat had become a good-luck charm. This November morning, I had placed it on my head again. Victor, Lucie, and I—as a family—were taking the train a bit down the coast to Vinh, a town near Cua Lo Beach. Victor said it was a wide white-sand beach, one of the best in Indochine, and was dotted with large villas built by the French. In two days, we were to meet Victor's young cousin Roland and his family, who were in from Clermont-Ferrand, the seat of the Michelin factories in central France. They were not Lesages like us. They were Michelins. The family was considering staying in Indochine for a month or two, and we were tasked with showing them the best of the country. In his letter to us, Victor's uncle Édouard—who was in truth his mother's cousin, but always called uncle out of respect—had made it clear that Roland and his family were to fall in love with the colony at once, as his nephew had found trouble in France in the form of an expensive, press-seeking mistress. He wanted Roland to disappear overseas for a stretch. He also wanted him to find a much cheaper mistress in the process, preferably one that knew very little French, apart from the dirty words.

"Best behavior," I said to Lucie as her servant, her *thi-ba*, bathed her.

Lucie tilted her head back for Cam to rinse it and closed her eyes, bracing herself in the long, claw-foot tub. "You're not allowed to speak English to me when we are on best behavior," she rightly pointed out.

"I'm well aware," I said, rubbing my eyes. I sat on the little pink chaise in the corner and inspected the white dress Cam had pressed for Lucie. When we had first arrived, the servants had consulted me about all of Lucie's clothes and diversions, but I soon learned that they knew much more about how rich little French girls should dress and act in the colony than I did. Seeing me touching the dress, Cam asked if it was to my liking—a mere formality, we both knew. I smiled and nodded, thinking for a moment about the shapeless, stained clothes I had worn as a girl. They were always too big—dark and practical dresses, pants rolled up at the hem so they would last for years instead of months. I had hated them. I touched Lucie's traveling dress, fingering the starched cotton skirt and white satin waist bow.

Just an hour later, Lucie was in her dress, trying not to crumple it, as we made our way in the Delahaye to the house of a hundred suns. Her dark hair was brushed and plaited, with white satin ribbons at the end, tied up in stiff bows that stood a chance of surviving the twelve-hour train trip ahead of us.

I told her to stop fussing and she inched closer to me, fanning out her skirt around her. I gazed out the window, pretending to observe the only other car gliding down our street in our quiet neighborhood, but I was mentally going through every ensemble Trieu had packed for me, making sure they were fashionable enough in the face of the Michelin fortune. Victor was a Michelin through his mother, Agathe. We were Michelins, too, he reminded us. But we weren't those Michelins. We weren't the ones directly descended from the Michelin et Cie founders, brothers Édouard and André Michelin. The pair had taken over the then fifty-year-old family rubber business in the 1880s and reinvented it. Michelin went from making small rubber items and farm machinery to popularizing the rubber bicycle tire, putting their rubber on the first automobile to run on pneumatic tires, creating the Michelin guides so no one had to eat or sleep badly on their journeys—they even built the first paved runway, and during the Great War helped the government design a plane and assisted in building nearly two thousand Breguet aircrafts in their Clermont-Ferrand plant. But Victor, and I, had been kept at more than arm's length from these activities for years. Unlike most of the family, we'd never been perched at the seat of company activity in Clermont-Ferrand, where the family and all their employees made the rubber tires spin. We were trying to change that with our efforts in Indochine. Édouard had told Victor that if he succeeded in the colony, then he could succeed anywhere, even in Clermont-Ferrand.

The evening dresses my servant and I had selected could be a problem, I worried. I'd been losing weight the last few months and had been afraid to try them on before packing them, not wanting to know if they were loose in the bust. But now I was angry with myself for such stupidity. The Michelin women were always so beautifully turned out, wearing the latest fashions from Paris, even though Clermont-Ferrand was miles from the capital, and I, with my American sensibility, never seemed to choose the right thing, even with the generous budget Victor provided.

I let my breath out slowly, desperate to calm my nerves, and tried to concentrate on the sensation of little Lucie next to me. She was moving her fingers absentmindedly against my palm, stroking my gold rings, as if she knew I needed to relax.

Lucie had taken to the country upon arrival, having always been too wild for the elegant streets of Paris. A tan thing with ink-black hair, she looked practically native from the back. Like us, she had studied Annamese for six months before leaving, important mostly for Victor, who wanted to have a basic understanding of the language before being surrounded by thousands of native laborers. I had first called the language Indochinese but was swiftly corrected by Victor, who told me that natives of Indochine were referred to as Annamite, their language Annamese. "It comes from the center region of Indochine, which is Annam. Sometimes the residents of Tonkin are called Tonkinese, and the residents of the south Cochinchinese. It's all terribly confusing but do try to say anything besides 'Indochinese' or else you will sound very new." Victor learned the customs and the language quite quickly, but nowhere near as fast as Lucie. In the two and a half months that we had been in Hanoi, Lucie had started speaking full sentences, even conversing at length with the staff, which made her a curiosity among *les indigènes* and a cause for concern in the French community, whose children were rarely allowed to learn the local language. The rich Annamites sent their children to France to be educated, not the opposite, the French women I had met reminded me, but I was never one to prevent learning. It was fascinating to watch the speed of the process, the wheels of her curious mind twirling like a pinwheel. One day she had been shyly hiding under the fabric of her servant's *ao* trying to string the few phrases she knew together, and a few weeks later she was telling the same servant stories in Annamese. Now all the servants, from the cook to the chauffeur, were teaching her to write Chinese characters and the more modern, simpler script, *Quoc Ngu*. She only wrote out a word or two a day, but I knew they were building up in her mind like a pyramid.

Lucie's nose on my wrist, smelling my orange-flower perfume, brought me back to the present, and I peeked over the bench at Victor, who was next to Lanh, fussing with a pile of papers full of figures. They covered his knees, resting precariously on his beige linen travel suit.

It was a familiar sight. I listened to the sounds of Hanoi as my heart beat quickly, my body refusing to calm down, as we waited for the station to come into view. It was Lucie who spotted it first. "*Regarde, maman*, the house of a hundred suns!" she exclaimed cheerfully. Since Lanh had told her about that name, she hadn't called it anything else.

"It's prettier every time I see it," I said and patted her exposed leg, thin and muscular like a dancer's. Victor had wanted Lucie to take ballet lessons, to do a few things in Hanoi that little French girls enjoyed in Paris, but she preferred to run wild—riding her bicycle on the wide streets of our neighborhood, buying penny candy in the open-air markets with the servants—and she was still young enough that her father allowed her to.

"Jessie, close the window, please," Victor said from the front seat, trying to hold his papers still.

I desperately needed the air but rolled it up immediately anyway. I tilted my hat so I could lean against the glass instead. Though it wasn't quite right for the winter season, the hat still felt like a talisman, something with a hint of magic instead of just a pretty geranium-colored accessory.

"Do you like the house of a hundred suns better than the Gare Saint-Lazare?" I asked Lucie quietly, getting in my last few phrases in English to her before we stepped into a public place and French took over again. Our home in Paris had been just a ten-minute stroll from Saint-Lazare.

"I'm starting to forget Paris," she replied in a tiny voice, not wanting to disturb her father.

"It has only been a few months, Lucie," I said, unable to hide my alarm. "And no one can forget Paris. It's the most wonderful place in the world. Spend just one day there and it finds its way inside you, even someone young like you. The memories you make in Paris are thicker than cartilage."

I could tell she was about to ask me what cartilage was, but she paused and laid her head against my arm instead.

"I remember that it rained every day," she whispered, "and that Mademoiselle DuPont would tell me not to play in the elevator or I would be trapped inside and have to live there forever. In the elevator. But no one lives in elevators, do they?"

"It did not rain every day," I corrected her.

"The bread in Paris was tastier. But I like rice, too," she said loudly, and then pressed her lips together when she realized her volume.

"Enough of that, *mes chéries*," said Victor, implying our English. "We're arriving."

Annamite men and women, most in their straight-cut traditional clothes, moved in a wave to make room for our car as we pulled up right under the station clock. Lucie smiled at the rickshaw coolies staring at us, and I turned to greet the porter who had approached the car, opening the door on Victor's side before Lanh had even turned off the engine. The man, whose eyes were friendly, though cloudy with age and cataracts, greeted us in Annamese and helped Lanh remove our bags from the trunk.

"Please be careful with that one. The handle needs to be repaired," I told him quietly, not wanting Victor to hear me. I knew he wouldn't be pleased that I had accidentally brought a broken suitcase on the journey. I could have blamed a servant, but it was something I never did, which was why they were so loyal to us.

"He doesn't speak French," Lucie said, stepping in front of me, translating what I'd said. The porter smiled at her and took the case into his arms instead of holding the crooked handle.

I reached into my purse for a tip but was interrupted by the stationmaster, who barked at the man to keep moving and hurried over to greet us.

"Madame Lesage, I saw the car and was hoping you were inside," he said, executing a quick, polite bow. "And your husband, of course," he added when Victor opened his door and nodded at him. "And Lucie," the stationmaster said, slipping her a piece of hard candy from his pocket. "The most intelligent child in Indochine." He added a phrase in Annamese, and she answered readily, pointing at her father behind her.

"Let me help you inside," the stationmaster said to me, ushering us in and shooing off the line of weathered men hawking food, fortunes, and shoe shines.

As I passed under the archway, I took a slow, deep breath, something that had become a ritual. The air changed a few inches from the train station. It was richer, as if the smells of the rest of the country had been brought up to Hanoi by the steam engines but weren't strong enough to make it farther into the city and mix with us.

"You're very kind to escort us in," Victor said politely to the stationmaster as we all walked, a tense half smile on his face. "But we will be fine from here," he said. He stopped and gestured to one of the waiting areas. "We wouldn't want to pull you from your duties."

He handed the man a few coins and nodded at him in a way that implied we didn't want to be bothered again. The man disappeared as quickly as he had come, managing a subtle wink at Lucie as he backed away. Victor was not a particularly tall or physically imposing man, but there was something in his demeanor that brought him an enormous amount of respect and obedience. Perhaps it was the scent of money.

"It's just part of his job," I murmured to Victor as we sat on the wooden benches.

"Yes, and he's very good at it," he said, smiling at me, his black hair slicked neatly with pomade. "But I need to get back to these papers. I don't have the patience for small talk today—except with you, *mon coeur*," he said to Lucie, who was hovering in front of him. Victor could have looked Annamite from the back, too, but he carried himself too rigidly—a posture that marked out well-bred Europeans in the colony. And from the front, his glacial-blue eyes gave him away instantly.

Lucie was still standing, shifting her weight from one thin leg to the other as if she were trying to float. When I realized it was because she didn't want to dirty her dress, I stood with her and kissed the top of her head, warm from just the few steps in the unforgiving sun. "You do know there's a half day's train journey ahead?" I said. "You'll have to sit sometime."

"Those benches over there look a bit cleaner," she said, pointing and pulling my hand. "May we sit there instead?"

I nodded yes, and we turned to the east side of the station, Lucie leading the way. We had almost reached the row of more modern benches when she was suddenly struck by a boy who was rushing toward us. She tumbled back, her body forcefully colliding with the wooden bench.

"Careful, boy!" my husband shouted after he heard me gasp, leaping up and pushing the child off of Lucie.

The boy, a shoeblack, grinned, not bothering to look at her, and suggested a shine, pointing at Victor's brogues.

"After this!" Victor snorted, pointing at Lucie and shouting out the few insults he knew in Annamese. "You're lucky I don't have you banned from the station."

He shooed the child away with one of his rolled-up papers, hitting him across the back.

I held Lucie by the shoulders. She was looking down at her dress in horror. On the upper part of her starched white skirt was a black checkmark-shaped swoop of shoe polish.

"*Maman!*" she cried, staring at the stain. "He ruined my dress," she whispered, tears quickly forming in the corner of her eyes. "I can't go on the train like this," she said, sobbing.

"No, Lucie, no, don't cry," I said, embracing her, but making sure to avoid the stain. "I'll take you to wash it. We can scrub it out, don't worry, *chérie*." I patted her on the shoulder.

"Take her to the washroom," said Victor, stroking Lucie's head comfortingly. "I'll wait here." He gestured to the bench closest to the bathroom.

I nodded and pushed Lucie the few steps to the door.

When we were inside, and luckily alone, Lucie pulled her skirt up and looked at the mark.

"Are you sure it will come out?" she asked, dropping the fabric and wiping at her tears.

"Of course," I said brightly, reaching for a hand towel. I wet it and soaped it up before starting to scrub.

We watched as my right hand moved back and forth and I tugged at the garment with my left. But all that did was spread the black stain, so I crouched down on the floor, hoping to get a better angle. It was not going to be easy to remove.

I scrubbed as hard as I could and listened as her sobs quieted. When I looked up and smiled at her, happy that the mark was turning gray, black spots started swimming before my eyes and I had to bend my head quickly down to avoid falling over.

"*Maman?*" I heard her say, but her voice sounded far away.

"I just feel a bit faint," I said, standing up carefully. Feeling dizzier, I gripped the sink and closed my eyes, letting my head drop heavily forward. With my eyes still closed, I turned on the water. I placed one of my hands under the stream, keeping the other on the sink for balance.

When I felt a little steadier, I bent down and drank from the sink, lapping the cool water in large gulps. I stayed like that for a few moments, feeling as if my thirst would never be quenched.

"I'm sorry, Lucie," I mumbled when I felt I could stand up again without help. I wiped off my mouth, glanced in the mirror briefly, surprised by my pale reflection, then whipped my head to my left.

Lucie was no longer standing next to me.

"Lucie?" I exclaimed, turning around to the stalls. They were empty. "Lucie!" I called out, running in a circle in the little room. She wasn't anywhere.

She was gone.

I ran out to the waiting room and checked the bench Victor had pointed to, but she wasn't there, either. Neither was Victor.

"Lucie!" I shouted, rushing between the benches, all packed with travelers, and out to the central space. "Victor!"

The station was crowded, and I suddenly felt as if I were swimming in a sea of bodies, when I should have been able to spot them so easily.

What could have happened? Lucie wasn't a child who wandered

off, but perhaps she had something pressing to say to her father or wanted our cases back so she could change her dress. Perhaps the shoeblack had convinced Victor to get a shine after all. I stared at the empty bench a few seconds more, then swiveled to look at the row of benches where Lucie had wanted to sit. They weren't there, either. I looked up at the clock inside the station. There were still ten minutes before the train down the coast was due to arrive.

It was a large station. And they could be anywhere.

Fearing the worst, I walked the length of the building, avoiding the small groups of Indochinese men in three-piece traveling suits, their hair deeply parted and slicked down, leather bags at their sides. I moved through the left and right wings, the center hall twice, then out the back door to the platform with the rows of tracks. They weren't there, so I hurried out to the front again to see if they were with the vendors. There were no children and no men who resembled Victor.

I looked at all the peasants peddling wares, some shirtless and half asleep in the shade, all too thin, their hands listless, their long yellow fingernails pointing down, their skin deeply darkened by the sun. I stopped and questioned the one nearest to the door.

"Did you see a man, a Frenchman, in a beige tropical suit and a little girl here?" I asked him, glancing at his calloused bare feet and his pile of sugarcane. Lucie loved sugarcane and was still taken with the fact that people consumed the sweet substance in raw form in Indochine. How I wished she were here now, chewing the fibrous stalk.

"Sugarcane, *madame*?" the vendor asked in French.

"No," I said, shaking my head vigorously. "But did you happen to see—"

He waved his sugarcane again, repeating his request through his smile. It was foolish to think the sugarcane vendor would have understood more than a few words in French. I repeated the phrase in Annamese, to the best of my abilities, but he just shook his head no. Lucie would have translated better than I did. Where was she? And where was Victor! I gave the vendor a few coins and backed away.

I ran back inside, my lungs tight, my breath shallow, and checked the clock above the ticket booth. The train to Vinh was set to arrive in two minutes. I rushed to the rear of the building, exited onto the platform, and inspected the scrum of travelers. One man I recognized from the French Officers' Club. He gave me a friendly smile, and I returned it but quickly twisted myself to the side to avoid his gaze, a new wave of panic crashing on me. I pulled down my hat and looked at every person standing on the platform except for him. I looked at them twice. I walked across the platform and stared at them from the other side. I even went to the edge and glanced down at the tracks, holding my breath, praying that my husband and child weren't lying there, unnoticed yet flattened and dismembered, but there was nothing but steel and tufts of grass poking up between the ties.

There were still no bells ringing to indicate the arriving train, so I slipped back inside to see whether Lucie might be in the ladies' room looking for me. She was not. I again covered every inch of the station, indoors and out. There was no Lucie, no Victor. My head felt heavy, yet I was filled with an almost painful energy that refused to dissipate. I ran back to the waiting area, sat on the wooden bench where we had left Victor, and started to sob. If Victor were with me, he would have been deeply mortified by the state I was in, but he wasn't. He wasn't anywhere.

I dried my face with the edge of my sleeve. My eyes were tired, unfocused, but I felt compelled to blink the feeling away and keep searching through the blur.

I stood up and darted off again, this time nearly tripping the stationmaster, who was headed to the main entrance, surely to greet another rich French family in hopes of a big tip. He stopped abruptly when he saw me.

"Madame Lesage!" he exclaimed, taking his handkerchief out of his pocket and pressing it into my hand in one elegant movement. "What is the matter? Please sit down here," he said, guiding me to a wooden bench in the waiting area.

"No!" I snapped through my sobs. "I need to sit there! Right there. They'll be coming to find me." I indicated the bench where Victor had been. He nodded, his hand outstretched to guide the way.

"Can I assist you in some way, Madame Lesage?" he asked after we sat, handing me yet another starched handkerchief as I continued to cry. I hadn't used the first one yet.

"Yes. I hope you can," I sputtered, clenching his handkerchiefs in my fist. "Something just went terribly wrong."

"I'm sure I can help," he said gently. "That's why I'm here. Please tell me what's upsetting you."

I looked up at his concerned face and tried to get the words out.

"Just a few minutes ago I went to the washroom to clean my daughter Lucie's dress," I said. "To get out a shoe-polish stain. A boy, a shoeblack soliciting my husband's business, had pushed up against her with his greasy brush, making a terrible mark on her white dress. But I couldn't wash it out. Then, I don't know what happened. I closed my eyes for a few seconds, perhaps a minute at most, and when I opened them, Lucie was gone. I ran out to find her, but she's not anywhere in the station—and I've looked everywhere—and neither is my husband, Victor, who was supposed to wait for us right here." I slapped the bench we were sitting on. "He's not here sitting where he's supposed to be waiting for me, and Lucie's not anywhere, either. I've been running all over the station for fifteen minutes now, but I can't find them. I'm alone, and we are going to miss our train to Vinh. We have to meet Victor's cousin. It's a very important trip, and now he and Lucie have disappeared. They're gone!"

The stationmaster nodded and looked at me, not unkindly but blankly, as if he had failed to follow me.

I stared back at him, thinking that perhaps I had mistaken idiocy for kindness.

"Why are you looking at me like that?" I blurted out. "Don't you understand me? Don't you *understand*?" I knew I sounded horribly rude, but I needed him to help me.

He shifted slightly but said nothing, and instead of crying again, I dropped my gaze to the gold nameplate on his jacket. Pham Van Dat. After nearly two months in Indochine and many hours waiting for trains, greeted each time by the same stationmaster, I had never bothered to learn his name.

"Monsieur Dat, I beg you," I said quietly. "Please help me find them. We have to meet Victor's cousin tonight. We must have already missed the morning train, but perhaps there is one later today? We must be on that one. Together. Please help me find them."

"You say that you are looking for your husband and daughter? Victor and Lucie Lesage?" he said slowly.

"Of course!" I bellowed. "You just greeted us outside a half hour ago! Who else would I be looking for?"

He shook his head and laced his hands together. "But *madame*, I'm afraid you're mistaken," he said, meeting my gaze. "I did greet you a half hour ago, as you said, but it was just you in the black car. Just you and your chauffeur. There was no husband and child. You were alone."

Alone.

It couldn't be. The stationmaster was mistaken.

"No, Monsieur Dat. You are mistaken," I said, shaking my head. "Of course they were with me. We are all journeying to Vinh together, as I said. To see Victor's Michelin cousin. A young but important one. He and his wife—she's from the La Trémoille family—they are *nhan vat quan trong*," I said, using the Annamese words for notable persons. "Victor, Lucie, and I—we are all here in this station somewhere. We came here, together!"

He shook his head again. "*Madame*, I saw the black car from my perch outside just thirty or so minutes ago," he said. "And even when it was still moving, I saw you and your red hat inside. I knew when I saw the hat that it was you, as I've seen you wear it before, on more than one occasion. And Madame Lesage," he finished up, his spine straightening, "do not think me rude, but I am sure it was you getting out of the Delahaye car. Alone. You are a difficult person not to notice." He looked at me with concern and repeated, "I am sure you were alone."

"That can't be," I insisted. "*You* are not remembering correctly."

I rested my heavy head in my hands, my vision blurring even more, and closed my eyes. "We traveled together to the station," I repeated, feeling queasy. "We came inside together. Victor, Lucie, and I."

I lifted my head with a jerk, propelled by a sudden idea. "Lanh will tell you!" I said loudly. "Please call my *tai xe* now. I insist. Phone our house. Lanh will have returned. And our servants saw us all off this morning. Please phone them," I begged. "Ask for Lanh, or Trieu. One of them should answer straightaway."

"Of course," he said, standing up.

When he had left, I looked at the restroom, holding my breath, waiting for Lucie to skip out of it. Was she still refusing to sit, afraid to wrinkle her now stained dress? Had they really wandered off? Or had something happened to them? Had they been taken away by force? Everyone knew who Victor was. Our wealth wasn't what some thought we had, but it was still more than nearly everyone else in Indochine.

I rubbed my eyes, but I still had to squint to see the stationmaster returning.

"Did you phone, Monsieur Dat? Did you speak to Lanh? Or Trieu?" I asked anxiously when he was close.

"Yes, Madame Lesage," he replied, his voice even. "I made the call myself and spoke to Madame Trieu. I'm sorry, but she said that she saw you off this morning, alone. That your husband and daughter are in Trang An for the day. To see the caves."

"Caves! What are you talking about?" I cried out. "They are here, with me. Victor doesn't have time to take Lucie to inspect caves. Please help me look again, please."

"Of course we can look again, Madame Lesage," he said kindly. "Perhaps they arrived in a separate car. Perhaps I just didn't see them."

In the center of the station, coming in from the five round archways, I spotted the porter who had helped me with my broken suitcase, the one with the cloudy brown eyes. I wanted to beckon him over. To ask him if he remembered Lucie speaking to him in Annamese. Little Lucie with her dimpled face, overly pressed and powdered by her maid. Lucie, who cared far more for Indochine than France now. But instead I turned away. I knew what he'd say, and I couldn't hear it from one more person. I clenched my teeth together and tried to set my mind straight. My roiling, heavy mind.

I straightened my back against the hard, polished wood of the bench.

"Yes, yes, I could be remembering it wrong," I said calmly, forcing a smile. But I knew I wasn't. We were together in the car. Lucie's hands were fiddling with my gold rings, her thin, tan leg was next to mine, her perfectly formed head against my shoulder. The way she rubbed her foot against my uncovered ankle, sitting so close even though the back seat of the Delahaye was very wide—I could still feel the sensation lingering.

"Come, we shall look again," said the stationmaster, waiting patiently for me to stand.

I rose but felt like screaming out in frustration. Even though I had just asked to, I did not want to search the station again, pecking my way through the crowd like a chicken without a head. What I wanted was my family next to me.

"When you helped me enter the station, did I have a suitcase?" I asked.

"You did!" he said enthusiastically. "It had a broken handle. You handed it to a porter here," he said, looking around for the man. "I explained to him that it was broken and that he should carry it from the base. Cradle it."

"You explained that to him?" I asked, feeling my stomach churn.

"Yes," said the stationmaster, his worried look returning. "Would you like me to fetch your suitcase for you? Perhaps that would help your mem—"

I found the strength to smile, the corners of my mouth quivering, my eyes blurring again, and interrupted him. "You've been very kind. I'm sorry to have been such a bother, Monsieur Dat. You're right about everything, I'm sure. I must just be remembering incorrectly. Perhaps I'm unwell."

"May I fetch a doctor?" he asked, stepping closer, but I shook my head and backed away from him. "I'm unwell," I repeated. "I must be. I'm terribly sorry." I turned around and ran as fast as I could in my brand-new, barely creased shoes toward the nearest exit.

I hurried to the left wing of the station, to the corner door that Lanh had pointed out to me on our first journey there, and slipped out, past the cars heading to the main entrance, past the line of coolies and the calls from the vendors, into the shadows of voie A. It was a narrow road that ran parallel to the large avenue that the station was on, the route Mandarine. Voie A, like the other narrow roads surrounding it, was full of Annamite workers shading themselves with newspapers or sheltering under tattered store awnings. I paused to catch my breath, my throat dry and aching from thirst, and shut my eyes tight, imagining Lucie's little voice, her hand on mine.

I wasn't unwell. I wasn't forgetting anything. My family had disappeared.

TWO

Jessie

September 2, 1933

Ⅰt's the *hoa sua* flowers. The lovely smell. That's what you paused to sniff, yes?" Trieu's pleasant voice came at me slowly, mimicking the breeze drifting in the open doors. "Milk flowers, in your language. But we say *hoa sua*." She overemphasized the pronunciation and nodded as I repeated the words, trying not to catch my tongue on the *S*.

"That's it," she said approvingly.

I smiled at the smooth, oval face of the girl who was employed as my personal servant. She was thin as paper and startlingly beautiful, her body managing to curve in the places that mattered, despite her slight size. When we were introduced in front of the house just that morning, I assumed she spoke almost no French. I had assumed wrong.

In the six hours that Victor, Lucie, and I had been in Hanoi, I'd already realized that I had incorrectly assumed many things about the country and its people. Or perhaps they were just described to me incorrectly by Victor's friends in Paris.

"At this time of year, they start to bloom everywhere," Trieu continued. "Even if there are no trees near, the smell is so strong throughout the city that it's as if they are growing in your own garden. Do you like it?"

She moved to the window, the skirt of her white *ao ngu than*, which was cut straight but slit high on either side, floating up behind her, a striking contrast to the black pants she wore underneath. She leaned forward and pushed the glass pane wide open. The wind responded by blowing in, and she breathed in slowly, moving her hands like a circulating fan to waft the smell closer to her face.

"I like it very much," I said, still surprised by her outgoing demeanor and perfect French.

"I will cut some and place them on your dressing table this afternoon. There are two trees that should be flowering in the far end of the garden," she said as she walked back to the bed. "They might not be fully open yet, but they can bloom here in your room." She unlatched the last of my trunks and continued folding my clothes, spraying them with floral perfume and placing them in the room's deep closet.

Victor had said that Annamite women were docile. Meek, he'd said. Do not expect the servants to speak more than a few courteous phrases to you, he'd advised. Just thank them and say no more. Do not wish them to become your friends or confidantes. They are employees; you are the employer. Their behavior will reflect that arrangement. But since we had arrived at our house in Hanoi that morning and Victor had left me alone with my servant, Trieu had not ceased talking, seemingly delighted to walk me through all three stories of the beautiful house. She had even chased Lucie down a hallway with Lucie's own servant, Cam, while the late-afternoon sunlight danced across the floor with them, following their laughter like tagalong children.

"When do the flowers die?" I asked Trieu as she motioned for me to sit in the intricately carved ebony chair at my dressing table.

"In December. By your new year they'll be gone. By our new year in February, Tet Nguyen Da, you won't even be able to remember the smell," she said. "They are not a cold-weather flower, so you must enjoy them now. Tomorrow, if you have a moment, walk around Ho Hoan Kiem, the lake," she said, gesturing to the dark blue water just three hundred yards from our house. "They are the prettiest when they lean toward the water, and something about the wet breeze awakens them earlier there than in the rest of the city. Close to Kiem, they should be nearing full bloom already."

She took a silver hairbrush off the table and started to brush my straight blond hair, placing a hand on the top of my head to keep it still.

I turned back to look at her, but she kept her eyes steady on the mirror. "Oh, no, thank you, but that's not necessary," I protested. We had servants in Paris, but physically they always kept their distance. They never touched me unless I asked them to, never locked eyes with me, let their gaze linger, or raised their voices. I could already tell that it was different in Indochine.

"It is necessary," she said, her voice still light and friendly. "You will dine at the Officers' Club, I am sure of it. The French always do on their first night. You will have to wear your hair like this," she said, holding up a strand and folding it in waves. "I will use the tool."

She went to the bathroom and brought back the iron rod that I had never learned to handle well, preferring to wear my shoulder-length hair straight and simple.

"Whatever you think is best," I replied, feeling that it was right to let her take the lead. Victor hadn't mentioned the slightest detail about our plans for the evening, but after our journey, I was hoping they involved a hot bath, a few stories with Lucie, and twelve hours' sleep.

"This is best for your thin yellow hair, Madame Lesage," Trieu said pleasantly. "It will make it look like there is more of it."

"Oh," I said, trying not to take offense. "I'm sure you know better than I do about these things."

"No, Madame Lesage," she said, positioning the wand in her hand. "But about the Officers' Club etiquette, perhaps I do. I worked for the last mistress of the house before you. Madame van Dampierre. She also went to the Officers' Club on her first night."

"How long did the van Dampierres live here?" I asked, trying not to move my head. Trieu tilted my chin up, and I fixed my gaze above. In the living room there was an intricate pattern in the coffered ceiling, but in the master bedroom the ceiling was smooth, high, and painted a fresh white, adding to its airiness.

"Four years," Trieu replied.

"I hope we will be here as long." I paused and looked at my reflection in the mirror, thinking about how many times Louise van Dampierre had done the same thing. "Were they happy here?" I asked.

"They were very happy for a time," she said thoughtfully. "And four years is not a short time in the colony. Many French women don't last more than a year or so in Indochine. Some, much less. They say it's too hot in summertime. They miss their food. They miss the European way of life. They want their children to grow up like they did. So they return."

"I'm not French," I said, pointing out what was obvious to the French but might not be to Trieu. "So I think I'll quite like it here. Food, heat, and all."

"Yes, Madame Lesage. I hope you do," she said, gently lifting another strand of my hair.

Lesage. I liked the way she said it, so differently than the Parisians, who paused between the *E* and the *S*. Trieu strung the syllables together like Christmas lights.

I leaned back, quickly growing more comfortable in her presence as she spiraled my hair with the wand.

Before this year, I hadn't thought much about our name. Not since my wedding day in 1925, when my last name was changed from Holland to Lesage. But on the boat ride over, Victor brought it up several times.

"Our last name is Lesage," he'd said, "but in Hanoi everyone needs to know that my mother is a Michelin. That she is a close, though much younger cousin to my uncles Édouard and André, may he rest in peace. She isn't Agathe Lesage. She is Agathe Michelin Lesage. Please remember to say her name that way."

He had reminded me of this detail in Paris while we were packing our trunks, again on our journey over, when a sleeping Lucie was curled at my feet like a cat, and yet again when we saw the white shores of Siam, the sand as fine as sugar. I thought he had done enough reminding, but he had whispered, "Remember, Michelin," when we were about to meet our household staff.

"They'll respect us more if they hear the Michelin name," he'd said as our new driver, Lanh, made his way through the narrow streets, our car gliding through patches of shadow and sunshine.

I was still shaken from the boat journey and too taken with the new world around me to care what my name was or wasn't. But as we pulled up to the handsome house with its center turret, and I saw the row of young Annamite servants waiting outside, their faces beaming, I'd put my hand on Victor's leg and said, "I think they'll respect us most if we are nice and pay them well."

"I'm always nice," Lucie had chimed in, which was mostly true.

"And I always pay well," Victor added. "I'm paying them all a quarter piastre more a day than the van Dampierres were. That's what people expect from the Michelins. Even in a global depression."

"What is the Officers' Club like?" I asked Trieu now, thinking that she already seemed so different from the person I'd stared at as we pulled through the iron gate. "Is it really so important that we go on our first night? Doesn't that seem a bit rushed?"

"I've never been inside," she said. "It's only for the French. But Madame van Dampierre seemed to care about it very much. It is where all the French go, especially the women, even though it was built for the men, I think. You will go there often with your husband, and nightly when your husband is away. You'll see."

"There are no Annamites there at all?" I asked, surprised. Victor told me that the French had created their own world inside a world, but from what I'd observed on our drive in, Indochine and its people seemed difficult to ignore.

"There are Annamites working inside," she clarified. "My cousin cleans dishes there. And a boy who worked here for the last family now serves drinks in the bar. But that is all they are allowed to do. Serve."

"What do the French women do at the clubhouse then?" I asked, imagining one of the beach clubs Victor and I had frequented on the Riviera.

"The club, never the clubhouse," she corrected me. "And they eat and drink too much. I think there are several tennis courts and a large swimming pool. They never bring children, even though their children would like to swim there, I think. There are rules against it. No children, no dogs, no Annamites."

"That seems a rather outdated policy," I said, holding my breath as the curling wand approached my ear. "I'm sure Lucie would love a swimming pool in this heat." I would ask Cam to find her one elsewhere.

As Trieu continued waving my hair, I tried to inhale the scent of the milk flowers the way she did, moving my hands slowly when the breeze came in. But after a few breaths I realized that what I was enjoying as much as the fragrant scent was the city's humidity. It was upward of 80 degrees outside, even in the late afternoon, and the air was thick with moisture. It was a dampness that was very familiar and never failed to remind me of being young. It felt like the summers of my childhood, like home.

Not Paris. If I closed my eyes, I was breathing the air of the small town of Blacksburg, Virginia. In that hilly southwestern corner of the state, where mountain laurel and black huckleberry bloom in the shadows of the Blue Ridge and Allegheny Mountains, there wasn't much to do but get lost in the wilderness and daydream about a bigger version of yourself.

I was never going to see Blacksburg again, and perhaps because I was so certain of that, I clung to little reminders of Virginia whenever I encountered them. Humidity was one of those memory triggers. On this evening, eight thousand miles away, I felt closer to my birthplace than I had in years.

By the time I was thirteen years old and the oldest of seven children, I knew I'd never stay in the South. Two years later, seven became eight when another girl was born. Girls were about as valuable as stray dogs to my parents. Another mouth to feed that would never be enough help on the farm. The house was crowded when we were three; when we were ten, closets had to be turned into bedrooms.

We were no different from the families we grew up around, all with too many children and not enough money. Except for one thing: our language. My mother was originally from Quebec, though she had spent most of her life in Virginia, having moved south with her father so he could work the tobacco farms. She had not passed on much to us, but she had given us French, spoken with a strong Québécois accent. She preferred to do her shouting in French, and the only reason we learned was because she was almost always shouting. Perhaps she would have restrained herself if she'd known that in the end it would greatly help to hasten my departure.

As soon as I could leave, I did, running down a path I'd carved using nothing but willpower and a fierce hatred of my circumstances. After I turned twenty, an age that felt like the true mark of adulthood, and had finished studying at the small teachers' college one town away, I traveled to Manhattan, a city that immediately started feeding my hungry soul. I spent two years teaching French in a high school above Central Park, too far north to be fashionable, and then used my savings to travel to Paris. In New York, I had lived in a boardinghouse for women near Grand Central Station, which allowed me to put aside enough money for my passage, as well as enough to survive on in Paris for exactly three months.

Just as I expected, New York helped me start shedding my skin, but I still felt too close to home there. Paris allowed me to embrace a new version of myself. It was the city that my dreams were made of. Before I sailed, one of my fellow teachers had gifted me a small leather writing journal and on the first page had written, in her beautiful looping hand, "Paris is the greatest temple ever built to material joys and the lust of the eyes," a quote from her favorite writer, Henry James. I didn't have enough money for material joys, but how right James was about lust of the eyes. Everything in Paris was beautiful. The people, the clothes, the food, but mostly just the city itself. The limestone buildings sitting tightly together along the Seine, the cathedrals commanding entire city blocks, and the river that you could walk along for miles, which seemed to exert a gravitational pull for the two banks it commanded. If Blacksburg, Virginia, had a complete opposite, it was Paris, France.

I went for a summer trip, I stayed for eight years, and now it was all oceans away. I had a new world to find myself in. Indochine.

I watched as Trieu worked magic on my hair, the soft waves she was creating, and had to admit she was right. It did look more polished. Fuller, too. I was going to say so when I caught a glimpse of Lucie's reflection in the vanity mirror. She was peeking in the scarcely ajar bedroom door with her beloved porcelain doll, Odile, in her arms and Cam right behind her.

"It's too bad we will have to send Lucie to boarding school now that we're in Hanoi," I said in a loud voice. "It's the only way she'll learn to be a proper French girl."

"No, *maman!*" Lucie cried, pushing open the heavy door and revealing her hiding place. "Don't send me away! Please let me stay!" Her little face contorted in panic, she threw Odile to the ground, causing the doll's big brown eyes to close. I laughed, motioning her over.

"Oh, Lucie, I'm kidding. I just wanted to see how accomplished you are as a spy. Turns out, very."

"Don't make me leave, *maman.* Please don't send me away," she begged.

"Don't cry, *chou*. I would never send you away," I said, opening my arms for her to run into. "You can be a wild little animal for all I care, play in the garden until nightfall and never read a thing, in French or any other language, as long as you're near me."

"I want to stay here," Lucie said, throwing her arms around my neck. She rubbed her face against my dress and hugged me. "I won't spy anymore," she promised.

"You can stay here," I whispered in her ear. "And you can spy all you want. But try spying on your papa next time. He's less observant than I am."

Once she was sure I wasn't about to ship her back to France, she pulled at my still warm hair and said, "Actually, Papa asked me to fetch you. I was fetching, you see. He wants to see you on the terrace. We didn't have a terrace in Paris," she added, rightly. "Now we do."

"Come," I said, taking her hand as soon as Trieu dismissed me from my chair. "Let's go together." Lucie held my fingers tightly as we walked down the wide corridor with its twenty-foot ceilings. In the upper foyer, where the tiles were a patterned black-and-white ceramic, she tried to hop from one square to the other. She gave up to descend the grand, half-spiral staircase, jumping from step to step.

"It's this way, *maman*," she said at the bottom, leading me to the double glass terrace doors with brass handles curled like figure eights.

"I remember," I responded, letting her drag me to Victor.

When he saw us emerge from the house, Victor folded his newspaper in four and said, "*Merci, chérie*," to Lucie. She sat next to him on his chaise longue and let him kiss her head. "For your hard labor, I present you with this cake." He lifted a blue porcelain plate with a pink pastry on it in the shape of a flower and handed it to her. "It's a mung-bean-and-rice pastry called *banh com*. A local delicacy, I'm told."

Lucie raised her eyebrows at the word "bean," but took the pastry in her hands. She leaned down to sniff it, gave it a lick, and then devoured it after she realized it was indeed made of sugar.

"There aren't beans in here!" she exclaimed to her father, eyeing the crumbs left on the plate.

"But there are, *chérie*," said Victor, pulling on her braid. "Why don't you go to the kitchen and ask how it's made? Then you can see the beans."

Lucie smiled and ran off as if she had lived in the tall yellow house for years.

"Don't you look beautiful," said Victor, tilting his head back and smiling at me affectionately once Lucie was out of sight. He was reclining on the metal chaise's black-and-white-striped cushions, smoking a cigarette. He alternated puffs with sips from his glass of white wine. On the boat journey over, I'd wondered if there would be French wine in Indochine, but that was a silly worry. The French wouldn't have bothered colonizing a place where they couldn't consume their own wine.

"Glad to be off the boat?" he asked, standing to kiss me before reclining again.

"To say the least," I answered, my smile feeling momentarily put on. I let the corners of my mouth relax, trying to forget the journey, and took in this new image of Victor. He had changed into beige linen pants and a crisp white dress shirt, the sleeves rolled up to the elbows, and he was surveying the small but well-manicured garden, the borders aflame with hibiscus. His shirt buttons were done up only to midchest, and he had a carafe of water full of lemon wedges positioned within reach. Next to it was a small silver bell.

"Do you think you'll like it here?" he asked eagerly. I could tell that he certainly did. We lived well in Paris, very well, even when the economic crisis hit the country two years ago, but it was already clear that in Indochine, where costs were so low, we would no longer live like Lesages. We would finally live like Michelins.

"I do," I said, sensing my happiness rise to meet his as we focused on the present, not the weeks we had spent cramped together on the bobbing ship. "The house is incredible, isn't it? Every room bright and full of light. And so much space. Lucie has her own wing on the third floor. But most of all, I like that it feels like a happy home."

"I'm glad you think so," he said, stubbing out his cigarette and putting his hands behind his head, the small family-crest ring he wore on his right pinkie quickly vanishing in his thick black hair. "I'm very glad we bought this house, despite those who advised me to rent it, not purchase it. 'Rent for a year, maybe two, then decide,' they said. They warned me that Indochine wasn't for everyone, especially the women. But they don't know me as well as they think, and they don't know you at all. You were born to see the world, and so was I." He smiled at me admiringly. "That's what you'd say in our early days, when I'd ask you if you were homesick for America, and look at us now. I'm sure that this house, and Indochine, will be right for us. Even if no one else in my family has dared to spend time here."

It was true. No other Michelins had spent more than a few weeks in Indochine, even Victor's uncles, Édouard and André, who had controlled everything in the twenties, including first buying rubber from the colony and then deciding to establish their own plantations in the French federation in 1924. They had spent over 200 million francs to acquire land in those early years. But Édouard was now seventy-four years old, André had passed in 1931, the younger generation was engaged in Clermont-Ferrand—and no one wanted to actually live in Indochine.

When they'd considered the colony as a place to set up their own plantations, rather than buying rubber from the existing plantations in Indochine, British Malay, and the Dutch Indies, they sent two executives—non–family members—on a boat, declining to make the journey themselves.

But in January, Victor had volunteered to come to Indochine, not just for a visit but to live. It was an idea I had planted in his head.

He had yet to obtain a high position in the company, kept out of the headquarters in Clermont-Ferrand, working in Paris instead. He'd been frustrated for years that we still weren't living in Clermont and needed a new approach for climbing the company ranks. Suggest a position for yourself in Indochine, I'd said one morning when Paris had surprisingly started to lose its appeal for me. I knew that there had been some significant difficulties on the plantations in the last few years, including worker strikes, even murder, mostly due to communist unrest. The Michelins had tried to stamp it out, positioning at the head of both plantations men who had been successful at keeping communism at bay among the workers in Clermont-Ferrand. But in 1930, there had been a very large strike on Phu Rieng plantation, one of the three they owned in Cochinchina, where the military had to intervene to put it to rest. Every paper in France had written about it that winter, and three years later, many still used it to highlight either the colonial or the native struggle, depending on their political persuasion. There had also been several deaths, one when a European overseer was murdered by coolies in 1927 and just this December when three coolie laborers were shot dead at Dau Tieng, the other large plantation. It was time that the family did more than observe from a distance, I'd said to Victor. I was no expert, but I had grown up on a farm. I knew that workers who had no face to put to a name could have difficulty with loyalty.

"But there are so many others in the family trying to get to management positions," Victor had protested, not seeing the opportunity that I was.

"None of your uncles' children have any interest in living in the colony," I had reminded him. "But I think they'd let you go. And if you went, and could keep things calm for several years, I'm sure you would be rewarded. Maybe they would finally offer you a position in Clermont-Ferrand."

Victor had resisted at first, but he finally built up the courage to speak with his uncle Édouard. Édouard's son Pierre had been delighted by the idea, having felt the pressure to at least visit the colony over the past few years, but having no interest in doing so. Once he had their approval, Victor became enamored with the prospect of life in Indochine. A few weeks later, he seemed convinced that he'd come up with the idea himself, which was perfectly fine with me.

I looked at him now on our new terrace, handsome and happy as he lounged in his new kingdom. "We are only seven and a half hours in, but so far I agree. I know that it's right for us."

I sat and took a sip of Victor's wine. It tasted crisp, despite the heat. Victor also didn't seem to remember that I had been the one who'd advised him to buy the house.

"Good. I was sure you would feel that way," he said. He was a man who always enjoyed feeling one step ahead of his peers, even if his wife was the one who had steered him to water. "After all, you already left your country once. Why not twice?" He took back his glass and pointed at my hair. "Did someone already tell you? About this evening?"

"Trieu. My servant," I clarified. "She said we would probably go to the French Officers' Club."

"Yes, we are. That's the etiquette it seems. No rest for the weary," he said, sitting up straighter. "There was a letter waiting for me when we arrived. We are to dine with Arnaud de Fabry, a very successful financier and the head of the chamber of commerce of Hanoi."

I nodded, racking my brain for any familiarity with the name. "But in his note de Fabry also said there's a chance that the governor-general will stop by to greet us. Pierre Pasquier. He's from Marseille, but he knows my mother. I thought it would be days before we met him, so this is a welcome turn of events. But still, even if we only meet de Fabry, it's important that we do. We need to be on very good terms with him. Not everyone who has a stake in rubber feels warmly toward us—ever since we began planting ourselves, we've far surpassed the competition in technology and production. Still, we need the other industries to support us. Especially in Tonkin—that's the region we are in now, Tonkin—as this is where we recruit many of our workers." He circled his finger around the rim of his glass. "I wonder if de Fabry has met *maman*?"

"Most likely. Everyone has met your mother," I said, moving to the edge of his chair.

"It does seem that way," he said, putting his hand on my shoulder and standing up. "It's a blessing and a curse. But here, I think, it will be a great blessing."

Victor's mother had grown to like me much more after Lucie became a toddler. It was hard not to love Lucie and impossible to ignore that she wouldn't be here if not for me. Still, I seldom traveled with Lucie when she went to visit Agathe, a distance we both appreciated.

"We dine in an hour," my husband said, pushing his sleeves higher. "Will you be ready?"

"I'm ready now," I said, motioning to my hair and lightly made-up face.

Victor reached for my hand and gestured for me to stand.

"Almost. You'll have to change your dress. Ask Trieu what to wear. I'm sure Louise van Dampierre put her through the wringer on etiquette and dress. She'll have an idea of what's suitable."

When we'd decided to come to Indochine, Victor's cousin Pierre, the younger son of Édouard and the new director of the company, had suggested that we reach out to the van Dampierres. Théodore van Dampierre, Pierre noted, had attended school with Édouard. They were the only good friends of the Michelins living in Indochine, Pierre had admitted. Théodore van Dampierre, who was working for the Banque de l'Indochine in Hanoi, wrote to us at once, even sending his letter by the new airmail system, which only took eleven days between the colony and Paris. A week later, we received a series of lovely letters from his wife, Louise, telling us all about life in the colony and why she'd enjoyed it so much. She even suggested that we stay for a time in their large yellow house, as they were headed back to France before we were due to arrive. She'd sent a few photographs of the home, so Victor had seen the large size of it, the many balconies and terraces, all looking like an invitation for the world to join us indoors. He was delighted with it, and I suggested that we do more than just stay there.

Why not purchase the lovely place? Firmly plant roots before we arrived. Since the price of everything in the colony had fallen drastically as the depression swept France, it was a fine time to buy. Victor had jumped at the idea.

We'd traveled down to Clermont-Ferrand to tell Édouard and Pierre in person, convinced that now that Victor had a special place in the company, we wouldn't be imposing.

Pierre was still getting his legs about him as director, as he had only taken over the position in September and for the worst reasons. At the end of August 1932, his older brother, Étienne, died in a plane crash. Despite being an expert airman, as many Michelins were, he'd lost control of his small airplane in dense fog and hit the ground in Saint-Genès-Champanelle, less than ten miles from the factory.

The management said they were all excited for us to go, and I could tell it was genuine, and an utter relief for them. *You can contract malaria instead of us*, their eyes seemed to say. But I'd dealt with far worse in life than a bit of a fever.

"I'm sure Louise was quite stylish," I said, returning to thoughts of the evening ahead. "But my guess is that Trieu simply has good taste on her own." I pictured her elegant black and white clothes, her dark hair a smooth curtain just grazing her shoulders.

"Either way," said Victor, letting my hand go. "She'll know."

As I made my way back up the stairs, I thought about the summer I met Victor. He had been drinking cold white wine with his shirt collar open, just like tonight. And even though July in Paris was usually quite pleasant, it had been a rare heavy day, and the air felt much as it did on this September afternoon in Hanoi.

It was a midsummer evening in 1925 when our divergent worlds collided with full force. I was sitting near the front window of Maxim's, the fashionable café on the rue Royale, drinking a glass of champagne, something I'd never had before. I also had never been to Maxim's but had passed it many times on my walks in the Eighth Arrondissement. I'd decided that since it was a month to the day from when I was due to leave Paris, I would spend foolishly and have a glass there. The restaurant was famous, and I wanted to tell the other teachers in the boardinghouse about places besides the usual cheap café in the Thirteenth where I dined nightly.

Victor came in a few minutes after I did, apparently with revelry on the brain. It was just two days before Bastille Day, so drinking and merriment had already begun. But unlike me, Victor did not walk in alone. He was with three rowdy friends, and they had quite obviously been guzzling wine, perhaps worse, for hours. They ordered enough food for ten men, sampled all of it, finished none of it, then smashed a bottle of Saint-Émilion Bordeaux onto the floor with the swing of an ill-placed elbow, causing a stream of blood-colored liquid to flood the polished parquet wood. The management wanted to drag them out by their shirtsleeves, but the men bought ten bottles of wine to apologize and proceeded to put one on every table in the room, much to the delight of the patrons. When the waiter began to open mine, an expensive Chablis, I shook my head, assuring him I had no need for it, but Victor leapt to my side.

"But you must take it," he said, leaning down and kissing my hand. "I only bought all these to impress you."

"What nonsense!" I said, laughing, suddenly quite glad that I'd worn my lowest-cut dress. "You bought all these to impress the proprietor, not me." My boldness fueled by the two glasses of champagne I had already consumed, I added: "And to keep from being tossed out on the street."

"Oh, did I?" he said, smiling in surprise. "You know what I think? I don't think you're French." He paused to reconsider his phrasing. "I think you are not French. I don't think . . . Wait. I don't know what I think," he concluded, sweat on his brow, his shirt askew.

"I'm American," I admitted, "though my mother is Québécoise. So, you're right, not French at all." It was something that my accent, French Canadian tinged with the drawl of the American South, gave away to most sober Frenchmen within a few words.

"American! Then of course you can drink this," he exclaimed. "There's nothing to do in America but drink."

"Actually, you can't drink in America anymore. Not out in the open anyway. Not since Prohibition."

"Which explains why a beautiful American like you came to France," he said, motioning to the waiter to finish opening the bottle. "Who wants to drink alone? Not me. I want to drink with someone charming, like you. Good thing we'd never pass a foolish law like that here."

"It is a foolish law," I admitted. Everyone in southern Virginia had just carried on making their own alcohol anyway, as they'd always done. "But American or not, I can't drink all this."

"Yes, you can. If you have help." He'd called over his friends, who all had the roguish yet polished look of rich young men with few cares in the world. After he'd persuaded me to have one glass, his light blue eyes gazing at me every time I spoke, he announced to his friends that we were abandoning them. He clasped my hand and pulled me along to the place de la Concorde, then through the Tuileries gardens, where my feet grew tired and dusty but my head, and my lips, were soon very much alive as he embraced me. I had kissed a few men before him, some handsome, but after kissing Victor Lesage, I forgot them all.

I did not sail back to America in August as planned. I resigned from the school where I taught French to children with strong New York accents, wrote to the boardinghouse to give my few things away, and married Victor four months later, to the horror of his mother. But even Agathe Michelin Lesage couldn't put out the flame of our newlywed bliss. Lucie was born the following year and became our light.

But all that was far behind us now, feeling almost as far away as haunted, humid Virginia.

THREE

Jessie

September 2, 1933

I looked back at my reflection in the mirror and turned to either side. Trieu had put me in a sleeveless, tea-length white crepe dress, cut on the bias.

"Are you sure this is suitable for evening?" I asked. "It seems rather casual. The length, that is." I looked down at my bare ankles. "All the women in Paris are wearing them long again at night. I had this dress made with cocktails in mind rather than a seated dinner. It feels far too informal."

"It is very hot here," Trieu said, pointing out the obvious. "Until November, the French women dress like this, even for dinner. This is the right one," she said firmly, and this time I nodded in agreement. I studied my reflection one more time, imagining what I'd be wearing if I were still in America, if I were being strangled by the poverty threatening to engulf the world. Victor and I had spoken often about how we were touched by the financial plague, but he'd reassured me that the family would never sink. The Michelins, like their tires, were hard to pop. The little that remained of my family in Blacksburg was certainly feeling the tidal wave of poverty. Even the recessions that only hit part of America had always sprinted toward us. An image of our farmhouse and the wild, wooded land around it flashed in my mind, sending a shudder down my spine. I never wanted to go back. Even Paris felt too close.

When Victor saw me descend the stairs to the landing, he whistled with approval. He raised his eyebrows at my hemline, but I repeated what Trieu had told me and he just nodded, leading me outside to the car. Lanh was already standing in front of it, his light gray uniform impeccably ironed and his hat set just so on his head. He did not need to ask Victor where we were going.

In the car, Victor put his strong arm around my bare shoulders and explained that we would be driving through a local neighborhood to get to the Officers' Club. Together, we took in the narrow pink and yellow houses with ceramic tile roofs, small terraces, and big green shutters, all pushed together. Moving in front of these tight, colorful rows were Annamites, many of the men wearing white pith helmets and the women conical straw hats or large disk-shaped ones that they tied under their chins. Around them, children bustled about, most of them barefoot. A jumble of telephone wires and streetcar wires snaked above us; below them were many storefronts with pieces of long cloth hanging in place of a formal awning, some painted with Chinese characters. And around it all was steam coming from various makeshift food stands. It could not have been more different from Paris.

"I like these other streets just as much as rue de la Chaux," I said, referencing our new street, in a neighborhood that had been reorganized by the French. As we turned south along the Red River, the sun was just starting to set in an orange-tinged haze above it.

"There's a more direct way to go to the Officers' Club," Lanh noted. "But we are a bit early, and as Monsieur Lesage requested, this way you can see more of Hanoi. The French parts, and the not so French," he added, braking gently to let a group of older Annamite women cross the busy road, their backs bent. I imagined it was less from age than from manual labor.

I turned to look at them, but Victor smiled and looked straight ahead as the group paused to ogle our big black car. Victor had purchased it from Delahaye and had it shipped to the colony six months earlier.

In Paris, Victor had managed a steel-frame construction business that André Michelin also owned. He was eventually allowed to transition to the central Michelin company, rather than André's other holdings, but his work had very little to do with the day-to-day rubber manufacturing operations down in Clermont-Ferrand. Instead, Victor assisted with updating the entries in the Michelin guides, which the company had been producing since 1900 to help travelers find suitable accommodations and dining establishments. Victor had said that it wasn't work for an engineer—he had earned a degree in engineering at École Centrale—but they had reminded him that thanks to years as a professional bon vivant in Paris in his early twenties, he knew all the best places in the capital city. It was a kind way of saying that his youthful antics were still keeping him from being trustworthy.

Eventually, Victor graduated from the guides and was allowed to work in advertising for some of the important Paris bicycle races that Michelin participated in, reminding the world that winning cyclists used Michelin tires, and that the company had, in fact, helped the world transition to pneumatic tires. After that he helped stamp the Michelin Man, Bibendum, as the French knew him, on just about everything. To his credit, it was work that he hated but did not complain about. Still, even his good attitude failed to move him an inch closer to Clermont-Ferrand.

Victor had never been too concerned with money, as he was sure we would always have enough, but I knew how easily money could come and go. Especially go, in an economic crisis.

Before I went to Victor with my idea, I told his mother, Agathe, presenting it in a way that I thought she'd be able to support. Everything that happened with Victor, besides marrying me, went through his mother first. Shockingly, she agreed.

Thanks to a push from Agathe, Édouard Michelin had granted Victor the newly created post of family overseer of the Michelins' two vast rubber plantations: the 22,000-acre Dau Tieng, where the deaths of the coolies had occurred in December—vast land due north of Saigon and over nine hundred miles away from Hanoi—and the 14,000-acre Phu Rieng plantation, another sixty miles northeast of Dau Tieng. He would also supervise the small 300-acre plantation, Ben Cui, that they had transformed into a company test station.

Dau Tieng was located in the gray-earth region of the colony and Phu Rieng in the red-earth, but both had performed well since the family started cultivating the land in 1926. Soon, the Michelins would no longer need to buy rubber from other sources. The importance of eliminating dependence was a business principle we had both heard time and again, but I now realized that it had been from men who had never set foot on their own plantations.

But we were changing that.

"The club is just here," Lanh said, taking a sharp left. Victor lifted his arm from my shoulders, straightened his jacket, and ran his right hand softly across his dark hair to make sure no strand was out of place, which it wasn't. It never was.

Lanh took another turn onto a nearly hidden driveway, which widened as we went, palm trees lining either side.

"Look," I whispered to Victor excitedly, pointing them out. When we'd first arrived in Indochine, docking at Haiphong on the coast and then traveling to Hanoi by train, I had seen many palms, but these were far more handsome—thin and tall and sinuous, trying to touch the sun with their leaves.

"Look there," said Victor, and I turned my head just as a white building came into view.

After years of living in France, I thought I was used to grandeur, but this was architectural beauty of a different kind. The building was softer, more welcoming than the hard-edged stone edifices of France. It sat on a vast green lawn, and the sight of the white-painted wood against the perfectly manicured grass radiated something I'd had trouble finding in Paris, especially of late: tranquillity.

"This may be my favorite building in the world," I murmured as we drove slowly up the road.

"I thought it was the Louvre," Victor said, putting his hand on mine.

"That is in the past," I replied as Lanh pulled up in front of the building. Three Annamite men in white uniforms with stiff mandarin collars and bright gold buttons came out to greet us, opening both car doors simultaneously.

"Welcome, Monsieur Lesage, Madame Lesage," said the third man as we made our way around to the right side of the Delahaye. I was surprised he had addressed us by name but knew not to show it.

"Thank you," said Victor, heading toward the club with an air of authority.

The building was long, with wings to the left and right that seemed to disappear into the trees and a two-story veranda punctuated by white columns running along the facade. Before we entered the main hall, I glanced up at the steeply slanted, red-brick-tiled roof that protected the veranda. Every part of the building was constructed with the natural elements in mind, yet without sacrificing beauty. I now understood why the French ran to the club as soon as their passports were stamped.

I followed Victor to the lower veranda. It was dotted with high-backed rattan chairs, sporadically occupied by men in tennis whites or casual tropical suits. There were also a half dozen women draped over the chairs as if they had melted into them. They were sipping cocktails, their hair short and casually styled or pinned up off their necks, conversing softly, all seemingly part of a sun-drenched world created with nothing but repose and revelry in mind. A few of the men and women glanced up as we entered, their skin turning a soft pink in the evening light, but not for more than a moment before they went back to sipping their drinks.

"Come in, please. This is the main room," said the man leading us upstairs as the hum of conversation faded behind us. "I am Teo. I run the club for Monsieur Maillard. You will see me often, and I will have the pleasure of seeing you often, too." He had that air of servility laced with confidence found among longtime servants fully aware of their competence.

"Of course," I responded politely. Next to me, Victor said nothing, his expression poker-faced, his chin slightly raised. Intentionally or not, his pose showed off his perfectly formed profile, the light blue of his eyes flashing in the dimly lit space. A teenage boy, also in a white uniform, appeared and offered tall glasses of water. "This end of the house is gentlemen only," Teo said when the boy had vanished around a corner. He gestured to the west wing. "The smoking room, the library, and the billiard room are there, sir," he said to Victor. "As are the guest rooms. The whole club was gentlemen only for many years, but the younger generation realized that the policy didn't allow for much fun," he said, smiling at me. "Now I think there are more women here than men during the week, even if they can't wander freely or stay the night."

"What time must the women leave?" I asked, looking down the long hallway.

"Two o'clock in the morning. Civilized enough yet uncivilized enough, as Monsieur Maillard puts it."

"I agree with that. Some of the old rules must apply, even if the world is changing," said Victor, finally breaking his pose. He reached for my hand, running his thumb over my large emerald Boucheron ring, a gift he gave me four months after Lucie was born. I closed my eyes reflexively, as my mind hurtled back to that chaotic time.

"Please come this way," said Teo. "The president of the chamber of commerce and his wife, Madame Marcelle de Fabry, are enjoying a drink outside. They are expecting you," he said, gliding silently on the dark wood floors. He led us through the main room, and this time eyes tracked us. I looked straight ahead the way Victor had done in the car, but couldn't help noticing that Trieu had been correct about the women. They were not wearing the backless silk and satin dresses in bright colors that were so popular in Paris. From what I could see, their dresses were white or a light pastel, and very few had the flared hem that had become a signature of modern evening dress in France. There wasn't one silk gown, but I spotted plenty of Paris chiffon and organza. I liked the look of it at once, as the light fabric made their tan skin glow. One older woman in a back corner was even wearing a white men's linen suit, her hair cut short to her ears. I tried not to stare at her, or the massed beauty in the room, and hurried closer to Victor.

Teo led us to an inner courtyard, lush with tropical green plants as large as boat oars and blossoming white flowers. I breathed in deeply, but the scent was different from that of the *hoa sua* around our house. Sitting at a lacquered table in the filtered glow of the remaining sun was a very attractive couple, the man a decade older than Victor, the woman not even thirty, judging by appearances. They rose to greet us when they saw Teo.

"Victor Lesage," said the man, whose light brown hair curled around his ears. It was loose, not back-combed and oiled down, as was fashionable in France. "You made it east in one piece." He held out his hand to Victor. "And you brought your beautiful American wife," he said in English.

"I did, but she speaks perfect French," Victor said, shaking the businessman's hand. "She's Québécoise on her mother's side, so actually, I'll correct myself and call it near perfect," he added, putting his arm around me playfully. He then leaned down and pressed his lips on my bare skin, sending a pleasant shiver down my arm. "My not only beautiful but also rather intelligent wife." He smiled at me, then turned back to Arnaud de Fabry.

"Welcome, welcome," said Arnaud, switching to French to introduce his wife. "Marcelle," he said, glancing at her, "the bon vivant of Indochine. No one can be around Marcelle and not enjoy this place. Especially *this* place," he said, gesturing to the building. "So, you are in good hands for your first evening with us, Madame Lesage."

I smiled and turned to his wife. Marcelle de Fabry was dark-haired like Lucie, though her perfect waves fell just above her shoulders, and had lovely pale skin set off by bursts of freckles. Her eyes were a golden hazel, and as I approached her, I could see that they were beautiful marbles of color, full of life. She stood up, her tall frame enviably thin, and greeted me like a dear friend. "Welcome to Indochine, Jessie Lesage," she said, gesturing to the inviting rattan chair with a grass-green cushion next to her.

"We just had the coldest Veuve Clicquot in the house brought to us. I like my champagne to be the temperature of ice cream," she said, smiling.

"To what are we toasting?" I asked as the four of us raised our crystal glasses.

"We are celebrating it being Saturday evening," Marcelle said as the men nodded and launched into an animated conversation. "And to being young and healthy and not so bad-looking," she said to me. "You're really not so bad-looking. I should detest you for it straightaway, but you seem far too lovely to hate."

"No, I'm—"

"Oh, darling, just say thank you," she said, still smiling. "It's not your fault you're pretty." Her tone sounded genuinely warm, even though it was obvious that she was the more stunning one.

"Thank you," I replied, sure that I was blushing. "And it is Saturday, isn't it? After so long on the boat, I can barely keep my days straight. But Saturday, that seems reason enough to have a drink."

"That boat ride over is dreadful, isn't it? Takes a lifetime to splash halfway around the globe."

"It wasn't ideal," I admitted.

I brought the drink to my lips and thought about how I wasn't just celebrating a day or a weekend; I was celebrating a new life, one I was very excited for. With that in mind, the Veuve Clicquot was even more crisp and satisfying here than it was in France. And it was almost the temperature of ice cream.

"How exotic of you to be American," she said, her freckles seeming to multiply as she smiled. "I just love America. I traveled there once with an American fashion designer, and I wanted to stay forever. Such an outgoing people, the Americans. I made a great many friends."

"When did you travel there?" I asked.

"Nineteen twenty-four. The spring of that year. I was barely nineteen years old."

"Yes, I imagine that one would want to stay forever in the New York of 1924."

"Were you there then?" she asked, her voice tinkling with excitement. "Maybe we crossed each other unknowingly on Fifth Avenue."

"I was," I said. "Wouldn't it be lovely if we had." I leaned back, sipped my champagne, and looked slowly around me. "This building is wonderful," I said, running my fingers along the carved wood railing next to my chair. "So welcoming, but still quite elegant."

"Isn't it gorgeous?" Marcelle replied, lifting her hands like a dancer's. "It was designed by a Frenchman who studied at the École des Beaux-Arts but then spent time in Ceylon and Singapore. That's why it doesn't look French at all. He learned from the British and the local builders in those far-flung countries. But it's for the best, I think, because the French don't excel in this indoor-outdoor architecture. We love to close doors and build the thickest walls possible, as if we are about to go to war and must keep the bullets out. And if we do build terraces, they are nothing like these verandas. They are so narrow one can barely fit a folding chair on them to enjoy a coffee in the sun. If there ever is any sun. It isn't very civilized."

"Everything French is civilized," said her husband, jumping into our conversation. "And they are only built that way because, as you presciently pointed out, my dear, in France it rains constantly."

"I won't bother arguing with you," she said, not turning to look at him. She put her arms on the table and stretched as we waited for our first course. "Hanoi is not New York, but she has her own magic," she said, raising her thin eyebrows. "I love it here. I was a bit wary of it during my first month, but now I'm utterly in love with the place. We've been here nearly three years now, and I don't ever want to leave."

"Really?" I asked, surprised. Hadn't Trieu told me most French women quickly soured on Hanoi?

"Oh, yes," she said, sitting back as the waiter placed our whitefish salad on the table. "The way we live here, we could never exist like this in France, even if Arnaud had a very good year. In 1933, that's just not possible in Paris. And culturally, Indochine is not lacking, either. *Les indigènes* are quite strong in the arts. In the mid-twenties we built the École Supérieure des Beaux-Arts de l'Indochine, and the school has already produced some fine talents. Painters, even sculptors. And our opera house is beautiful—it rivals Garnier. You must take in an opera from the first-tier box, on the right side if you can. It's like jumping inside a lorgnette, the view is so good. The companies performing are world-class, too, not some singers they picked up off the street. The administration ships the performers in from France or even more far-flung places. Then there's the sunshine and freedom on top of it. It's proven to be my recipe for happiness."

"My recipe for happiness is a happy wife," said Arnaud, interrupting us. "You'll learn that soon enough, Victor. Keep Jessie content, and life in Indochine will be marvelous for you. Because some of the French wives, forgive my honesty, but they have a bit of trouble with it. With our way of life here."

"Jessie won't," said Victor looking at me. "She has an adventurer's heart. But if Jessie were ever unhappy, I'd swim back to France with her the moment she desired. That's just the type of upstanding man I am," said Victor, placing his hand on mine.

"When did you two marry?" said Arnaud, laughing. "Yesterday?"

"Something like that," murmured Victor. "It was actually Jessie's idea to come here," he continued, looking at me appraisingly. "I'll deny that if you repeat it outside of this little foursome, but Jessie saw the potential in Indochine before I did. My family, of course, has seen it for years, but Jessie decided we shouldn't just leave the plantations to be run by others. And after what happened at Dau Tieng in December—very unfortunate, those three coolies—it's important to finally have a family presence here. To have someone with the Michelin name, even if it is sandwiched between Victor and Lesage."

"Quite right," Arnaud chimed in. "Nor do you need a repeat of that enormous coolie strike you all dealt with in 1930. Bit of a fiasco."

"It was," said Victor. "That's what we most certainly want to avoid. Terrible press we received from all that. A bit exaggerated, in France at least. But we want to avoid that type of thing altogether."

Marcelle turned to me. "Well, you may be an adventurer, and adored by your husband—how lovely and *rare*," she said, shooting her husband a sly smile, "but you still look as if you just stepped off the boat. First things first, Jessie, that posture must go. Far too perfect." She moved forward and placed her warm hands on my shoulders, pushing them down gently. "Relax, my dear," she said. "You're on vacation, for as long as you want to be. This is Hanoi. It's so much better than real life."

"It does seem a bit like a vacation," I said, feeling my tired body bend under her hands. "The palm trees on the way in were a sight to see. As is all of this." I allowed myself a glance over my shoulder toward the dimly lit dining room, which despite the shadows was alive and buzzing with conversation.

"I'll never tire of it," Marcelle said. She looked up into the last rays of sun and closed her eyes. When she opened them, she leaned in and whispered, "You know, I'm from somewhere exotic, too."

"Are you? Where?" I asked curiously.

"Lille," she said, laughing. "It's exotic to Arnaud. He doesn't know that our country extends past Paris. He thinks that Italy borders the Thirteenth Arrondissement."

"Were you in Paris before coming here?" I asked, enjoying Marcelle's animated manner.

"*I* was in Paris. But Arnaud was in Burma," she said, pushing the hair from her forehead. There was no way to avoid sweating if you were sitting outside, but Marcelle didn't seem to mind. "The government sent him there to deal with some financial nonsense. Burma is British, as you know, but the French can't escape a few economic entanglements."

"You didn't follow him to Burma?" I asked.

"No, I didn't," she said, catching her husband's eye and smiling at him. "I was scared of such a faraway place at the time. I was young, and there are almost no French there. Especially French women."

"But you came here," I said, looking around us.

"Yes, because it's the crown jewel in our colonial empire. And in so many ways it's just an extension of France," she said, following my gaze.

"I don't quite see it like that. Yet," I admitted.

"You've been here mere minutes. You'll see. It's even better than France," Marcelle said. "I have quite a few local friends. I don't live in this little colonial castle like so many of the wives do. And I don't just brush off the people here as useless mites—that's short for 'Annamites,' or the natives, as many like to say. You've seen a map of the colony, I presume? Annam, Tonkin, Cochinchina, Cambodia, and Laos all broke apart when the French colonized the region formally in 1887, though we forgot to grab Laos until '93. Some of the regions are considered protectorates, some simple colonies. Annam, where the emperor rules, or where we let him think he does, is a protectorate, and that's where the term 'Annamite' comes from. And 'mite.' But really, it's not a very nice term."

"Enough of that history lesson," said Arnaud. "Let's ask the mites for more champagne," he said, grinning at his wife, who rolled her eyes and turned back to me.

I nodded, thinking of all the reading I had done about the colony before we'd come over. I was trying to come up with an intelligent response when Marcelle leaned in close and whispered again, as if it were quite normal for us to share secrets: "But all that is just geography. If you want to see the real Indochine, just tag along with me. I would be happy to show it to you."

"I would like that very much," I replied.

"Stick close to my wife," said Arnaud, again interrupting our little tête-à-tête. "She knows this city like a native now. I shouldn't let her run so free," he said, looking to Victor. "But she's much happier when uncaged."

"You didn't marry a housecat, I'm afraid," said Marcelle, laughing.

"Jessie would love a tour guide," said Victor. "We have both been trying to learn about the colony since we decided to come over six months ago, so we are quite familiar with the geography. We even took language lessons."

"Did you?" said Marcelle. "How fascinating. I've been here so long, and I still don't speak it well. Difficult language."

"Jessie was a teacher," said Victor. "She eats up knowledge."

"How lovely for you," said Marcelle, not unkindly. "And lucky for Victor to have a clever wife."

After the fish salad, we dined on three more courses—trout in jelly, leg of lamb, and profiteroles with crème anglaise, all taken with too much wine and champagne.

When we had finished, sipping strong coffees to temper the alcohol, Arnaud gripped Victor's arm. "You're wanted for billiards, my man. Are you any good? Everyone would like to know, because if you're not, they are ready to take your money, what's left of it, anyway. The rubber men were more fun to play with before '28, when the economy was booming, but we know you're not flat broke yet. The government has been handing you money left and right. All the planters, but especially the Michelin machine, n'est-ce pas? Loans from the Banque de l'Indochine that they never expect you to pay back. Not to mention those lenient tax rates. Simple rice farmers have higher taxes than Michelin et Cie."

Victor opened his mouth to protest, but Arnaud had strong ties to the government and knew of what he spoke. I could see him recalibrate.

"We appreciate all the support the state has given us since we decided to start planting ourselves. Because really, what is good for Michelin is even better for the state," said Victor confidently. "For France. If we win, the colony wins, and the country. We invested 200 million francs here before 1925 alone, and the number has just gone up. Even if our rates are low, that's still quite a lot of money paid in taxes. Which is fine. An honor even. That's always how we've viewed things. Country first, then Michelin."

"Of course, of course. Your success is our success," said Arnaud, pulling his elbows off the table. "I understand the Michelin strategy. You've now taken ownership of your product from start to finish. You've always been innovators. The pneumatic tire has changed the world. And my wife is a fan of those guides of yours. She was in France, anyway."

"Yes," said Marcelle, smiling kindly. "It's a brilliant idea. Arnaud has always been fond of driving in circles. Who knew a simple road map and a few restaurant recommendations could save him? And me."

"You women don't understand the roads," he said, winking at his wife. "Too bad about Étienne, though," Arnaud said, addressing Victor again. "Had great potential. But at least he was able to put a bit of a mark on the company's actions out here. To help direct your planta-tions from afar. The other planters were less than thrilled to lose your business—I still hear about it. You really need to join the Union of Rubber Planters, by the way, even if your family has refused in the past—you are wise enough to do what is most lucrative."

I nodded along. I knew how proud Victor was that Michelin was still able to make a profit in a difficult economy.

"It wasn't just the potential profits that motivated us," he said. "It was the quality of the rubber. We'd been receiving subpar rubber from the planters here for years. Surely you know that, from your union. But with our methods, our research, that will cease to be an issue in a few years' time."

I nodded my head politely and noticed that Marcelle's eyes were starting to glaze over.

"Come. Let's talk of other things," said Arnaud, glancing at his wife. "We're boring the women. In fact, we should leave them to their own devices so that Marcelle can say all the scandalous things she reserves for the company of the fairer sex. So, billiards?" he said, glancing behind him at where I guessed the room was. "Are you halfway decent?"

I looked at Victor, who had the gleam in his eye that I recognized from his nights out in Paris with his friends. He thrived on competition. And like most boys who grew up rich and bored, he was unbeatable at billiards.

"It's been a while, but I do play a little," said Victor, standing up. "You'll just have to remind me which end of the cue to use." He winked at me and brushed his hand across my bare arm as he walked out.

Marcelle and I watched the men go, pushed aside our coffee cups, and finished off the champagne.

"Freedom, finally," said Marcelle, smiling. She pulled out a cigarette from a handsome silver case, placed it between her fingers, and offered it to me. "It's my last, but please," she said. I declined, and she shrugged, placing it between her lips. It was immediately lit by a waiter. "I love Arnaud dearly, but it's almost strange to have him around as much as he has been lately. Usually he loses himself in his work. Most men do here, I'm afraid, and I'm sure Victor will have no choice but to follow suit. He's to work down in Cochinchina? At both plantations?"

"Yes, but I don't know how often," I replied. "We hope he can do much of his work from Hanoi."

"I don't think so, my dear," said Marcelle, after she exhaled a small stream of smoke. "The plantations are a two-day train-and-car journey away. And that's just to Saigon. He will have to motor on again from there. So you'll find yourself alone, and here, quite often, I'm afraid."

"Perhaps," I said, though Victor had promised that he would split his time evenly between Hanoi and the plantations in the south.

"Victor must have been spending most of his time in Clermont-Ferrand before you left? Though maybe it wasn't so noticeable. Being alone in Paris as a pretty young woman is never a bad thing. Feels more like a gift, really."

"He didn't, actually," I said, hesitating slightly. I knew Victor wouldn't want me to reveal how far he'd been kept from the operations in Clermont-Ferrand all these years. "He worked closely with his uncle André in Paris, so he never worked outside of the capital."

"Of course. We all knew of André Michelin. Was he really Victor's direct uncle? He and Édouard?"

"Not exactly, but André especially treated Victor like he was. And he really let Victor become his right-hand man," I said, embellishing a bit for my husband's sake.

"It's quite smart of Victor to have taken on that role," said Marcelle kindly. "You would be much less glamorous if he'd forced you to spend your pretty years in Clermont-Ferrand. I've never been taken with L'Auvergne. All those mountains. Isn't there a volcano, too?"

"There is," I said, smiling back, grateful she didn't question my explanation further.

"How savage," she whispered. She took another pull on the cigarette and blew the smoke into the night sky. "Nice of Victor not to put the family in Saigon. There are many of us there, too, but it's much more fun in Hanoi because the government is here, which means the wives are here. It makes it feel much more like home. And of course, we have the club. They have one, too, the Cercle des Officiers, and I'm sure Victor will spend much time there when he goes. They also have Le Cercle Sportif Saigonnais. It's another chosen meeting place of the French elite. But it's so sports-oriented. The men are always sweating, and not in the way you want them to. Not from huffing and puffing in the bedroom, which is the acceptable kind of sweating, of course. It's just . . . well, it's simply not this place. Neither is."

"If you love it so much here, I'm sure I will, too," I said, trying not to show how surprised I was by her colorful references.

"Of course you will." Marcelle gestured behind her and suggested we move to the bar.

"It's a delightful room," she said as our heels clicked on the wooden floor. "But darker. Better for deception. Besides, we can parade you around properly there. The women in the dining room all look as if they have nothing better to do than count their sun freckles, but I know they are all dying to meet the beautiful American—Canadian American—who swept Victor Lesage off his feet. At least they are staring at us as if they are."

"I doubt they know Victor," I said as I followed her.

"Perhaps not, but they certainly know *of* him. Your imminent arrival made many of the papers here. Don't worry, the picture they ran was quite flattering. And sometimes just knowing someone through a photo and a few words is more fun. More cause to speculate and invent stories about him, and you. Try not to be too nice. They'll be disappointed." She grinned as we passed the last of the dining tables.

As we walked into a smaller room, dominated by a long wooden bar and stiff straw fans spinning overhead, Marcelle surveyed a small group of people, some men but mostly women in pale-colored or white and ivory gowns, with more skin showing than I imagine they would have dared in Paris. They were standing by the open windows, their bodies close together as if they always moved as a pack. They glanced at Marcelle, but they stared at me.

Marcelle leaned into me as if we were old friends and put her hand on my arm. When we turned away from them, she whispered, "They're friendlier than they look, the wives. But on first meeting, alcohol will help."

"Alcohol always helps," I murmured.

We had drinks presented to us before we even reached the bar.

"How convenient," said Marcelle, taking a long sip of a lavender-colored cocktail. "I know the French think we invented hospitality, and many other things, but the Annamites have us beat when it comes to service."

"The staff here is very attentive," I said, draining the cocktail. "Our staff at the house are lovely, too. Or they seem to be thus far. I'd look all wrong tonight if my servant Trieu hadn't dressed me. There's a fashion all its own out here, isn't there?"

Marcelle nodded. "A lot of white. We are like ghosts floating around this place. And thank goodness for servants, they often do know what's best for us. You're in the big yellow house. Number 131 rue de la Chaux, right?"

I gave a slight nod, still taking in the crowd around us.

"Your staff worked for the van Dampierres then, so they must be the best. I'm sure they were well trained when the van Dampierres inherited them, but you can bet that it was Louise who perfected their skills."

"Were you friends with them? Théodore and Louise?" I asked, hoping to learn a bit more about the family that came before us.

"I'd say friendly more than friends," said Marcelle, swirling the ice cubes in her drink, her diamond bracelets clinking against the tall glass. "But they are family friends of yours, or of the Michelins, aren't they?"

"Yes. Well, Victor and I have never met them, but they are close friends of Édouard's. Théodore van Dampierre attended the same school as him, though a decade later."

"Must be quite the school to produce Édouard and Théodore, who was practically the head of the Banque de l'Indochine."

"Indeed," I replied, starting to suspect how important the bank was in the colony.

"He was quite an animated man, considering his rather serious job," said Marcelle pensively. "And Louise, she was lovely. Very elegant, very popular among the older wives. She certainly ruled that set. A smart woman, too. Did a bit of charity work when she was here, with orphans. There are so many. Mixed-race children mostly. Abandoned little things. She was known for that, and for being part of a less wild crowd here. Elegant woman, but staid. Quite religious, I think. And because of that, I heard that she didn't take well to certain things. And her husband, as kind as he was, he took to them too well." She raised her eyebrows at me and leaned against the bar, which we had sauntered over to.

"What sort of things?" I asked, leaning like Marcelle. She seemed like the kind of person who expected emulation, and I was happy to go along.

"Those sorts of things," said Marcelle, whispering again. She nodded over my shoulder. In a corner was a Frenchman who looked well over forty. He had a young native woman, a waitress, backed up against a wall, his body trapping hers in the shadows.

Before I could register what was happening to the *indigène* girl, a woman appeared beside me, her eyes on Marcelle.

"I didn't know you were here," she exclaimed. She was a striking woman with alabaster skin and light red hair that tucked delicately in toward her chin. I wondered how she was able to keep her skin so white despite the constant sunshine.

"Caroline," said Marcelle, jutting out her chin to kiss the woman on each cheek. "Where else would I be on a Saturday evening?"

"I've heard your social life doesn't have borders, *ma chère*," the woman responded playfully, rapping her painted nails against her perfectly curved hip.

"One shouldn't listen to all the rumors," said Marcelle. Caroline shrugged and smiled at me.

She had a stunning face, and a plunging, amply filled-out décolletage that I was sure she'd relied on for years. I returned her smile and tried to forget the image of the girl pressed against the wall. I hoped she had escaped.

"You're Victor's American wife," Caroline said. "Aren't you pretty." From the way she said it, I understood that it wasn't a compliment.

"Thank you. But compared to French women, I always feel very plain," I replied honestly. "We just can't quite keep up in America."

Allowing a trace of a satisfaction to show, she dismissed my comment politely.

"Did you arrive today? You must have. And then you're dragged out to the jungle on your first night in Hanoi."

"I don't mind," I lied.

"No, of course you don't," Caroline replied coolly. "Besides, this place is lovely, even if it's a world apart from Paris. Though I imagine Paris was quite different from wherever you grew up."

"Hanoi *is* very different. But I'm finding it fascinating," I said, pretending I didn't hear her last phrase.

"That it is," she said, exhaling and dropping her cigarette in a nearby ashtray. "I was dining casually downstairs, otherwise I would have met you as soon as you walked in. I've known Victor for years. He just poked his head out of the men's wing to say hello to me, in fact. Quite sweet of him."

He had? He had interrupted his billiard game to see this woman, but had not bothered to check on me? Even after that show of affection when we'd first sat down? I bit back my annoyance and smiled.

"Oh?" I said. Victor hadn't mentioned knowing any women in Hanoi, especially not one who looked like Caroline. "You and Victor are acquainted?"

"I knew him as a child," she said, reaching for one of the lavender drinks on a waiter's tray, "but my family moved to Marseille when I was fourteen. A terrible time to be pulled out of Paris. I still haven't quite recovered from the shock."

"I see. Well, being a child in Paris must have been lovely. And with Victor, too. As a friend," I said, babbling on. I had no idea what to say. Why hadn't Victor mentioned her?

"It has been years since our paths crossed, which is no surprise, as I imagine he's spent much of his time during the last decade in Clermont-Ferrand."

"I'm sure he was happy to see a familiar face," I managed to say, my own face frozen in a put-on smile.

"It's a small world, our community in Indochine," Marcelle jumped in, clearly trying to shift the conversation.

"Isn't it, though," Caroline replied. Something about her tone made it clear that it wasn't my community yet. "But to be quite honest, I never thought a real Michelin would ever make it over here. They don't seem too concerned about the press they've received since that incident in December. I suppose why would you if the money is still good."

"They do care, quite a bit. That is why—" I started, but Caroline spoke right over me.

"What surprised me even more than his swimming over to the colony was to hear that he'd been married off. I never would have expected Victor Lesage to be married, and with a child already. I heard he was such a womanizer in Paris. That no girl stayed on his arm for more than a week. I thought he'd be a bachelor until fifty, at least." Leaning in and lowering her voice, she whispered, "Tell me, dear, how did you tame him? You must be exquisite where it counts. Is that something they teach you in America? The sexual arts?"

"Caroline!" Marcelle exclaimed, pushing in front of me. "How many of these purple cocktails have you had? Have you gone mad? You don't even know this poor woman."

"It's just talk, Marcelle," said Caroline, laughing and taking a step back. "No reason to run to her rescue. She's a Lesage, isn't she? I'm sure she can handle herself perfectly well."

Marcelle took me by the arm and turned to pull me away, but I stayed where I was, staring at Caroline.

"People change," I said flatly, thankful for Marcelle but not willing to let this horrible woman's first impression of me be that of some meek wife.

"Not the people I know," Caroline countered. "Not his set."

"Enough, *chérie*. You're boring me," Marcelle said to Caroline. "You're going to make Jessie think that all the French women in Indochine are beasts like you. Scurry on, please, so I can introduce her to someone less intoxicated."

"I'm not intox—" Caroline fought back, but Marcelle had already pushed past her.

"What a way to begin your time here! I'm terribly sorry about that," she exclaimed once we were on the other side of the room. "I'm pretty sure she's on a boat back to France in three months, so don't even worry about her. She just thinks she's the prettiest French woman in Hanoi, and she clearly doesn't want any competition as she finishes out her spell here."

"I'm quite sure *you're* the prettiest woman in Hanoi," I said, reaching for a much-needed drink. "And thank you for coming to my rescue. Frankly, I'm in shock. Why would Victor forget to tell me that he knew a woman like her?"

"I'm sure he was in no hurry to bring that up," said Marcelle, grinning. She pushed the thin straps of her dress higher onto her shoulders and stood a little straighter. "And thank you for the compliment. I'm attractive in a way that looks nice in pictures, magazines. I was modeling a bit for Lanvin and Patou when I met Arnaud. Striking in front of a camera, but perhaps a bit too thin in real life. Caroline and you, you are beautiful in real life."

"I'm not sure that Indochine is real life," I said, looking around us.

"You're right about that," she said, opening her cigarette case again. She saw that it was empty, snapped the case shut, and grabbed my arm. "Listen, were you serious about what you said at dinner? That you wanted to see the real Indochine?"

"Yes, I was," I said, starting to smile again. "I didn't come here to pretend I was still in France."

"Come, then," she said excitedly. She glanced at the people around us and then leaned in close to me. "Do you want to see the men's wing? There's a service hallway we can sneak through. You have to peek at least once." She dropped her voice even lower. "Why not now?"

"But won't we get in terrible trouble if they catch us?" I whispered back, looking around instinctively. "Embarrass our husbands?"

"Yes. If we got caught. Which we won't. Or most likely won't. Come! The risk is half the fun."

Before I could answer, she pulled me out of the cocktail room and down the hallway. Something told me not to let go.

"This is it, here," she said as we reached a nearly invisible door in the white wall, a tiny latch barely discernible in the center molding. A boy eyed us as Marcelle leaned against it, and she quickly reached into her little purse and slipped a few coins into his hand.

With only a few workers at the end of the hallway, she hissed, "Don't just gawk at them! Come on!" and pulled me through.

My pulse rising, I stood close to her as she shut the door behind us, trying to adjust my eyes to the dark.

"They use this corridor for formal functions, the types of to-dos where the staff are supposed to look as if they emerge from the walls," she explained.

"Do they have to carry trays of champagne in the dark?" I asked, holding on to her shoulder.

"They do, but they're used to it. They've got black eyes that can see in the dark."

"How convenient."

"The bedrooms are farther down, but the billiard room is just a few paces from here. It's the first room in the men's wing. Come, let's see if our husbands are up to no good."

Despite what that wretched Caroline had said, Victor hadn't been "up to no good" since before we were married. He had changed. Marriage had changed him. Becoming a father even more so. And I doubted that an hour in a billiard room would reverse that.

Marcelle paused and put her ear to the wall. "Yes," she said, reaching down to feel for a latch. "It's just here."

She placed her ear to the wall again, and when there was laughter loud enough for both of us to hear it, she flicked the latch and pressed the door the tiniest bit open.

I peeked in over her shoulder, staying back far enough so that if one of us tumbled in, it would be her. The room was beautiful, done out in a tropical dark wood that resembled mahogany. There were bookshelves lined with books, but all had light gray dust jackets on them, the titles written in cursive on the spines in brown ink. There was a large billiard table in the middle, and rattan chairs and couches with cream-colored cushions lined the walls. The table might have looked out of place if the felt was green, but it had been covered in gray instead, a light, handsome gray that matched the soft surroundings. It all had the look of an eternal summer, which, compared to Paris, Indochine was. I spotted Victor, cue in hand, waiting to take his shot. In his other hand was a tall glass of water, which meant that he definitely wanted to win.

I looked for Arnaud, but before I could spot him, I saw a young native woman perched on one of the couches in the far corner. She was leaning against a man at least twice her age who looked like so many of the men in the room—tan and utterly carefree. He seemed far more interested in her than in the billiards.

"That's the girl from the bar," I whispered, taking a step back. "Is she allowed in here?"

"Allowed?" Marcelle said, pulling the door shut again as we spoke. "I'm sure she's encouraged. Didn't the women in Paris warn you about anything?"

I thought of my friends in Paris, all the right kind of women who said and did the correct things. They were, in Victor's eyes, my close friends, but because I started life as a girl *not* saying or doing the right things, I never allowed myself to become truly close to any, growing even warier of them when I learned that they'd all been handpicked as companions for me by his mother. Perhaps with someone like Marcelle, someone who clearly did not care about etiquette or rules, I could find true friendship.

"The women I knew in Paris?" I replied. "They warned me about malaria."

"Right, malaria . . ." she said, her voice trailing off. "It *is* a bothersome infection. But not as bothersome as syphilis. Come, our husbands seem focused on the game. How boring. Let's go to the bedrooms. If you think this is scandalous, I'm sure worse is going on there. And it's not even midnight."

We crept farther down the hidden passage and turned a corner. In this section, a bare bulb hung from the ceiling, illuminating the numbers written on the unpainted walls.

"Now, *you* push one of the doors open. It won't bite. Just be sure to do it slowly, and as soon as you see a sliver of light, stop."

I pushed the first one open and stopped prematurely. Marcelle pushed it the rest of the way, stopping as soon as we could see light. She peeked in and came back immediately. "Empty," she whispered. The second room was, too. But when I pushed the third door open, we were flooded with light, and more than just moonlight. I pulled my hand back as if I'd touched a hot stove.

"Just look quickly and then pull it shut," Marcelle whispered excitedly. I leaned in, suddenly feeling the way I had with my sisters growing up, enjoying the silliness that could be had when our brothers disappeared. I put my eye to the door and pulled back, slapping my hand over my face to keep from laughing out loud.

"What, what?" Marcelle pushed me out of the way, looked in, too, then fell back against the wall laughing. "Come, quickly, shut it. Let's go. We're certainly not going to outdo that."

We ran toward the hidden service entrance, both trying to suppress our laughter.

Room three was occupied by a portly man, completely naked and sunburned, lying on his back on the bed, his genitals fully exposed and one very formal shoe still on. Our eyes watered with laughter as we headed back to the kitchen. Marcelle peered out, and when she saw there was again no one but staff, she opened the door fully and pulled me out by the hand. She closed the door with her slender hip, then put her head on my shoulder, convulsing with laughter. "That was the *vice-ministre des colonies!*" she said, barely able to get the words out.

"The deputy minister of the colonies?" I said, pulling away from her. "No!"

"Yes! He's here visiting from France. We attended a reception with him just last night. My goodness, I can never look at him the same way again. Do you think he always sleeps with one shoe on or just when he is very intoxicated?"

"We don't even know that he was," I said, laughing again. "Maybe that's his normal nightly routine."

Marcelle put her hand on my arm. "Come, Jessie Lesage. We are going to have far too much fun together, that's obvious. Let's get a strong drink before our husbands force us home."

Victor came to fetch me an hour later, and my heart was still full, my cheeks aching from laughter.

I had never met a woman like Marcelle. If anyone was going to convince me to relax the boundaries I always seemed to set around my friendships, it was her, I was already sure of it.

I grabbed Victor's hand joyfully, and he kissed the inside of my wrist as we slipped out of the building. Nuzzled in the back seat of the Delahaye, I fell asleep against him before we'd even left the grounds of the club. When we arrived home, we went straight upstairs and collapsed into bed, a pile of sweat, alcohol, and exhaustion. We found just enough energy to make love in the heat, quietly, not yet sure of what the walls did and didn't keep out.

"Did you enjoy our rite of passage?" Victor asked as he turned onto his side and closed his eyes.

I thought of Caroline. Of the biting things she'd said. Then I thought of running behind the walls with Marcelle, and I grinned. "I did," I said. "I had a wonderful time with Marcelle. She's rather intoxicating. So is the club. The whole world here, really."

"I agree," said Victor. "Aren't we lucky that it's our world now?"

FOUR

Jessie

September 4, 1933

When I woke up, I wasn't surprised to find an empty space where Victor had been. I knew he was due to leave at sunrise, but the bed in Indochine seemed bigger than ours in Paris, and suddenly I felt very much alone.

At the end of the bed was a tray with breakfast on it, a real French breakfast of fruit, croissants, and strong black coffee, which I devoured, placing my silverware on the plate silently when I'd finished. Victor had taught me how to put down my cutlery without a clink, as if we were eating with feathers, and now I did it that way even when I was alone. It was one of the many things Victor had had to teach me when we were married, but to his delight, and mine, I was a quick study.

I pushed the covers off my legs. All the linens on the bed were white, as was the mosquito net covering it and the curtains on the two French doors. I looked down at my nightgown, cotton with delicate silk edging. It seemed to have been made to match. It was a welcome gift from Trieu, who said it was too hot in Indochine to sleep in anything else. She was right again. I gathered the skirt and stared out at the sweeping city view. I knew I shouldn't step onto the front balcony in my nightgown, so I let my eyes take in the buildings from bed—the mismatched rooftops and shutters closed to block the sun, the slice of the lake we could see from our perch, and the white masses of milk flowers that seemed to have blossomed overnight. In the bright morning light, I could see farther than the evening before, past the smart avenues to the east of Hoan Kiem Lake and into the crowded local neighborhoods far west of it. I stood, wrapping myself in my blue silk dressing gown, the same one I had worn after Victor and I made love. We'd spent the next day in a haze of exhaustion, the weight of our journey and our night at the Officers' Club hitting us, but now, on this Monday morning, as the city woke up below me, I felt well in my skin again. I opened the door to the balcony and tried to spot Hanoi's landmarks, ones I had read about in travel books on the boat journey over—St. Joseph's Cathedral, the Hotel Métropole—but I was distracted by the lovely view of the opera house, which was just at the end of our street.

I had just glimpsed a rowboat bobbing in the lake when I felt myself gripping the iron railing. It had been on the boat journey from France that things had turned difficult. On a rainy afternoon, alone in our cabin, I had accidentally picked up Victor's papers, documents penned by Michelin management. What I saw had tainted the journey over, but I was determined not to let it wedge itself inside me for good. They were just notes on the past, Victor said when he'd found me reading. He was going to Indochine to change things.

I gave up looking for landmarks when I grew distracted by the morning's noises, including the sound of Lucie pushing open my door, still sleepy-eyed in her pink nightgown. She wandered in, looking a little off balance, Cam behind her.

"My Lucie!" I said, tying the belt of my dressing gown in a loose knot and meeting her by the door. I had barely seen her the day before as she had slept on and off for hours. I leaned down and kissed her warm cheek. She still smelled like the same Lucie, even in a new country full of different air, different odors. "Are you hungry? You must be. I just ate, but I'll make you anything you like if we can find the ingredients. What would you like to have for breakfast, *ma chérie*?"

"Oh, *madame*," said Cam, putting her hands on Lucie's bare arms. "You do not have to worry about Lucie's meals. The cook will take care of them. We should have informed you yesterday."

"Thank you, Cam, but I don't mind," I said, placing a hand protectively on Lucie as well. "I like spending time with my daughter in the kitchen."

"But the lady of the house is never in the kitchen," said Cam. She smiled at me and respectfully removed her hands from Lucie.

"Oh," I replied, feeling embarrassed. Cam was, of course, only doing what she was trained to do. They all were. "If that's the way it's done here, then of course. I will stay out of the kitchen and just join her for breakfast on the terrace."

"If you would like to," said Cam politely. "But don't you have many things to do today?"

I thought for a minute, fiddling with the watch Victor had given me before we left Paris, a new model called a Reverso. The jeweler had told him that no other modern wristwatch kept time as well. On the back of the watch face, Victor had had engraved a simple image of an orange, a nod to my maiden name, Holland. The watch was novel in that it could flip around to show the orange, not the time, a feature that also protected the face.

"No," I said to Cam, glancing down at the watch, which, now that I had no appointments or visits with friends or family, seemed more like jewelry than something I depended on. "I don't have anything to do today. I suppose I'll just explore this little neighborhood of ours. I can't really learn too much about it from up here, can I?"

Trieu slipped in the door, surely having heard our voices, to start getting me dressed. Cam played with Lucie and her doll at the foot of the bed as Trieu helped me into my undergarments, and I watched them while standing in my slip, Lucie dissolving into giggles as Cam pretended that the doll was doing somersaults.

When my dress was on and Trieu was brushing my hair back, pinning it out of my face, Cam put the doll in Lucie's arms and turned and looked at me with curiosity. "Did you cook the meals when you lived in France?" she asked, drawing a quick reprimand in Annamese from Trieu.

"Sometimes," I said, not bothered by the question. "I've always enjoyed cooking. We had help, but I often just did it myself."

"I didn't know the French knew how to cook anything," said Cam.

"I'm not French, remember, Cam," I said. "Where I'm from, we cook."

I thought of my mother, who, despite having lived in two different countries and being fluent in two languages, had never known anything but an impoverished rural life. Her father had grown tobacco on their farm in Joliette, near the St. Lawrence River, fifty miles north of Montreal. But when his crops failed, he moved the family to a warmer climate, finding work on a large tobacco farm in Mount Airy, North Carolina, near the Virginia border. It was there that she'd met my father, whose people also worked that land. Together, they attempted to farm their own land in Virginia. It was hard for me to picture my mother doing anything but working. All through my childhood, until my siblings and I were old enough to help, she killed chickens herself, cutting off their heads with as much emotion as she exhibited when plucking a weed. She would de-feather the birds, butcher them, and fry them for all her hungry children, keeping the heads and feet for stock and the feathers to stuff pillows with. As I grew older, and she grew more exhausted with each succeeding pregnancy, that duty fell to me. I did not miss that kind of cooking one bit.

"Perhaps the Americans are more like the Annamites than the French are," I said. Or perhaps poor people were just the same the world over.

Cam took Lucie downstairs for breakfast once Lucie had tired of watching me get ready.

When my hair was done, my favorite rings were on, and a pair of small emerald earrings were glimmering on my earlobes, Trieu walked me down to the kitchen. All through the empty house, the fans were blowing up the thin curtains in the sitting rooms like the skirts of twirling children.

When we reached the open door to the kitchen, I looked in and saw Lucie, Cam, and our cook, Diep, clustered closely together. Diep was flipping a fried egg into the air, much to Lucie's delight. She was seated on Cam's lap, her back arched happily like a cat's. I stood silently and watched Cam's hand moving in gentle circles on Lucie's spine. My stomach tightened at the sight, and not even the sound of my daughter's laughter, or her enthusiastic phrases in Indochinese, could stop the jealousy that pricked me.

"*Nũa!*" Lucie shouted, shrieking for more, as the egg landed precisely in the center of the pan. The cook cracked another one so she could continue charming Lucie.

"We are so in awe of Lucie's Annamese," said Trieu quietly as she watched them. "What an intelligent child. How did she learn?"

"We all had lessons with a tutor before we came," I said. "I picked up quite a bit, but Lucie started speaking it with impressive ease after just three months of study. She was like a little parrot with her tutor. She's quite good, isn't she?"

"Excellent. And she will be happier here because of it," said Trieu. "It's rare. But it is a gift." We watched as Lucie gave the cook a hug after she flipped an egg onto her plate.

"The van Dampierres' children loved Diep, too," said Trieu. "Though they only had boys. Poor Madame van Dampierre. She was such a feminine woman. She deserved to have a girl. As for Cam, even though she's so young, she treats the children as if they're her own. She is the oldest of ten children. That's why she's so motherly." Trieu stepped into the kitchen, motioning for me to follow.

"Mama!" Lucie exclaimed, not moving from Cam's lap. "Look at what Diep can do with eggs! They fly like birds. It's magic."

"It really is," I said, watching the second egg land in the pan, its yolk intact.

"Shall I sit with you while you eat, darling?" I asked her. "On the terrace?"

Lucie hesitated, then looked at the cook. "I want to stay here and see the eggs," she said, leaning her head against Cam's shoulder. "May I?" she said after my face fell. "Just for today?"

"Of course, darling," I replied, forcing a smile. I had counted on her taking to the staff, but perhaps not so quickly. "How amusing," I said. "Flying eggs."

I made my way back upstairs, walked down the tiled hallway, stepping only in the middle of it, the slight clack of my low-heeled day shoes the only sound in the house. When I reached the end of the hall, I paused in front of the master bedroom. I leaned against the doorway and looked inside. I'd never had such a large bedroom. Our apartment in Paris was beautiful, but the French didn't build the same way in their country.

I closed my eyes a minute, remembering my childhood bedroom. In our neglected farmhouse, the walls were a mix of old chipped paint and water leaks. In the bedrooms, there were creaky metal beds everywhere with sagging mattresses that felt like sleeping on wet cardboard. Like the rest of the house, my bedroom was inhabited by children of various sizes with too little space and privacy to properly grow.

I looked at my new bed, already made by one of the servants, the light streaming in to kiss the room, and wished I could transport the restless child that I had been to this place. But it wasn't worth looking backward. My childhood was lost, but I had Lucie. She, I had vowed when I started to feel her move in my stomach, would have everything I had not. She would be the opposite of me.

I walked into the bedroom and put my hands on the bed. I was tempted to climb back in, my body still not set to the hours of the Orient, but I noticed there was a door to my left slightly ajar. I thought it was the closet, but quickly realized that it was the door to the adjoining room, the small one that Victor had taken for his study. One of the servants must have opened it and forgotten to close it when I was downstairs.

Below the only window in the room was a large wooden desk, simple but well polished, which must have belonged to Théodore van Dampierre. On top were a typewriter, a navy-blue blotter, two of Victor's pens, and a few Michelin guidebooks. I looked down at the familiar red covers, the picture of the Michelin Man—André and Édouard had noticed one day that a haphazard stack of tires resembled a figure—printed on each cover. I picked up the most recent guide, its familiarity giving me a certain comfort, and ran my thumb over the price indicated on the cover. Twenty-five francs.

There were three drawers on each side of the desk and one wide, shallow drawer between them. Only one had a small silver keyhole in it. Instinctually, I reached for it, but it was locked. I opened the drawer below it. Empty. Then I opened the middle drawer. Inside was a small silver key. I took it up quickly, pressed it between my fingers, and then slipped it inside the keyhole. It unlocked without a sound, and I pulled the drawer open.

Inside was a stack of papers, held together with a metal clip. On the top of the stack was a document I had seen before. I had read it on the boat. It was an internal report that had circulated through the company. There was nothing out of the ordinary about it except that instead of focusing on the factories in France, it went into detail about the plantations in Indochine.

I knew much about the company. But I had never read an internal memo before. All I had ever read were the guidebooks.

But halfway into our boat journey, that changed.

Victor and I had left the small window of our cabin open, and late in the day, despite blue skies, there was a sudden downpour. I jumped up from the top deck and headed down to close it as soon as I felt the drops on my skin, but when I arrived, I was too late. The rain had come in and soaked a folder that was on the small table right below the window. I grabbed it, wiped off the table with a bath towel, and opened the folder to see if there was anything important inside.

It was full of Victor's papers, and the top one was a memo penned by his uncle Édouard. I scanned it quickly to see just how significant it was, worried that the water stains might upset Victor.

There was quite a lot of damage in the middle, but it was still fully legible. I started skimming from top to bottom. There were a few suggestions for Victor as he headed into his new position and a short economic overview of each plantation. I stopped there, seeing no need to keep reading, but just as I was moving the paper off to dry, a phrase jumped out at me. A moment later, I was sitting on the floor with the paper in my hand reading it carefully.

"Race primitive."

A primitive race.

When I was a child, I'd been called primitive many times. It didn't have to do with my race, but something else I couldn't control. Poverty. "The primitive country children"—I'd heard my teacher say the phrase when I was thirteen or fourteen to speak of my family and others like us. My sister had asked me whom exactly she'd been talking about, and I hadn't had the heart to respond, "Us, of course." I'd just shrugged.

"Paresseux." Lazy. That term, according to the memo, best described *"les coolies tonkinois,"* the laborers from Tonkin, the northern region where Hanoi was located and where the majority of the Michelin plantation workers were recruited. It went on to describe a typical day's work for a coolie, beginning at 4:45 a.m. and ending at 5:30 p.m., including nearly two hours of walking. The coolies received five days off a month, but only half days. On those days, they were required to clean their accommodations as well as the homes of the French over-seers. Next came recommendations on how to save more money in this time of economic crisis. Perhaps a shorter pause for lunch could be implemented now that the mishap of 1932 was further behind them, allowing more rubber trees to be tapped in a day? Already the plantations were ahead of their competition, the Michelin coolies able

to tap over four hundred trees a day when the coolies on competing plantations owned by the Société des Terres Rouges couldn't even tap three hundred. It was stressed that Victor had to maintain or improve those numbers.

The memo also mentioned the salaries on the plantation, which had recently been cut. Despite that, Victor would be making a salary that was equivalent to the pay of 4,500 coolies. The coolies made two and a half francs a day. In Clermont-Ferrand, the lowest-paid worker made nearly forty francs, they noted, but Indochine was different. Cost of living, it said, was very low. It was a fair wage.

I planned to stop reading then, but at the bottom of the page I saw the words "*nombre de morts.*" Death toll. It was noted that in 1927 alone, 17 percent of the labor force at Phu Rieng had died. And more recently, it had been 25 percent.

I was so fixated on the figures that I didn't hear the cabin door open. But I heard it shut.

Victor was standing there, watching me. He didn't say anything. He simply stared at me, looking from my face to the papers I was holding.

"Did they get wet?" he asked.

"A little," I managed to say.

He walked over, taking what I was reading out of my hands and closing the envelope.

He placed it under his arm. "It is no great secret that things haven't been easy on the plantations, for the workers or for the management. You may not have known to what extent, but you've read the newspapers. This should not come as a shock."

"I have," I managed to say, though they certainly had not printed the mortality rate for coolies.

"I am going to try to change many aspects of our operation, including the welfare of the workers. But the most important thing, taking precedence over everything else, is that the plantations continue to make money. If we don't have profit, we can't even feed our men. The second priority, which is equal and forever linked to the first, is to keep the communist element from rising up. After what happened in December, that is imperative. I don't know what you read from this," he said, patting the folder, "but you should already know that."

"I did know that," I said. "But it's helpful to be reminded," I added honestly.

He nodded. "You're always a wonderful vehicle for change, Jessie, and you have helped me realize that I've been complacent in my career. Relying on my bloodline to keep me afloat but not taking it as far as I can. If I succeed in those two tasks, I think we can have a very nice life."

"I will do anything in my power to help you," I said earnestly. Victor's success mattered even more to me than it did to him.

"Good." He turned for the door. "But please don't read my papers," he said without looking back at me.

After that day, I'd felt Victor watching me. When we were alone together, his eyes gave off electricity. I'd felt it when we first met. He would track me, not out of suspicion but out of lust. Now he tracked me out of something else. It felt like suspicion at first, but I realized that it was just contemplation. He was wondering at times who this wife of his was.

When we'd reached Indochine, excitement had replaced the discomfort of that day. But as I looked at the papers again now, my eyes sought the same word on the same water-stained paper. "*Primitive.*" I flipped the page, not liking the way that word turned my stomach. I was now reading a 1927 report of the Michelin plantations, done by an inspector named Delamarre on behalf of the colonial government. At the top was written "Extremely Confidential."

I loosened my grip, afraid to wrinkle the pages, and started to read, but nearly dropped everything when I heard a sound at the door.

"Jessie."

Victor's voice broke me out of my state. Every fiber in my being stood on end as if I'd just been thrown into a frozen lake.

I looked up at him. He didn't look angry, just surprised.

"What are you doing?" he asked, his voice still calm.

He looked at the exact sheet of paper I was holding.

"I thought you were traveling to the plantations today," I said helplessly.

"Yes. I am," he said, watching my nervous movements. "But I'm taking the evening train. I received a phone call this morning and was advised to stay in Hanoi through the afternoon as there's an important meeting that I should attend. Informal but important. The government man I met with this morning suggested it."

He watched as I struggled with the clip, trying to make the papers look like I had when I found them. I bent the top page accidentally, smoothed it, and started the process over again.

"Let me," said Victor, reaching out for the papers. He took them gently out of my grasp, placed them in the first drawer, closed it, and locked it with the little silver key. This time, he put the key in his pocket.

I turned away from him and began to walk back into the bedroom, but he caught me by the shoulder.

"Jessie. This is a complicated business. You know that. But I'm here now. I'm going to try to make our plantations both lucrative and peaceful. That's what I said on the boat, remember?"

"Of course," I said, relaxing under his touch.

"The men my family has put at the helm, as plantation directors, Theurière at Dau Tieng and Soumagnac at Phu Rieng, they're an engineer and a military man respectively. I've never met them, but my guess is that while they are certainly intelligent, they might lack compassion and economic know-how, the kind that I gained from working with André all these years. All this," he said, pointing to the stack of papers, "is just an attempt to educate myself about what I'm walking into. Our company isn't perfect, but we are trying. And succeeding. We're still turning a profit, more than any other plantation in Indochine. So I don't want to change that. I want to improve upon it.

And avoid a repeat of 1927, when the French overseer was murdered by the coolies, and 1930, and last year."

I felt very silly. We had spoken at length about the three coolies who had been shot at the end of last year, the very unfortunate result of 1,200 coolies stomping in anger past a guard on the edge of Dau Tieng plantation. Michelin had reduced their rice allocation by a hundred grams and lowered their pay from 0.4 piastres a day to 0.3. It was unfortunate, but the economy dictated it. But the coolies didn't understand that. Some of the 1,200 men were just angry; others were communists trying to incite change. Men like them were very dangerous in communities like plantations where people lived in close quarters. Victor had to keep things like that from happening again. But I hoped he wouldn't use the word *primitive* when he did.

"I didn't want to get you caught up in all this," said Victor, running his hand softly across my hair. "I wanted you to just get settled in our pretty house, enjoy lazy days at the club, and spend time with Lucie."

"But I care about your work, too," I said, which I did, far more than Victor even knew.

"I know you do. And I need your continued support," he replied. "I've always had that from you."

"Of course," I replied, looking up at him. "You always will."

I was going to say more when we were interrupted by a knock on the door.

"Yes?" Victor called out.

"I'm sorry, sir," said Trieu, appearing at the door. "A note was just left for you. The man who delivered it said it was important."

Victor motioned to her to bring it to him and opened it before she left the room.

"Wonderful news," he said without looking at me.

"What is?" I asked, trying to glance at the paper.

"The governor-general can meet me today. In an hour. I put in a request with his office just this morning. It's not why I stayed in town, but it's a nice turn of events. I will just have to forgo my other meeting this morning. Unless—"

Victor glanced at me, all worry gone from his face.

"Unless you would like to go for me. It's just speaking to one of our security contacts about a man who has been making things difficult for us on the plantations. You just need to write down what the officer says. It's like secretarial work, really. Would you mind terribly?"

"But won't he be expecting you?" I said, feeling uneasy.

"He will be. But you can explain that I had to meet with the governor-general. Besides, look at you," Victor said, grinning. "He'll be thrilled to speak to a beautiful woman instead."

"I just have to write things down?" I asked. After my years of teaching, I had often wanted to be more involved with the family company in France, to feel productive and useful. Though Victor was open to it, his mother was strongly against it. She refused to have a daughter-in-law who did anything to get her hands dirty. I once suggested that I teach again instead, and she looked at me as if I'd proposed working as a chimney sweep.

"Yes," said Victor, still clutching the note about the governor-general. "But you must be there at eleven o'clock sharp. Very sharp. You know how these men in uniform are. He's no longer in the military, but the habits tend to linger."

I wanted to help Victor and, more important, wanted him to trust me after two incidents where I might have inspired mistrust. "Of course, I'll do it. Thank you for asking me," I said brightly, though nerves were pricking at me. I couldn't have anything go wrong.

"Good," he said, kissing my forehead and then taking a step back. "Bright as you are, I suppose it would be a waste to just have you recline by a swimming pool all day."

"That doesn't sound too bad, though," I said, smiling.

"Let's make sure you do that this afternoon then," he replied. "Keep me company while I change," he said, walking toward his large dressing room, "I'll explain everything. But like I said, it should only take a matter of minutes. Have a cocktail while you're at it. Secretarial work, I hear, is far more interesting with a drink in you."

––––––––

"Trieu," I said after I rang for her and she hurried to my room. Victor had left a few minutes before, staying only long enough to set the course for my morning. "I need Lanh to chauffeur me somewhere, a neighborhood south of the train station, and I must arrive a few minutes before eleven. Could you alert him?"

"Yes, *madame*," she said, turning around quickly.

There was still over an hour before I had to leave, but I couldn't bring myself to do anything except alternate between sitting on the bed and sitting on a chair on the large balcony off the bedroom. Even though I told myself it was ridiculous—I was overqualified to take dictation, as Victor had described it, even if it was in this entirely foreign place—I could not stop feeling nervous.

At twenty minutes past ten, I exited the house and climbed inside the Delahaye.

"Did you take Monsieur Lesage to the governor-general's house?" I asked Lanh brightly as he started the engine.

"Yes, I did, *madame*," he replied without looking at me.

"Oh, good. He's very excited about it, even if he's not letting on."

"I did detect that, yes," said Lanh. "As he should be."

He maneuvered the car onto the street, and we moved through the neighborhood slowly as I tried to enjoy the view of the large houses and the few elegant women I saw strolling down the sidewalks. That was what I might have been doing if I hadn't read the dossier.

I flipped the face of my watch mindlessly. When I looked up again, we were in a local neighborhood. I lowered my window a bit, but when Lanh turned a corner abruptly, an animal carcass hanging on hooks outside of a butcher shop hit the car, causing me to yelp.

"I'm sorry, *madame*, such tight streets here. Maybe better if you roll up your window. Can you do it yourself, or should I stop and help you?"

I rolled it up quickly without answering.

"Are you certain that this is the neighborhood you're due to visit today?" Lanh asked, still keeping his eyes in front of him.

"Yes, quite sure," I said, feeling utterly unsure all of a sudden. "In fact, I think this is the correct street, no?" I said, glimpsing a row of noodle stands. Victor said I would know I was in the right place by the noodle vendors.

"It is, yes. At least it is the address you provided," said Lanh, slowing down. "And this is the café that you mentioned."

I looked down at my watch. I was twenty minutes early.

"You can let me out just here and then drive on, Lanh," I said.

"Yes, *madame*," he said, stopping the car, exiting, and opening my door. "I will return in an hour then. That's what you would like?"

"That is. Thank you, Lanh." I watched him climb back in the car and drive off.

The street was sunless and narrow, with wobbly bicycles and rickshaws weaving among the pedestrians. Men and women carried bundles on their backs or slung on wooden rods that they balanced on their shoulders. Among them darted rickshaw coolies in worn shoes or wearing no shoes at all. I tucked myself between people until I was against the row of rusting iron tables in front of the café. There was no terrace, so the tables and chairs were placed on the road, pushed up against the café's front wall to take up as little room as possible. There was a young woman leaning in the door frame, with a tray dangling from her hand. Café Mat Troi. I checked the sign, to be sure I was in the right place, and then slipped into an empty seat and smiled at the waitress.

"A whiskey, please," I said as she approached me, my smile tight. I said it in French, but I was quite sure that "whiskey" was a universally known word. She shook her head no. "*Pas de whiskey ici*," she murmured. "*Café. Thé. Eau.*" "*Eau,*" I replied. She nodded, went inside, and returned quickly with a chipped glass and a carafe of water.

When she was out of view, an *indigène* man next to me reached into his jacket pocket and handed me a dented metal flask.

"You French own the alcohol. We Annamite are not allowed to sell. Can't pay the taxes. They have it here. Bootleg whiskey. But she won't give it to you."

"Why not?" I asked, watching him pour whiskey in his water glass. He rubbed the rim between his fingers and handed it to me.

"You are French. You can report her for selling alcohol. And then the café owner must pay heavy fines. Maybe worse. You'll never be served whiskey, or anything else, in a café like this one. You go to the nice hotels, the ones built for you. There you can drink it. But today I'll help you."

"Thank you," I said. Victor clearly had no knowledge of these rules or he would have warned me.

"A little more," he said in French, refilling my glass as the waitress eyed him angrily.

On this tight street, life seemed to be lived on the pavement as much as it was indoors. It was loud and chaotic, and there was not a face like mine to be seen.

I tried to drink my second whiskey slowly but drained it in a matter of minutes and received a third from the man without even asking.

Feeling slightly numb, I was finally able to sip instead of gulp, mindlessly spinning my emerald ring on my finger. It was something I often did to soothe myself.

There was no trace of the scent of *hoa sua* flowers here, no one in formal clothes, and only a few cars tried to inch through. Instead there were barefoot children running around, women in conical straw hats or with rags on their heads pouring out buckets of brown water, men with greasy gray hair hurrying here and there with cigarettes dangling out of their mouths, and a few establishments, like Café Mat Troi, that catered to them. I thought about how strange it was that this world apart existed just a twenty-minute drive from my new home. It was also odd that the policeman wanted to meet Victor in such a neighborhood, but perhaps he was patrolling it. What did I know of life here yet?

"Are you lost?" I heard a voice say to me in perfect French. I looked up to find a Caucasian man in a three-piece cotton suit staring at me with interest. I had not expected anyone to speak to me except the man I was meeting, and my pulse quickened at the sight of him. "It's five blocks that way," he said, pointing. I looked in the direction he was gesturing, where the street seemed to grow even narrower and more packed with willowy Indochinese bodies.

"What is?" I asked.

"Luong-Vuong," he said, matter-of-factly. "*Pour le chandoo.*" He looked at the nearly empty glass on my table and repeated the word "*chandoo.*"

"I'm not looking for Luong-Vuong," I replied. I tried to sound as if I knew what he was referring to, even though I hadn't the faintest idea. "I'm just enjoying a drink."

He shrugged. "You don't have to keep it a secret here, my dear. These people don't care." He waved at the Annamites around us, none of whom were looking at us, and then quickly left, hopping in a rickshaw just a few steps away.

"*C'est quoi Luong-Vuong?*" I asked my waitress, who I hoped spoke enough French to understand me.

"*Une fumerie d'opium,*" she replied, barely looking at me. "*Chandoo c'est l'opium. Et Luong-Vuong est une fumerie très connue.*"

She ran her hand over my table with a rag and then took a few piastres off the table next to me, which was leaning askew, one of its legs broken. Luong-Vuong was an opium den. That man thought I was going to smoke opium, *chandoo,* at 10:57 in the morning. I wondered what exactly about my appearance gave him that grim impression.

"It's why a French will walk down this street," the waitress added, as if sensing my confusion. "Not why you here?"

"Me?" I said, looking up at her. Why was I on this street? Because I was helping Victor. Because I had made a life for myself supporting my husband. Because my old life was something I could never return to. And perhaps most importantly, because I spent countless hours thinking of my childhood self and how I didn't want to disappoint her. But perhaps opium was an easier explanation.

I looked down at my watch, wondering if it was eleven yet, when I heard a car engine roaring. It grew louder, and I turned to see a large black Citroën making its way down the street, forcing people to press against the buildings so it could get by. It slowed just one door past the café, in front of a run-down row house with light blue walls and faded, peeling shutters. It jolted to a halt, and the back door, the one closest to the café, was flung open. A French policeman in a black uniform with bright gold buttons and a wide belt emerged and banged on the roof of the car.

I stood up quickly and smiled at him, giving a friendly wave, as he wasn't expecting a woman. The front doors of the Citroën opened, and two more officers, one French, one native, climbed out. The Annamite policeman walked around to open the other back door before soundlessly dragging a man out of it. Wearing only a black stretch of cloth tied around his lower half, the man wasn't putting up a fight. He wasn't moving at all, his body heavy in the officer's arms. He was dead. I sucked in my breath and gripped the table. This could not have been what Victor was expecting. All I had to do was write things down, he'd insisted. Secretarial work. Instead, I was looking at a dead body.

The dead man's face as they moved him, battered and burned, was visible to all of us on the street.

I stared, frozen. I watched the police, the dead man, the Annamite men and women coming up to see, the few children whose eyes were being covered by their mothers' hands, and then I opened my mouth and screamed, gripping my chair for support. Embarrassed, I moved my hand over my mouth to make sure I didn't emit another sound.

I watched as one of the French policemen helped move the body, grabbing the dead man's ankles. Together, the officers sauntered a few paces, looking as if they were holding prize game, not a human being, and deposited the man in front of the blue door. He fell with a thud, his head rolling in the direction of the café, and I could see how badly bruised it really was. The burn marks around the man's eyes and mouth were still raw. He clearly had not been dead for long. The older policeman, who hadn't yet touched the body, put his boot against the man's torso, rolling it even closer to the door, exposing the back of his head, which had large patches of hair missing. From the bloody flesh that was exposed, which looked sticky and not the least bit scabbed over, I guessed it had been pulled out just a few hours ago.

"Victor," I whispered, not sure why I said it. He certainly couldn't help me now.

I heard another scream, and then another. A woman shouted something in Annamese, and I saw someone hurry out the door to my right. It was a young woman dressed in a brown *ao*. She ran to the dead man's side, slumping against the door of the blue house. I held my breath as I watched a rush of grief hit her.

She pulled the man's body into her lap. She was facing me now, and I saw that she was quite pretty, perhaps in her early forties, with her hair tied back at the nape of her neck. She was weeping. The three officers said nothing, stepped over her, and climbed back into their car, driving off, their speed slow and leisurely.

I removed my hand from my mouth and shook my head. She had to be his wife. "Help her!" I called out in French, taking a few steps toward them. The café server followed and pulled me back to my table, wordlessly refilling my drink. This time she gave me whiskey.

I looked at her, picked up the glass, finished it in two swallows, and held it out for yet another pour. She motioned for me to sit back down.

"Communist," she said, refilling my glass again when I was seated. "He is a member of the Indochinese Communist Party. They want him dead for long time. Now, he dead."

"Communist?" I whispered, looking up at her.

"Yes, communist. Men in that party getting killed now. It's very dangerous to be in the party. Especially to be in the party and to be talkative. This one talkative."

"It's this dangerous?" I asked, still whispering. I knew what a problem communism was the world over, but I didn't think that in a French colony the consequences could lead to what was in front of me.

"They want independence," she said as another patron lifted his glass to her for a refill. "From you," she said without glancing at me. "The police in the black car, they *Sûreté générale indochinoise*. Political police. Dangerous police. This is how they do it. Kill people."

"Because the people who die want independence?"

"Yes. Independence and more. They want the workers to lead the country and they want you out. But communists, they are stupid people. They won't have it, never. Independence. You French. You are too strong for us."

"I'm not French," I said. "I'm American."

"American," she said, stopping to think about what that meant but evidently coming up with nothing.

"The wife there," she said, nodding toward the sobbing woman. "She must forget it. If it is not the French in Indochine, it will be another. The Chinese again. Or the British also very greedy. Worse than the French, I think. Maybe they want us, too, and then we speak your language. I don't want to learn another language. And it's an ugly language, yes? English."

"I don't know," I replied in French, standing up and strewing more piastres on the table, my hand unsteady. "I barely use it anymore."

FIVE

Jessie

September 4, 1933

"M adame Lesage!" I heard Lanh cry out. I turned to see him rushing toward me. "What happened?"

"I don't know," I said, feeling completely lost. "I was supposed to meet someone on Victor's behalf, a policeman, but he never came. Or I don't think he did. Other policemen came. And I was waiting longer than I thought I would be, so I had a drink. Many drinks," I admitted. "Then this," I said, gesturing to the man's body and the grieving woman in the street behind us. "It's horrible."

Lanh took a few steps away from the café, guiding me with him. "I heard a police siren. I should have known to turn back. Is he dead? How terrible," he said. He stopped a passerby and spoke to him in rapid Annamese, then turned back to me, shaking his head.

"The dead man is a communist leader," he confirmed. "He was a political prisoner before but managed to escape. The police have made it very clear what happens to these men, these communists trying to spread their message. They want to put the country in the hands of the peasants, and the French, and many Annamites, do not agree. I'm terribly sorry that you had to see this."

"Are there . . . Does this happen often in Hanoi?" I asked, wondering if Victor could have had any idea about what I was going to witness.

"No," said Lanh. "Not on the street anyway. But it is a mounting problem. I believe it is a bit of a problem on the rubber plantations, too, no?"

I nodded my head yes. Clearly, it was a very big problem.

Lanh offered his arm. "I should have found you sooner. I was circling the neighborhood, but I should have sped over when I heard the siren. Please forgive me."

"Of course," I said, but my voice sounded weak. The whiskey was suddenly catching up with me, and I felt off balance. I desperately needed something to eat and my bed.

Lanh walked me to the nearby car and helped me lie down on the back seat. I nodded off immediately, and when we arrived home, he offered me his arm as we climbed up the stairs to Trieu and Cam, who got me out of my dress and into my bed. I took two bites of a warm chicken bun that they brought up and fell sound asleep.

When I woke up, my head heavy as lead, Trieu was perched on a seat by the window, arranging a cluster of photographs I'd put there. She was positioning the one of Lucie so that it was more visible from my bed. When she saw I was awake, she came to me and fluffed the three white pillows behind my head.

"I have something for you," she said, picking up a ceramic cup from a tray near the frames. She brought it to me and wrapped my hands around it. Inside was a pungent broth.

"It's a local recipe. We fetched it from the herbalist while you were asleep."

"That's thoughtful," I murmured.

The cup, which had no handles, was extremely hot.

"It's part of learning to live in Indochine," Trieu said, watching me turn it in circles. "You need to become accustomed to drinking from cups like this. What is inside is *thuoc ta*," she said of the broth. "That's what we call our traditional medicine. We use many kinds of herbs, but this one is special. In your language, it's called the king's herb. We drink it after we've had a shock—the death of a child, the news of a very bad illness, any strong shock that won't leave us. This will help it pass from your body."

"But I haven't experienced either of those things," I protested, sniffing the dark liquid, its scent like wet earth. "I've just had too much to drink."

"Maybe," she said. "But I think you are also sensitive to death. Even a stranger's death. Maybe you've never seen someone like that man. A dead person."

I thought back to Virginia, to our farm and the woods beyond it. I had seen death before.

"It's not the first time. But he was so badly beaten. His face, and the back of his head—he had to have been tortured for hours for it to look that way. And then just left by the police, dead on the street."

Trieu watched as I rested my chin against my chest, trying to get the ceiling to cease spinning. "Lanh said he was a communist. A very active one. Running a large underground cell. That he'd been imprisoned before."

"Is that a death sentence?" I asked, lifting my head. "Talking about something like that?"

"Of course," she said. She looked at me as I lay there still holding the cup but not drinking from it. She sat on the edge of the bed and mimed tipping it back, encouraging me to try it. I took a small gulp. It was hot and bitter, as I'd expected, but not unpalatable.

"I don't understand," I said, handing her the cup when I had emptied it. "Why should it be a death sentence?"

"*Identifying* as a communist isn't a death sentence. But being an active communist is. Being vocal, trying to turn other men into communists, too. Especially young men. That there are certainly consequences for. We are all aware of it."

"Is that what he was doing?" I asked, thinking about the problems that had occurred on our plantations in the last six years.

"I think so. He's been in the newspapers before. I don't know that much about it, but the police are perhaps more fearful of communists now because the party unified three years ago and is more threatening. The French and the emperor in Annam, Bao Dai, they aren't happy either."

"The French like the emperor very much, no?"

"Yes, they do. He is practically French himself. He went to your country when he was nine years old and has spent most of his life there. Everything he does is in agreement with the French. Some say that that's why they continue to allow him, the Nguyen dynasty, to keep some power." She turned the empty cup around in her hand, then placed it on my nightstand. "More than a third of the country has that last name. Nguyen. Almost none of them are related to the emperor."

"Do you like being French?" I asked Trieu, watching as she fussed around quietly with my blankets and sheets. "Living in a protectorate that feels controlled by the French, I mean. Do you mind that?"

"I enjoy it," she said, smiling pleasantly. "I attended a very good school here. With financial assistance, of course. I speak two languages now, rather well, I think. I have a nice job. If my education had been left in the hands of my people, I would not have received one. You French care more about the education of girls than we do. Much more."

"I certainly do," I said.

"Today was very unfortunate. Lanh is embarrassed that he wasn't there to help you earlier."

"It wasn't at all his fault," I said.

"Still, we all want you to recover quickly. And you shouldn't worry too much about politics," she said. "It's not good for the stomach."

"I'll try not to," I said honestly.

"Just don't become a communist," Trieu said, smiling.

"Sound advice," I replied, starting to find my strength.

"You have a visitor downstairs," Trieu said when she'd finished smoothing the bed. "A woman named Marcelle de Fabry. I told her she shouldn't wait, that I wasn't sure how long you would be resting, but she insisted. Would you like to see her, or shall I send her off?"

"Marcelle is here?" I said, surprised. I knew I looked and felt a mess, but seeing her could shift my day for the better. Put today's unwelcome episode behind me.

"It was nice of her to stay," I said, pushing my covers back. "I hope she wasn't waiting long."

"An hour or so," said Trieu. "Lucie was here for a short time and spoke to her. She was very polite. And we've given her plenty to eat."

"Oh, good. Then yes, please send Madame de Fabry upstairs," I said, feeling more stable and refreshed already. "But please give me my hairbrush and dressing gown first."

Trieu helped me cover up and arranged my hair herself.

"I'll bring her here then. Your friend," she said, and left.

———

After an hour of gossiping, with Marcelle doing her best to cheer me up, she walked over to look at the photographs on the table that Trieu had rearranged, her elegant green silk dress flowing around her. She ran her hand over the frames, then picked up the one of Lucie. "I'm so happy that I met your daughter," she said. "She's a very polite child. And such a beauty. She looks like Victor, doesn't she? The lovely hair, and the cheekbones already so prominent. Striking on such a young child."

"Yes, thank you," I said, watching as she studied the picture. "I'm glad you were able to meet her, too. And that she was polite. Sadly, the only thing Lucie inherited from me are my dark eyes. Pity, considering Victor's."

"Oh, she'll survive," said Marcelle, fluttering her lashes over her own hazel ones.

"That picture was taken last year," I said. "She was photographed by Henri Cartier-Bresson, a good friend of Victor's mother, when we were on a trip to Marseille. He had just returned from the Ivory Coast and was recuperating from something or other. But he was good company. He's quite in demand in Paris now. The photo was a present from Victor's mother to Lucie for her seventh birthday, not long before we left for Indochine. It should really be in her room, but I'm very fond of it."

"I see why," Marcelle said. "And looks change. Perhaps she will look more like you in her next portrait."

"Perhaps," I said, leaning back on the bed, the strange memories of the morning receding. Marcelle was light and witty, two things that Victor wasn't particularly. He was thoughtful and smart, which I appreciated, but I needed a counterbalance every now and then.

"Do you and Victor plan to have more children?" Marcelle asked brightly.

"Oh, I don't know," I said, feeling a flash of panic, as I always did when asked that question. "Perhaps. But we are happy just with Lucie at the moment."

"But you said you're thirty-one, didn't you? Is there much time left?" she asked, turning toward me.

"I hope so," I said, my rote answer.

"Was it difficult for you to have your daughter?" Marcelle pursued, turning around to put the picture back. "Is that why you only have one?"

"No, with Lucie, we had no problem conceiving," I said. Marcelle turned back around and looked at me expectantly, waiting for me to go on. I didn't.

"That's good to hear," she said after a moment's pause. "I've heard some terrifying stories of giving birth. And then after birth, when the doctors and nurses are gone—I've been told that can be even worse."

"After birth?" I said, my stomach lurching.

Marcelle nodded and came to sit on the edge of the bed, leaning back on her hands, her thin arms rigid behind her, as if we were two young girls gossiping in boarding school.

"My mother had problems after the birth of her first child, my oldest sister," she said. "She explained to me when I married Arnaud that things can be difficult once a baby is born. How a woman can lose a bit of herself, start to feel more sadness than usual. In the worst instances, a mother's sanity can completely go. There was a horrible story last summer that was even printed in the newspapers here. A woman in Lyon killed her two-week-old baby, strangled her when she wouldn't stop crying. Infanticide, they called it. Do you remember that?"

I shook my head no. "Did it happen to your mother? Some sort of difficulty like that?" I asked, my voice too soft, overcompensating for the level of panic I suddenly felt. This was a very different feeling from the emotion of the morning.

"Not to that extreme, but she did feel an overwhelming sadness," Marcelle said breezily. "That's what she called it. But it happened only with her first child, my sister Alice, and only for a month or so. Of course, she had four more of us after Alice, poor lamb, so that probably affected her sanity permanently. But you just have the one, and she seems quite manageable, so no wonder you're doing fine."

"Yes, thankfully," I said, trying my best to smile. "I am the oldest of eight, so I am in no hurry to have a large family."

"I can imagine," said Marcelle, looking at me and smiling sweetly.

I moved my thumb to my index finger, but my ring wasn't on. I reached up and touched my ears. My earrings had been taken out, too. Trieu must have removed everything while I was asleep. I glanced quickly at my nightstand and saw that she had placed all the jewelry there on a little porcelain tray. I grabbed the ring and put it on my finger, feeling Marcelle's eyes on me.

"I don't like to take it off," I said, putting the small earrings on, too. "I will have to explain that to Trieu. My servant."

"Oh, yes," said Marcelle. "All these servants need a bit more training when there's a new family. Even if they were very good with the last."

I put my hands under the covers and sat back again.

"I'm sure you are a wonderful mother to Lucie," said Marcelle, looking at the picture again. "And if you did decide to have another child, and something ever did go wrong for you, the world is very modern now. We have something to help fix everything these days, don't we? Even women's trouble like that."

"Indeed," I said, looking at the way she was running her thumb rhythmically over the bedspread as she spoke. It was very much like how I was touching my ring under the covers.

"I don't know what kind of care is available here in Indochine," Marcelle went on. "I imagine most local women simply have to deal with these realities in a primitive way. But for us French—or almost French," she said, grinning, "things are better. My mother is very well-informed on these developments, as she is constantly pressing me to have a baby, even though I'm so far away now. My sister Alice worried when she had her first son, because of the way our mother suffered. There was talk of sending her to Switzerland, just to be safe. Leaders in such care, she said. And that's not so far from France, is it?"

She stood up and stretched, glancing at the portrait of Lucie again. "Anyway, I don't know why I've been going on so much. I suppose I always enjoy talking about such things with women who already have children, as I consider taking the plunge myself. I will be thirty in two short years, after all. How terrifying. I remember when I turned twenty, it rattled me. And back then I was sure that thirty meant that a woman was practically deceased. Turns out we still look all right at this advanced age, don't we?" She turned back to me and smiled. "Anyway, I'm sure Victor would want you to return to Paris if you were to become pregnant again. He seems very protective of you. You're quite lucky."

"Switzerland?" I asked after too long a pause. I knew it was too long. I shouldn't have said anything. I should just have nodded and changed the subject. But I wasn't myself, I was a shaken version of me, and it tumbled out. Three syllables fell out of my mouth, and as soon as they did, I knew it was a mistake.

"Oh, yes," Marcelle said, her expression turning sunnier. "You know the Swiss. So advanced with medicines and therapies. We should probably all be giving birth there, instead of under a bush in Indochine."

"It's a different experience for everyone, I imagine, but I love being a mother," I said, trying unsuccessfully to keep my voice steady. "And

I'm sure when the time comes, you will, too. Even if you have to give birth under a bush," I added, forcing a smile. If there was a moment not to show how rattled I was, it was now.

Marcelle went to close the window, saying something about the heat. As she did, she changed the subject, telling me a funny story of her early courting days with Arnaud in Paris.

I watched her carefully as she walked around my room, pulling the curtains closed, giving them several tugs so no light shone through, chatting easily as she did.

Something in her carriage, her very upright posture, her tense arms as she pulled that material, struck me as confident. Too confident. Too rigid. Her body was different than it was the night we spent laughing together at the club. Her thumb, moving back and forth as if to the beat of a song as she sat next to me, had been a hint, but now, with the way she moved her shoulders, her legs, the quickness of her voice as she spoke, it suddenly became obvious.

She knew.

When Marcelle turned back, her posture had changed. The tension in her body was gone. She'd ridden the wave of adrenaline and managed to beat it down in a matter of seconds.

"I should be off," she said, straightening her dress. "I don't want to keep you up. That is, if you really are feeling better. You are, aren't you?"

"Much," I said, smiling, the corners of my mouth strained. "I'm so lucky you decided to call on me today. You helped me take my mind off the difficult morning."

"I think we're rather lucky that we found each other," she said, coming to kiss my cheek. "Send a note over when you're fully recovered. We will go to the club and wreak havoc. Perhaps we can stow away and spend the night. Find out what really happens between the restricted hours of two and seven in the morning."

"I would love that," I said, managing a laugh.

After Marcelle had left, I counted backward from one hundred, slowly, trying to calm myself, waiting to hear the click of the front door. As soon as I did, I rang for Trieu, who appeared in the doorway seconds later.

"I need to speak to Victor, at once," I said. "Please send Lanh to find him. He must be done with the governor-general by now. He may have already left for the plantations, but I hope he hasn't."

She nodded, two strands of her hair out of place. She caught me looking at them and tucked them behind her ears. "I'm sorry, *madame*, the hallway windows are open and the wind is picking up."

"Of course," I said, instinctively trying to glance outside to see how windy it was, but all my curtains were drawn. "Just please fetch Victor quickly. I'm afraid I'm feeling ill again."

When Victor rushed into the bedroom an hour later, he took off his suit, draped it over a chair, and lay down in bed next to me, even though it was the middle of the afternoon.

"I had no idea that the policeman I—you—were supposed to meet would be bringing a dead communist with him," he said apologetically. "I suppose I don't know how things are done here just yet. I would never have sent you if I knew—"

"It's not that," I said, leaning into him, my weak voice almost disappearing before it reached his ear. And it wasn't. Everything that had happened on the street this morning was practically forgotten.

I pushed back the covers and stood up, gesturing for Victor to follow me. Together, we walked into the bathroom and I pulled the door shut. I turned the water on in the tub, which came out in a loud rush, and looked at my husband, finally letting the tears fill my eyes. I cupped my hand over my mouth to stop the sound of myself screaming. He reached for me, his face flush with concern, holding me up, and I moved my hands over his right ear instead.

"Marcelle de Fabry knows about Switzerland," I whispered, my hands shaking. "She knows."

SIX

Marcelle

September 5, 1933

Switzerland. It had been foolish for me to say anything, but I couldn't help myself. I've always been impulsive. These days that was a dangerous thing to be, but there it was—there *I* was—unable to keep control when it was most important to do just that.

I poured myself a glass of water from a crystal pitcher and looked out at the brick terrace where I was sitting. Our home was much smaller than the Lesages' enormous one. The van Dampierres had five children; for them the large house on Rue de la Chaux made sense. For the Lesages, it was absurd. The Lesages. The *Michelin* Lesages. I leaned back in my chair and smiled, thinking about the way the muscles in her neck had tensed as I'd let it slip. Switzerland. I had almost laughed when I uttered it the first time but had managed to suppress the urge, smiling idiotically instead, though she didn't seem to notice, too caught up in her own distress as soon as I pronounced the word.

It was ill-considered. Stupid, really, but I had to do something to smash her smugness, and that certainly did the trick. There she was lying in her palatial bedroom, propped up in her bed like a little marquise, emeralds strewn by her side, her blond hair, far too long for her age, arranged around her face like a halo. As soon as I walked into the room, I wanted to rip out those smooth golden tresses. But instead I said the one thing that I knew would shake her to her core, and that was even better.

Months before Jessie set one little foot in Indochine, I knew about Switzerland. I knew about every dark period of her life, but I knew that one incident had disturbed her like none of the others. That it still had the power to shake her.

Money was the grease that kept my world in Indochine on track, and six months ago, money helped me get inside the mind of Jessie Lesage. A picture of the Lesages had run in *La Revue Franco-Annamite*, the French colonials' newspaper of choice, when it was announced that Victor would be coming to Indochine for an indefinite period, the first in his family to bother setting foot in the colony for more than a few days. A real honor for us all. I immediately clipped it out and sent it to the best private investigator in Paris. He was a quiet but thorough man, I was told, someone that a former neighbor of ours had used when she was sure her husband was having not only an affair but an affair with a man. He had been.

I needed to find out everything I could about Victor and Jessie Lesage, I'd written to the investigator. Payment would be generous.

A month later, he'd responded. Victor Lesage was interesting by birth, but seemed to be scandal-free of late, having given up a rather fast lifestyle after he married. His parents were divorced, and his father, a bit of an eccentric, perhaps even a bit mad, lived in Marseille. But it didn't much matter since his mother was the Michelin, anyway. Victor, he said, was just a cog in the family company, though. Not remarkable, not unremarkable, just there. After tailing him and speaking with the utmost discretion to old school friends, the investigator found no traces of affairs, money mishandling, gambling, homosexuality, illness, drug use, or anything else untoward. But he still requested a large sum of money because what he'd found out about Jessie was worth it, he stated. He'd been able to track down a doctor she'd been seeing weekly for the last seven years. "Weekly," he'd underlined. The doctor was a psychiatrist, and the investigator had managed to pay him in exchange for Jessie's files, including her medical history. It was "an abundance of riches," he'd written.

Her childhood had not been an easy one. The trauma from that lingered. But mostly the nerves she had, the tics, stemmed from what happened in Switzerland. He could send me the file, he'd said, but he demanded the money first. I immediately sent a telegram to my sister in Paris, telling her that if she could deliver a specified sum to the investigator, I would pay her twice that amount. All she had to do was obtain it from Arnaud's banker. The promised compensation was almost as much as her husband brought home in a year, so I knew she would say yes.

It took over two months, but when it arrived, I read that file until it was nothing but creases and fingerprints. The doctor's notes revealed that Jessie wanted to leave Paris. "A traumatic incident that brought up difficult memories from the past," he had written, "made her suddenly sour on the city." She was from then on "desperate for a change of scenery." At the club, after Victor had praised his wife as some kind of latter-day goddess, rather than a simple farm girl who was lucky enough to be pretty, he'd told us he wouldn't even be in Indochine if not for her. That it was she who'd suggested they come. I knew that no Michelin actually cared to see the realities of their plantations. It was far easier to ignore the atrocities from abroad. But Jessie's desire to move made perfect sense. She didn't want an adventure; she wanted an escape.

Switzerland. It could have been a coincidence, of course. That's what Jessie would be thinking. Trying to decide whether there really was a case of new mother's depression in my family, wondering what type of person my mother was, what exactly she had endured, which clinics Alice had sought information about in Switzerland, wondering and wondering.

But I wasn't wondering about the kind of person she was anymore. Jessie Lesage wasn't just going to be one of the wives swimming laps at the pool and developing an alcohol dependency; she was going to be involved with the plantations. Why else would she have been there when the police tossed Huynh Dinh's body onto the street?

It hadn't seemed like she knew much about Michelin or her husband's professional life when we spent the evening together at the Officers' Club. Most women wouldn't have cared about the details anyways, just what the profits could buy them, and I'd assumed she was one of those women. She was tightly wound, but open to having fun. Self-centered but, admittedly, also easy to like.

That part bothered me the most. Easy to like. Because I *had* liked her when we dined together. I had enjoyed our time spying on the drunk minister, so peaceful with his flaccid penis out and his one perfectly polished shoe on. I had liked laughing together, clutching hands so we wouldn't fall, watching our husbands, two of the most powerful men in Indochine, shooting billiards together. And I'd enjoyed watching her stand up to Caroline when she branded her as some American temptress.

I was open to giving her the benefit of the doubt. She could, in fact, be a very separate entity from her husband. The woman whose dossier I had studied over the last several months had suffered difficult circumstances. Perhaps she was a misunderstood woman who wanted to get out of Paris, slightly cracked around the edges but decent at the core, unlike the family she had married into.

But no. I was with her this morning, though she couldn't see me, in an inconspicuous Peugeot with wheels that deflated too quickly— shoddy Michelin tires most likely—and rust on the hubcaps. I had been skulking around her neighborhood out of curiosity, wanting to learn more about her, when she'd flown out of the house looking nervous. I'd decided to follow her expensive car through the French corner of the city, staying a few feet back. When she headed to the local neighborhoods and driving became a challenge, I'd followed her under the shade of a conical straw hat that I purchased right off the head of a noodle vendor, staying behind a large, rowdy group of young people.

She did not see me trailing her to Café Mat Troi. On foot, I was able to tuck myself away in an alley across the street, a favorite shortcut for the *pousse-pousse* drivers, which gave me a direct view of her. She could have seen me, too, if she had only thought to look my way, but she was obviously concentrating on something else.

She'd stood up and screamed when she saw Huynh Dinh's body dumped by his front door. It was the correct response considering what was in front of her, but it felt muted. The Michelins practically held a parade every time a communist was killed, especially one as powerful as Dinh, who was accused of distributing communist literature not only in Tonkin but also down on the rubber plantations, concentrating on Michelin's. Jessie hadn't celebrated, but something was off.

Before she'd screamed, Jessie had looked at her watch. A quick, furtive glance seconds before the car carrying the policemen had pulled up. She had known about the body being dropped; perhaps the Michelins even had something to do with it. I'd watched in horror as she'd smiled at the first policeman. She had even waved, like he was an old friend. Jessie Lesage was not separate from the Michelin machine. She was helping to turn the crank.

SEVEN

Jessie

September 9, 1933

Confirm. That was what Victor had said when I told him about Switzerland. See Marcelle de Fabry again, straightaway, and confirm. One mention of Switzerland could be a coincidence. Two slips could not. But Marcelle didn't seem like the type of woman who, if she had slipped, would do it again.

Victor had apologized repeatedly for asking me to go to Café Mat Troi. He should not have sent me without having first met the policeman himself. He'd acted foolishly. He had since found out what the mix-up had been. The man he had communicated with, a policeman who was also paid by the company to help with certain arrangements, thought that it would be *amusing* for Victor to see what they did with overzealous communists in Tonkin. A bit of a fun surprise for the new Michelin in town, he thought. No one had been expecting me to go in his stead. The man, Thomas Brignac, apologized to Victor and sent over a very nice note, full of spelling errors, about how embarrassed he was.

I told Victor I had stopped caring about that dead communist. I understood that the police couldn't let men like that take over Indochine. It was Switzerland that was yet again my source of anguish.

It was a month after Lucie was born that I was sent to Switzerland. I had an easy pregnancy, nine months of staying active and well, enjoying the kicks and grumbles of the baby who was quickly forming inside me and then wiggling so much I knew it was desperate to see the world. I had an uneventful labor, too. I was nervous, of course, alone in the delivery room with only my bloody bedsheets to grip and tear at when the contractions seized me, a pain so intense I had to look at myself in the mirror that hung near the bed every few hours to remind myself I was a woman and not an animal at the slaughter. But I had witnessed my mother giving birth to all my siblings. I knew I would survive the ordeal. And when they placed Lucie on me, a little white bonnet on her head, her tiny body wrapped up, her eyelashes barely grown in, I knew none of it mattered. I knew I would never be alone again. She was perfect. She had Victor's dark hair under her tiny hat, a pile of it, dark blue eyes when she finally opened them, and a mouth that was like the first bud of a perfect pink rose. She was my Lucie. She would be Victor's, too, but my body had made her. That meant she would always be mostly mine.

We were very happy in the hospital, in our own little world, baby Lucie and I. Victor fell in love with her as soon as he entered the room, smelled her intoxicating baby scent, and heard her warbling cry. He would visit us all seven days that we were tucked away there. When we left, driven home by Victor himself, not trusting his chauffeur to it, I thought everything would be the same at home. Better even, as I was feeling stronger and more myself when we arrived. But our little blissful world was shattered the very next day.

Victor's mother, Agathe, came and stayed with us, even though she lived just a mile away. She was constantly present, taking Lucie away from me whenever she pleased and demanding that the baby be fed on a set schedule. When I wanted to sleep with Lucie in bed with me, she told me I was a fool. That I would crush the child and that she had to sleep not only in her bassinet but also in an entirely different room. My parents had done very little right, but because we were in a small house, we were always sleeping close to someone, piled up like puppies comforted by heartbeats. Lucie needed to hear my heartbeat; I knew she did.

Despite Agathe's threats, I would sneak into Lucie's nursery when her nurse was asleep, lift her little body from her bassinet, and bring her back to bed with me to breastfeed. Soon that, too, was deemed disgusting by Victor's mother. She forced bottles on Lucie, and I started to panic. Postpartum hysterics, Victor's mother called my reaction. *Fits.* I heard her use those words constantly to Victor and to Lucie's nurse. Then, one night, just after Lucie had turned a month old, I was consumed with a nervous energy that woke me up with a start. I went to Lucie's room, sure that everyone was sleeping, picked her up, and brought her to my bed. I meant to keep her there for an hour at most, but I fell asleep, so soothed by her presence. Agathe caught me with Lucie in my bed the next morning, my arm draped over her body, which was tucked tight against my torso.

Agathe was outraged. "You're suffocating her!" she'd screeched, waking us both up as she ran into the room. She tried to grab the baby, but I wouldn't let her go. In the struggle, I lost my grip on Lucie and she fell to the floor. Victor insisted on calling the doctor, and the next day, Agathe took Lucie away from me.

With Lucie's doctor's word to support her, and my husband in agreement, it was decided that I was a danger to the baby and needed treatment, the best available. I was to be sent to the Prangins Clinic in Switzerland, a mental health facility near Lake Geneva. I was to stay for an undecided length of time, and Lucie was not to go with me.

On the morning Victor and I left, I was hysterical on the way to the station, as they hadn't even let me see Lucie, kiss her good-bye. I remained inconsolable on the train, barely staying in my seat, constantly pacing the length of the car. Victor tried to stop me, embarrassed by my behavior, my tears, but after an hour, he gave up and let me grieve.

He fell asleep when we were nearing Lyon, and I watched him

rest peacefully for a few minutes. But when his face changed into an expression that reminded me of Lucie, I threw myself over him, crying and pounding his chest. "Who has the baby now, Victor? Who is feeding her?" I yelled, my breasts still producing milk as I cried.

On that endless journey, everything smelled like Lucie. Every woman suddenly looked the way I imagined Lucie would grown up. I didn't have a picture of her to take with me. I had nothing of her but my changed body, which, just a month after the birth, was still recovering.

When I arrived at the clinic, they dressed me in a shapeless blue gown and gave me a sunny room with windows that didn't open. The doctors who tended to me, drugging me, said many women felt sadness after they delivered a child and became mothers. They asked if I felt as if I were losing a part of myself. Did I want to end my life? The baby's life? No, I did not want to end our lives; I wanted to end Victor's mother's life. I wanted to take my baby and hide with her, away from the Michelins and their money, their bourgeois rigidity and rules. I had grown up with nothing, but that also meant that I had grown up with few strictures besides raising my siblings as if I were their mother and helping to put food on the table. I got as far as I did through honed instinct, not by following the decrees of someone else. But the Lesages did not operate in that fashion. They told me which women to befriend, where to dine, which activities to take part in. Tennis was an acceptable sport for me. Shooting, something I'd excelled in from my youth in the countryside, was certainly not. Work was out of the question. If I had to do something with my days, I could volunteer with orphans. Most of the time I understood their advice. I had infiltrated their world, and I genuinely didn't want to disturb it. But I would not be told how to care for my child.

I never wanted to see Agathe's pinched face again. I wanted to live far away from her. And if Victor was strong enough to choose us over his family, then he could come, too.

In Switzerland I stared at a bare white wall and cried for two weeks.

I spoke to the specialists, I submitted my tired body to their ridiculous examinations, and I begged to go home.

No, I was told by my doctor. No, I was told by the chief of the hospital. I was nowhere near well enough. I would have to stay longer, perhaps a month more.

That was when everything went wrong.

According to a report they sent Victor and Agathe, I attacked the chief of the clinic in a way that only their most deranged patients dared. I managed to break two of his fingers and scratch his cornea before they were able to restrain me.

I don't remember any of the confrontation. I barely recollect that doctor's face. All I remember thinking was that they didn't care that a baby had been torn from its mother at the most critical time in its life—and that the chief of the clinic must have very brittle bones.

And I remembered the medicine, of course. I could practically still taste it. They wanted to turn me into a near corpse with no worries and barely a heartbeat. I took what they wanted me to the first time, and then never again. I silently threw it up in a plastic bowl every time they administered it, then dumped it in the toilet when I was allowed to go. I had to at least hold on to my sense of self.

After the incident with the chief, I was restrained and forced to take extremely strong barbiturates, which numbed me and made me fall asleep for days. When I finally woke up, I was no longer permitted to go anywhere alone. I was restrained, tied to my bed like a murderous criminal. I was released only to use the bathroom, and that had to be done in the presence of two female nurses. I wanted very much to break their fingers, too. It was in that state that I realized I had to change, or at least pretend to change, or I would never see Lucie again.

My crying ceased. I admitted that I was wrong to have taken the baby into bed with me. That I should have released her into Agathe's loving arms that morning. That a woman who had borne four children of her own, three of them girls, knew better than I did. They all knew better than I did, I said.

Two weeks later, they released me to Victor, who took me home. I never slept with Lucie again. At least, not until she was nearly five years old and could sneak into my bed on her own. When she did, I pulled her tight against me, our bodies curved together as they were the night everything went wrong. For the rest of my life, I knew, I would be trying to get back that month in Switzerland, loving Lucie with all my heart, always trying to make up our lost days.

When I came back to the house in Paris, tiny baby Lucie was smiling. I held her and laughed with delight while Victor and his mother watched me, examining me for signs of mania. I could never again give them a reason to send me away. But that night, alone in the bathtub, all the world's tears fell into the water. Lucie had changed. Not only could she smile, but she now looked more like me. Her eyes had darkened and even though her hair was black, she reminded me a bit of the girls in my family. Especially my youngest sister, Eleanor, the one I missed the most.

I told Victor a month after I returned to Paris, to our marital home, that I was completely cured. Switzerland was a distant memory. But the truth was that it had pushed me off center and I was quite sure I was never going to come back, not without help. My powers of renewal were lost. I never showed any signs of nerves in front of Victor, terrified that I'd end up restrained to another hospital bed. But I had to break sometimes. I'd learned that after Virginia.

I started consulting a doctor, once a week, far in the Eighteenth Arrondissement, and with him, I cried. I talked about the waves of anxiety that would come over me if I smelled a baby or saw a child fall in the park—and, sometimes, for no reason at all. I talked about the fear I still had of losing my child, and my mind along with her. And I spoke about Virginia. The memories that still punched at me, and all the things I had kept from Victor. That I would always keep from Victor. I spoke about my worries, my secrets, to no one but him. I was very thankful for the outlet. Knowing that I had a private ear every week, I was able to find myself again. But Victor could never know about the doctor, about how much I needed his counsel, and he could certainly never know about certain pages of my life from before I met him.

In the seven years since Switzerland, Victor and I had talked about having more children, but I refused to while we still lived in Paris, just around the bend from his mother. If we go to Clermont-Ferrand, or somewhere even farther, I had told Victor, maybe I'll be ready then.

It had taken months, but one day he walked into our living room in Paris, sat on the floor, and apologized. He understood, he said. He understood how his mother had contributed to my weakened mental state. He gave me the emerald Boucheron ring and promised to try to keep his family out of our private lives. He begged me not to lose myself to emotion again. He said that my state had terrified him. He admitted that he'd only seen one person in a similar condition—his father, right before he left the family. "They said it was mania," he disclosed. "I call it selfishness, but perhaps it was mania. All I know is that it terrified me. And then I had a new baby and a wife in the same condition. I'm sorry I sent you away, but I panicked. I don't want you to be my father. I want you to be you. Adventurous but balanced. Supportive. And in love with me." I'd looked at him, a man who had given me everything I had, including my child, swiveled the ring around on my finger, and nodded. Yes, I was that person, and something like Switzerland would never happen again. I was completely in control of my emotions, I assured him, a sunny smile on my face. As for loving and supporting him, that part was easy.

Our marriage commitments when we first made them had felt rushed—genuine, but perhaps devoid of deeper thought. On that day, when Victor sat at my feet—though I still had to keep certain realities from him—it felt as if we were finally truly married, love and sacrifice bonding us to each other.

He put his hand over my ring, and together, we swore never to speak of Switzerland again.

EIGHT

Marcelle

September 12, 1933

We already know about the kind of man Victor Lesage is,"
Khoi had said when we'd read the shocking news about
his impending arrival in the colony. "But let's wait and
see about his wife. Let's find out what we can about her now, but when
they arrive, let's get to know her before jumping to conclusions. After
all," he had said, "think about how little you know about Arnaud's
work. About his decisions. You don't play a role in any of his professional ones and very few of the personal. Let's imagine the same is true
for her." I agreed. Arnaud lived a very separate life from me; the same
could be true of Jessie and Victor Lesage. I hired the investigator in
Paris, but I did nothing further. Since we'd met, I had valued everything that Nguyen Van Khoi said.

His words, his actions, his presence in my life—they had transformed me. He had made me a person who wanted not just to taste
the world, but devour it. Perhaps I had shown hints of this person
when I was a child in Lille, a rebellious girl who grew up too quickly,
but Khoi brought her out fully. Then he kept pulling and saved me
from the petit bourgeois, narcissistic existence I was destined to have
as Arnaud's wife.

My connection to Khoi was stronger than anything I'd ever felt with Arnaud. And I knew it from the day we met.

It was October 23, 1926, the kind of autumn day that was meant to be etched in one's memory. The leaves weren't browning yet, just flaming at the edges with oranges and reds, and the air was crisp and clean, as if there wasn't one car humming around us, one fire burning. It smelled like the countryside even though we were in the heart of Paris.

I was twenty-one years old, recently engaged, and, because of the promise of my future life, feeling very grown up and sure of myself.

I was running an errand for Arnaud, who had been having trouble tracking down a book he needed, written by an obscure economist. He thought perhaps bookstores on the Right Bank would have it but didn't have time to look himself. Arnaud was thirty-two and a rising star not only in business but also as an adviser to the government, and was full of confidence for our country as it flourished along with many others during those years.

With more time on my hands now that I no longer had to seek out a suitable husband—a pursuit my mother had forced me into as if it were a profession—I volunteered to look for the book. I was still working as a fashion model, but Arnaud wanted me to put an end to that when we were married, so I was already slowing down, saying no even to pictures for *Vogue* magazine.

If Arnaud had known what would happen that day, he would have let me say yes to *Vogue*.

Perhaps I'll look near the Sorbonne, I thought, in one of the bookstores frequented by students. Of course, most of them did not follow Arnaud's line of thinking about France—he was a man who embraced economic liberalization, not socialism—but bookstores in the Latin Quarter always had so many titles in stock, since students were the most voracious readers in Paris, I'd been told, even reading things they didn't agree with so they could grow stauncher in their positions.

I walked down boulevard Saint-Michel, with a particular store in mind, and passed small groups of students in animated conversation, their clothes a bit worn and purposefully oversized. I was certainly dressed more nicely than they were, thanks to my work and, of late, to Arnaud, but I felt a tinge of jealousy as I passed them, especially the women. I would have loved to have been one of those students, but that was never an option for me. To marry well, that was the only thing that would enable me to overcome my lower-class start in life.

As I turned onto the rue Serpente, I spotted a rather charming café and decided that if I found the book, I would treat myself to lunch there. Arnaud wouldn't mind. Even though we were only engaged, I was already drawing an allowance from him. It was generous, but not too generous—he was an economist, after all.

I never found the book. I didn't even make it to the store. But I did make it to the café.

I was just a few paces past it, still on the rue Serpente, when I saw him. He was a student, I thought, since he was carrying an armload of books, but nothing else about him blended in with the surroundings. Not his clothes, not the way he wore his hair. For others, the fact that he was the only *homme Asiatique* on the street might have made him stand out, but not for me. It was his carriage, the way he walked, even the way he held so many books with ease. Everything about him was elegant and effortless. I stopped to look at him, holding him too long in my gaze, and when he looked back at me, I didn't turn away. Perhaps because of my boldness, he walked up to me and asked whether I was lost. Whether I needed help. And in that moment, I felt as if I *was* lost; I *did* need help—just not the kind he thought I did. What I needed was to be saved from the life I was about to make for myself.

As soon as he spoke that first sentence, I knew everything was going to change for me. I knew it the way I had known I was not going to spend my life in the wrong corner in Lille, and the way I had known Arnaud was going to ask me to marry him. I was just sure.

Because of that, I did the oddest thing. I started to laugh.

He looked at me oddly, then started to laugh, too.

"I know why you're laughing at me," he said, without any hurt in his voice.

"You know?" I repeated, suddenly worried that he could hear my inner thoughts.

"Yes. Because I am a foreigner, while you, I am assuming, are French, and here I am offering you help," he explained. "You think that's quite strange."

"That is why I'm laughing," I said, though it wasn't. "But I don't think you're strange. I think it's very kind of you."

"The secret is," said Khoi more softly, his French as pointed and perfect as a Parisian's, "that you should always ask foreigners for directions. We had to learn the city, not just have its compass automatically built into our French souls. So, I'll repeat my question. May I help you find something, *mademoiselle*?"

"I was searching for a book," I said, staring at the stack in his hand. "But then, to be honest, I glimpsed this little café a few steps back, and I stopped thinking about the book and started thinking about how lovely the place looked and how much I would like to have lunch there. And then I saw you, and I suppose I started thinking about something different altogether."

"Café du Soleil, yes? With the red-and-white-striped awning? I've eaten there several times and it is quite good."

He hugged the books closer to his chest and added: "I'm Nguyen Khoi. Or Khoi Nguyen, as the French prefer to say it. As you might have guessed, I'm a student here."

"I did, but only because of the books," I said. "Nothing else about you says student."

"No?" he asked. "And I've been trying so hard to look like one. It's embarrassing to admit, but I've been in Paris for years. I went to the Lycée Condorcet before coming here, but I'm still trying to conquer the student look. I even scuffed up these old shoes to get the right effect. How is it you all describe it? The shabby intellectual."

I looked down at his wing-tip oxfords, which were immaculate except for a small scuff on the side of the left one, and laughed. "Are you trying to look poor, Nguyen Khoi?" I said, trying to pronounce his name the way he just had. "Because I don't think you know how to. And from what I've learned in Paris, poor boys certainly don't attend Condorcet."

"I think I'm just trying to get these to blend in," he said, waving at his clothes, "because this never will," with a gesture toward his face. "Not that I mind," he clarified.

"Neither do I," I answered, my eyes locking on his dark ones for several seconds.

He looked at me differently after that. We went to the Café du Soleil and stayed for four hours. By the time we left, I was quite sure I was in love with him.

Our affair started a week later. I wanted desperately to call off my engagement to Arnaud as soon as I tumbled into bed with Khoi, but Khoi advised against doing anything irrational. He pointed out that I wasn't due to be married for a year or more, and that perhaps there would be other ways to handle our love by then. That's how he said it: "handle our love."

What I didn't know then, and what would take me months to figure out, was that Khoi could never marry a Western woman. He was from a very prominent Annamite family. His marriage would be an arranged one, with a girl as close to him in social stature as possible, and if he resisted his parents' wishes, he would lose everything he stood to inherit. They were in the silk business, he said, and had managed to hold on to everything despite the rapid French colonization that began nearly forty years before. Not many Annamite families had been able to hold on to their land, their factories, or increase their wealth; perhaps five or ten thousand in a country of nearly twenty-three million had managed. I quickly got the impression that the silk Nguyens were in the upper echelon of those families, although that, losing that stature, he said, wasn't what weighed on him. What he didn't want to lose was his family.

But until he went back to Indochine, we could pretend that the world wasn't against us.

We made the most of our time. We made the most of being in love. And almost as impactful for me as being in bed with Khoi, as breathing in, trying to absorb such a fascinating person, was the shift out of Arnaud's moneyed but incredibly boring world into Khoi's passionate, academic life full of people as wonderful and as curious as him. And because Arnaud was far more focused on work than he was on me, he didn't even notice my dramatic turn away from him.

I would not have found myself in Indochine years later if it hadn't been for the little community Khoi had built in Paris. Khoi shifted my world, but his friends were the ones who managed to spin it in circles.

A month after Khoi and I met, he woke me up abruptly at four o'clock in the morning. I wanted to chastise him, but he was grinning and I couldn't bring myself to do anything but laugh.

"You want that, this early?" I said. "I should send you to Pigalle instead."

"An innocent foreigner like me? A docile *Asiatique*? I don't even know where that is," he replied, lowering his body on top of mine.

"And I do want that, I always want that with you," he said, and I could feel just how much he did. "But that's not why I woke you up. I thought it was time you get to know a bit more about me. And the best way to do so is to meet the misfits I've been keeping up with in Paris."

"You? Misfits?" I said, trying to imagine Khoi fraternizing with anyone who wasn't the height of sophistication, as he was. "But what would Nguyen Van Thanh think of that?" I said, referencing his father, whom he had only recently told me about.

"My father would swim here with a pistol tied to his hand if he knew, but that's why I keep my letters home mostly about my studies and the weather. My parents think it rains every day here. I've told them that it helps me stay studious."

"Studious indeed," I said, my hand moving down his naked body.

"This first," he said, moving it all the way between his legs, "and then I will show you why I woke you at this cruel hour."

We made love as quietly as two people who have just started making love could, and while still breathless from having climaxed, Khoi pulled me out of bed and helped me put on my dress from the night before, as it was conveniently on the floor. I pulled on my coat and a hat and watched as Khoi wrapped a scarf around his neck.

"What are we venturing out to do exactly? Ski?"

"No. We're off to Pigalle," he said, straight-faced.

"Khoi. You can't be serious."

"I'm very serious," he said, grinning and pulling his hat on, too. "Well, not Pigalle exactly, but to the Eighteenth. We have a party to attend."

"At this hour?" I asked as we walked outside, the Seine at our feet and the ornate cedar spire of Sainte-Chapelle shooting toward the sky behind us. Khoi hailed an old black taxi, and we jumped inside. "Who has a party that starts at four thirty in the morning?"

"Who said the party began at four thirty?" he countered, giving the driver the address. "It started yesterday evening. But you and I were . . . a bit busy," he said, running his hand between my legs. "So I thought we'd sleep a little and catch the tail end. Or probably the middle. These parties sometimes go on for a week and only fizzle out because someone has to go to the hospital."

"Whose party is it?" I asked as the taxi slowed down as we turned onto the rue Frochot. "Bacchus's?"

"That's not a terrible comparison, actually. But no. It's Cao Van Sinh's party. He is my brother here, as close as my real brothers. You can call him Sinh. Or brother Sinh. He's Annamite as well, though I suppose you guessed that," he said, grinning. "Our names haven't really caught on *en métropole*."

"No? Well, I plan on naming my firstborn Khoi."

"Wouldn't that be nice," he said, taking my hand. "As for Sinh, I didn't know him before I came to France. We met two years ago, when he moved here for university. His family is very well-off, but he managed to stay at home for his early schooling. Boys like him who live near Quoc Hoc in Hue—that's in the protectorate of Annam, where the emperor lives—get to do that. It's a very elite school. But he came here for university, his parents insisted. Sadly, he's not studying economics with me. He's learning law. Or how to break laws, if we're being quite honest."

"He sounds charming," I said, trying to picture Hue on the map of Indochine that Khoi had drawn for me during an early encounter. "Why have you kept him hidden away?"

"It's you I've been keeping hidden. The last thing I need is for Sinh to fall in love with you. And how could he not?" he said, squeezing my hand. "But I ran into him yesterday and he told me that he was mad for a French girl named Anne-Marie de la Chaume. A fellow student and a bit of a rabble-rouser, from how he described her. He asked me to stop over tonight to help convince her to fall in love with him."

"Maybe you should have drunk less last night, then," I said as we exited the taxi.

"No, I'm fine. And he will be, too. You'll see. It's actually very hard not to fall in love with Sinh. But please don't. My heart couldn't take it."

"You do know I'm due to marry next year," I said, instantly regretting having brought it up.

"I know," said Khoi. "But you don't love Arnaud. And I won't love my wife either. This," he said, touching my heart, "will always exist for us."

Hand in hand, we walked inside the building and took the little elevator to the top floor. We could hear the noise from the party growing louder as we climbed higher.

"Don't the neighbors complain about the noise?" I asked, the music playing from the phonograph perfectly audible before we even knocked on the door.

"The neighbors? I'm sure they're all here, and intoxicated," he said, not bothering to knock.

I hesitated to walk inside the large apartment, something I had done very few times in my life. But I had never seen a party quite like the one that was suddenly playing out in front of me.

"Where is Sinh?" I asked after a moment. Khoi pointed to the couch.

I looked and saw a slim Annamite man folded around the body of a girl, in passionate embrace.

"Anne-Marie?" I asked, smiling.

"Who knows!" said Khoi, laughing. "But let's find out."

A Frenchman in a smart suit was standing next to me. It took me a moment to realize that the pants were three inches too high on his ankles, and there was a small monkey, wearing a purple sweater and matching knit hat, perched on his shoulder. I inched away, moved through the group of bodies, trying to attach myself to Khoi. When we reached Sinh, Khoi slapped him on the back with gusto.

"You're here, you filthy bastard," Sinh said after pulling his friend onto the sofa. "And at just the wrong time, as always."

I was intrigued by Sinh, but I was transfixed by the woman he had just stopped kissing. She had stretched out on the couch and had her hands behind her head as if she were in a hammock. Her brown hair was very short and slicked over to the right in a deep part. She was petite, very slight, and wearing a man's tuxedo, though the crisp white shirt was barely buttoned above her naval.

"Hello," she said, registering that I was staring at her. "I'm Anne-Marie de la Chaume."

"Marcelle Martin. A friend of Khoi's," I said, returning her smile.

"Oh, a friend, are you?" she said, batting her lashes over green eyes. "How lovely. Well then, I suppose I'm a *friend* of Sinh's. He and I only met formally, and by formally, I mean physically, this evening, but he's been following me around like a lost dog for months. I don't think he thought I noticed, but I certainly did. How can you not with someone like him?"

I didn't think anyone could be more appealing than Nguyen Khoi, but I could see that Sinh was strong competition.

"So, you're why I haven't seen this utter fool for a month," said Sinh, standing and kissing my hand. He wasn't nearly as tall as Khoi, who was a bit over six feet, but he had broad shoulders and was wearing a three-piece suit that fit him exceptionally well. "I see why he's kept you hidden."

"You are very pretty," said Anne-Marie, rearranging her shirt to show even more of her flat chest, "and perhaps, pretty as you are, very married?"

I peered at Khoi, who had clearly told his friends about me, unfortunate details and all. He glanced my way and gave an innocent shrug.

"I'm not. Yet," I said, not feeling the need to lie to them.

"How delicious," she said, stretching her body out even more on the small sofa. "I simply adore an affair. 'Lover' really is a far more charming term than 'husband.'" It was then that I noticed that her feet were bare and that she had several gold rings on her toes, one of them in the shape of a snake. Behind us, someone had changed the music to Gershwin's *Rhapsody in Blue*, and it was playing so loudly that it felt like the clarinet was lodged inside my ear as it embarked on its glissando.

"Why don't you two head to the bar, which I think is now set up in the bathtub, and fix yourselves a cocktail," Sinh said, winking. "I have a bit more kissing to do before I can have a conversation. You don't mind, do you?"

"Of course not," said Khoi, standing. "I think if I don't leave, you'll drive a stake into my heart. Come, Marcelle, to the bathtub."

The bar was, in fact, set up in the washroom, which was packed with a mix of mostly French and international students, predominantly Annamites, many of whom lived in something called the House of Indochine at the Cité Internationale Universitaire.

"It looks like something plucked from the countryside of Tonkin," said Khoi, explaining it to me. "It was built by the school, or the government perhaps, to make the Annamite students feel more at home. A lovely but absurd idea. As if we can only exist inside a pagoda. Our minds work perfectly well inside stone walls with gray zinc rooftops, too."

"Take me to see it?" I said as I drank down a concoction that tasted 100 proof.

"Of course. But Sinh should take you. He used to live there, so he'd make a superior tour guide. That is if they let him in. He was asked to leave his lodgings last year."

"Too many parties?" I asked, looking around the washroom, which we still hadn't left. "Too many livers gave out?"

"No, I don't think they minded that. What they didn't tolerate is that he's a communist. Actually, he became a communist while living there. And a vocal one at that."

"Is he?" I said, unable to hide my surprise. "I didn't think the Annamites as rich as you all were communists."

"I'm not a communist," said Khoi. "I was very much a collaborationist until a few years ago, basking in my French education, loyal to the civilizing mission that France has embarked on in the colonies. But befriending Sinh changed all that."

"So now you're an almost communist?" I asked, smiling. The man with the monkey perched on his shoulder had entered, and the animal was dangerously close to jumping into the bathtub and ingesting a gin rickey.

"I suppose I'm still finding my way," said Khoi. "But I think the rhetoric that some of the nationalist parties espouse makes sense. There are intellectuals in Hanoi associated with the movement who are first and foremost calling for freedom of the press, an end to the colonial government's oppressive censorship. But it's still a small movement, and from what I've read, they're a bit disorganized. All these more moderate parties may have to fly the flag of the communist party eventually. I think their ideology will spread quickly now that the French are profiting so much from the colony and other Western countries pay handsomely for our rice, our rubber. We shall see. But the communists already have a very vocal brother in Sinh."

"Do you think Anne-Marie knows he's a communist?" I asked as Khoi refilled my drink.

"Anne-Marie?" Khoi said, laughing. "She's practically a Bolshevik, according to Sinh."

"Is she?" I asked, shocked that a girl wearing gold rings on her toes was ready to paint the town red. "Well, I think she's wonderful. Both of them. All of this," I said, gesturing to the people packed in with us. On the other side of the bathroom, sitting on a small child-sized chair wedged against the sink, was a very blond Frenchman wearing sunglasses. His feet were propped up on a Victorian-era top hat, and he was playing a ukulele left-handed. "Even when I socialized with photographers and other artistic types when modeling for *Vogue*, I never saw all of this," I said, zeroing in on a man whose shirt seemed to have gone missing. He had a very muscular torso, and no one seemed to mind.

"Maybe it's time for you to become a student of life then," Khoi said, leaning in and kissing me.

"Thank you for finding me," I replied as we exited the tiny space.

"There had to be some reason for me to be in France," he whispered back. "Turns out you're it."

Khoi and I spent the rest of 1926 tied up with each other, and very often in the company of Sinh and Anne-Marie, who had fallen completely in love with each other by the time I finished that terrible drink mixed for me in the washroom. But it wasn't until the early spring of 1928, when I was about to turn twenty-three and Khoi had celebrated his twenty-fifth birthday, that the loose knots joining us together were pulled tight for good.

It wasn't apparent at first that Anne-Marie was rich. She did a very good job hiding it the first year that I knew her. She seemed very intelligent. Certainly well-read and well-bred. She had a little top-floor apartment, a former maid's room, near the Palais Royal, and we spent many nights there with Khoi and Sinh on her tiny balcony, drinking wine and feeling like we were dancing on top of the world together. I was quite convinced that Anne-Marie had grown up without much, like I had, but had shed her past faster than I'd managed to, thanks to her curious nature and the luck of getting to attend university. Perhaps her family cared about the education of their girls, I thought, unlike mine. But in March of '28 I spotted her on the street near the Arc de Triomphe. She was with a woman whom I assumed was her mother, as she was the right age, and they had the same small straight nose with a perfect swoop at the end and a comfortable intimacy between them. Anne-Marie was not dressed in men's clothing that day. She was dressed very smartly, in a cherry-red crepe de chine dress. I barely registered what her mother was wearing, too distracted by the flash of the candy-sized diamond earrings she had on. Out of instinct, I opened my mouth to greet Anne-Marie, but closed it as soon as she looked at me with a panicked expression. When I walked past her, she winked at me quickly, but didn't utter a word.

The following day, she visited my apartment, a small but comfortable place in the Eighth that Arnaud was renting for me. She had a bottle of wine in hand and an explanation at the ready.

"My parents don't know," she said before the wine was even open. "They don't know that I dress the way that I do when I'm out late at night, that I cavort with foreign students, and that I refuse to act like a repressed French woman. I will not be like the past generation, like my mother. And they certainly don't know that I joined the French Communist Party, that I write for *L'Humanité* under a nom de plume, and that I've participated in rallies and protests with the Annamite students. And most of all, they do not know that I'm sleeping with Sinh. Or that I'm in love with him."

I looked at her curled up on my couch, her thin body draped in a suit that I noticed must be custom-made, and suddenly she looked like a rich little girl, more scared than she had ever let on, instead of the confident, intelligent woman I had come to adore. "Who are you?" I said finally. "Whoever you are, I'm absolutely in love with you, we all are. But we might as well know all of you if we're going to keep on this way."

"I'm Anne-Marie de la Chaume, and one day my parents are going to have me beheaded for all this," she said, relaxing a bit. "But I don't really mind. I mind enough to lie for now, to still keep things cordial with my parents, to pretend I'm just another girl at university. But that's all I can muster. When they're not looking, I can't live the life they want me to."

"Is it that bad?" I asked, thinking that all most parents wanted for their daughters, mine included, was a rich husband, healthy children, and stability.

"It is that bad. I won't live like that. I would probably not be going on with this charade—it can be rather exhausting—if my circumstances were different, but my father is a senator, and I love him enough to not want to ruin his career. He's worked very hard for what he has."

"Is he?" I asked incredulously, thinking about how at the last party we'd all attended, Anne-Marie had asked an art student to paint the night sky on her bare back and then, after two cocktails, had added that the sun should be rising on her breasts. "Your father is representing Paris?"

"Doubs. In Franche-Comté."

"And your mother?" I asked, trying to remember the face of the polished woman I had seen.

"Oh, my mother," she said, lighting a cigarette. "My mother is his loyal servant. Isn't that what all our mothers are? No work outside the home, no free thought, just bowing at their husband's feet all their lives, letting them ravage their bodies and souls with baby after baby in their youth and then drinking the days away to try to forget it all later on."

"What will you be then? Because I quite like the you that I know. I wish that you would just be that version of yourself instead of that one I saw yesterday. The little girl in the starched pinafore."

"I'm not quite that, I hope," she said, looking down at her clothes. "But I suppose being financially beholden to my parents is part of the problem. I don't need much, but I do need to eat and pay for school. I enjoy school. I'd like to remain a student as long as I can."

"Your mother looks like she could provide that to you by sneezing."

"Oh, no, *ma chère*, she would never do anything as unladylike as sneeze," said Anne-Marie, wrinkling her nose. "But it is my mother that provides for us, you are correct. She's the wealthy one."

"Royalty?" I asked, reaching for a puff from Anne-Marie's cigarette.

"Sadly, not," she said, waving at me to keep it. "Maybe then they'd just laugh off my behavior as eccentric. Too much intermarriage and all that, so my brain didn't come out quite right."

"Well, you're also just too pretty to be a royal," I said, grabbing the bottle of wine from my small dining table. It was almost empty.

"How rich coming from the fashion model," she countered. "My father ran as part of the *Bloc national* on an anti-communist platform. Me being a communist is worse than me being a murderer."

"How did you become a communist anyway?" I asked, sipping the last few drops of Pinot Noir.

"How does anyone? You educate yourself about the world. You realize that while you have privilege and opportunity, a possibility to create a life that is better than what you were born into, most of the world does not. And then at university, I've met many communists. What they say makes sense, they are pro-labor and anti-colonialism. And as you know, I met foreign students, most from countries we have colonized, chopped up as we wish to scrape them apart for our economic gain while we starve and impoverish generations of people, who we don't really see as human anyways, because they are a bit darker or a bit yellower than we are."

"I don't think we are chopping them up," I said, raising what was left of my eyebrows at her.

"Trust me, in some places, like plantations, coal mines, we are killing people—sometimes we don't even bother to chop them up because that might cost more."

"And here I thought that all girls did at university was read Molière and meet their husbands," I said, smiling.

"Perhaps I have done that," she said, grinning.

"So, your father is on the far right. And your mother?" I asked.

"My mother, too, of course. She is whatever my father is. But she's also richer than he is. She's a Michelin, of Michelin et Cie, the tire company, on her father's side. That's one of the main reasons I care so much about the colonies. About laborers being treated worse than farm animals. Because I am distantly attached to the whole thing. I am an oppressor through blood."

"I see," I said, remembering the colorful advertisements the company had all over Paris. "These Michelins are not communists, I take it," I asked, running my finger across the top of my now empty glass.

"Far from it. Do you read *L'Humanité*? What we are doing over there, as in my family," she said, pointing to her chest, "is slavery under the guise of patriotism. And the men managing the headquarters in Clermont-Ferrand, these third and fourth cousins of mine, they've been on the right for a long time—all these industrialists are. I remember my father talking about them when he explained the Dreyfus affair to me. He and the Michelins were all anti-Dreyfusards, *mais bien sûr*. They've already forbidden me from ever dating a Jew, can you imagine what they'd do if they knew I was bedding an Annamite?"

"You fascinate me," I said, pointing at her bare feet, her toes still adorned like they were her hands, "and now how you became you fascinates me. After seventeen months, you're still surprising me."

"Like I said," she continued, closing her eyes for a moment, "I met students who had defied their families and inched over to the left. Some to the very far left. One of those students was another named Nguyen, no relation to yours. A very intelligent boy from a small town in northern Annam. He was the one who really changed everything for me." She leaned into me, her cheeks flushed from the wine. "You need to educate yourself about the colonies, Marcelle," she said. "Especially Indochine, since one of the best and the brightest it ever produced is in your bed every night."

"We speak of the colony, sometimes," I said. "He's told me about the growth of the industries, the opium. Silk, of course."

"'Growth'?" she spat out. "France is profiting off peasants, Marcelle. We are taxing the masses at such an obscene rate that they lose their homes, their lands, and become tenant farmers enslaved to their French masters, forced to give them at least half their output. As for opium, yes, it's a growing industry, because we're drugging them, too. The French have actively tried to turn the peasants into opium addicts because the tax on it is exorbitant. Opium, alcohol, and a pinch of salt here and there provide half of the colony's revenues. It's what got the colony out of the red thirty years ago. And while our government does all that, they also force them to practice Catholicism, then to abandon their language, their way of governing, all while we strip away their livelihoods and dignities. It started with religion, why we put our toes on that land in the 1600s, and now it's all about money. It always is."

"Have you been to Indochine?" I asked.

"No," Anne-Marie said defensively, curling her bare feet underneath her. "But I don't need to. I read everything I can about it. And in Paris, conveniently, Indochine has come to me."

"I suppose I don't know much about it," I said. "I'm embarrassed, but most of what you're saying is new to me."

"You and Khoi need to educate yourselves further," she reiterated. "I think most days Sinh and I speak of almost nothing else but colonialism. Unless we're discussing sex. Or food. Or if we should put another bottle of gin in the bathtub," she said, smiling. "To which the answer is always yes."

"Of course," I said, laughing. "Just try to keep the circus animals away from it."

Anne-Marie looked at me and grabbed my hand. "You're very important to me, Marcelle. This last year and a half, the four of us practically living together, it's been a dream. But you're too smart to just have a life built around only love and joy. You need to know what is happening in the world. And to be involved. I also think it's high time Khoi descend from his throne and realize that men like him, the collaborationists, are a large part of the problem."

"I don't think he's that anymore," I said. "But we will start talking about it more. Reading about it like you and Sinh do. I promise."

I kept that promise.

In the haze of my new life, and rather enjoying my unofficial college education, I married Arnaud at the end of 1928, having pushed off the wedding as long as he would let me. In December, I formally moved in with him, making my trysts with Khoi, and my nights out with Sinh and Anne-Marie, much more difficult, but I still found a way. And the universe seemed to bless my illicit union by cooperating.

At the beginning of 1929, Arnaud had to travel to Burma for a year at the behest of the government, and I refused to go with him. There were no French women for me there, I reminded him, and I was scared of going somewhere so far-flung. Surprisingly, he believed me and sailed alone, while I sailed right back into Khoi's apartment, and into his bed, with its view of the gray skies and the lazy river. On my first night without Arnaud, we mixed drinks in his bathroom, him fully clothed in the tub, while I sat on a small chair and tried to play the ukulele.

In the company of Khoi and his friends, I had started to become someone different from who I was when I was a single girl working in Paris, or newly engaged to Arnaud. I was someone I liked much better. I was less inhibited, more curious, wittier, and very much sexually alive. That was it. I finally felt fully alive.

We all were. There was a shared electricity between the four of us as long as we were together. And with Arnaud in Burma, Anne-Marie only in her second year at university, and Khoi and Sinh considering extending their studies to spend a few more years in France, it felt like we had time on our side.

I was feeling wrapped up in luck one cold day in March of '29 as I walked home from the market on the Left Bank when I heard someone call my name. I turned around to see Sinh waving at me in his wool overcoat.

I hooked my bag of meat and vegetables onto my shoulder and rushed to him.

"Khoi told me you'd be here," he said, greeting me. "I was looking for you."

"Were you?" I said happily. I had, over the two and a half years I had known Sinh, spent most of my time with him in the company of others, so I felt a certain rush of delight to hear he'd been looking for me alone.

"I'm headed to the Musée Cernuschi near Parc Monceau and thought you might like to join me."

"Yes, I would, of course," I said, flattered. "It's just that I went to buy tonight's dinner, so I'm afraid I have meat in my bag."

"Here," he said, taking it off my shoulder. "I'll run it up to the apartment. Wait on the bridge a moment."

I watched him hurry across the Pont Saint-Michel and tried to picture the Musée Cernuschi. I didn't want to admit that I had no idea what it was.

He returned empty-handed five minutes later and nodded toward the rue de Rivoli. "It's at least an hour's walk up. Shall we take a taxi?"

"Let's walk a bit," I said, starting across the bridge. "And when my feet give up, I will admit defeat."

"Even a little before then is fine," he said, following me east.

It wasn't until we were crossing over the rue Royale that I admitted knowing nothing about our destination.

"And why would you?" said Sinh kindly. "It's certainly not the Louvre. It's a little museum, just one man's collection, displayed in his former home. Quite a grand one, though. And it's all art from the Far East that he collected, or stole, on his nearly two-year sojourn there. Depends how you view that sort of thing."

"And how do you view that sort of thing?" I asked, indicating that I was ready for a taxi.

"I think you can guess," he said as one pulled up near us. "But it doesn't mean I don't enjoy looking at it."

When we entered the beautiful neoclassical-style building with two mosaics on the facade, one of Aristotle and one of Leonardo da Vinci, the first thing I saw was an enormous bronze statue of the Buddha.

"Are you a Buddhist?" I asked Sinh, suddenly feeling quite ignorant and silly for having asked.

"I suppose my family practices some form of Confucianism," he said thoughtfully, not regarding it as a foolish inquiry. "As for me, I'm in the phase of asking many questions instead of adhering to one particular religion."

"I've always liked that about you," I said. "You do ask many questions. Anne-Marie always wants to *do* things. But you seem to want to know *why* we do things."

"Yes," he said, smiling, "I suppose that's true."

"You'll make a very competent lawyer one day," I said as we walked toward a small grouping of jade items.

"I sadly don't think I'll ever be able to practice law," Sinh said, looking down at a small Japanese vase and pointing out the very faint painting of a crane on it. "My father is in the colonial government, he's about as high up as they will let a native man climb. And all he desires in life is for me, his only son, to follow him there. We must serve our country, he believes, even if our country is no longer a country and we are really just serving France."

"Does he know you feel that way?" I asked.

"No, of course not," said Sinh, catching my eye again. "I am a loyal son in every way except right here," he said, pointing to his head.

"At least that stays hidden," I replied, thinking how different Anne-Marie and Sinh looked, but how similar they were, both with fathers in the government, both rebelling against them but determined not to embarrass them.

"When I was a student at Quoc Hoc in Hue," said Sinh, "I had some classmates who started speaking out a bit against our teachers. Some of our teachers, this Frenchman from Lille in particular, were very harsh with us because they truly thought we were incapable of learning at the speed of French students. Because our cheeks weren't pink, our eyes not round, it must mean our brains were different, too.

This man from Lille, he would shake his head when anyone made a mistake and call us '*les jauniers.*' The yellows."

"Did Khoi ever tell you that I'm from Lille?" I asked, grinning.

"Are you? How stupid of me to say that. I hope he's no relation," said Sinh, putting his hand on his heart and bowing in apology.

"No," I said, "certainly not. My relations barely attended school, they certainly did not teach."

"Well, there's a lot to learn outside of a classroom, too," he said, gesturing at the art around us. Sinh stayed quiet as we moved on to admire some antiquities from China.

"The boys who rebelled against that teacher from Lille, they started rebelling against the whole French system. They criticized the fact that so few young people were being educated in our country, or whatever it is you want to call it now. And that it was only boys, and a few girls, like us, who received an education. People with means that the French thought would serve them well in the future. That's what most of our fathers were already doing. But I didn't agree with the boys who spoke out. I was happy to get such a good education and to be deemed worthy of holding an important job one day. I was like Khoi. But here, in Paris, I met boys who did not attend schools like Quoc Hoc. I started thinking outside of myself, and my upbringing, and about the lives of the majority of my countrymen instead. Khoi and I, we are very bad examples of true Annamites. The average man is a rice farmer who can no longer afford the land his family has farmed for generations. Now I act with them in mind. And with Anne-Marie, of course. She is always on my mind, too."

"She does have that impact," I said, heading up the museum's stairs. At the top, I stopped and looked at Sinh. "Do you remember one evening, one of the first we spent together, where you helped a young French woman with her son?"

"I think so," said Sinh, seeming unsure.

"The four of us were walking near your apartment in Pigalle, and a young woman's little son suddenly ran out into the street. You darted off after him, grabbed him by the arm before he was flattened by a truck, and delivered him to his mother. But when you gave him to her, your hands brushed against hers and she flinched, jumping backward. She actually jumped. Do you remember that?"

"Now I do," he said thoughtfully. "She had clearly never touched the skin of a *jaunier* before. Maybe she thought my skin color was contagious."

"Yes. I thought that—that she'd never touched even the hand of an *Asiatique*. It could have remained very uncomfortable, but you smiled at her, and explained that you were a student here, and that you loved Paris and were thankful to be allowed to study here and then did something with your hat to make her son laugh, and we all parted five minutes later like dear old friends."

"Most people have good hearts," he said thoughtfully. "They just need to be reminded that our differences are charming instead of menacing. I hope to always be charming instead of menacing, even when it comes to politics. I believe in fighting with the voice, the pen, never the sword. Unless it's in self-defense, that is."

"But you accomplish that. That's just what you do," I said as we walked on. After a few moments of quiet, I paused in front of the large windows overlooking the park. "Just by being you, you remind the world, or at least everyone you meet, that our differences aren't menacing. That they're wonderful."

"That's a rather thoughtful thing to say," he said, putting his hand kindly on mine for a moment. "It's really quite unfortunate that you're married and that Khoi has to marry someone back in Indochine, one of these days. Even an unofficial diplomat like me can't fix that reality."

"Please don't remind me," I said, gazing out at the beautiful city below us. "I'm so enjoying living this dream for now."

"I won't remind you again. But I do have a favor to ask you," he said, matching my gaze. "It's a question really, since I'm so good at asking them, according to you."

"Please do ask," I said, smiling again.

"Watch over Anne-Marie for me, will you, Marcelle?" Sinh said, tilting his head back a bit. "She needs watching over. Just this morning I found her eating ice cream in her bathing costume on the couch."

"I'd laugh if it didn't sound so like Anne-Marie," I replied. "But aren't you the one who looks over her? I feel like she looks over me rather than the reverse. I don't know if she would welcome the change."

"I do, and I'm happy to, but I have to travel home for a month. And with the journey, that means three months in total. I've been avoiding going home since I fell in love with that utterly delightful creature, but I can't say no to my mother forever."

"I'll watch her, of course," I said. "If she'll let me."

"I think you'll find that she will," he said, leaning against the window.

Sinh sailed for Indochine two weeks after we spoke, at the end of March. He promised to write to all of us. He told us that the letters might take a month to arrive, though, so we shouldn't worry. Two months later, we hadn't heard anything. Khoi and I fretted. Anne-Marie was distraught.

"Khoi, send a telegram," Anne-Marie said to Khoi one evening when she'd joined us for dinner in Khoi's apartment. She had clearly been with her parents, as she was wearing a dress and was also quite drunk. "To his father," she clarified, putting her hands on Khoi's shoulders. "He will respond to you. He must know of your family."

At this point, both Anne-Marie and I knew that all the important Annamites, and even many of the French in the country, were acquainted with Khoi's father's family, the Nguyens. It was the most common last name in the country, but they were the silk Nguyens, who had spools of thread hand-painted on the porcelain dishes in each of their homes. Khoi kept a small set of such plates in his kitchen, tucked behind his extensive whiskey supply. I'd come across them one day, and Khoi admitted that all the Nguyen family's dishes bore this signature.

"Contact his father? Down in Hue? I don't know," said Khoi, the joy of the day already drained out of it. "His father often works with the emperor, or that's what Sinh said. I don't think he'd deign to read a telegram from me. He might not even accept it. But I will try," he said when Anne-Marie let out a desperate-sounding squawk. "Of course, I will. I'll leave right now to do so," he said, walking across the room for his hat. "Don't worry, Anne-Marie. I'm sure Sinh hasn't forgotten about us. Well, me, maybe," he said, smiling. "But not you."

"It's impossible," I said, sitting next to her. "I've never seen two people more in love than you and Sinh."

"That's only because you can't see yourself," she said, seeming slightly relieved. "Too bad you're so utterly married."

"It is quite a pity," I said, not disclosing that I had been thinking very often about how to get unmarried over the last year and a half.

We didn't receive word back from Sinh's father for another month, a month that Anne-Marie and the two of us spent worrying and drinking in excess, both noon and night. Anne-Marie's grades started to reflect her mental state, and her parents forced her to spend time with tutors instead of her friends.

We saw less and less of her, so when we finally received a letter from Sinh's father, Anne-Marie was not with us to open it. We had, in fact, not seen her for a week. Khoi ripped the letter open, walking toward me as he did, but as soon as he'd read a few lines to himself, he stopped in the center of the room, his face ashen. It was as if he'd just been handed his death notice.

His hand barely able to hold the paper, he read on, turning the pages over. There were three in total. He walked to the kitchen, poured himself a whiskey, drank it in one gulp, then poured another and handed it to me. He watched me drink it and then started reading the letter aloud. To my surprise, the note was in French.

Dear Monsieur Nguyen,

I would first like to thank you for the friendship you showed my son during his years in Paris. He mentioned you in his letters many times and praised you for being not only an upstanding student, but a model representative of our people in France. I am afraid I only know your father by reputation, but I hope I have the chance to meet him, and you, in the near future and express my gratitude in person.

Unfortunately, the good news stops there, for this letter is a letter no father should ever have to write. Your dear friend, my son, Sinh, is no longer with us.

"What!" I said, gasping. "No." I started shaking my head. All I could say was no. I kept repeating the word quietly as Khoi continued to read, his voice breaking.

I never saw Sinh when he arrived back in Indochine. His boat docked at Haiphong at the end of April, and he was immediately brought into police custody. The reason, I was later told, was because he was in possession of communist literature. He had several copies of L'Humanité, a French communist publication, with him.

"He took Anne-Marie's writing home!" I exclaimed. "Why would he do such a thing? He should have known not to."

"How could he not have taken her writing?" said Khoi, letting his arm bend down for a moment. The letter dropped to the floor. "He couldn't bring her, so he took her words instead. I'm sure he thought if anything the newspaper would be confiscated on arrival. Not that they would lead him to a death sentence."

Khoi bent down, gathered the pages, and kept reading.

The police telephoned me when he was in custody and informed me of what had happened, a courtesy made only because of my position in the government. I told them to please hold him overnight and that I would come to take him in the morning. I was in Hue and it would take me that long to travel north. I asked them to keep him in custody overnight as I was very angry with him. How could the son I raised be so foolish? I was sure that a night in prison would help set him straight and put a stop to the communist filth that had taken over his mind in Paris. Perhaps you can better inform me on how he fell into such a thing when we meet.

When I arrived in Haiphong the following day, I was informed that Sinh had died during the night. That he had started arguing with one of the officers, who told him that he would never be able to return to France again now that he was a known communist. Then, I am told, Sinh physically attacked him. Another policeman acted on an order to protect his comrade and shot Sinh. The bullet, unfortunately, found its way through his back and into his heart.

I was able to see his body the evening I arrived and have it moved for proper burial at home. The government has been very supportive of our family as we grieve, and over the last several months, there has been a thorough investigation, which concluded that it was as they said, just a terrible accident. The policeman in question remains in the service, though I'm told his mental state is quite fragile and that he is filled with remorse.

In most circumstances, news like this would have made it to the newspapers in France, but I asked the police for discretion during our difficult time, as I did not want Sinh's mother to have to deal with further grief at seeing her son's memory, and our family name, forever associated with communism. I ask that you please consider her and be equally discreet with this awful news.

Again, we are thankful that Sinh had such a loyal friend while he was in France. It is a comfort for the whole family to know that in his final days Sinh may have been misguided, but he was happy. That came through in the many letters he sent to us and his siblings.

We look forward to welcoming you in Hue the next time you find yourself in Indochine.

Cao Van Quang

"Khoi," I managed to say between sobs when he was quiet. "How will we tell Anne-Marie?"

Khoi shook his head, as if he couldn't even think about such a thing yet. I continued to sob, while he remained alarmingly quiet, and an hour later, when our grief allowed us to, we tried to figure out how to tell her the awful news. In the end, the burden was lifted, and Anne-Marie came to us. She had known about Sinh's death for several days.

Four days before we received the news, she had finally admitted to her parents, Charles and Joséphine de la Chaume, that she was worried about an Annamite friend, and it was her anxiety about his safety that had put her in a nervous state for several months. As soon as she'd said "Annamite friend," her father had erupted.

He informed Anne-Marie that they knew about her relationship with Sinh. That they'd known about it for six months, after a neighbor had seen Anne-Marie holding hands with an *homme Asiatique*, while herself dressed in men's clothing. The neighbor had been in Pigalle to meet "a friend," who was certainly a prostitute, which perplexed Anne-Marie's father even further, he admitted. Not believing the neighbor, as he was sure his daughter was at that moment asleep in her apartment near the university and very much dressed as a girl, he had started following her the very next day. He soon learned that not only was she certainly having an affair with an *Asiatique*, she was also involved in not-so-clandestine communist activity. That she and her lover were, together. As soon as he had seen it with his own eyes, he set about doing the only thing that made sense to him. He made plans to get rid of the yellow pest.

"That was how he said it," Anne-Marie told us, no longer crying. Her face was just deeply filled with anger. "He framed his outrage about it all as being about communism, about how he was sure this *Asiatique*, this activist, had turned my head. But I could see what he was most angry about. It was that his only daughter had been ravaged by a *jaune*. He looked at me like I was sullied forever because I'd let Sinh inside of me."

Anne-Marie's father had admitted nothing more than that they had asked for advice from their powerful Michelin cousins on how to handle "the ugly situation." André Michelin had been particularly helpful. His answer to Charles de la Chaume had been not to worry. That these types of things took care of themselves.

"I think it was them who took care of him," said Anne-Marie, stone-faced. "Took care of him until he had a bullet in his heart."

"No," said Khoi, shaking his head. "That can't be it. You read the letter," he said, looking at the sheets of paper now on the dining table. "Sinh's father said the government did a thorough investigation."

"Sinh's father is more loyal to France than to his own son!" Anne-Marie yelled. "Isn't that apparent? He doesn't want to lose his place in the government, his stature. He didn't even question it when they told him that Sinh caused his own murder."

"No," I replied. "One's love for their child surely trumps—"

"You don't know what it's like there," said Anne-Marie. "Even you," she said, looking at Khoi. "You, who should know better, you haven't even taken the time to know."

"I have changed, Anne-Marie," said Khoi calmly. "You helped change me. Sinh changed me."

"How about we change you for good then? Both of you. This will change you for good," said Anne-Marie, turning around and reaching into her bag. She grabbed something from inside it angrily, then turned back around and handed Khoi a stack of papers. They were wrinkled, but from the look of the first page, we could tell it was an official government document. I moved and read over Khoi's shoulder.

"What is this?" I asked Anne-Marie.

"A government report I stole from my father's office. This," she said, pointing, "all this was produced by the colonial government. One of their twice-yearly investigations of the Michelin plantation, but as you will see on the third page, the plantation managers are told about them in advance. So all this was observed *despite* the fact that these plantation managers, that all the staff, *knew* the inspectors were coming."

The document was dated less than a year ago, 1928, and was indeed the findings of the general inspector of labor of the two large Michelin plantations in Cochinchina. At the top of the report, I saw the words "Very Confidential."

The man in question, a government appointee named Delamarre, had visited the plantations over the course of several days. After a rather soft introduction to his colleagues, Delamarre wrote at length about the scars and signs of abuse he observed on dozens of workers.

"One of the coolies," he'd written, "spoke to me on behalf of his comrades and said that, unfortunately, the workers were horribly treated on the plantation. I asked him if he or his comrades were showing signs of blows, but he said that that very morning, the coolies marked by the blows they received were evacuated by car. But the management had forgotten some," he noted.

The report went on, with Delamarre writing:

> The coolies are subjected to harsh, frequent beatings, and often put at the bar of justice, which is a wooden plank attached to the ground with narrow holes in it to restrain them, and tight wooden restraints around their necks. I asked where the bar of justice was now and two replied that it was installed in their sleeping compartment.
> I saw in one room a bar of justice pierced with nine holes. I was in the presence of the plantation overseer, who contemplated the room with utter surprise. Then I heard moans coming from the next room. This door being opened, I saw that the second room was also equipped with a bar of justice including nine holes. A man was attached to it. He was lying on his back, with both feet hobbled in the bar, the lower part of his body naked. He was very thin and visibly sick and carried six deep marks from a rattan cane on his back.
> Later I visited the hospital and in one of the rooms I found twenty-nine coolies that had been evacuated the day before my visit. I had them undress and saw that fifteen of them had, on their backs, traces of sharp blows, more or less recent, and of varying numbers

and seriousness. A twenty-year-old boy, Tran-van-Chuyen, had on his back eight scars caused by blows from a stick that had deeply cut the flesh. Another one, of the name of Vu-Viet-Thu, aged twenty-one years, had on his back the trace of fifty-six strikes of cadouille, a large wooden stick used for beatings, and had six wounds covered with scabs. He also had two deep wounds on his right cheek.

Later I was informed by one of the plantation officials that several suicides by hanging had recently taken place at Dau Tieng plantation, an epidemic which he said was surely provoked by a strange superstition among the natives. There were six suicides by hanging in less than a month at that plantation. I had many conversations with the coolies and it seems that these suicides had begun shortly after the arrival of a Monsieur Baudet, who was placed as assistant at the head of a team of three hundred coolies. The coolies told me that this young man was very cruel and had beaten them on the soles of the feet with a rattan, and that he forced the men thus chastised to run in circles in order to restore the circulation of blood so that no mark could subsist. The managers knew of his methods, and the suicides, but had sent him to do the same work at the other Michelin plantation, too.

Before I departed, I advised the overseers to learn the basics of the native tongue, which would give them the means to be easily obeyed by their men and to better control what is happening around them.

I looked up at Anne-Marie, speechless.

She was anything but. "At *L'Humanité*, we have received anonymous letters from men who were coolies and spoke enough French to write in the language," Anne-Marie explained. "They wrote of this treatment. And worse. Things that I'm sure the leadership succeeded in hiding from this work inspector. Women raped in the fields, even at the hospital. Pregnant women being beaten until they miscarried, rice rations infested with vermin, and pay that isn't enough to feed a dog. But I always wondered a little, of course. Were these reports escalated at all by the editors at *L'Humanité*? I just didn't want to believe it was as bad as they said, since in the end, I am related to these Michelins. But when all this comes from a government inspector who is investigating a plantation that has already hidden the men in the worst condition because they were warned in advance, then how can you deny the truth."

She pushed the papers back in her bag.

"Do you think there will be one of these official documents about Sinh's death, Khoi?" she said angrily. "Or will he just be another nameless dead man. On the plantations, these men don't even have names. They just wear numbers etched into a plank of wood around their necks. Don't you think that's what Sinh is to the French government?" she said. "Do you really think that the bullet lodged in his heart was an accident and that the policeman in question is consumed by guilt? Or do you think that's an utter farce made up either by the police in charge or by Sinh's own father so that he can sleep at night?"

"Of course, it's a farce," said Khoi finally. "Of course."

I looked over at Khoi, whose voice seemed changed. And who, I would realize as the years went on, was forever changed by that day.

"Khoi," said Anne-Marie, in a calmer voice, "you must go to Indochine and figure out what happened to Sinh. You are finished with your studies in two months. I know you thought of continuing them, but now you can't. Please do not. You must go home. I won't be able to survive if I don't know what happened to him, what really happened to him." She turned her face and looked at me desperately. "Arnaud is in Burma. You could join him there and then move on to Indochine. You could go, too. You have to help me," she whispered.

It could have been Khoi, I thought as I looked at her beautiful face, tight with grief. If the world were tilted just the slightest bit differently, it could have been him instead of Sinh who was dead.

"I will go. *We* will go," I said, looking at Khoi.

"Until I have enough money to leave, I have no choice but to stay here in Paris under the watchful eye of my parents. But I'll have enough money soon. I'll see to that. And I will never set foot in their house again. As for the rest of them," she said, looking at the crumpled inspector's report in her bag, "these Michelins counting their money in Paris and Clermont-Ferrand while their workers hang themselves. This so-called family of mine. Please burn everything they have to the ground."

At the end of 1929, with his degree completed, Khoi sailed home. One year later, I followed him with Arnaud. By then Arnaud knew about Khoi, and I knew that he'd had a string of affairs with local women in Burma. He even admitted to impregnating a particularly young one and having to pay her family off. We both accepted these not-so-hidden activities as part of our lives. He wasn't loyal, Arnaud, and of course neither was I, but he was smart and fair. And even knowing that he would lose me completely to Khoi when we went, he still brought me to Indochine.

In February of 1931, Khoi and I finally found a policeman who had been working in the station at Haiphong the night Sinh died. For a fee, he gave us the dossier of the man who he was sure had shot Sinh. This man, Paul Adrien, was no longer living in Indochine. He had sailed back to France the year before. Anne-Marie, it seemed, would have to be the one to find him.

But she was proving very good at finding things. When the private secretary of André Michelin was no longer employed, as her boss had died in April of '31, Anne-Marie located and befriended her, with the help of some sizeable bribes. This led her to discover a letter that a senior official in the *Sûreté générale indochinoise*, the secret police, had sent to André Michelin, in response to one of his telegrams.

"The boy in question will be banned from ever setting foot in France again. Your niece will be banned from ever coming to the colony. All parties will be the better for it. And from now on," the letter read, "as you requested, we will be in touch with your assistant, Victor Lesage."

NINE

Jessie

September 18, 1933

"Where shall I deliver this note?" asked Lanh politely as he took the small white envelope, my initials engraved on the back.

"To the home of the president of the chamber of commerce, Arnaud de Fabry. It's for his wife, Marcelle. Do you know the address? I'm afraid I haven't had time to find out."

"I know it," said Lanh with a smile. "I will take it there now."

I looked at the envelope, white against his white gloves, a perfect image of the way two women began a friendship. But that was not the purpose of the letter. "Thank you. Please, if you can, make sure that it is delivered to Madame de Fabry herself, not to a servant."

"Of course," said Lanh, turning toward the front door. "Even if she isn't in, I will wait until she is."

I had hoped to meet Marcelle at the club, which I had visited every day since she'd called on me, but she was never there, morning or night. Victor had left on his long journey down to the plantations, and I had no one to confer with. See her as soon as possible, Victor had said. Do anything you can. He wanted to help, but he no longer had time. In the south, there was even more for him to worry about. He was finally going to see the plantations, to meet the two men running them and the thousands more working them. I had to deal with the question of Marcelle de Fabry alone.

This was not how I had dreamt about my time in Indochine beginning. It was supposed to be a safe world. A reprieve from Paris. Instead, everything that had gone wrong in Paris seemed like it had followed me across the ocean. Switzerland had finally started to feel far in the past, but here it was again. The memories had stowed away on the ship, refusing to be forgotten.

I looked at myself in the mirror and saw that my face had lost its color. I pulled my hair away from my face. It looked suddenly longer and unstyled. Stringy. I inspected myself from another angle, but I still looked lost and dead behind the eyes. I looked like my mother. If there was anyone on earth whom I could not resemble, it was my mother. And if there was anything I liked to think about less than Switzerland, it was her. Both of my parents.

I ran out of the room and let my shoes clack down the stairs the way Lucie did. It was not ladylike, but there was something rather satisfying about the sound. I was in Indochine, and even if my time here had not started off well, I could change things quickly. I had certainly proven to be the master of my own destiny over the years. I had put myself through school, then found a way to New York, to Paris, into the arms of the right kind of man, and now to the colony. I could start anew yet again. But first I needed Trieu to transform me into a woman who looked nothing like my mother.

I called for her when I was downstairs, but she did not come running as she usually did. I rang the silver bell that had been placed in the living room, but still no one came. I wandered into the kitchen, opened the door with more force than I meant to, and Diep, our cook, jumped from surprise. Standing next to her was a young girl whom I'd never seen before. Trieu was not with them.

"Diep," I said, surprised to see a stranger in the house. "What is this? Who is this girl? I was ringing the bell," I said, feeling as surprised as Diep looked.

"I'm very sorry, Madame Lesage," she said as the girl moved behind her. Diep squawked at her in Annamese, and the girl stepped back to her side. "This girl, she is Lanh's younger sister."

"And where is Trieu?" I asked. "I need her to help me . . ." My voice trailed off as I looked at the girl. I needed Trieu to help me with more than just my appearance. I needed her calming presence to set me right for the day, her knowledge of how French women could thrive in the colony to rub off on me. Instead, I felt shaken by the sight of the girl. Her body, her posture, the tired shine to her eyes— she looked nothing like me, but she reminded me painfully of myself when I was her age.

"Lanh's sister," I repeated, taking my eyes off the girl. "Does she come here often?"

"No!" Diep exclaimed. "Never. But she had nowhere to go today, as her older sister moved south to Saigon on Saturday. Lanh is finding a place for her, but she is too young to stay at home by herself today. She won't be here more than a few hours. Just as long as Lanh is working."

I looked at her again, huddled behind Diep, her simple cotton dress neat but pulling at the hems, at least two sizes too small.

"He should have informed me," I replied, irritated that I was out of my depth even among the servants. "I'm to know everything that goes on in this house. Especially when Victor is not here. I'm new here, I know, but it is still my home."

"Of course, Madame Lesage," Diep said. "That was very unwise of Lanh not to tell you." From the way she said it, it was obvious she'd known he hadn't told me—had perhaps even advised him not to.

"How old are you?" I asked the girl, taking a step toward her.

"*J'ai neuf ans*," she replied in unaccented French. I nodded and looked at Diep.

I thought of myself at nine. I had been home without parents daily at that age and had babies to take care of, too. It seemed very over-protective of Lanh to feel his sister couldn't do the same, but it also felt nice to know that there were people who were protective of children. Especially poor children. "I think it's best if you escort her home and spend the rest of the day with her," I said. "You can have the day off."

"Yes, Madame Lesage, I'm very sorry," Diep said, bowing her head.

As Diep led her toward the side door, the servants' door that opened into the small yard, I looked at the girl with her dark hair, her thin form. There was something about the way her knees went in, almost hitting each other as she walked, that made me feel like I was looking at my sisters. Those thin legs. Too thin. Coupled with a timidity, a feeling that you just knew the world wanted you to disappear. Poor people, especially girls, really were the same no matter where they lived.

"Wait, Diep," I called out. "Doesn't she attend school?" I asked. "Shouldn't she be there now? Lucie is at school."

"She had a place at a school for natives. For girls," said Diep, as Lanh's sister leaned against the door looking at the floor. I wasn't sure exactly how old Lanh was, but he looked to be nearly my age. I wondered if they had the same mother, even with a twenty-year age gap. The girl had the same wide-set eyes as her brother, the same elegant line to her nose, so perhaps they did. "But now she needs a boarding school, since her sister can no longer care for her and Lanh is of course busy here," Diep continued. "And very thankful to be," she added, daring a smile.

"Where did you attend school, Diep?" I asked. "Did you go to a school in Hanoi?"

"No, I'm from the countryside," she said, glancing at the girl behind her. "My cousin went to school for one year, in Hanoi, but it wasn't a very nice place. It was actually quite awful."

"Are there nice places in this city?" I asked, gesturing for the girl to come back into the center of the room, away from the door. "What's the nicest native school where this child could board and allow Lanh to keep working here?"

"Dong Khanh is the best school," Diep said immediately. "The girls in the royal family go there."

"That seems a bit out of reach," I said, thinking of the simple schoolhouse where I had been educated as a child. "Her brother is a chauffeur, her parents are—"

"Dead," the little girl said in Annamese. "*Chet ca hai.*"

"I see," I said, pausing. I should have guessed as much if her sister was taking care of her.

"I'd like some water," I said to Diep as I thought about what to do. "I imagine she would, too." The girl nodded, and I instructed her to sit on a simple wooden chair, one of six around the table where the servants ate together. "And perhaps something to eat."

I gulped down the cool water, watching the girl eat a plate of vegetables and cold fish that Diep had served her.

She barked at the girl, who sat up straighter, placing her napkin in her lap and her hands on the table, then accompanied me out of the kitchen.

We went to the living room, where I sat on a large couch next to the telephone. She watched me as I sat back and placed my forearm on the armrest.

"Call the school, please," I said, lifting a finger and pointing to the phone. Diep was a short woman and quite stocky, an unsurprising trait for a cook, but she had a pleasing face, which was right now pinched into a look of determination.

"Which school?" she asked.

"Dong Khanh. The one you spoke about. Call that one."

Diep walked over and picked up the phone without hesitation. She spoke to the operator in French, one of the *dames téléphonistes* whose pleasant voices were always there to connect you. When she was on the line with the school a few moments later, she introduced herself in French and then switched to Annamese. At a pause in the conversation,

I leaned over and said, "Just tell them that her studies will be financed by her brother's employer, the Michelin family. Say the money is coming from Victor Michelin Lesage. Be sure to say 'Michelin.'"

She turned back to the receiver and spoke very quickly before covering it with her hand.

"They said before that there was no space for a boarding student available. But now they just said that there is."

"What a pleasant surprise," I replied. I left Diep on the phone and walked upstairs. I opened Victor's top dresser drawer and pulled out half of the pile of piastres that he had left for me in case anything should arise where I needed more than my standard allowance.

When I came back downstairs, Diep had finished speaking but was still gripping the receiver.

"They can take her then?" I asked, just to be sure.

"They can," she said, an incredulous expression on her face. "They said she could come today. That she could sleep there tonight."

"Good," I said. "And how much are they asking for tuition?"

"It is four hundred piastres for the year," she said, after a moment's hesitation. "Quite a sum. Perhaps I should have asked before saying that we would bring her today."

It was far less than what I was holding.

"Take this," I said, pressing it into her hands. "Enroll her for the rest of her schooldays, then. We will settle the rest of the bill later."

Diep looked down at the money, then back at me, but did not move.

"Go enroll her," I said firmly.

"But Madame Lesage, are you sure?" Diep said, gripping the money tightly, as if she was worried that it would fly away.

"Yes, of course," I said, not meeting her stare.

"But you must want something to eat first? Isn't that why you ventured into the kitchen? Let me make something for you before I go."

"I'll just prepare myself a sandwich," I said, starting to walk away from her.

"Madame Lesage," she said, causing me to turn around. "Lanh will be so surprised. So thankful. He will—"

"You may say the money is from me," I said, interrupting her. "I don't want him to think that you robbed the Banque de l'Indochine, but I'd rather not discuss it with him. Please ask that he doesn't mention it or thank me in any way. I think that might make the time that we are in the car together a bit uncomfortable. For both of us."

"Of course, *madame*," she said. "Rest assured that he will never mention it to you or Monsieur Lesage."

We walked back to the kitchen together, Diep insisting that I let the little girl thank me. She stood up as soon as the door opened. Diep spoke to her in Annamese, her words coming quickly. The girl stared at me, this time square in the face instead of at my midsection.

"*Merci*, Madame Lesage," she said softly.

"You're most welcome," I replied. I was not going to let the capable mind of another penniless girl go to waste. Indigenous or not.

I went back into the living room, thinking of the nature of women. Of mothers and the motherless. Of young girls navigating the path from infant to mothers themselves. I had walked a very broken path to get to our beautiful house in Indochine. When I was very young, my life was about survival, though I didn't fully understand it. Now I saw that surviving in the same house as my parents, with so little money, was a feat in itself. When I turned seven or eight, my attention shifted to the survival of others. There were four of us by then, and my parents were certainly losing interest in tending to babies. My mother delivered them and soon went back to trying to feed the mouths instead of kissing the mouths. She was constantly fighting, my mother. Fighting with her husband, fighting with her children, and fighting with herself. And along with this fighting nature came the push to try to fend off the anger and depression that so often comes with poverty. Almost every day, she lost the fight.

When I was a teenager, then the oldest of eight, my childhood was gone. All I focused on was how to keep my siblings alive, how to bring them some joy, and how to get myself out of Virginia so that I could eventually pluck them out, too. I realized that the only thing that made me the least bit special was that I could speak two languages. I took my ability to speak French, the one gift my mother had given me, and did everything I could with it. I became a teacher. I became a working woman with my own humble means. But I wasn't making enough money to support my siblings—not one had managed to attend college besides me—and as a teacher I never would. I needed more. I needed something outside of the country, the social system I had always known. When I finally got to Paris, I became a woman with only two goals: to stay there indefinitely and to marry a man who could provide very well for me. I found that in Victor, and almost as soon as I did, he provided Lucie, too.

I went back upstairs and thought about the girl in the kitchen. I had hopefully just changed her life for the better. Alone in my bedroom, I looked in the mirror and managed to smile. Maybe I didn't look that much like my mother, despite my dirty hair. Perhaps I didn't look that bad at all.

TEN

Marcelle

September 20, 1933

T o the Nguyen home?" my driver asked me as I rolled up my window. When I first arrived in 1930, I always drove myself to Khoi's house, but with the amount we drank, it proved to be a problem when one night I drove my little red car right into a lamppost. Luckily, the damage was minimal, and Khoi had the car repaired for me before Arnaud even noticed, but he insisted that if we were to drink, I had to use a chauffeur. He said he really preferred my body with my head attached.

"Yes, to Mr. Khoi's, please," I told Tuan, trying to sound nonchalant. I slipped him enough money in addition to his salary to know that he would always be discreet and wouldn't spread the news of my affair all over Hanoi, but I still couldn't shake my discomfort. Arnaud still liked to remind me that before the French colonized Indochine, local women accused of adultery were given a death sentence. And not just a simple bullet to the head. These temptresses were trampled to death by elephants for their sins. When Arnaud thought I was being too flagrant with my affair with Khoi, he would make an elephant noise and wave his arm like a trunk. At least he had not lost his sense of humor in Indochine.

As we rode out of the city, I watched as the buildings started to thin out, the grass growing greener and the trees taller beyond the city limits. Very few of the French lived so far out. This part of the city, the area to the west of the Grand Lac, was reserved for the old world, the moneyed Chinese and Tonkinois.

When we were in Paris, we never bothered to leave the city. We barely left Khoi's apartment on the Île de la Cité, or Sinh's or Anne-Marie's apartments, always aiming for discretion, especially for Anne-Marie, so that her double life would stay hidden. But when Khoi and I finally found ourselves in Indochine together, it was like a whole new world was waiting for us. One lived outdoors. I discovered a side of Khoi that I hadn't known before, like that he was an exceptional swimmer who could practically breathe underwater. He also knew the names of all the flowers that bloomed around his house, and didn't mind sitting in the blazing sun for hours. The only times he really came inside were when I visited, and then it was usually right up to the bedroom. After seven years, that part of our relationship hadn't cooled in the least.

But now, with Jessie and Victor in the colony, we had far less time for days spent in the bedroom. We had much more work to do.

Since Khoi and I had been reunited, we'd been trying to fulfill our promise to Anne-Marie to find out what really happened to Sinh, which had proved, so far, to be an impossible task. We knew Paul Adrien, the man who had killed him, was in France. To avenge our friend's death, we turned our energies to spreading the message of communism through the growing cells embedded on the plantations, all while bringing major instability to the Michelin machine.

For several years, we'd known that a large communist uprising could be enough to push Michelin out of the colony, to sell their massive holdings. The strike in 1930 involving 1,300 men at Phu Rieng during Tet had nearly caused Michelin to leave. They had viewed it as a communist uprising, when really it had just been their employees asking for basic rights.

Anne-Marie confirmed through company documents she was able to obtain that Michelin management were seriously considering leaving despite the millions they'd poured into their holdings. Even the French newspapers I'd read said the rubber men in Clermont-Ferrand were terrified. That was when we realized that a mass strike, undeniably fueled by communist sentiment, could scare the Michelins out of the colony, the best revenge of all.

Their plantations would take on other ownership, yes, but they would surely bring more humane labor practices. The other plantations in Cochinchina had a retention rate of nearly 90 percent of workers. On Michelin plantations, only 30 percent signed another contract, and those who did so simply couldn't afford the train journey home. Laborers were better off anywhere but Phu Rieng and Dau Tieng.

After Anne-Marie found the reports, Khoi started to give more money to a communist party member who made frequent trips from Hanoi to the plantations. He also increased the payments to a man he'd hired, Tran Van Sang, to be his eyes and ears on the plantations. We needed a repeat of the Phu Rieng strike, but this time, it needed to occur on both plantations.

But with Victor's shocking move to the colony, things had changed again. It was imperative that Michelin be turned upside down, and that Victor be viewed as the one who let the communists light the match. For Victor was nearly as complicit in Sinh's death as André Michelin.

In 1930, Anne-Marie had discovered that Victor had actually transmitted every correspondence between Michelin and the secret police. He had even sealed the envelope that held the death warrant for Sinh. The men in power at Michelin had decided to execute him, but Victor had been the messenger. Now, he was in Indochine to bring peace and prosperity to the plantations and then be rewarded when he returned to France. I was hell-bent on making sure that it never happened. Victor needed to be seen as the family failure, and soon.

Tuan opened the car door for me when we pulled up to Khoi's

home, then drove off to idle elsewhere, as he knew we preferred. I had sent Anne-Marie a photograph of Khoi's house when I'd first arrived a few months after the 1930 strike—I wanted so badly to feel like we were still tied together, still as close as we'd been in Paris—but she'd never acknowledged it. A different world had started absorbing her by then.

Before I could ring the bell, the imposing front door was opened by Khoi's head housekeeper, Kim Ly.

"Monsieur Khoi is finishing his morning swim," she said as she opened the door wider, expressionless as always.

She walked me through the three sitting rooms, even though I could have found my way in the dark, and opened the large glass door that led to the backyard. Unlike in central Hanoi, where Arnaud and I lived, with little space for gardens, Khoi had several acres.

Kim Ly left me silently, and I propped myself against a chair, still in the shadow of the house's deep roof. I looked out to the pool and watched Khoi's body move fluidly as he did his laps. Khoi was the only Annamite in all five regions to have a private swimming pool, another detail that made him legendary. He swam another hundred meters before he noticed me, then stopped in the middle of the pool and did a few quick strokes to the edge. He braced his muscular arms on the side and pulled himself out in one smooth motion, then stood up and shook out his thick black hair, which seemed much longer when it wasn't combed back with pomade. A boy rushed over with a folded white towel and Khoi's metal-rimmed sunglasses. He put them on, quickly used the towel, and walked up to me in his bathing trunks.

"Hello, darling," he said in his deep voice, pulling me against him and laughing as I squirmed at his wet touch. "You're early, yes?"

"I'm late," I countered.

"Are you? How unlike you," he said, smiling. "Would you like to swim? The water feels perfect on a day like this. Scorching, isn't it?"

I looked at his broad, dark shoulders, glistening with beads of water that he had missed with the towel. They trickled down his firm back like tiny pieces of glass.

"Scorching," I replied.

After seven years, I still had trouble taking my eyes off Khoi. Every inch of him still mesmerized me just as it had the first time we had been naked together. It had been in Khoi's apartment, in the middle of the day, and when he asked if I wanted to draw the blinds, I'd said no. I hadn't considered how it would make me sound. My carnal instincts were winning over my modesty, and I'd very much wanted to see him, all of him, in full daylight. As flooded with light as it was in Indochine, it was still how we preferred to make love. That hadn't changed, but so much had. Our relationship felt far bigger than just us now.

"Let's head upstairs," he said, putting his cold lips against my neck. "You can help me get dressed, and I can help you get undressed."

After we had made love for nearly an hour, we pulled apart on his bed, and one of Khoi's servants rolled us cigarettes. As soon as he had finished, he lit mine and then Khoi's.

"I'll light the rest of Madame de Fabry's cigarettes," said Khoi. "Thank you." He dismissed him with a nod.

"Apologies," he said, propping himself up higher. "He's new."

When I started coming to his home—or La Maison Lua, the silk house, as the outsiders called it—I had been shocked by how many servants he had. None of us had had any in Paris, which had just added to our sense of wildness and freedom. But that was gone here. In Khoi's house, I soon learned that even when he dismissed them, they stayed right outside the room, waiting in case he called for them. This meant that we wanted for nothing, but they could hear us making love. It was a very strange adjustment after the anonymous student life we'd lived together in France, but Khoi said they were his father's servants, as was the house, so everything had to remain as it had been.

I fell in love with the silk house immediately. But I found it strange that Khoi lived in it alone while the rest of his family lived in the city.

"My father wants me to live here, and live this way," Khoi had explained. "In many ways, he is a collaborator just like Sinh's father. Perhaps not to that extreme, but just one step beneath. As I am his eldest son, he insists that I live like a little French nobleman. He thinks it's important for me, as the most Western of us all, to entertain the government officials, show off my perfect French, quote their great writers, eat their food in front of them so they think of me as one of the good ones. So that they consider me a friend—inferior, of course, but still a friend. That way, if the colonists succeed in producing silk, like they did rubber, perhaps they'll let us keep a finger in it. It's a business decision, and he expects me to play along."

"But you don't mind," I'd said, looking around the house. "Admit it."

"I used to," he'd replied. "After Paris, where I embraced a far simpler lifestyle, I minded very much. But now that you're here, I mind less. Besides, if I say yes to everything my father asks, he tends to ignore my personal life. And right now, we really need him to ignore our extracurricular activities."

I turned around in bed and looked at the wall to the right of us. On it was a framed picture of Anne-Marie and Sinh. She was in her usual tuxedo, and he was carrying her in his arms like she was a new bride. They were barefoot, and he was walking down stone steps right into the Seine. I remembered the moment so vividly. It had been a few minutes past dawn, and I was just outside the frame as Khoi shot the photo. At first, the two were simply dancing around by the banks, and by the end of it, they were swimming in the river. When we'd heard a police whistle from a nearby bridge, all four of us had run, Khoi dropping the camera but going back for it. It was as if he knew that the film inside would one day be precious to us.

Since leaving Anne-Marie in Paris in 1930, we had had long periods where we'd lost contact with her. She had at first remained in her parents' home, finishing her university years and adhering to her parents' demands while still secretly writing for *L'Humanité*. But in 1932, her parents had discovered that she was still involved with the paper, that she was continuing to spread a communist message in direct opposition to her father's political beliefs, and this time from right under their roof. Furious, they'd shut her out of their home. With no family, and Paul Adrien still unfindable, there was nothing left for her in Paris. The last we had heard, she was in Rome, having joined an Italian underground political group fighting against Mussolini and fascism.

In the last letter that I received from her, sent from Rome, she had written, "I do dream about coming to Indochine one day, despite my banishment from the colony. I feel perhaps my body would be revived if I went there, if I saw Sinh's world, met his parents, if they would even meet me. But the truth is, I know my soul wouldn't make it. You wouldn't recognize me, Marcelle. I'm a shred of myself."

"We will just have to be the ones to carry on then," Khoi had said after we hadn't heard from her for four months. "We must succeed in pushing the Michelins off their thrones."

The whole country needed to be taken out of French hands—it became our ultimate goal, because it had been Sinh's dream. To put the country back in the hands of its sons and daughters. There were over twenty million Annamites in the colony and less than thirty thousand French, and yet they, we, controlled it all. That had to change.

"I want to talk about Victor Lesage," Khoi said, turning back to me, his body wrapped up in the silk sheets. I nodded. I had thought of little besides the Lesages since they'd arrived.

"That night at the Officers' Club, he said—"

"He said, according to Arnaud, that he's determined to make the plantations more profitable than they are. 'Increase our profit margins, by any means necessary, even in a time of economic crisis.' He's also panicked by labor unrest, about the negative newspaper stories that come with it. He deemed all that to be as pressing as their margins. And then he beat them all flat at billiards."

"Nothing about actually helping the men themselves then," said Khoi.

"No," I replied, looking again at the photo on the wall. "Does that surprise you?"

"Nothing about that family surprises me anymore, except how a lovely creature like Anne-Marie came from it."

"I miss her," I said, wishing I could do more than just look at her picture. "Victor is who we assumed he would be. Our plan to sink his family's company, and with it his career, is still the right one. I still see him as the man who mailed Sinh's death warrant, but we can't only focus on him. He and his wife are very much a pair."

"You're quite sure?" said Khoi. I thought of Jessie waving to the policeman right before Dinh's body had been left like a sack of garbage in front of his house. That genuine smile. The way her eyes shone with excitement.

"I'm sure," I replied.

Khoi stood up, pulled on a pair of linen trousers that were hanging over a chair, and fell back on the bed, flicking the ash from his cigarette in the small porcelain dish on his side table. The hand-painted spool of silk thread now forever tied us back to our days in Paris.

"I need to go into the city today," he said, speaking at a normal volume again.

"Whatever for? I just got here."

"Business," he said. "If I don't want you to be in head-to-toe French silk, then I need to focus as much as I can on Lua Nguyen Thanh, too."

For the past twenty years, the French government had been trying to break into the local silk industry, setting up a trade group and medium-sized factories in Nam Dinh and Ninh Binh. Their efforts had gone nowhere at first, but since the 1920s, when a French silk company founded in Lyon began investing heavily in the colony, the government had been trying with more gusto to expand its mulberry plantings so it had something to send to the factories. They had even opened a new factory in Phnom Penh, in the far-flung western territories of Indochine, in Cambodia, no longer satisfied with their investments in the north.

"Would you like to stay in the house or come in, too?"

"I'll go back," I replied.

"Come, let's find the rest of my clothes," he said, jumping up and grabbing me by the hand. We tumbled in our respective states of undress into his closet, and I ran my hands against his suits, all arranged by color, the whites shading into black.

Khoi no longer tried to be the shabby Right Bank intellectual. He now dressed like the man his parents had raised him to be.

I don't know what I imagined he would become when we were finally in Indochine together. I knew he was not going to be waving a French flag, nor could I see him following Sinh and raising a red one. But now that Khoi had been home for three years, his intentions had crystallized: to work for both his family and his countrymen, refusing to give up the first for the second.

"Are you meeting your father?" I asked, moving over to where Khoi's silk shirts and jackets hung in his closet, many Nguyen green.

"I am. It's our weekly conversation where I try to pull him in my direction and he attempts to hold me back. But he's coming around to investing more money in outside industries."

"Good, considering that the French are grabbing at silk."

"It's not just because of silk, though. It's not just for us. We must prosper so that we can lead the country out of this darkness. If the communists seize power, how will Indochine survive in a global economy? We will have our independence, but we can't eat it, can we. I want to make sure our country doesn't sink when our current captains are forced out," he said, his voice seeming to bounce off the closet walls.

I knew that Khoi could distinguish between French colonialists and me, but my heart seized at the thought of being evicted with the rest of them. I watched as he turned to the mirror, picked up a comb, and ran it through his thick hair. "Except for me," I said as breezily as I could. "You can convince the government to make an exception for me. And Arnaud, I suppose."

"I promise," Khoi said, smiling. "Even Arnaud. Though he will most likely try to murder me at a chamber meeting before we get to that point."

"He will not. He's too lazy."

"Fine, he will hire someone to kill me, then. But before I convince a new governor to pass the de Fabry law, we need to focus on how to make Indochine an economic power, how to export our products successfully, the very ones the French are robbing us of right now."

"Like Nguyen silk. Paint the world green," I said, running my fingers over his jackets.

"Silk, but not just," he said, watching me. "Resources, but not just. We need to be ready to lead both economically and politically. Right now what do we have? Annamite puppets."

"Not you," I said. Khoi was in the chamber of representation of the people of Tonkin and part of the chamber of commerce which Arnaud led.

"Please," he scoffed as I took one of his blazers from the hanger and put it around my shoulders. "You know as well as I do that the chamber of representation is toothless. We meet once a year and the French don't even bother consulting us then. It's an embarrassment. If Sinh hadn't turned me into an anti-colonial, being a part of that group would have done the trick. And the chamber of commerce only half listens to me, and only because of certain connections," he said, an amused smile on his face. He slipped the green jacket off my shoulders and put it on his.

"But you're still part of both chambers."

"Of course," he said, looking for shoes that matched. "One, because that way I can remind Arnaud that I am younger and far more virile than him," he said, grinning. "And two, because when the country is finally ours again, I will already be in a position to help push it the right way. Right now we are forbidden from having political parties. Anyone who tries to organize is followed by the secret police. We can't even whisper the word *independence*, or organize without landing in prison."

"I know all this," I said, pointing to a pair of brown shoes. Khoi nodded and reached for them.

"Well, my father certainly needs to be reminded. He needs to see that we need more than silk."

In labor practice, the Nguyens were already closer to a communist model than the punishing ways of the French. Khoi's family knew the importance of keeping workers for the long term. Theirs was an industry where constant retraining of artisans and laborers was a financial burden. It was in their interest to build loyalty. The French, by contrast, and the Michelins especially, seemed convinced that profits came from spending very little. And the least always went to the workers.

"So, books?" I asked. "Is that next?" Last year Khoi had thrown a thick tome into his swimming pool while rather intoxicated to test the quality of the paper. Since then, he had invested a considerable sum into publishing. Linguistic nationalism was part of economic freedom, he said. Using the Quoc Ngu script. The money in publishing was going to increase tenfold in the coming years, he was sure of it, so why not become an investor, a backer of words, of ideas.

"Yes, books. Paper. But also mining. We're already invested in Nouvelle-Calédonie, and now the rumor is that they've struck gold in Laos. We need to be part of that, too."

"Gold? Really?" I said, laughing. "Is that what Sinh would want? Mining for gold? Is that going to further the global communist call?"

"It's not like I personally want to fill my pockets with gold, Marcelle," he said, taking a step away from me. "It's for my family in the short term, and my country in the long. I can't think about the global communist cause right now. I know that's what Anne-Marie wants. What I imagine you want. The whole world turning together."

"Of course. Any true communist desires that."

"Well, I think we both know I'm not a true communist. I'm a true anti-colonial," he said, calming down. "And right now, supporting the global cause does not support me or Indochine. I need to think about how we will feed ourselves after independence. I need to think about how I can help. I need to think bigger. For my family, and then for my people."

"Sounds like something Jessie Lesage would say as she extols the benefits of capitalism," I said, trying to keep the petulance out of my voice. Khoi and I were partners in all the ways that mattered, but his goals were, first and foremost, to protect family and country.

"Ah, the mystery of Jessie Lesage. I think that even before I meet Victor, I need to meet his wife. If you believe she's complicit, perhaps she is. Can you arrange it?" he asked.

"Of course." I paused for a moment and looked out the window at the shining water in the swimming pool below us. "Your boat. That's where we should take her," I said, smiling at the thought. "She'll be quite thrown off guard if you can invite the right characters."

"I'll do my part," said Khoi. "But you should invite Red."

I kissed him and smiled. "I will definitely invite Red. I hope she hasn't met him yet. This town is about as large as a butter dish."

"Take a chance," said Khoi, grinning. "Red is always a chance worth taking."

ELEVEN

Jessie

September 21, 1933

T his was left for you by the de Fabrys' driver." Trieu placed a
thick blue card on a silver tray on the end table in the sitting
room.

I opened it and read the short missive.

*Thank you for your note. Of course, I would like to see you again.
Did you know that they serve breakfast at the Officers' Club? It's the
best time to be there. It opens around seven. Come tomorrow. Bring
your appetite, and your bathing costume.*

Marcelle

I was there at 7:01. When I got out of the car and stepped onto the
empty veranda, the grass still wet, a haunting mist rising just above it,
I sensed at once that Marcelle was right. This was the best time at the
Officers' Club. Suddenly it had gone from private club to a home. And
this time I seemed to fit right in. I had had Trieu make me look clean,
rich, and confident, all the things that pushed the lingering image of
my mother far from my mind.

"Madame Lesage," said Teo when he caught me halfway up the

stairs. "Madame de Fabry is having breakfast by the swimming pool. You will join her, yes?"

"Oh," I said, realizing I had yet to set eyes on the club's pool. "Yes, of course."

Teo led me back down the stairs, through an airy sitting room with high-backed rattan chairs, all empty. As we walked along a stone-tiled path, a boy in a white jacket handed me a glass of ice water with a sprig of rosemary in it.

"It is two hundred yards west," said Teo as we made our way along the even stones. "Will you be able to make it? Driving is a possibility as well."

"Of course, Teo," I said, laughing. "Where I'm from, we do a lot of walking." I had a sudden memory of hiking up into the rolling mountains with my brothers and sisters when I was younger, wishing we could keep walking away from our town forever.

When we reached the swimming pool, tiled a bright turquoise with a star pattern at the bottom, there was no one in it and only one person lounging beside it. Marcelle. A bright red bathing costume hugged her tall, slender body, and a large straw hat shielded her face. She was the image of easy youth, tucked fetchingly under a blue-and-white-striped parasol topped by a small white flag flicking in the breeze. She looked nothing like a woman who would have ferreted out my darkest secret and baited me with it. I relaxed slightly at the sight and walked over to greet her.

"I'm nearly speechless," I said, kissing her cheeks. "This is heavenly."

"Isn't it, though?" she said, lifting the brim of her hat to see me better. "Most of the wives spend their mornings sleeping off the wine from the night before. I don't know why they even open the club at this hour. I suppose for the men who stay overnight, the ones with and without clothes," she said, grinning. "But I doubt any of them emerge from their private wing before ten o'clock."

Embracing the quiet, Marcelle and I swam lazy laps, pausing at the end of the pool, our arms up against the sides for support, to rest and talk. After thirty minutes in the water, we were speaking more than moving, as new friends tend to do, and my mind, which had been flustered and in a state of paranoia this morning, relaxed more. Marcelle was just an outgoing person, I told myself, the type who shared too much and asked too many questions. I had panicked too quickly. Besides, I had been extremely rattled by what I had witnessed that morning. I had been in a state, and that was why I had jumped to conclusions about Marcelle.

She spoke of being a newlywed alone in Paris, just as I had been. Lacking in community, and in female friends especially. She had lived with her in-laws at first on the rue du Beaujolais behind the Palais Royal, but she had felt stifled there.

"My mother-in-law prefers to frown," she said, plunging her head underwater, despite not having a bathing cap on.

"She can't be worse than Victor's mother."

"Of course she is," she said, slicking back her wet hair. "Victor's mother is a Michelin. All of Victor's money is hers, yes?"

"Most of it," I said, which was true. "She is related to the very rich aunt, on their mother's side, who gave a large sum and helped Michelin reestablish themselves in 1889 when the brothers took over the company and renamed it. So Victor is a bit of a distant cousin, but he's the right cousin."

There was money on the Lesage side, too, but Victor's father had kept the bulk of it with him when he'd left the family a decade before.

"Then she is better, Victor's mother, even if she is worse," said Marcelle. She moved her hat brim higher as the only cloud in the sky passed over us. "Did the family mind that you worked before you were married? That was such a point of contention between Arnaud, his family, and me. They thought being a fashion model, even one for the best designers, designers they wore themselves, was on par with being a prostitute. *Une pute.*"

I looked at her animated face as she attempted to walk alluringly in the pool, both of us laughing as she tried to sway her hips.

"In all the years we've been married, Agathe never brought up that I was a teacher," I said, thinking back. "It was unsaid, but quite obvious, that she liked me to pretend that I was rather unformed before encountering Victor. That I was just floating around waiting for a husband. She did tell me I was never allowed to work as a married woman. She said that even before Lucie was born. But I don't think a woman like her could understand that aspect of a woman like me. Or you. I really did enjoy my job. I liked being around young people, and I loved giving another language, another culture, to children. I had French growing up through my mother, but I was so starved for everything else when I was young. I was given the language, but no view of the world that went with it. We never traveled north to Quebec. We certainly never went overseas. So I spoke a language that only got me from one end of my house to the other. And that was about thirty feet." I didn't usually admit the circumstances of my childhood so readily to people, especially well-to-do women, but there was something about Marcelle that indicated that she hadn't grown up wealthy, either. She seemed far too carefree.

"But then New York," she said, stretching out her arms as she spoke.

"Well, first the local teachers' college. That's what really helped me escape my small, rural world. But yes, then New York."

"Then Paris, and now you're here. Starving no longer," she said gaily. "If awful Caroline had known all this about you on your first night, she wouldn't have wondered why Victor picked you over all those dim-witted socialites back home that were surely buzzing around him like gnats."

"Sometimes I still wonder," I said, smiling.

"No," she said, shaking her head, her wet hair stuck together in thick strands. "Brains are more effective than beauty. Only the world tries to make women forget it. They don't want us to be too smart," she concluded. "They're scared that if they encourage it, we'll end up more intelligent than the men. With the big secret being," she said at a whisper, "that we already are."

Victor had picked me, she'd said. And it was true; he had.

Ours was a believable enough scenario, I always thought. I was pretty enough. Clever enough. And of course, I was also starving enough. That was the part Marcelle couldn't see.

Victor had told the story about how we met at Maxim's by chance, just before Bastille Day, countless times. But it wasn't true. There was nothing chanced about it.

It was true that I had never set foot inside Maxim's until the night we met. But I had been outside the establishment many times. On most days of the latter half of June, I stood across the street, waiting to see if Victor Lesage was going to enter. About twice a week, he did.

I wasn't picky about who would help me complete the one very important detail of the plan I'd created when I was still at the teachers' college. I was convinced that becoming a French teacher was my ticket out of Virginia. Then in New York, I decided that since I was having no luck meeting rich enough men in Manhattan, where the men seemed to be able to size up your pedigree in a single glance, I should move my sights to France, where there was a history of American women reinventing themselves. I set my sights on Paris.

I could have saved up more money before I sailed, but marrying well had become imperative. Life at home in Virginia had become unbearable for my siblings. I had to get them out, and in a matter of months.

When I arrived in Paris, I started reading the society pages voraciously. Anyone with a title was excluded from the list of potential husbands that I'd started on the back of a sturdy bag from a *boulangerie* in the Thirteenth. They would be too snobbish. I was looking for someone who would indulge himself in the form of a pretty American who came from humble beginnings but had learned how to hide it. And I needed someone who wanted to tumble into bed with me immediately, because I knew that the only way a woman like me was going to marry the type of man I wanted was to become pregnant with his child. And even that was no guarantee. But I was my mother's daughter, and she'd birthed eight children.

During my first week in Paris, the Michelin name popped up in the newspapers several times. It was the summer of 1925, not long after the family had acquired its first acres in Indochine. According to reports in *Le Figaro*, they had their eyes on even more land in the Orient, with plans to plant rubber trees on a massive scale. The family, it was said, had wealth already through their tire production—it was the height of the automobile boom—but Indochine provided great potential for more, as the Michelins were very technologically advanced, far ahead of the planters they'd been buying from for years to make their tires in Clermont-Ferrand. And it was abundantly clear by the mid-twenties that rubber was destined to become white gold for the colony.

The reporter had been kind enough to mention all the members of the family who were not yet married and had even managed to pull a few sentences from Victor. When asked whom in his prominent family he admired the most, he'd said Thérèse Michelin, the wife of his uncle Édouard, who had been a teacher before she married. Victor had called her "the most curious person I know." After reading that, and seeing a picture of Victor in the same newspaper, one that confirmed that he was not only wise but exceedingly handsome, I knew whom I had to go after.

I began by turning into the kind of woman Victor admired, and soon I knew where Victor ate lunch. I knew the route his driver took to his office. I knew where he had his hair cut and the names and measurements of all the girls he took out for dinner. And when the moment felt right, a moment that coincided precisely with my running out of money, I went into Maxim's and made quite sure that Victor fell in love with me.

I was living in a tiny *chambre de bonne* near the place d'Italie. The room had a leaky roof and a toilet far down the attic hallway that somehow managed to be ice-cold in summer. If I could play my hand right, I would not be living there much longer. Luckily, Victor fell for me like ripe fruit.

"Jessie?" Marcelle said, nudging me. "You haven't fallen asleep, have you?"

"Not quite," I said, pushing my mind back to the present.

"Thinking about Victor?"

"I was actually," I said, smiling.

"I guessed so," she said. "You had a dreamy sort of look on your face, one where you had to be thinking about a man. He's in the south, though, right? He mentioned he had to go soon when we met at the club."

"Yes, he is. And he hasn't informed me when he'll return. I hope it's not too long, but I suppose I understand if it is."

"His first trip there, I imagine it might be," she said. "But I'll keep you busy here. Come," she said, shaking the water out of her ear. "Let's stop swimming for a bit. My muscles feel too well exercised. I need to abuse them again with the consumption of morning alcohol." She got out, wrapped herself in her towel, and bent her knees so that her long, slender legs formed a bridge on the chair.

"Will Victor sleep on the plantations?" Marcelle asked, turning her head toward me and pushing her wet hair from her face.

"Yes, he will," I said, still surprised by his decision myself. "He said that's one of the most important things for him to do. To be seen by everyone. The managers, the overseers, the junior overseers, the coolies themselves. To make it feel like someone from the family really cares about the community."

"I suppose after that unfortunate incident last year that that's for the best," she replied thoughtfully.

"He is very committed to preventing anything like that from happening again. The deaths of those men, it was horrible. He has to stay abreast of any rising unrest, any communist activity. It's been hard for the company to keep such a thing out. But I'm sure it's been hard for everyone. Arnaud must speak of it, too."

"Of course. The chamber discusses it regularly. It's been a problem in the mines, and in the factories, too," said Marcelle breezily. "But of course, it's a problem in France as well," she noted. "All over Europe."

"Less so at the factories in Clermont-Ferrand, Victor says. There is a real company loyalty there. And diversions, too. They have many sports and leisure activities to engage in after working hours. It's something that the company has recently implemented here as well, and according to the overseers, the groups are thriving."

"How lovely," said Marcelle, smiling. "It can't be all work and no play. What kind of activities do the workers get up to now?"

"All sorts of things," I said, trying to remember what Victor had said on the ship over. "Renovation theater, Annamese opera, soccer. They even play teams from other plantations. It sounds a little silly, I know," I added, thinking about how I'd pulled a face when Victor told me the coolies were spending their leisure time singing *Hat Tuong*, a type of opera. "But I think sometimes people drawn to communism are just desperate for community. Poverty can be so isolating. Then they are sold the notion that everything will be shared, that they won't be wanting anymore, but what they don't realize is that it simply doesn't work. They'll be enslaved to the state, and in the end, they won't have any freedom left."

"You seem to know quite a bit about it," said Marcelle, rapt.

"Before coming here, we had to educate ourselves about it. I suppose I didn't have to, but I've always been a reader."

"Me, too," said Marcelle. "In recent years anyway, after I stopped being a human coat hanger."

I smiled at the thought. "Poor people the world over are susceptible to the kind of rhetoric that the communists espouse. But what the far left doesn't tell them is how much better their lives are because of things like the French *mission civilisatrice*. Some French, I know, say it's a burden on the Europeans to have to bring social reforms, teachings on new industries, fresh political ideas, religion, and even modern thinking about women to the colonies. But I think it's wonderful that the French can help change lives. Look at Indochine now. The hospitals are better, their transportation is faster, even the life expectancy for natives is longer since the French have come." I thought about the care that I received at home in Virginia. I only remembered ever seeing a doctor once, and it was after I had broken my arm when I was eight and would not stop crying. My father had finally admitted that the doctor's bill would be less painful than the sound of me wailing. On the Michelin plantations, Victor had told me, everyone, families included, received free medical care.

"But the worst part is," I said, thinking back to the only thing that proved true sustenance to me in my youth, "if you take away a person's dreams about what they might be able to achieve with personal and economic freedom, then the light inside them will die. They won't have the hunger to better their lives, or their family's future. I didn't have it easy as a child, but at least I had the chance of something better. I value that over everything. The coolies working on the plantations now, they have that, I imagine," I said, surprised that I was going on as I was, but Marcelle seemed riveted. "That's why they come south, I think. To make more money than they can in the north and then take it home to their families. That want for something more is an innate human quality, whether you are a coolie in Indochine or a poor girl in Virginia. I know, just as well as the men working for Michelin, how heartening dreams of a better future can be."

"I admire you, very much," said Marcelle, smiling. "I know we've just met, but we share a similar trait, don't we?"

"I think we probably share many," I said affectionately.

"I don't doubt it," she said. "But I'm thinking that at the end of the day, we could do many things to help ourselves, but to ultimately ensure our economic freedom, we had to marry well. That is the plight of women the world over."

"It is," I said. "But at least we had freedom of movement. We were able to have careers and move out of our hometowns and meet men of worth. We were able to dream about our futures and then execute on our dreams." I let my mind wander back to Victor.

"What would my world be if I hadn't had the opportunity to better my lot in life? I want the men in Indochine, and the women, to have that, whether they work for Michelin or not," I said, feeling rather emboldened.

"Sometimes I really think I'm the dullest person in Indochine," Marcelle said with a half smile.

"You! You're—"

"Intellectually," she said, interrupting me. "I know I'm not dull, say, in conversation, but I never went to university. I barely finished lycée. My mother was happy to have me run off to Paris to model instead of attending classes, as she thought it would help me marry well. Annoyingly, she was right," she said, grinning.

"Come," she said, standing up. "You wild lady capitalist. We will only be able to better ourselves, and our positions in life, if we eat something. Starving women simply do not get ahead. Unless you're a fashion model. Then that actually does help quite a bit. Even if the magazines insist that with these new silhouettes we're allowed to have breasts again."

"I don't think the fashion world is in my future," I said, smiling. I very much appreciated Marcelle's self-deprecating nature. This morning, she seemed far away from the kind of person who would use something menacing against me.

"Let's go have breakfast then," she declared. "If we ask nicely, they will make us local food."

"I like local food," I replied as she started fussing with her hairpins. "I had my driver, Lanh, take me to a native restaurant last week, as all my cook prepares is French food. He ordered everything and it was delicious. Flavorful." She nodded and assured me that my cook could make her own food very well, but that most likely no French woman ever asked her to serve it.

When her hair was restored, she sat up, and I watched as her back curled erect, her vertebrae just apparent, indenting her bronzed skin.

"We can change here." Marcelle pointed to the small pool house a bit set off down another path. "Did you give your bag to the girl when you came down?"

"Lanh did," I said, thinking how I'd barely noticed him handing it to a young woman.

"Good. They will have hung your dress here," she said, gathering her things and heading over.

Dressed and with our still-damp hair pinned up under cloche hats, we made our way back up to the clubhouse in our flat day shoes.

"Do you like it better at this hour?" she asked. "The club?"

"I love it at this hour," I said, looking out at the lavender planted to the east of the building.

"Just like Provence," she said, following my gaze. "A slice of home for all the homesick colonials. But don't worry. That will never be you."

She had no idea how right she was. I might have started my time in the colony in a shaky way, but I was very grateful to be here. I had heard other women say that their friendships helped bring out the best in them. I had never felt that way before, but in the company of Marcelle, I was starting to understand the sentiment.

When we were upstairs, I turned toward the dining room, but Marcelle caught my arm.

"First, to the bar," she said. We waltzed in, and I offered a faint smile to the four other women seated inside. I sat with my back to the bar, and we ordered two highballs, which arrived ice-cold. I had planned on drinking nothing. I wanted to stay sharp, observant, but Marcelle's vivacity had already worn me down. Suddenly, it all felt very silly, my paranoia. I enjoyed laughing with her, speaking frankly with her. I was relieved that I could now do so without analyzing the intonation of her every word.

"To a morning of self-betterment, to discovering our similarities. And, of course, to freedom," Marcelle said, clinking her glass against mine. "And also, to making it all the way to this evening after drinking these."

"Strong," I said, taking a sip, trying to stifle a cough, which turned into a laugh.

Marcelle smiled, and when we were seated comfortably, she launched into a tale of the first time she'd come to the club—like me, on the day she arrived in Hanoi. She was describing herself as pale and terrified when she'd driven up the palm-tree-lined road, before stopping midsentence and breaking into a bright smile.

"He would be here," she said, looking past me. "I bet he slept here."

"Who?" I asked.

"Red, of course," she said, raising her eyebrows.

Cautiously, I turned and followed her gaze. A man with unkempt blond hair was sitting at the bar, his back to us.

"Red," Marcelle called loudly, causing the man to pivot in his seat. He looked from her to me and gave us an easy smile. Immediately, something about him unnerved me.

"Marcelle de Fabry," he said, rising and walking over to us. I noticed a mound of light chest hair creeping out of his white shirt, which was unbuttoned at the collar and tucked into his beige chambray pants.

He took Marcelle's hand in his and kissed it.

"I'm happy to see you," he drawled. "I thought it was going to be a dull morning, but no longer."

"It's almost afternoon, Red," she said. "Did you just wake up?"

"Something like that," he said, raising an eyebrow.

"You're the color of a sunset. In fact, you *are* red," she said, looking at his deeply tanned, slightly burned skin. "Sandalwood and turmeric. Mix it and apply. Then you'll look less lobster, more European."

"Did you get that recipe from a Tamil coolie?" said Red, looking down at his arms. "We used to do that in Burma."

"You should do it again here," she said, touching his skin. He grabbed her hand, squeezed it tightly, and then turned to me when he dropped it.

"We haven't met, have we?" he asked, blazing holes into me with his dark blue eyes. They were nothing like Victor's nearly translucent ones, beautiful by their absence of color. This man's were like a storm brewing in daylight.

"Or have we?" he asked, when I didn't answer right away.

It bothered me the way he phrased it. As if I weren't memorable. But I didn't like that it bothered me.

"We haven't," I said coolly, reaching out and shaking his hand.

"No kiss?" he said, looking down at our interlocked hands and grinning. "You can't be French."

"I'm American," I said, dropping his hand. "And French women don't kiss strangers. Neither do Americans."

"But I'm not a stranger. I know Marcelle very well. We go back years, don't we? To the wild days?" He looked at her, earning an eye roll. "Oh well," he continued, leaning down and kissing both my cheeks. "I'm British, so we should really be speaking English, but Marcelle here barely knows a word of our barbaric language, so we won't. For now."

For a moment we locked eyes but said nothing. When I felt my skin prick, I blinked and said, "Do the British kiss in greeting?"

"*Est-ce qu'on fait la bise?*" he repeated in his low voice. "Oh, no. We British aren't allowed to kiss at all. We even marry without kissing first. Then we make love to each other through a hole in the sheet. A rigid people, aren't we?" He looked at Marcelle, who nodded her agreement.

"Though you're about as rigid as spaghetti," she added.

He opened his mouth to speak, but she cut him off.

"Cooked spaghetti," she clarified.

"I still haven't been told your name," he said, looking at me again.

"I'm Jessie Lesage," I offered. "I'm—"

"You're Victor's wife," he said, and I couldn't tell if the crackle in his voice was excitement or disapproval. "I should have guessed from your pretty face. I've heard about you." He leaned in and said in a loud whisper, "The French women hate you."

"They do not!" Marcelle interrupted him. "I adore her."

"You adore everyone," he said good-naturedly. He turned back to me. "Women are just given to jealousy. Especially here. But pay no mind. I'll like you perfectly well, I can already tell."

"That's reassuring," I said, my heart beating quickly.

"Will you join us for lunch, Red?" Marcelle asked, gesturing to the three empty chairs at our table. "Or do you have a railroad to build?" She turned to me. "Red is trying to help our government complete the rail line down the coast. As it stands now, when we travel to Saigon, there's a big hole between Tourane and Nha Trang, forcing us to drive in the middle of an already horribly long train journey. But they should have it done, with Red involved, in about two thousand years, isn't that right, Red?"

"Three," he replied, smiling. "And no, thank you, I'm still recovering from last night. This seems to be helping, though." He raised his hand to show the cocktail he was holding. I hadn't even noticed the small glass, as I had only looked at his face.

"Suit yourself, but at least sit for a little, please," said Marcelle. "I need to say hello to Madame Clerc, who just came in. Her son is on his way here. He was no better than a criminal in Paris, but in Indochine they are going to make him the king or something like that. You know how it is here. Anyway, Arnaud would have my head if I didn't say hello. You'll keep Jessie company while I do, won't you, Red? You two can speak your funny little language to each other."

"If I must," he said, winking at me and sinking into the chair beside me.

"Jessie Lesage," he said, allowing a hint of a smile. "How did a pretty little American girl like you get caught up with these big bad Michelins?" he said, switching to English.

"Big and bad?" I replied lightly, trying not to show offense. "We are big, perhaps, but bad, certainly not. We, my husband's family, are as committed to the success of the colony as those in the railroad business are, I gather."

"Of course. We all are. Everything we do is for France. And her loyal subjects," he said, smiling. "But still, you don't seem like the kind of girl who would have married a Michelin."

"You've known me less than ten minutes," I replied. "And have you ever met a Michelin?"

"Not yet," he admitted. "Your family doesn't make it over here very often. But you don't have to meet them to know about them, do you. The Michelins have provided colonial and French newspapers quite a few dramatic stories over the past few years."

"I suppose I haven't paid quite enough attention," I said, smiling, though of course I knew exactly what he was referring to. "I stayed rather busy in Paris. Women's things, you know."

"You might want to change that here," he advised. "Just so you won't be surprised if people talk at the club. Though I'm sure your husband will make improvements. And it would be unfortunate for a beautiful woman like you not to get to enjoy women's things."

"Is your drink orange?" I said, hoping to shift the conversation to a lighter topic. I leaned in to smell it cautiously, but the man overpowered the scent of the drink. Red smelled like Indochine. The other Western men all smelled like imported European soaps and powders. Red was different.

"This? Yes, it certainly is orange," he said, holding it in front of him. "Would you like to try it?" I took the small crystal glass he offered me and sniffed the liquor in it again.

I put it to my lips and raised my eyebrows at him, smiling, just before I let the cold drink touch my tongue. It was much stronger than I had expected.

"It's a Pegu Club," he said as I scrunched up my face. "Lots of gin. I grew a bit too fond of them in Rangoon."

"Is that where you've come in from?" I said, handing him back his glass. "Burma?"

"Indeed," he said. "A year ago, but yes. It's a wonderful place, Burma. You should visit. You and Victor," he added. "I thought I'd stay there for years more, but it turns out the French can't build a railroad properly without an Englishman's help."

As a waiter approached, Red raised his glass and asked for another Pegu Club. "Two," he corrected himself. "This young lady needs to be initiated." He threw his forearms on the table with a bang. They were as hairy as his chest. "I think you would like Burma. You have a wild air about you. You're trying to hide it, but I see it. People like that thrive in places like Indochine and Burma. Personally, they suit me better than home. I'm just too undomesticated for London, or Paris for that matter. I tried that one, too. Wasn't a good fit."

"You should work on your accent then," I said, trying to break myself from his spell and hold up my end of the conversation. "It's much too proper. You won't convince anyone—or at least me—that you're a savage if you sound like King George."

"Hard thing to shake, an accent," he said, sipping the last of his drink.

"I've been told that a few times," I agreed.

"Your accent becomes you," he said, looking at me quizzically. "To be honest, I've never heard an American speak like you."

"You've only met New Yorkers probably."

Red twirled his glass in his hand and leaned back. "I met a man from California in Rangoon. Railroad man."

"As in he worked on the railroad or he owned the railroad?" I asked.

"I believe he owned it," Red said, laughing.

"Then he definitely didn't sound like me."

"What do the French think of your accent?"

"Some think it's terrible, others find it charming," I said honestly. It was mostly the men who found it charming.

"It's quite obviously the latter. And your French is extremely good. Almost as good as mine."

"It's not quite, but thank you. It's my favorite language, even when spoken with an American accent," I said, turning up the drawl.

"It's everyone's favorite language, trust me. When French women find out I'm a Brit, there's nothing I can do to compete with their countrymen," he said, shrugging.

It was clear from the shrug that he didn't believe that for a second. Red had obviously come out on top most of his life.

He pushed his dark blond hair out of his eyes and nodded to a man who had just walked in.

"That's the *résident supérieur* of Tonkin," he said. "Stodgy grump when he's sober but marvelous when he's drunk. So, avoid him during daylight hours. You can tell that to Victor, too. If he needs to work with him, it best be between one and three in the morning."

"I'll pass along the advice," I said. "Where are you from in England?" I asked.

"Buckinghamshire."

"And where did you go to school?"

"Cambridge."

"Are you married?"

"Never," he said softly, leaning toward me. He picked up my glass and drained it for me.

I laughed, and he laid his hand on my shoulder. Firmly.

"That's my cue," he said, keeping his grip on me. "Marcelle is on her way back, but I just got the prettiest woman in the room to laugh. Now I can start my day properly. A pleasure meeting you, Jessie Lesage. I'm sure I will cross your golden path again soon."

TWELVE

Marcelle

September 24, 1933

S ang has been found out."

"What?" I mumbled, Khoi's words startling me awake. Since
he had returned in 1930, one of Khoi's first missions was to
study the management pyramid of the Michelin plantations, which
was easily done by traveling north into the rural provinces of Tonkin
and finding former coolies who had worked there and were willing
to talk for a modest sum. On each plantation, the laborers were divided into villages to live and then into smaller teams of ten to work.
Each team of laborers was overseen by a foreman, native like them.
Above the foreman was an overseer, who was usually mixed-race and
spoke French. These overseers reported to the chief overseers. Above
them all reigned the plantation manager. The Annamites could not rise
above an overseer position, but those overseers were at least given their
own rooms, unlike the laborers, who slept fifty to a barracks and had
only a few square feet of living space to call their own. The mixed-race
overseers came from varying backgrounds, unlike the French, who for
the most part had gone straight from the army to Michelin. Plantations followed a strict hierarchy, and the number of men on them was
massive and, according to the French, needed to be controlled. A mere

civilian would not be capable of enacting such control. Those with military training, it was believed, might fare better.

Tran Van Sang was the mixed-race overseer at Phu Rieng who had agreed to send reports with any details he could uncover about the plantation management, but most of all, he was there to support covert communist activity in the plantations. He was to help hide such activity from upper management and to encourage the laborers to re-cruit more men into their fold. Khoi had paid Sang since he returned in '29. He was our most important link to Michelin. Now Khoi was saying that his game was up.

"Are you sure?" I asked Khoi. He had been out late, and I'd fallen asleep waiting for him to return. I still hadn't told him how Jessie ex-pounded the praises of Michelin as the benevolent freedom-givers to thousands of coolies. Now none of that seemed important. Sang was our physical link to everything Michelin.

"I'm very sure," he said, sitting up on the edge of the bed. He still had his beige suit on, the tie slightly loosened. "I received a note from my driver when I was at the Taverne Royale a few hours ago that I had an important telephone call, and we were able to connect. Sang is now in Saigon."

"How was he found out?" I asked, already knowing the answer.

"Ask me instead *who* found out."

"Victor Lesage."

"Indeed. Victor Lesage. He has only been down on the plantations for a few days, but he already figured out that Sang attended a com-munist meeting that took place in village three at Phu Rieng under the guise of a play rehearsal."

"A play rehearsal?" I said, remembering what Jessie had said at the club.

"Yes. A play rehearsal. They have recently added leisure activities to their slave labor. You know, fifteen minutes here and there where they can kick around a ball or sing a song. The overseers smugly assume that their benevolence will keep communism at bay, when really, it's a perfect time for men who seldom meet to gather and spread their message."

"Well," I said. "Then I suppose I support this rise in the theater."

"Yes, but Sang says Victor has figured this out, too, that plays and soccer games have become excuses for covert meetings of the communist party, so now he is putting an end to it all."

"But how did he figure it all out?" I asked, trying not to become distraught. "Sang has been so careful. There have been no close calls at all in the last few years."

"Victor Lesage attended this meeting, under the pretense that he is passionate about bringing art and culture to the workers, and it turns out he speaks enough Annamese to understand them. They had no idea and were still speaking freely."

"Well, that's extremely unfortunate," I said, suddenly remembering how Victor had said that the family took language lessons in Paris. How could they have learned so much in only six months? I had been foolish not to pass that information on to Sang. "But how did he learn about Sang specifically?" I pressed.

"Victor didn't discover his role right then, but he gave one of the laborers in attendance a handsome payout and money for a journey home if they could speak after the meeting was over. The man talked, of course, and he fingered Sang. Luckily, the worker had some shred of a soul left and told Sang what he had done, giving Sang time to run. He beat Victor to the plantation periphery, and because he's not just a laborer but an overseer, they let him out. Now he's hiding in Saigon, but we're figuring out how to get him north quickly. He'll be arrested and imprisoned immediately if not. You know what happened to the men who organized the labor strike in 1930."

I did. Five years' imprisonment in the French political prison on Con Son Island, a hell floating below Cochinchina.

"I did not expect him to act this way," said Khoi. "Victor. I imagined he would barely spend time on the plantations at all, and not understand a word of Annamese or attempt to interact with the workers. With his background, I thought he'd spend his days at the Officers' Club here and at Le Cercle in Saigon, focus on building relationships with government and business officials. Pocketing more people through bribes and cajoling. There must really be pressure on him from Clermont-Ferrand to keep the peace. No repeats of the murders and communist strikes. And he must have a handsome paycheck waiting for him if he succeeds. Now we have, well, I don't know what we have. A disaster, I suppose."

"We need someone to replace Sang," I said, terrified not to have a contact on the plantations.

"We do," said Khoi. "But he is irreplaceable. We won't find anyone as capable. Still, as pressing as that is, the first thing to do is help Sang leave Indochine for a spell."

"Of course," I said, worried for a man I had never met. I looked at Khoi, who had lain back on the bed, exhausted. "Three days ago, I spent the morning at the club with Jessie Lesage," I said quietly. "You should have heard her. She went on and on about how the capitalist system in America allowed her to change her own life. To bootstrap her way to the top. She is quite sure that what the Michelins and the rest of them are doing is paving the way for great opportunities for the poor. Smart as she claims to be, it's impossible for her not to know that the Tonkinese coolies on their plantations went there because our colonial policies drove them to desperation. That we brutally eroded their way of life, their subsistence farming, and then imposed draconian personal taxes that have to be paid in cash and lead directly to financial ruin. Of course, that works out just fine for us French because it means cheap slave labor for the plantations. She refuses to admit that. Oh, how I wish you'd heard her. It was just awful, Khoi. Her blind idealism about how anyone can improve their station in life if they just work hard enough. As if there is some teachers' college around the corner all the laborers can attend, and some rich savior a bit further down the road for them to marry if they just work hard enough. Indochine is not America. I don't care where she's from, whatever it was like, I know she had people to help her. Teachers who taught her how to read at the very least."

"I believe it," said Khoi. "But she is still not the one who licked the stamps sealing Sinh's death sentence. Remember that."

"I remember," I said, growing frustrated. "But she married the man that did. And she's supporting him now, fueling him, every step of the way."

Khoi took off his clothes and lay down next to me.

"I'll leave the house again in an hour. Try to sort out this whole mess with Sang. But I need a minute of rest first." He laid his head on my chest and let his eyes focus on the picture of Sinh and Anne-Marie, which was half glowing in the moonlight.

"I miss Anne-Marie so much," I said. "Spending time with Jessie— even if she's untrustworthy—is reminding me what it's like to have female friendship. I want that back."

We were both quiet for a moment, listening to the whirl of the metal fan in the far corner of the room. Before there was electricity, Khoi told me, the rich *colons* used to have servants tie one end of a string to their big toe, the other to the fan, and pull all night while their masters slept under the cool breeze. He'd assured me that the Nguyens had never bothered with such a service.

"We need Victor to disappear," I said quietly. "Both of them need to disappear."

"He is proving to have a knack at quickly undoing everything we have spent years on," said Khoi. "It terrifies me to think that all our efforts could fall away in such a short amount of time, and that Victor could rise to the top in the process, when all he deserves is to sink. I really was expecting him to be far less interested in being present on the plantation. It's almost like he's not a Michelin."

"He is certainly a Michelin," I said. "They both are."

"This way of ours," said Khoi, starting to fall asleep, "it's exhausting."

"But it's the only way," I said.

"I know," he murmured. "And it's the right way. But this is a battle with many fronts, and I'm trying to win them all. At this rate, I think I'll be dead by thirty-five."

"Never say that again," I said, kissing his forehead. "You have two lives to lead now. Yours and Sinh's. So you'll have to live to be at least two hundred years old. On that note, we should probably stop drinking so much."

"Never," said Khoi, smiling. "It's too much fun. At least the French haven't taken that away from us yet."

I waited until Khoi fell asleep and then got out of bed, too restless to lie still.

I walked toward his dresser, and the ukulele propped atop it. It was the same one that had been played the first night I met Sinh. Khoi bought it for a few francs from the partygoer, who had become a friend, after Sinh had died.

I ran my fingers quietly over the strings, the lightness of that phase of our lives feeling so far behind us.

I didn't know what to do about Sang, or how to find the man who had put a bullet in Sinh's chest. It seemed like the latter would elude us all forever. I didn't even know what to do about Victor and Jessie, but I was certain of something. The Lesages' visit to the colony would have to be a very short one.

THIRTEEN

Jessie

October 2, 1933

I'd like to pay, please," I said, nodding to the young waiter. I was at the restaurant of the Hotel Métropole on the boulevard Henri Rivière, a favorite haunt of the French community in Hanoi. He was standing just a few feet away in his crisp white uniform, his arms at his side like a soldier's yet with a practiced smile on his face. In his right hand was a small wooden tray, which he held against his thigh like a shield.

"*Bien sûr, madame,*" he said, hurrying over to my small marble table and producing the check for my meal. I left my piastres next to it and stood, in no rush to leave. I had been on my way to the dressmaker to pick up several new day dresses that I'd ordered. I seemed to be losing weight in the heat, and Victor said that instead of taking in my clothes, I should just purchase more. The dressmaker had a studio very near our home, so I had insisted on walking, despite protests from Lanh. I was hoping to get back in time to greet Lucie when she returned from school, but before I even made it to the dressmaker's, I glimpsed a man who looked very much like Red cross the street and make his way up the front stairs of the hotel. I did think he was perhaps too slight and too young—I guessed Red was at least thirty-five—but the blond hair and half-rolled-up shirtsleeves squared with my memory.

I'd walked through the hotel lobby, to the bar and then to the back garden, but didn't see the man again. He must have been a guest returning to his room rather than a resident of Hanoi in need of a stiff drink. When the French hotel manager came up to inquire if I needed assistance, I'd said I was interested in a late lunch at the hotel's Brasserie de l'Étoile and found myself ordering several courses just so I could linger and watch for the man.

In the ten days since I'd met Red, I had been thinking about him far too often. My mind nearly cleared of my worries regarding Marcelle and her oddly deep knowledge of Swiss mental health facilities, I was free to start enjoying my new world in Indochine, and to let Red swim through my thoughts.

He was a type, I told myself. Too smooth, too good-looking, too skilled at finding the bon mot, the kinds of words and phrases that struck women the right way, even ones like me who weren't built to fall for a good line or a handsome face. I was certainly not the first woman he had rested his hands on the day he'd met her. His was a thoroughly practiced touch. But the problem was I didn't care, and I doubt the women who'd come before me had, either. Since I'd met him, I hadn't been able to shake him.

I had never had time in my life for spontaneous assignations. Every time I'd gotten into bed with a man—there were four of them, including Victor—it was because I hoped he could help me in ways that had nothing to do with sex. What I had needed was a husband with means. Enough means so I would never have to worry about money again, something I had spent every day of my life thinking about, to some degree. I had fallen easily into Victor's bed, but because I could not yet break my agreement with the school that employed me in New York, the only source of income I had, I had just a month left in Paris, which translated into six days to get pregnant, if the medical books I'd consulted back in New York were correct.

When I was in bed with Victor for the first time, just three days after we met, I made a show of using the diaphragm kit I'd obtained from a female doctor in Manhattan who was sympathetic to poor, unmarried women. Then I inserted it sideways. It wasn't going to block even the laziest sperm. It took sleeping with Victor constantly—and eating almost a full jar of honey, a secret fertility source, I had read—but it worked. By the following month, one of the steamiest Augusts Parisians could remember, I was pregnant.

Victor was less than thrilled at first. He felt tricked, deceived. Which, of course, he had been. But he was also in love with me. He stayed mad for a week, and then he'd come up to my little apartment, the first time he'd ever visited, his head practically touching the top of the door frame as he came in, and had kneeled in front of me and put his head on my stomach.

"You should probably change your clothes," he'd said after I'd stopped crying. "The dress you're wearing is a bit too informal to get married in."

In the years since we'd married, my dependence on Victor had turned to love. Real love. And I knew he felt the same. His affection for me wasn't just passing lust or something born out of obligation. Ours was a union that felt unbreakable, even if it had been built from a few half-truths.

Since we'd been married, no other man had rattled me. Until now.

I nodded at the hotel manager on my way out and, with my stomach painfully full, made it back to the house at four o'clock, too late to see Lucie bounding up the stairs after Lanh fetched her.

I went to my bedroom to change out of my street-stained clothes before retiring to the terrace in a pair of loose silk trousers. There, I used the bell that always sat on the iron table and rang for Trieu. She appeared a few minutes later with a chilled bottle of white wine. As she poured, I asked her to bring Lucie to me.

I heard my daughter's feet on the tiles before I saw her and turned just in time to watch her leap through the glass doors from the bedroom. She smiled when she saw me and threw her arms around my neck. Her hair was loose, and she had changed from her school uniform into an airy white dress that made her look like an ethereal sprite who had flown in to keep me company.

"Would you like to hear my latest phrase in Annamese, *maman*? I'm getting very good," she said, nuzzling on top of me as I reclined in Victor's favorite chair. He was on the train up from Saigon, due to return in a few hours, after two weeks away. Sitting in his chair gave me comfort while he was gone, and sitting there with Lucie even more. I tilted my head back as Lucie caressed my temples.

"Of course I would," I said, breathing in the scent of her hair. By evening, all the perfumed soaps and powders applied by the servants had worn off and Lucie smelled like a child again.

"*Người làm bánh đau nặng. Ông bị ung thư họng vì hút thuốc phiện nhiều quá,*" she said with a voice full of emotion, shaking her head as she finished the phrase.

"That sounds very authentic," I said, laughing. I appreciated the distraction, the humor that Lucie always brought to me.

"Thank you, *maman*," she said, putting her finger right on the tip of my nose. "Diep has been helping me with the different sounds. I mean tones. That's what they're called. And that sentence is something they've been saying a lot in the kitchen."

"Have they?" I said, picturing Diep. She had not said one word to me about the money for the girl, and neither had Lanh, but I had noticed that our food had gotten noticeably tastier since that day. "What does it mean, that funny phrase?" I asked, grabbing her finger and pretending to bite it.

"It means 'The baker is very ill,'" she said, sitting up. "He has throat cancer from smoking too much opium.'"

"Lucie!" I exclaimed. "What on earth!"

"But it's true, *maman*," she said, throwing herself back down on my body. "The baker *is* very ill. He does have throat cancer from smok—"

"Yes, yes, *chérie*. I understand," I said, covering her mouth with my hand as she tried to look at me. "But opium isn't a good topic of conversation for a little girl."

"Okay," she replied, disappointed. "Though it is quite a profitable commodity for the colony." She wiggled so she was lying sideways on me, her legs folded awkwardly so that she just fit against my torso.

"Who have you been conversing with?" I asked her, too amused to chastise her again.

"Everyone I meet!" she said, laughing. "There are so many people to meet here."

After delighting me with other phrases in Annamese that she'd picked up from the staff, Lucie kissed me good-bye, off to the kitchen for more language lessons with the cook. I kissed her head again, barely grazing it as she was in such a hurry to get to her private world.

Alone, I took a large swallow of wine. It was already too warm, losing its fight with the latitude of Indochine. I held the glass between my palms and looked out at the world below me, happy to experience Hanoi from my perch. After a month of living in the capital, I was starting to memorize its movements like a bird of prey.

After I'd refilled my glass twice, the scene below started to blur pleasantly, and I relaxed, willing my mind to stay right where I was, in my home, on my husband's chair, with my daughter downstairs.

I closed my eyes, letting sleep creep over me, until I felt the warmth of someone nearby. As I stirred, I felt a blanket being draped over me and Victor's comforting touch. I slowly opened my eyes to see him standing above me, still in his light gray traveling suit with a faint pinstripe, his wide silk tie slightly loosened. His black hair was deeply parted to the left and oiled down, as usual.

"Look at you here with the city at your feet," he said, leaning down to kiss me. "Like the queen of Hanoi."

"How was it?" I asked, turning my head up to kiss him back.

"Extraordinary. The plantations are just incredible. The breadth of them, it's like they creep all the way to Saigon," said Victor, his eyes animated. He motioned for me to move over and joined me on the chaise, which was wide enough for two. "I'd seen pictures over the years as the land has been cleared and planted, and I heard much about it from Uncle André, but nothing prepared me for the vastness of it. The modernity. And the sheer number of people working the land. There are five thousand coolies at Dau Tieng alone. Four thousand more at Phu Rieng. The amount of rubber trees still being planted is astounding. It feels as if the forests come down in a day, replaced with fields of saplings."

"And you lived among all those men these past few days?" I asked, still having a hard time picturing Victor breaking bread with thousands of natives.

"Of course not. I stayed in my own very civilized bungalow. It was built for me when we sent word that I was coming. It's rather handsome. Made of brick. Not too many insects. There are these horrible ants the size of a franc down there, but they've been directed to stay out of my house and they seem to take orders well."

"That's a relief," I said, smiling.

"The two overseers, Theurière and Soumagnac, they're not the most personable men in the world, but since the strife last year, they really have done much to modernize the plantations. Especially with the hospitals. The health care is world-class. And I was told the food is much improved as well. There are canteens serving meals of rice, meat, fish, and a brown sauce they all go wild for called *nuoc mam*. There are also doctors and nurses who live at the site, working in the large infirmary, stores where the coolies shop, separate little villages for them to sleep in—it's very well laid out. And we've improved the housing, too, there are now thatch-covered mud houses with gardens. And we were able to build them for a third of the price than other plantations spent, since we had the coolies build them themselves. It's quite rewarding, I imagine. To be able to build your own house. Really, it's all quite impressive. There have clearly been great strides made by the overseers."

"I'm happy to hear it. Very happy," I said, thinking again about the horrible document I'd read on the boat. Victor had had no control over that era, I reminded myself. Now he did.

"But there was one very unsettling thing that happened. It's why I've had to stay away as long as I have."

"Which was?" I said, my nerves instinctively jumping.

"Something shocking, actually," he said, reaching for the glass of wine that had just been brought to him by Trieu. "I suppose it shouldn't have been shocking, considering all the papers have reported about the spread of communism on our plantations, and others, but still."

"What was it?" I asked, my concern mounting. "You have to be very careful, Victor."

"First, I need to thank you because if you had not forced us all to hire that tutor and learn as much Annamese as we could in six months, I would not have realized what I did."

"Which was?" I didn't know how much of his talking in circles I could take.

"The makings of another communist uprising. I'm sure that's what it was."

"No," I said incredulously. "Like 1930?" The strike had been five days long and thousands of coolies had shown up with a list of demands on the manager's lawn. There were so many that Soumagnac and all the managers had fled the plantation and the government had to intervene with military force. To the joy of the coolies, some of their demands had been met. But not all. Michelin was not about to reward such behavior.

"Most likely worse. A few days ago, I found out that one of the mixed-race overseers at Phu Rieng, who had been considered very loyal since he'd just renewed his three-year contract, has been helping the coolies under his direction hold communist party meetings, and encouraging them to recruit more into their ranks. And on top of that, one of the coolies told me that he's being paid to do so."

"By whom?" I asked, shocked.

"I don't know. He was able to escape. A grave oversight on our part."

"What will you do now?" I asked, inching closer to Victor instinctively.

"I've notified the police, but I don't think they'll try too hard to find him. They're busy with bigger fish in that domain. I'm just happy to be rid of him, though exercising some punishment would have been helpful for prevention. These men, they really learn by example. I need to show them that I am lenient, but not weak when it comes to those who would instigate uprisings."

"Of course," I said, thinking about what Victor had said on the boat.

"I've left it all in the hands of the overseers now, and I think they're capable of keeping the peace. I hope so, anyway. Despite that mishap, it was a fascinating trip."

"Then you're glad we came. To the colony."

"Yes," he said, smiling at me. "I'm glad you convinced me. And I do see now that it could change the trajectory of my career forever."

"It's the right thing to do," I said, my heart fluttering. Victor thought I'd pushed him toward Indochine because I saw great career opportunity for him. And I did see it. But I'd also had a very private reason to leave Paris.

After six years of giving me sanctuary, my memories had finally followed me there, and they had taken up house.

It was November 1932, and Lucie and I were walking home from a visit with her cousins. She was busy running her hand along an iron railing near the Grand Palais, soiling her white cashmere gloves.

"Lucie, please don't touch anything," I had hissed at her, tired and frustrated from a conversation I'd had with Victor that morning. His position in the company, now that André was gone, was starting to feel shaky. The younger generation was taking over in Clermont-Ferrand, and Victor was not close to them. I was thinking about how to improve our circumstances when I heard someone say my name.

The voice came from behind us, and it was certainly not French. I heard my name again and froze, grabbing Lucie's hand instinctively, nearly pulling her to the ground. The woman who had spoken had an unmistakably Southern accent. My accent.

I turned around slowly and came face-to-face with my past.

"Jessie Holland?" the woman said, looking at me incredulously. "Am I dreaming, or is that really you?"

It was I who wanted to be dreaming. But she was there, no dream, looking as if she was ready to embrace me—Dorothy Davis, one of my schoolmates in Blacksburg. She looked nothing like the girl I had known, always in a dirty dress, shoes a size too small. She had always had a pretty face, though, and I saw that it was even prettier now, especially when set off by an expensive-looking wool hat and broadcloth coat with fox trim. She was with another woman, who was equally well turned out.

"I heard a rumor in Blacksburg that you lived in Paris now, but I never took it to be true," she said, still looking at me in shock. "But it is. It really is. You're right here."

"Yes, it is," I said, trying not to look as stunned as she did. "This is my daughter, Lucie," I added before sending Lucie off to play with the railing again. She could have licked it for all I cared at that point. I just wanted her away from the woman and the conversation I was sure we would have. I knew it would be impossible for Dorothy not to mention it. Not to mention them.

"What a beautiful child," she said, looking at Lucie playing. "She looks like one of you. The Hollands. Especially the eyes."

"Maybe a bit," I said. "But she really resembles her father."

"Does she? Who is her father?" she asked, trying her best to make it sound innocent.

"A Frenchman. Parisian," I said, smiling tightly.

I could tell she wanted me to elaborate on the man who had plucked me from my hell in Virginia, but I did not go on. Because really, I had plucked myself from all that. We spoke about Paris a few moments, and when her friend walked off to admire the Grand Palais, Dorothy of course brought up our shared hometown.

"After I finished school, I moved to Richmond," she said. "It felt so cosmopolitan to me, if you can believe it."

"I can," I said, smiling, moving a step back to indicate that I was ready to close the conversation, but Dorothy went on. "I first married a veterinarian who had studied at the Polytechnic Institute in Blacksburg. He did very well for himself, thankfully."

"How nice for you," I said, taking another step back, but she matched me, like we were fencing.

"It was a fine marriage," she said, warming to her topic, "but, well, it wasn't a *coup de foudre*, as the French say. And I'd always dreamt of bigger things than being a veterinarian's wife. But I got very lucky. Girls like us really do deserve luck sometimes, don't we?"

"What was this stroke of luck?" I asked, cursing myself for my curiosity.

"When I turned twenty-three, my husband flat out died!" she exclaimed. "He fell off a horse and God just sucked the breath and heartbeat right out of him. Can you believe it? God must be a woman," she said, looking up at the sky as if she might be struck by lightning there and then for saying such a thing.

"Oh, how dreadful, I'm terribly sorry," I said, feeling like that was probably a better fate for the veterinarian than to be married to Dorothy for the rest of his life.

"Don't be. After that I took a page out of your book and left the state entirely. Though I went to California. Los Angeles. I met a wonderful man in the picture industry, Nick Lesser."

She paused as if the name should mean something to me. It did not.

"Anyway," she said, gesturing dramatically with her slender, gloved hands. "Nick had a few smashing successes in America, which put him in high demand all over the globe, including here. So now he's in Paris helping the French make pictures, too. He wasn't going to leave California, his career was going *so* well, but with the money the French offered him, and with the economy so dismally bad and so many people barely able to afford a ticket to the pictures at home, how could he turn it down? They assured him that the economy in France was better off than in America, and they were certainly correct. Just look at that bridge," she said, pointing to the Pont Alexandre III. "At home, people would be chiseling that gold right off."

"I don't think it's real gold. I think it's just gold paint—"

"All that is to say," she said, interrupting me with a giddy smile on her face, "that I live here now. In Paris!"

My heart stopped.

"You *live* in Paris?" I said, nearly choking on the words. "How surprising," I said, trying to find oxygen again.

"Surprising for both of us, I'll say. Do you ever go back to Virginia?" she asked with feigned sweetness.

"No," I replied bluntly. I gestured to Lucie to come back to me so that we could run off together, but she wasn't looking in my direction.

"I've returned once since we moved to Paris last year," Dorothy said. "My parents are still in Blacksburg." She'd looked at me differently then. Making sure our eyes didn't just meet but locked.

"How nice for you," I said, inching a bit closer to the bridge where Lucie was.

"I saw your mother while I was there," she said, her voice growing louder.

I didn't respond. I hadn't seen my mother in over ten years.

"She doesn't seem too well. My mother said that she is constantly wandering around town muttering French to herself, her long white hair unbrushed and dirty. There's talk in town that she's sick. In the head. Sick in the head," she repeated. "I saw her myself actually, from a distance, but even from there, I have to agree."

"She hasn't had an easy life," I started. "And she still struggles with cultural differences. Even after all these years."

"Trust me, my dear," she said, trying to hide her disdain for my excuse. "This isn't a cultural difference. She's not well. Naturally, I didn't see your father," she added in the same breath.

"Yes, well, things were difficult after all that," I said quietly, looking toward Lucie. How I wanted to disappear in that moment. Or, better yet, to march Dorothy to the Pont Alexandre III and shove her into the Seine. The bridge wasn't very high, but people had lost their lives from even shorter falls. I could not have her speaking about my parents to my daughter or husband, and I could definitely not have her living in the same city as me.

"People still talk about it in town," she went on, looking at me with false sympathy. "How can they not? So, I understand why you wanted to leave so badly. I wouldn't want to be talked about like that."

"I wanted to leave well before all that happened," I said, knowing that her little pea-sized brain was recording my every word, ready to dish it all in letters to her friends and mother in Blacksburg.

"Don't you miss that open space, though?" she said when she noticed Lucie was walking back to us. "The smell of the grass? It's pretty here, but there's hardly anywhere for a child to play. I don't have children yet, so for me it's just fine. But that poor little one looks like she's desperate for wide-open spaces, no?"

"We don't need grass," I said sharply. "We prefer gold bridges."

Lucie stopped walking and instead pointed to the bridge. "May I play there?" she called out in French.

"Of course, *chérie*," I replied, watching her turn away from us. "I should go with her," I added, making my excuses. "But what a lovely coinci—"

"I never see your sisters and brothers around," Dorothy said, interrupting me. She had to say it. Her mouth now looked fat and chapped rather than pert and pink, as it had when she approached me. "Did you bring them all here with you? Maybe I can say hello to them when I call on you."

"They don't live here," I said with finality and started to walk off.

"You haven't told me where to call on you!" Dorothy yelled out, stopping me.

"I think it would be best if I called on you," I said sharply, not bothering to ask for her address.

"Whatever suits you best, dear," she said, picking up her pace behind me. We reached Lucie at the bridge together, and Dorothy held out her hand to her.

"And what's your name, darling?" she asked before I could cut her off. "You're very pretty."

"Lucie Lesage," Lucie answered immediately.

"Lesage," said Dorothy, with a victorious smile. "Jessie Lesage then. Has a nice ring to it. If you don't call on me," she said, reaching into her purse and handing me her card, "then I'll be sure to find you. I really must meet your husband. I'm sure he's a wonderful man."

"He is," I said.

Dorothy looked at me appraisingly, and I could tell she was trying to calculate how much I had spent on my outfit. I cursed myself for having chosen my most expensive coat that morning.

"Jessie, you really have changed, haven't you?" she said.

"I just have nicer coats now," I said. "As do you."

"Yes," she said, rubbing her gloved hands together. "Well, I must be off, but it was wonderful to run into you like this. I'll be traveling a bit for the next few months. To Spain, then Portugal, perhaps even farther afield to Morocco. But when I return, we really do have to introduce our husbands. I just know they'll get on. And I'm sure your husband will want to hear all about our childhoods. There really are so many stories to tell."

"Indeed," I said. A few months. How long was a few months? Could I get out of Paris before she returned? Or could I see to it that she never returned? She could not tell Victor about my mother—or, worse, the things I couldn't even bring myself to think about.

Victor was terrified of "episodes," as he called them. Mental illness. Of what had happened with his father. Of what had happened to me in Switzerland. If he knew that it ran in my family, that my mother had been sick since I could remember, that my brother Peter, the second oldest, had never been able to work a day in his life because of his streaks of mania, then what? Would he leave me for good? Would he be waiting for signs of it in Lucie? Would he love her less, afraid that she was wired more like a Holland than a Michelin? That thought alone made me want to jump into the Seine and just keep swimming.

I had told Victor, the very first night we'd met, that both my parents had died. That they were long dead. It was much easier than the truth. He could never know the truth. Never. But Dorothy was ready to deliver it to him like a Christmas hog. That was painfully obvious.

After that terrible chance encounter, I spent many sleepless nights trying to think of a solution. Then one day, Victor had left a newspaper on the table that he said featured a disparaging article about Michelin, focusing on their activities in the colony. In Indochine. No one in Victor's family had any desire to live in the colony. But they clearly needed someone on the ground who might be able to prevent another communist uprising. I put the leftist paper back on the table and started to formulate a plan.

The following day I summoned my courage and had lunch with Victor's mother. Would Victor keep his employment much longer without André to advocate for him, I asked, or would he be pushed out like an old tire? I told Agathe that if Victor could prove himself in the colony, make himself indispensable, then surely he would be rewarded upon his return.

She nodded while sipping her tea, the cogs of her brain spinning slowly. I watched, fighting the urge to scream that good logic aside, she owed me after what she'd done when Lucie was born. And if she cared about me keeping my sanity in the long run, she had to help me.

"I think it's a very smart idea," she'd finally said after slowly draining the entire cup of tea. "It's one I've often had myself."

"Yes, I assumed you had," I replied, even though I was quite positive that no such thought had ever entered her head.

"You suggest it to Victor, and I'll second it when he comes to ask for my opinion. I'll also push for it down in Clermont-Ferrand if need be."

"Thank you," I said, bowing my head slightly in the type of show of reverence that Agathe adored.

Six months later, Dorothy had not called on me and I was on a boat to the Far East.

FOURTEEN

Jessie

October 3, 1933

I know you've had Lucie to look after, but have you been getting up to much in my absence?" Victor asked me over breakfast the morning after he returned.

We had fallen asleep early the night before, while still discussing his discovery on the plantation.

"I've been to the Officers' Club a bit," I said, "but Lucie loves to play here, so we often do." I certainly did not intend to tell Victor about who I had met at the Officers' Club.

"Now that I'm back in Hanoi for a spell, I can go with you to the club if you'd like."

I nodded but didn't look at him.

After Trieu had cleared our breakfast and closed the glass doors behind her, Victor gestured for me to come closer.

"And Marcelle?" he asked quietly.

"I do think it was just an unfortunate coincidence," I said just as quietly, remembering our lazy hours by the pool together. "We went to the club together once, and I saw that she speaks frankly with everyone, sharing snippets about her life that most women would want to keep secret, and also giving a lot of unsolicited advice. She told one of the guests to apply sandalwood and turmeric to a sunburn. Likened them to a lobster. I've seen others taken aback by the things she says. But I'm sorry I was so dramatic about it all," I said with a genuine laugh. "You don't have to worry. I'm back to my usual self."

"That's a tremendous relief," Victor said, leaning back again. "I understand why it worried you, of course, but it did seem highly unlikely to me," he added. "I thought about every scenario. Could she know someone at the clinic? Could she know a friend of my mother's? Someone *maman* could have confided in about you?"

"Whom would your mother confide in?" I asked, trying my best to remain outwardly calm. I was back to normal, after all—I'd just declared so to Victor. I couldn't seem worked up about his mother. "Didn't you once say that she never spoke of it because she didn't want a stain on her family?"

"Yes, and I'm sure it's true," he said hastily. "But you were so distraught. I was just trying to get to the bottom of it."

"I am sure it's nothing. Just an odd coincidence that brought back old memories."

"I think these are just the kinds of things that women talk about. Especially women like Marcelle. The bold, loud kind. You weren't spending time with women like that at home." He put his hat on as the sun moved over us, the parasol no longer fully covering our faces. "My mother kept you around all those aristocrats in Paris."

"Marcelle isn't exactly a street urchin," I countered.

"No, but she's a little more common than the ladies you saw at home. A little more eccentric, no?"

"I don't think I can label anyone common," I said, thinking back to my beginnings. Victor knew that I had not grown up with money, but I had told him nothing beyond that. It was all he needed to know.

"Some people shed their first skin better than others," Victor said, his arm brushing against mine as he reached for his coffee. "I did ask around a bit about Arnaud. He's quite the ladies' man, it seems, but one of Governor-General Pasquier's closest economic advisers. He remains prominent in the Alliance Républicaine Démocratique. He was also in Burma for a few years, one of the only Frenchmen there. It's a bit of a unique position, since we have such little presence in Burma, but he seems to have come out of it well."

"A ladies' man?" I asked, remembering what Marcelle and I had seen in the billiard room.

"Those might just be rumors," said Victor. "Men like to start such rumors about themselves when they're abroad and there are willing native women in such large supply."

"I hope they are just rumors, for Marcelle's sake."

Victor nodded. "On a different note, I have a proposition for you. A bit of a redo of that terrible situation that I put you in with the policeman. If you're up for it, that is."

"A redo? As in I have to live that nightmare again?" I said, my heartbeat picking up.

"No, I phrased that badly," he said, smiling. "But I do need your help. We need your help," he said, referring to what was bigger than us, "and this time I promise you'll enjoy it."

For many years I'd wanted to be more helpful to Victor, in his working life especially, but Agathe had always forbade it. Finally, she wasn't here.

"What is it?" I asked, appreciative of Victor's trust in me.

"I need someone to travel to Haiphong, eighty miles east of here, and meet with a man. He helps with recruiting and worker transport in the rural parts of the region. I'm told that he has some important papers for me, but I can't make the journey myself, as our overseers down in Cochinchina are insisting I come back to the plantations straightaway. The hospital expansion at Phu Rieng is finished, and I'm to give the governor-general a tour. He is very invested in how we are bringing modern European health care to our workers. I can't tear myself in two, but I don't want our man in Haiphong to hand off the papers to just anyone. I want them in the possession of someone I trust. And given what happened with that overseer at Phu Rieng,

I'm more cautious. But I know whom I can always trust. I can always trust you."

"Yes, you can," I said, feeling a rush of love and pride. "You can always trust me."

"Plus, it would allow you to see more of the country," said Victor. "Take the train and spend a bit of time relaxing. We can set you up in a lovely hotel and you can contribute to our success here in a more concrete way. You'd like that, wouldn't you?"

"Very much so," I said. Victor knew that I wanted to feel useful, to exercise parts of my mind that I'd ignored since we'd married. The parts that only belonged to a working woman.

Haiphong. I thought about the commotion on the docks when our boat had finally anchored in the port city. I'd barely slept the night before, anticipating our arrival at dawn, as the captain had promised. When the boat started to slow, I expected to pull into the quiet of the Far East, greeted by gentle waves, the murmur of soft voices. Instead, we heard loud shouting and the bang of metal containers moved around on the docks. There were huge cargo ships, piled high with wares—from household goods to bags of dried rice—and men running shirtless on the decks and below, wrapping rope around large containers, others trying to pull them to shore. The few women appeared to be carrying loads of at least fifty pounds on their backs, weaving unsteadily between the men, trying to keep their balance. There was nothing quiet or gentle about it.

But this trip would be different. I was no longer a stranger to Indochine. It was starting to become my home.

FIFTEEN

Jessie

October 4, 1933

Have you ever been to Haiphong?" I asked Trieu as I prepared for the journey. It was just past seven in the morning, but I was already dressed.

"Yes, I've been," Trieu said. "With Madame van Dampierre. She attended a party at the opera house there, *Nhà hát Tây*—or the Western Theatre, in French—and Cam and I traveled with her since she insisted on bringing all the boys. I think what you are doing, traveling alone, is a better idea. It's very modern for a woman to travel alone. A foreign woman especially."

"Yes, I'm excited, but I'm a bit anxious about silly things," I said, sure that my nerves showed. "Such as, what if I miss my train or can't find the hotel that Victor has reserved for me?" I went on. "Part of me wishes he was coming along," I admitted. "Though that doesn't sound very modern of me, does it?"

"If something like that happens, then you just ask for help," Trieu said, kindly. "And all the *pousse-pousse* drivers know the Hôtel du Commerce. It's the prettiest in Haiphong. It's even prettier than the Métropole here. They'll expect that that's where you're going. Unless Lanh has arranged a car?"

"No, I asked him not to. I prefer to take a *pousse-pousse*. You can see so much more that way. Hear everything, too."

Trieu nodded and looked at my outfit, my gray pants and short-sleeved white blouse with a slightly puffed sleeve, all cinched by a thin alligator-skin belt.

She pointed at my head and turned back to the closet, emerging with a hat, a bright geranium-colored straw boater with a narrow gros-grain ribbon that edged the crown. It was designed by Reboux and cost a pretty penny, but I hadn't worn it yet, wondering if it was a bit much for a day hat. It was wide-brimmed, with a dramatic dip on the left side, but I had to admit it was striking.

"You should wear this," Trieu said. "*Un canotier en paille.* I think it's your prettiest straw hat. And you'll feel confident in it. The color is something only a self-assured woman would wear. One who doesn't get nervous."

She placed the hat gently on my head, so as not to muss my waved hair, and I looked at my reflection in the mirror.

"Isn't it pretty?" asked Trieu. "There's something about the color that makes it even lovelier."

"Yes, there is," I said, smiling. I looked at it from all angles and then moved to my dressing table. I reached into a drawer and applied a bold lipstick to match, my hand trembling slightly.

"Beautiful," she said approvingly.

When Trieu was gone, I checked my suitcase again and added one last thing to my handbag. Victor had left me an envelope with 1,000 piastres, the equivalent of 300 American dollars, in it. He said I was to give it to the contact as a bonus.

I placed it carefully inside my bag, both wishing I didn't have to carry such a sum of money with me and reminding myself that I was foolish to let my nerves get the better of me. How many husbands let their wives be involved in their work? Especially such important work. All Marcelle did was sun herself at the club all day. She certainly wasn't allowed to have any involvement with Arnaud's business dealings at the chamber of commerce.

I had decided to come to Indochine, and I had to be devoted to us prospering here. I looked at my reflection and saw a very competent woman looking back at me.

"Off to the house of a hundred suns?" said Lanh when he opened the door of the Delahaye for me. I got in slowly, then sat up rigidly in the back seat.

"The what?" I asked. "The house of a hundred suns?"

"That's what I call la gare de Hang Co," he said, closing my heavy door. He sat down in the driver's seat, turned the key in the ignition, and gently moved the car out of our driveway, launching into the story of why he chose that moniker.

I smiled, thinking about a young, hopeful Lanh. Haiphong was just a ray, then. A simple sun ray.

At the station, Lanh didn't leave my side until he'd made sure the stationmaster was there to take care of me. In fact, the stationmaster and a porter met the car as it pulled up in front of the elegant building, then stayed with me until the train arrived.

Once inside the black steam-engine-powered train, I again sat rigidly, my back barely grazing the seat behind me, highly aware of the amount of piastres I was carrying.

The car was half full, and I was thankful that so far no one had sat beside me, or across the aisle. I felt a breeze and looked up to see eight fans on the carriage's ceiling, one on either side of the four round light fixtures. The walls were a polished wood, the windows large and separated by decorative mirrored paneling—it looked as elegant as any train I'd ridden in France, perhaps even nicer.

A few men in light traveling suits boarded, hanging their hats on the hooks near every window. I watched for other female passengers, but there was only one in the car, and she seemed to be accompanying her husband. I kept my head in my book, *Journey to the End of the Night*, by Louis-Ferdinand Céline, which I'd brought with me from France.

As the steam engine hissed and the train started to move, the wheels chugging beneath us, I turned to watch the house of a hundred suns slowly disappearing, and then the city of Hanoi receding, too, as the train made its way to the mile-long Paul Doumer Bridge. In the distance I could see a tennis club, home to a game that was as popular in Indochine as it was at home. The train pushed past it quickly, and the houses and buildings thinned out even more as we started the bridge crossing. Below us flowed the Red River, palm trees leaning from its banks. The water, which looked murky during the day, especially from a distance, looked bright and dusted in yellow sunlight as we rode over it.

Beyond the river, the view gave way to rice paddies, the earth tamed into squares, the people working the land bent over, shielded by their conical hats while their feet sank in the mud. The rice paddies were almost an iridescent green, the plants pointing straight up into the sunny sky.

I didn't close my eyes on the four-hour journey, as the sight of the countryside proved to be very calming. But eventually open space gave way to the sights of a city and the nerves crept my way again. When we stopped, I rushed off the train, the first to disembark. I reached for my bag, ignoring the porters trying to help me, and hurried across the station lobby's marble-tiled floor.

I still had three hours before I had to meet the recruiter, but I quickly hailed one of the waiting rickshaws, climbed in with the driver's help, and turned to look back at the facade of the small station. This particular sun ray was bright yellow.

After a quick ride through the city, which felt tiny after Hanoi, I checked into the hotel, the Hôtel du Commerce, an ornate white building that resembled a grand hotel in Venice.

After a long nap, made possible with the help of a very large whiskey, I changed into fresh clothes, a pair of white trousers, wide in the leg, and a dark blue blouse, perfect to set off the hat, which I wanted to keep. Trieu was right; it was something a confident woman would wear.

At five p.m., with the money tucked into my bag, I headed off in another rickshaw. I knew that somewhere behind me was the grand opera house Trieu had mentioned, and beautiful homes painted with yellow and orange ochre, like ours, but I wasn't going anywhere near them. Victor had told me that the address I was headed to housed another café. The Café Mat Troi—it had the same name as the one where the communist had been thrown in Hanoi. He apologized but said that all cafés in Indochine seemed to have the same name.

"I suppose it's high time we import our creativity, too," he'd said, giving me a kiss on the head.

I sat at a glass table outside the café and ordered a Pernod and soda, not allowing myself anything stronger, as I knew it might push me from feeling bold to feeling sick.

"Madame Lesage," said a Frenchman approaching me. He was tall and handsome and dressed more like Victor than someone who spent time with coolies in a port town. "Welcome back to Haiphong. I take it your journey was a pleasant one."

"It was," I said, his presence putting me at ease. His movements suggested that he'd been in Indochine for many years. He sat and ordered a *fine à l'eau*.

"I won't keep you," he said. "I'm sure you have better things to do than spend time by the dock, but this is the paper your husband requested. It's very important," he said quietly. "Though I suppose he knows that since he sent you."

"Thank you," I said, taking it from him and placing it in my bag. As I did, I reached for the money and handed it over quickly, relieved to have it out of my possession. "May I ask what exactly it is? This paper?" I said, realizing Victor had never told me. Now I felt rather embarrassed that I didn't know what I was collecting.

"It's a list of names," he said. "Men that already work for you, but that are perhaps up to something untoward. Men that shouldn't be trusted. They should, if possible, be sent back north, away from the plantations, away from you," he said, smiling. "Men like that are capable of starting an uprising. Or worse."

I reached back into my bag, unfolded the paper, and looked at it.

"All of these?" I asked glancing up at him. There were ten on the page. "Are you sure?"

"All," he responded firmly. "That is what the recruiters who work farther north, on the rice farms, said. They get their information directly from men who were on the plantations but have come back home."

"I suppose I'm glad we have such capable people working up north, then."

"We have to," he said. "It's 1933. The northern corners of the country are about to ignite."

"Well, it is I who won't keep you," I said. "Will you be traveling today?" I asked as I stood. "Or do you live in Haiphong?"

"I live here," he confirmed. "I know most of us live in the bigger cities, but I've always liked Tonkin. The climate is much better here, and the pretty women all eventually make their way through," he said, smiling at me. "On their way into the colony, or on their way out. Less malaria, too."

"A winning combination," I said.

"I think so," he said pleasantly. "Will you be all right walking alone? Can I accompany you to your hotel or somewhere else? Or fetch you a taxi?"

"That's kind of you, but I'll be fine," I said, feeling relief. I'd had nothing to worry about. There seemed to be no corpses ready to land at my feet.

"Well, then," he said, reaching for my hand, "I hope our paths cross again soon."

I walked slowly back toward the center of town and then, on a small side street near the opera, stopped to sit on a sunny bench and fully exhale. What had I been so nervous about?

I left the city after that, in a taxi with all the windows open, my hair flying everywhere, and spent the rest of the day in the countryside, wanting to see more of what I'd passed on the train. I was a helpful woman. A good wife.

SIXTEEN

Marcelle

October 4, 1933

Ｈow do I look in this hat?" asked Khoi, picking up a straw boater from an end table and setting it squarely on his head. "You look like a very handsome naked man wearing a straw hat," I said, grinning at him.

He had been able to get Sang on a boat to Japan, and we were celebrating his freedom and our own. This meant giving all of his staff the day off, except his chauffeur. We then proceeded to take off all our clothes and swim naked, Khoi lapping me again and again. We stayed unclothed and roamed wherever we pleased. It almost felt like life in Paris.

"Let's scream like animals while we make love again." He'd pushed me against the door as soon as he'd closed it. An hour later, we were reclining in the living room, idly drinking lemonade spiked with gin.

"You should empty the house more often," I said, stretching my legs onto his lap. "I like being able to do this." I waved my hand above my head, indicating all the space that was temporarily ours.

"But how will we eat?" he asked, laughing.

"We'll just have to cook. We do know how to cook. Or at least I do. We should be forced to do it every now and again, so we don't forget."

"I cooked for us in Paris," said Khoi. "Is that already forgotten? I made you shark fin soup."

"I'm pretty sure that was a diseased minnow that you and Sinh fished out of the Seine," I said. "But no. That is not forgotten. I will never forget anything about those days." I inched my legs higher on his lap. "Ever."

"Do you think Anne-Marie is still in Italy?" Khoi asked. "Or maybe Spain? I wish I knew. I wonder if she's even aware that Victor Lesage is here."

"I don't know," I said. "I just hope that wherever she is in the world, she's found some happiness."

"What about you?" he said, pouring me another drink. "Are you happy?"

"Me?" I said, smiling. "You and I are alone. Whenever that happens, I'm happy."

"Good," he said. "Because while everything we are doing is extremely important, this," he said, gesturing to me and then to himself, "is the most important."

"Of course. There is nothing more important to me. And there's no greater love in Indochine than this one," I said, "though I can see that Jessie Lesage is convinced that what she and Victor have is the most passionate love affair ever written. But I'm trying to change that slowly. She met Red at the club the other day, and he clearly had an impact on her. As soon as I can, I'll get them both on your boat."

"Good," he said, eyeing me. "And your impression of her is still the same?"

"Khoi, that woman is calculating. I can see it. Every move of hers is considered. That guise of docility that she puts on, like she's some rule-follower tiptoeing through her new country. I don't believe any of it."

"Maybe," said Khoi, looking at the smoke he was exhaling instead of me.

"'Maybe'? Please. How did that woman convince Victor Lesage to marry her? She's pretty, yes, and has that female softness that men so often mistake for a gentle maternal quality, but that can't have been enough. She comes from nothing. She surely relied on the age-old art of conceiving out of wedlock. He loves her now, that's quite obvious, but I am sure he didn't from the start."

Khoi puffed on his expertly rolled cigarette and remained silent.

"What?" I said, annoyed.

"It's just that when you told me about your time together at the Officers' Club, it sounded as if you'd enjoyed yourself. As if you welcomed her company."

"I do not enjoy Jessie Lesage's company," I spat, although I recognized as soon as I said it how unconvincing I sounded. "I'm telling you, she's calculating. I'm sure she got pregnant on purpose. She probably hid half naked in Victor's bushes and then threw herself on him when he was two bottles of wine in."

"Oh, yes, with all those bushes in Paris," said Khoi, laughing.

"You have too much sympathy for the devil sometimes. She sold her soul long ago. Are you forgetting the family she married into?"

"Of course not," he replied. "Of course not."

He kissed me on the cheek and walked upstairs to get dressed. I watched him disappear, his presence still lingering below. Sometimes I was quite sure that I loved Nguyen Khoi too much.

SEVENTEEN

Marcelle

October 4, 1933

I stretched my hands out wide on Khoi's dining room table, enjoying the smoothness of the blood-red lacquer under my fingertips. Khoi told me that actual human blood was mixed in with the paint to make it such a color, a claim I liked to believe, even though it probably wasn't true. It gave the piece even more history. Khoi had gone into the city to tend to some paperwork regarding the family's factory in Nam Dinh. "The timing isn't ideal," he'd said after he'd received a phone call, "but we will do this again. And more often. It's time our life in Hanoi resembled our life in Paris a bit more closely."

Sitting at Khoi's beautiful dining table made me think about something I'd been trying to push out of my head since arriving in Indochine, because I knew how unrealistic it was. Still, I couldn't help but fantasize: What would it be like to eat a meal as Khoi's wife instead of his lover? I would never know. It was the one thing I simply couldn't will into being.

In the early 1920s a French woman married an Annamite man—the only such intermarriage in the colony, the newspapers had reported at the time. The French government intervened to stop the wedding. They succeeded the first time, but the lovebirds tried again, this time with the bride's father declaring in writing that his daughter was of sound mind. It still remained true that while Frenchmen were allowed to impregnate any *indigène* woman who so much as sneezed in their direction, we French women weren't allowed to marry their countrymen. We could only marry men like Arnaud and follow them to the colonies, provide a stable home for them, and help them be model colonists who wouldn't grow lonely and seek local girls at night. That was our role.

But I had never been good at filling the roles assigned to me.

I heard a faint knock at the door and jumped. No one ever knocked at Khoi's house. The door was always opened by an attentive servant before the visitor's knuckles hit the wood. I rushed to answer it, suddenly aware that I was still wearing my dress sans undergarments. I flung the door open anyway and stared at the man in front of me, someone I never thought I'd see on Khoi's doorstep.

"Madame Lesage boarded the morning train to Haiphong," he said before I could bark at him.

The man's name was Pham Van Dat, and he was the manager of the Hanoi train station. For the past two years, Khoi and I had been paying a small but regular amount for him to keep an eye on who came and went from the train station. He knew what the policeman who had killed Sinh, Paul Adrien, looked like, and he knew that if he was ever spotted, there would be a significant payout. Last month I had added two names to his watch list: Victor and Jessie Lesage. I had given him the formal portrait that had run in the newspaper when it was announced they would be coming to live in the colony. The reproduction was grainy, but Jessie was unmistakable.

"Are you certain?" I asked, after ushering him inside.

"Of course," he replied. "And before you ask me why I appeared on Mr. Khoi's doorstep, his valet was in the station today with his mother, helping her board a train for the coast. I heard him mention that all Nguyen Khoi's servants had a day's holiday."

"But how did you know *I* was here?" I pressed.

"I assumed someone would be here if the servants were not," he said. "You or Mr. Khoi."

"So it was Jessie Lesage? You're one hundred percent certain?" I said.

"Madame de Fabry," he said patiently. "Please. Would I travel all the way out to Nguyen Khoi's palace if I had any doubt? It was her. A man who was half blind would recognize her. And she was wearing a big red hat, as if she wanted to call even more attention to herself."

"Wait," I said, putting my hand on his arm. "Did you say the morning train? Then she left hours ago."

"Yes," Monsieur Dat confirmed. "The nine o'clock train. It left exactly seven minutes late. No fault of mine. There was a child who refused to step away from the door. A French child."

"But why are you telling me this just now?" I asked angrily.

"You do not pay me enough to allow me to abandon my post and risk being fired. I just finished my work. As soon as I did, I came here. By bus. There was a chicken on it. It wasn't pleasant."

We paid him plenty, but I couldn't argue now.

"When is the next train to Haiphong?" I asked.

"Tonight," he said, adjusting his tie. I was very happy he had thought to change out of his uniform. "It's a night train. Very slow, with a long stop in Hai Duong. You won't arrive in Haiphong until morning."

"I'll be on it," I said, then thanked him. "Wait here," I added. I ran upstairs and took a handful of piastres out of the bag of notes Khoi kept in his dresser.

"Thank you," I said, pressing them into his hands. "And next time, just leave your post."

EIGHTEEN

Marcelle

October 5, 1933

I was groggy when the train pulled into Haiphong shortly after seven in the morning. After leaving Khoi's, I'd had just enough time to rush home and change my dress. I'd left Khoi a note saying that I was spending the night on the coast, but didn't elaborate. I knew he would think I was acting too hastily, that Jessie was probably just taking a train to explore her new country. But I knew it was more than that. She was not the type to sightsee in Haiphong, nor was she of the character to travel alone for no reason. She was going to Haiphong to do something for Michelin.

I had been to Haiphong many times over the last couple of years. The city, just east of Hanoi, was where all large ships traveling to the north of the country docked. It was also where Sinh had been killed, and where most people accused of communist activity were detained upon entry to Indochine. The poorest areas around Nam Dinh and Nghe An, also in the north, were still considered the largest red threats, but the party, even though they'd been forced to go underground, was spreading throughout Indochine, all the way to the edge of the sea. The party's leaders in the north and elsewhere were educated men and women from the upper middle class, their members urban *petit bour-*

geois and rural peasants. And an increasing number of those peasants had worked on plantations. The north was certainly prime recruiting ground for Michelin. In the 1920s, the truth of what life was really like on the plantations, the horrors, didn't make it up north very fast, as the plantation recruiters had been able to sign hundreds of illiterate men to three-year agreements, which had no out clauses at all, except by escape or suicide. But when the first group of men arrived home at the end of the 1920s—a much smaller group than had left due to the high number of deaths—they brought the truth of life on a Michelin plantation with them. If they hadn't interacted with underground communist cells when they were on the plantations, they were waiting for them when they got home.

I was the first passenger off the train at 7:20. I grabbed my small bag from the porter and hurried out of the yellow-painted station. With its palm trees in front and white stucco details, it looked as if it should be in Nice. Of course, I knew that I, too, looked as if I should be in Nice.

A driver in a private car tried to wave me over as soon as I emerged from the station. I would rather have taken a *pousse-pousse*, but I knew I could be fighting time. I had already cursed myself on the train for not driving, though I was a decidedly terrible driver.

"L'Hôtel du Commerce, *xin vui long*," I said. "Please."

"*Oui, oui, madame*," he responded, stepping on the gas as we roared off in the direction of the famously beautiful hotel. Jessie Lesage was undoubtedly staying there. Anyone who could afford it did.

As the man drove, I stared at every Western woman I saw, but there were not many on the streets at such an early hour. Suddenly, the car turned sharply off the boulevard Paul-Bert and squeezed into a road barely wide enough for it.

"Why are you taking the back streets?" I shouted to the driver. "Please stay on the main road!"

"Quicker here, *madame*," he said in French, navigating a bend expertly.

"I don't like this route," I insisted. "Please go back to boulevard Paul-Bert." Jessie had only been to Haiphong when she arrived, and

I doubted she'd seen more than the route from the docks to the train station, and that from the back of a car. She was unlikely to be wandering the back streets at an hour past dawn. If she was walking anywhere, she would be walking on Paul-Bert.

I looked down at my watch again. It was 7:35.

But the man was right. This way was quicker. We arrived at the hotel in just ten minutes. He helped me out, and a porter from the hotel ran out to greet me, his crisp white jacket almost glowing in the morning light.

I looked up at the mansard roof of the grand, cathedral-like baroque-style structure. It was striking, but so European. In a city that did not yet feel completely taken over by the colonists, the sight was jarring.

After I paid the driver, I walked up the steps, into the grand foyer, and straight to the front desk.

"I'm afraid I was not able to telephone ahead," I told the hotel manager who greeted me. "But I would like a room for the night. Or perhaps two nights. I'm not sure yet."

"*Mais bien sûr.* That can be arranged, *madame*," he said, his square jaw worked into a smile.

"Madame de Fabry. Marcelle de Fabry," I said, trying to sound pleasant. After I'd said it, I regretted it. The man would certainly know the de Fabry name. Arnaud was often in the newspapers.

"I'm meeting my friend here today," I said as coolly as I could manage. "Her name is Jessie Lesage. Could you tell me if she's checked in?"

The man consulted the large guest book in front of him.

"Yes, she checked in yesterday," he said, running his finger down the list, written in large script, "but she checked out this morning."

"What?" I said. "No, that can't be."

"Yes, she did. I see it right here. She spent last night here but checked out an hour or so ago. Perhaps earlier. I can't quite read the script. I was not the one to assist her, I'm afraid."

"But you're sure?" I said, trying to get a look at his book, which he inched away from me.

"I'm certain," he said, closing it.

"Have any boats from France come in since yesterday?" I asked, trying to think of every reason Jessie could have come to Haiphong.

"No," he replied. "But one is due to leave in a few hours."

"I see, thank you," I said sweetly, trying to seem more like a dim-witted colonial wife and less like a huntress on the prowl.

Haiphong was not like Ha Long Bay or the caves of Trang An, places that attracted foreigners seeking sights. It was industrial. It housed rice factories and large storage facilities. It had pockets of charm, but it was essentially a dirty working city. Michelin, however, sent hordes of new coolies from Haiphong on boats south. Perhaps she was here to observe one of their slave ships?

I turned down the *pousse-pousse* drivers jostling to get a fare and walked quickly toward the harbor precinct. When I reached the crowded docks, I stopped for a moment and watched the boats coming in, full of wares rather than passengers.

I didn't see any men in large groups who looked like they were on their way to the plantations. I turned to the east and walked to the canals, a more tightly packed section of the port where smaller boats docked. The crude wooden crafts, shaded by thatched bamboo roofs, bobbed in the midmorning sun, some overflowing with goods, others with people. I watched as men loaded cotton sacks of rice onto wide carts, then ran off, somehow able to pull five times their body weight.

Khoi wanted me to be patient. For two years I had let him determine how we could create some meaning from Sinh's senseless death. But it was time for me to act without him as a constant guide. As soon as I'd realized the kind of woman Jessie was, and had confirmed that Victor was, in fact, the man we had assumed, I had begun acting on my own. Clearly, it was the right decision. It had brought me here.

I lingered for a moment, looking in the shadows for a European woman, but I was one of the only ones walking the docks. When the sun grew too strong, I walked back to the side of the port that had cafés and restaurants, catering perhaps to the people who had just completed a long journey and were eager for a meal at a table that wasn't bobbing up and down.

I stopped in front of a rather pretty one, one of the few with an awning. Café Rodier, it said. I looked the patrons over but still saw no foreign women, only men.

That's when I spotted it. Café Mat Troi. It had the same name as the one in Hanoi where Jessie had seen the dead man tossed onto his doorstep.

"May I help you?" said a man in heavily accented French. "Hungry this morning?"

"Oh, yes, why not?" I said, glancing at him and then at the sign again. "Can I ask you what that means? The name of the café. Mat Troi. What does it translate to in French?" I asked, wanting to confirm that what I was thinking was correct.

"Sun Café," he said, smiling. "Very popular name. I think there must be ten more cafés in town with that name."

"Of course," I said, still looking up at the large metal letters.

I didn't care how many more cafés there were in town with the same name. Jessie had been at this one. I could sense her.

I was about to sit when I stopped abruptly.

There were times in my life when I feared my heart might burst from shock—when my father died, when Khoi read me the letter from Sinh's father, and then when he sailed for Indochine without me. But this moment eclipsed them all. My heart, I was sure, would burst.

"Are you all right?" the man sitting in front of me asked. His back had been to me when I approached the café, but I could now see his face.

I was looking directly at Paul Adrien, the man who had shot Sinh dead and changed the balance of my universe, of so many people's universes, forever. This man calmly drinking in the bright morning sun had taken one of the country's strongest rays and extinguished it in an instant.

I had given up trying to find him. We all had, believing he had vanished. Back to France, we were told, except he couldn't be located there, either. And now, when I had stopped looking, when I had put all my efforts on bringing Michelin to its knees, Paul Adrien had appeared in front of me.

What kind of man could put a bullet through someone's heart? I wondered as my own heart rattled inside of me. Especially the heart of a stranger? Sinh had provoked him, the report had said. I knew it wasn't true. Sinh wanted to change a lot about his country, but he had never planned to do it through violence.

"Can I help you?" Paul asked, peering up at me.

"I'm sorry," I said, trying to manage my shock. "I felt a bit lightheaded." In truth it was far worse than that. I felt like I might just crumple at his feet.

"Here." He stood. "Let me help you to a table. Or would you like to join me?" he asked. "I was just finishing my drink here and would be happy for some conversation."

"That's very kind," I managed to say, not understanding how I was able to get the words out. "I'd like to."

He pulled a chair out for me and introduced himself.

"Paul Adrien," he said.

"I'm Alice Bisset," I said, giving my sister's name.

"Are you waiting for a boat, or do you live in Haiphong?" he asked, his voice calm and easy.

"No, I'm just passing through," I replied, desperate to say as little as I could. I needed to regain my composure and then make him talk as much as possible.

"I see," he said, seeming to understand that I wasn't much of a conversationalist. "Perhaps you would like a drink as you pass through?" he asked, gesturing to the waitress.

"A whiskey. A double. Neat," I said as Paul raised his eyebrows at me. "If they'll serve me."

"A good breakfast," he said, grinning. "And they will. I know them well."

"I've been up for a while," I said, which wasn't a lie. "You must live in Haiphong?" I asked, hoping it sounded natural. Easy. This man had an easy air about him, which I hadn't expected, and it bothered me. According to Sinh's father, he'd been plagued by his actions. It looked like the only thing plaguing this man was a life of leisure.

"I do, but I've just recently returned. To Haiphong and to Indochine," he said. "I lived here before, in Haiphong, but I returned to France in 1929 for a time."

"But you came back to the colony, most people do not," I said, taking a big gulp of my strong drink.

"I was hesitant. I didn't love my early years here, but the economy is difficult in France now. There is more opportunity here."

"May I ask what you do?" I said, my shock having transformed into a quiet rage.

"I used to be a policeman. I was a *militaire* in France, the army, and then I came here because it seemed full of adventure. And again, the money was better."

"It's important work," I said, practically choking on my words.

"Yes, I enjoyed it. And it is important, thank you for saying that. But it was difficult, too. I think it was right for me to stop." Finally, his face turned stormier.

"And now you work on the docks?" I asked.

"No, now I work for Michelin et Cie. The rubber company," he clarified. "I was just meeting with one of the plantation's owners earlier today. Actually, I don't know exactly what her role is. But she was very pleasant. Everyone at Michelin is. I've been lucky."

She.

She *had* been here. Jessie Lesage had come to Haiphong to meet with the man who killed Sinh. I took another drink and forced myself to speak.

"Oh, lovely," I said, trying to nod.

"Anyways, I help keep order here, which is a bit like policing, I suppose. Mostly when they send boats down to the plantations. New workers. Today, no ships are sailing, so I have a bit of a day off, which is most welcome."

"How did you choose this particular job?" I asked, the patio starting to feel like it was narrowing in on me. I had to leave soon. I could not keep up this charade for much longer.

"I suppose in a way it chose me. The Michelins approached me for it because I speak the language. Annamese," he specified as if I thought they spoke German in the colony. "That's why they hired me."

That, I was very certain, was not why they hired him.

"It must be steady work," I said, shifting in my chair and reaching in my purse for money for the drink.

"It is steady. I lost myself a bit back in France after my first sojourn in the colony. I was in need of something steady."

I nodded, now at a complete loss for words.

"I'm sorry. I don't know why I'm going on like this," he said, grabbing his drink and swigging the rest of it back. "You most likely did not come to a café alone looking for conversation."

"I think I was just looking for a drink," I said, staring down at my near-empty glass. "But the conversation is an added pleasure."

"Still, I'll leave you in peace," he said, standing. "I hope we meet again." He looked at me meaningfully. I realized that I wasn't wearing my wedding ring; I had left in such a hurry.

"I'd like that." It was the first true thing I'd said since we met.

He put his hand on my shoulder before he left, and then walked off.

I took a *pousse-pousse* to the hotel where Jessie had stayed the night before. I did not have time to wait for an evening train, opting to hire a car instead. The weight of all the years of searching and waiting was crushing me. I needed to be home. I needed Khoi next to me. I was willing to act alone on some things, but this was not one of them. I did not have the capacity to handle this alone.

After an agonizing trip back to Hanoi, I rushed into Khoi's house, nearly trampling his housekeeper Kim Ly.

"You've been where?" he started, but I didn't let him finish.

I threw my arms around him and put my mouth to his ear, my body exhausted.

"I saw him. Khoi, I saw him. Paul Adrien. Jessie Lesage was in Haiphong to meet him. She sat with him and talked to him. And so did I. I had a *drink* with him."

"You what?" he said, grabbing my arm. "Are you certain?"

"Khoi, he introduced himself to me," I said. "After all this time, he was there in front of me, all because I was chasing Jessie Lesage."

"What do we do?" Khoi whispered.

"We have to tell Anne-Marie."

"How?" said Khoi, asking the question that I had been turning over the entire journey in the car.

"I don't know," I said. "We don't even know which country she's in. Or if she's alive," I said, finally uttering the one fear we never dared voice.

"We'll find her," said Khoi. "Together."

NINETEEN

Jessie

October 16, 1933

A group of us are taking a boat out on Ha Long Bay. Have you been yet?" Red asked when he found me on a sun lounger near the club's swimming pool eleven days after I returned from Haiphong. I shook my head no.

"You must," he said, sitting down next to me, his gaze lingering on my bare thighs, which had become leaner and tanner since I'd moved to Hanoi. "It's like heaven on water. Please come. Your husband will let you, won't he? In fact, bring him. He probably hasn't seen it, either."

He slid his sunglasses down his nose so that I could see his eyes.

"He's in the south," I said. "And will be for the foreseeable future. He was home for a week, but he had to travel down to the plantations again, so it's just me. But I would love to come. I'm sure he won't mind."

He wouldn't mind because I certainly wouldn't tell him until after the trip was over.

Victor had been very pleased that everything in Haiphong had gone so well. "If we didn't have Lucie," he'd said to me, "I would simply hire you to work beside me." Maybe one day, despite Lucie, we could arrange that.

"Good," Red said, touching my bare knee as he stood. "You'll like the group. They're a little eccentric, but that's welcome here. We're far away from the Eighth Arrondissement, *n'est-ce pas?*"

"Very far," I said.

"Marcelle and her man are the ones behind this trip, so don't worry too much about the eccentrics. She was going to send you a note, but I told her that I wanted to be the one to invite you."

"How thoughtful," I said, smiling. "Of them. And you. But eccentric? Maybe Marcelle, but Arnaud seems anything but."

"Did I say Arnaud?" Red countered, backing away with a smile. "I don't think I did."

He turned before I could ask more.

"Saturday at seven a.m!" he shouted, his back still to me as I watched his strapping figure disappear.

————

"Have you really not been to Ha Long Bay yet?" asked Marcelle as we made our way in the Delahaye to Quang Yen Province, of which the bay was the crown jewel. "What is Victor doing with you? Keeping you chained in the cellar?"

"Me, chained? No, quite the opposite," I said, suppressing a smile. "But I can't believe it's taken me this long to find my way here," I said, pointing out the window as the water came to view.

"In the end it's for the best. This way you can experience it for the first time with me. And the others." Marcelle paused briefly and took my arm. "You do understand about Khoi, don't you? It's not that I don't love Arnaud. It's just that I couldn't take any more of his behavior without replicating it on my own. I tried to be the patient wife and all that, but I couldn't stand it anymore."

"Has he had many . . . lovers?" I asked, unsure how to phrase it. There was plenty of adultery in Paris, of course, but the parties involved didn't flaunt their betrayals as the French seemed to in the East.

"Many!" Marcelle said, laughing. "I think every *fille indigène* under twenty-one with questionable morals or a need for some quick money has been in his bed."

"Does he pay them?" I blurted out.

"He doesn't *not* pay them," Marcelle said. "I haven't ever looked into his arrangements, but I think he helps pay off certain debts their families may carry, that sort of thing. It's not a direct exchange, but a more circuitous one." She stroked the leather of the car door. "When I put it that way, it actually sounds quite benevolent, doesn't it?"

She lowered the window a bit and we both breathed in the air, which had become fresher as we moved farther out of the city. "Khoi doesn't pay me, if you're wondering. But he could certainly afford to."

"No. Of course," I stammered. "I assumed as much."

I looked away from Marcelle, closed my eyes, and thought of Victor. We had never been tempted. But we'd never been in a country like Indochine, either.

"What are you thinking about?" asked Marcelle. She must have been watching me.

"I'm just thinking of Victor," I said quickly. "I hope he has a chance to see all this soon. The scenery is so beautiful."

"Liar!" Marcelle replied, laughing. "You're thinking about Red."

"I'm not," I said, shifting on the seat. I glanced up at the rearview mirror, afraid that Lanh had heard us. Of course he had.

"I don't believe you," Marcelle said mischievously. "And look, you're already flustered. Relax, I'll tell you everything I know about him."

I should have stopped her, especially with Lanh listening, but I didn't. I was curious. I looked ahead and said nothing, waiting for her to go on.

"Red," she said in a singsong voice. "Well, his real name is Hugh Redvers, which is much too proper for a man like him. That's why in Indochine, he is always just called Red."

"Convenient," I said, still not meeting her eye.

"I think he would prefer to hear you say 'mysterious,'" she purred, leaning into me, forcing me to turn in her direction.

"I'll try to remember that," I said.

"Yes, do," she said, practically grinning. "What else? He loves listening to American jazz music, especially Duke Ellington. The Duke, he calls him. He has an enormous phonograph, which he had sent all the way from America. If you ever make it into his apartment, I'm sure he'll show you," she added in a whisper.

I turned scarlet, and she started to laugh, inching away from me.

"All right, all right," she said, putting her hands up in mock surrender. "Look, I'll just tell you these things, and you can do what you want with the information. So, besides jazz, and beautiful women, he likes a very spicy noodle soup called *bun rieu cua*. He consumes it at an alarming rate. I think he believes it makes him more virile, but I'm surprised it hasn't caused him to breathe fire. He drinks room-temperature water with no ice, even on the hottest days, something he picked up from a Chinese woman he was bedding for a few months, and yet he takes those Pegu cocktails of his ice-cold. A man of mystery."

She grinned, warming to her theme.

"He barely works, which is why those train tracks down the coast still aren't finished. He smokes opium nearly every day, drives a dark green MG with plenty of room for another person in the front seat. And when he's not in Hanoi, he's traveling the Mekong Delta on some adventure for lost men who never want to be found."

She stretched her left arm along the top of the back seat, letting it hover just over my shoulders.

"What else? Oh, yes, this is probably the most important point. Every single woman who comes to Hanoi between the ages of fifteen and fifty falls in love with him at first sight, so don't feel too guilty. He never wants to be married, but he really does enjoy being loved. Or at least lusted after."

"I don't feel guilty at all," I replied. "I don't fall in love with strangers. I'm in love with Victor."

"Aren't you lucky," she said breezily.

"So Red will be there, and Khoi," I said, pronouncing his name just as Marcelle had. "Who else?"

"You don't care who else," said Marcelle, still smiling. "But you're sweet to ask. Don't worry, you'll like everyone. Very pleasant people. As for Red, I asked Khoi to put you in adjoining rooms for the night. Only a few hanging silk drapes will be separating you, and those can be removed with a flick of the wrist." She slapped my arm lightly.

"You didn't!" I exclaimed, waiting for Lanh to tap the brakes out of shock, but the ride remained smooth. Lanh, I had learned, was unflappable and discreet. He had never mentioned his sister, not even a thank-you in passing, just as I'd requested.

"Oh, Jessie, what a terrible prude you are," Marcelle said, taking my hand. "There are no adjoining rooms, don't worry. Besides, I'm sure you have a chastity belt of some sort in that large valise of yours. Or maybe you have it on now. Is it uncomfortable?" she teased. I didn't answer. "Every woman falls under Red's spell for a little when they arrive," she continued. "Your reaction is normal. Maybe you've even walked past his charming little place on la rue Jacquin hoping for a glimpse of him."

"I've done nothing of the sort," I answered, not admitting that I had looked up his address in the telephone book. "Besides, by your description, he sounds like a fantasy concocted by some bored women."

"Red? No. He's better than that. And what French woman in Hanoi is bored?"

I shrugged and reached back to fix a hairpin.

"I don't mean to tease you," said Marcelle. "The myth only lives because he is so charming. Humorous and quick-witted. The best party guest one could ask for. You'll see. But he's a bachelor for life, that one."

"And I'm married," I said as the pin I was adjusting stabbed me in the scalp.

"Yes," said Marcelle evenly. "I know."

After a few minutes of silence, she grabbed my shoulder and pointed out the window behind me. "Look!" she said as I turned my head.

We had been driving by the water for some time, but when Lanh slowed the car after Marcelle raised her voice, I saw the boat. It was a beautiful wooden structure, painted white, unlike the other boats around it, which were made of unpainted dark wood. The white boat had three sails of bright orange cloth, open and flapping wildly against the blue sky, like emblems of an endless summer. There were three levels and a deck and white wooden railings that encircled every level to meet at the prow, where a long wooden spar stuck straight out.

"Pretty, isn't it?" said Marcelle, following my gaze.

"Pretty? It's magnificent," I said. "What does Khoi do again? Is he the emperor?"

"No, darling. The emperor is in Annam. His name is Bao Dai, and he isn't even twenty years old yet. Khoi's family owns most of the silk industry in this country. Everything soft that you touch was originally chewing on his mulberry trees."

"Seems lucrative," I said as Lanh opened the car door for me.

"For now," Marcelle said before following me out.

"The party has arrived!" a man's voice sang out. It was definitely Red. I saw him waving at us from the deck. A half dozen others stood nearby, but I could barely make out their faces.

"In force!" Marcelle shouted back.

Red cupped his ear and shook his head, indicating that he couldn't hear and instead waved us toward him.

The sparkling blue waters of Ha Long Bay played with the light, the sun bouncing off it in undulating lines and shapes as we made our way onto a wide plank to reach the boat.

"This is breathtaking," I said as Red took my hand. He gripped it tightly and held it until someone else approached us.

"I'm glad you like it," said a strikingly handsome Annamite who took my bag from Lanh and handed it to a boy behind him. His jaw was square, and his cheekbones, just prominent enough, were so perfectly placed that they looked almost painted on. I could see right away why Arnaud was a mere companion for Marcelle now. "It's called a junk," he went on. "A term that comes from the Javanese word for 'boat.'" He reached for both my hands, shaking them and bowing his head as he did. "I'm Nguyen Khoi," he said. "And you're Jessie Lesage. Marcelle is so fond of you. We're very glad that you could join us. In Indochine and on this little boat."

"It's marvelous," I said, nodding good-bye to Lanh, then stepping on board. The floor of the deck was dark wood, the narrow planks buffed to a shine.

"I'm quite fond of it, too, Madame Lesage," he said as another boy came to collect my shoes. Khoi explained that no high heels were allowed as they dented the wood and instead gave me a pair of navy-blue silk slippers to wear. They were my exact size.

"Jessie, please," I said to Khoi.

"Jessie, then," he said, indicating the deck. "Come, Jessie, I will introduce you to our friends."

I walked behind Khoi and Marcelle as we made our way up the stairs to the sundeck. Marcelle's white dress was very pretty against the backdrop of the orange sails and the wooden boat, but I couldn't keep my eyes off of Khoi's clothes. His jacket, cut in a Western fashion and paired with wide-legged white trousers and a white jersey shirt, was made from the loveliest light blue silk I'd ever seen.

"That fabric, your jacket, is beautiful," I couldn't help saying as we stopped for Marcelle to rearrange her hat, which the breeze wanted to blow off. "I've never seen silk quite like that." It was true. It looked almost like linen, or cotton, with no sheen to it, but up close it was unmistakably silk.

"Thank you," Khoi said, looking down at his sleeves and smiling. "It was made especially for me. A gift from my father on my thirtieth birthday. I shouldn't wear it out, especially with the water spraying into the boat on occasion, but I don't believe in keeping beautiful things in boxes. And now that it's nearly November, it's finally cool enough to wear something like this."

"I agree, about beautiful things. We must enjoy what we have," I said, looking around at the boat. There seemed no doubt that Khoi was a man who enjoyed what he had, and he clearly had a lot.

"Yes. Although I would be rather devastated if anything happened to the jacket, so I'm forced to change for dinner. We only had a hundred yards of this particular silk. I can't have another one made."

"We will all be changing for dinner," said Marcelle, taking him by the hand. Their fingers wound tightly together, they approached the other guests, who were sitting on teakwood-and-rattan veranda chairs with rounded, carved armrests in a modern deco style. Next to them, on a square table, was enough champagne to last a week.

Khoi stepped away from Marcelle when we reached the group so that I stood between them. "Madame Lesage. Jessie Lesage. May I present Jacques Barbier, who is with the press. He just started work at a new newspaper, a monthly, *L'Information d'Indochine*. The first issue was printed just a few weeks ago. Next to him is his lovely friend Pham Hanh. And Monsieur Renaud and Madame Claire Angevine," he continued as they all stood to greet me. "Renaud also works in textiles. And of course, Wang Jing from Saigon and his wife, Wang Li," he added as a Chinese couple stood up. "Monsieur Wang works in . . . natural relaxation remedies."

"A pleasure. So lovely to make your acquaintance," I said in a loop, greeting the crowd that Marcelle already seemed to know intimately.

"I will just show the ladies their rooms," said Khoi, turning to his servants and saying something in Annamese. They put down our bags and crossed to the table, removing the covers from two silver dishes nestled among the champagne bottles. They contained perfect pyramids of cooked and seasoned clams. "*So huyet,* which translates to blood clam, named for the red flesh. A delicacy of the bay," Khoi said. He picked up our bags himself. "Ladies, please," he said to Marcelle and me.

This man, though I'd only been in his presence mere minutes, seemed tailor-made for Marcelle. Though I didn't wish ill on anyone, it did seem unfortunate that Arnaud hadn't just conveniently fallen off a horse, like awful Dorothy's husband had. The hand of fate really chose the wrong woman to bless.

As we walked, Khoi pointed out features of the boat to me: a round window where there was a particularly dazzling view of the water, the bathrooms and the kitchen if I should find myself hungry in the middle of the night. "There will be someone there to make you a meal at any hour," he added, without a hint of boastfulness. Marcelle and I were shown to two separate bedrooms, although I doubted Marcelle's would be used for anything but as a place to set her bags.

I thanked Khoi as he left, then sat down on my bed, which was covered in silk linens, all a deep inky blue a few shades darker than my slippers. The bed itself stood on a wooden platform, rounded at the edges, with a subtle foliage motif along the base. I quickly freshened up, changing into a pair of high-waisted striped trousers and a matching blouse, taking a light jacket with me, too, in case the weather turned cooler. I paused in the doorway of my cabin, where Marcelle stood waiting. I might as well have been a million miles from my farmhouse in Virginia.

"What a whirlwind this all is," I said to Marcelle, looking around the cabin. "Even this bed looks too beautiful to sit on. And the people upstairs. Everyone is so handsome. And such a diverse group. I didn't know that such things happened in Indochine." I was referring to the sight of *Asiatiques* socializing with the French. "Of course, I knew it happened behind the scenes, like you and Khoi, but not so openly. I certainly haven't seen it at the club."

"Not everyone has the Michelin name to uphold," said Marcelle. "They're not afraid to live a little. Besides, aren't we still behind the scenes here?"

"I suppose," I said, looking around again. "Although one of those men is a journalist, is he not?"

"Don't mind that journalist," said Marcelle, slipping her hair out of her pins. "All he reports on is conflict, and not the domestic kind." She pointed upstairs. "You just don't know about all this," she said, "because those sorts of couplings don't happen at the club, unless it's a Frenchman pulling one of the poor working girls into his bed at night."

By the time we joined the group on deck, the sails were tight, and the boat had pushed off, being steered steadily by the native crew. We were floating between limestone peaks, most covered in bright green foliage. I had no idea they would be so green, having expected smooth gray rock instead of the jungle that seemed to be growing out of the water.

"These are called karsts in English," said Red, who had taken the seat next to me. He had a pair of sunglasses on, his shirt untucked and a glass of his terrible orange drink in his hand, as he always seemed to. His face was very attractive, that was undeniable, but his look was one of studied slovenliness, as if he'd applied the faint stains on his pants himself. "They are limestone, like all these isles."

"They're marvelous," I said, looking at them, so dramatic despite their relative lack of stature. Their sheer number, color, and brilliance made them seem otherworldly.

"To the rock wonder in the sky," he said, lifting his glass in the air.

"That's a nice way to put it," I said, marveling at the beauty.

"I stole it," said Red, lowering his sunglasses and grinning. "It's from an old Annamese poem. A very old one, but quite famous."

"He steals words along with hearts," said the journalist, breaking in with a laugh. "Anything authentic in there?" he said, pointing to Red's head. "Or did you smoke all the good stuff away?"

"This from a journalist," said Red. "Selective truths are worse than lies."

The two men laughed and continued to exchange light jabs. "Legend has it," the journalist told me, "that the bay sprang into being when a naughty dragon plunged into the sea and thrashed his tail around, cutting apart the land and creating these little islands. There are over a thousand of them. 'Ha Long' itself means 'where the dragon descends into the sea,' so don't believe this 'rock wonder in the sky' nonsense from Red. Actually, don't believe anything Red says," he added with another laugh.

The two men conversed, and I listened more than I spoke, as we all had champagne and finished the delicious clams Khoi had served. We all spent the day drinking and sunning ourselves, engaging in light conversation, falling asleep in the cool breeze, and then starting the process over again. Red kept a respectful distance, and I found that I was the one moving physically closer to him, so that by the time it was late afternoon, we were sitting only inches apart. At five o'clock, Marcelle disappeared below board while we spoke and reappeared a half hour later with a camera in her hands.

"Let's take a few pictures before the sun sets. So that we can remember a time when we were all young and beautiful. Well, the women, anyway," she said, grinning.

I stood closer to the men and then was joined by the rest of the party. "But you have to be in it, Marcelle," I said.

"Trust me, I've been photographed enough for one lifetime. Those flashbulbs have probably taken half my soul with them, but all right."

She took off her hat and tied a green ribbon around her dark hair, then came and squeezed in right next to me, not separating me from Red, who was on my other side. Marcelle smelled like gardenias and the spice of local food, a perfect mix of East and West.

When a small silver bell rang indicating dinner, Marcelle took my arm and held it tightly. "All we do on this boat is eat," she said. "Well, at least until the sun goes down. But it's worth adding a pound or two. The food is the best you'll taste in Indochine."

We ate dinner early in a capacious dining room downstairs where the tall, open windows framed a view of the sun, just beginning to set. Afterward, the whole group moved down the hall to an elegantly appointed sitting room with low couches, reclined chairs, and piles of silk pillows. I sat on the largest pillow and stroked the fabric, sure that it was the finest silk I had ever touched.

Khoi said something in Annamese to a girl in a bright pink *ao* who had appeared at the door. She ran off, returning a few moments later with another girl. In their hands were several long wooden pipes, each with a small ceramic bowl attached to a saddle on the top.

"Opium?" I asked Marcelle quietly as the others chatted animatedly around us, suddenly feeling quite out of my element.

"You still haven't smoked opium?" said Marcelle. She laughed but lowered her voice when she saw me flush. "I'm sorry, that was rude. I'm just surprised. They practically shoved one of these in my mouth as soon as I arrived. But I'm happy to be the one to initiate you. First, I show you the Officers' Club—well, the good parts anyway—and now this. There's almost nothing left for me to teach you concerning the vices of Indochine. Almost," she said, glancing at Red.

"No," I said, watching as he lay back on a pile of pillows, one of the young native girls coming over to tend to him. "I've never even smelled it before." I knew there was rampant opium use in Indochine and that the Europeans indulged in it as much as anyone, many of them becoming addicted. But after seven weeks in the country, I still hadn't seen it. My closest encounter—and that was secondhand—was with that overly bold Frenchman on the day I witnessed the delivery of the dead communist.

"The wood those pipes are made of is very ornate," I said to Red as he inhaled and closed his eyes.

"It's not wood, it's bamboo," he said, exhaling and rearranging the pillows the better to sink between them. "Beautiful, aren't they?"

"Yes, surprisingly so," I replied, marveling at the way his face and body already seemed more relaxed.

Within a few minutes, everyone was smoking except for me and, I noticed, Khoi. He had left the room after seeing that his guests were attended to. A piano melody was playing softly on a phonograph, and the conversation had died away. Red motioned one of the girls over and whispered something to her, his hand on the small of her back, rubbing her dress in a gentle circle.

When the girl asked me if I would like a pipe of my own, I shook my head and pressed against the wall, feeling light-headed and a little nauseated.

"I think I'll go back up to the sundeck," I said to Marcelle, not wanting to see her or Red like this. Marcelle nodded but didn't reply, her eyes half closed, her head back against a mound of bright cushions.

When I reached the deck, Khoi was sitting alone with a cocktail.

"Don't you smoke?" I asked after he'd pointed to the chair next to him.

"Rarely," he said, handing me a glass of champagne that he'd poured himself, waving off the boy. "It bores me a bit. Perhaps because I grew up around it. I do indulge occasionally, but less and less often as I get older. It just doesn't have the same exotic appeal for me that it does for foreigners. Colonials behaving badly and all that. Of course, the French also love that it's a very profitable commodity for them. The colony would have taken far longer to become profitable if they hadn't levied the opium tax, and managed to put the substance in so many people's hands. It's sticky, in more ways than one. But you're smart not to smoke it. You're too charming to let your mind be dulled."

I liked Khoi. Besides his mesmerizing looks, he had a self-assurance that the rich French lacked. All the fuss, he seemed to shrug, was a little tedious, even though he was the one providing it.

"May I offer you something other than champagne?" he asked, looking at my full glass. "I'm sorry, I just assumed."

"What are you having?" I asked.

"Lemonade," he said, holding up the tall glass with a grin. "I loved it as a child, and I'm afraid I never grew out of it. I had a French cook—isn't that funny, a French cook for an Annamite boy?—who made the most delicious kind, with lavender in it. I have no idea where he found the lavender. This one lacks the herb, but it's still quite good. Please, try it."

"This might actually be better than the Veuve Clicquot," I said after he handed me his glass and I took a sip.

"Here, you can have both," he said, gesturing for another glass.

"So, I hear you own a Delahaye," Khoi resumed, watching me drink. "It's a beautiful car."

"Do you know the company?" I asked. I hadn't seen any other Dela-hayes in Indochine.

"I do. My father is quite an enthusiast himself. He owns three."

"Three!" I exclaimed.

"He tends to do things in excess. At least when it comes to cars."

"This boat isn't excessive, though," I said, looking around us. "It's perfect."

"Thank you. I chose the boat."

He looked at me, with a glance that seemed to flicker between admiring and appraising.

"Please don't think me rude, but your French is so perfect. Did you live in France?" I asked him after he'd finished sizing me up. "I wish my accent was as Parisian-sounding as yours."

"I quite like the way you speak," he replied, pouring himself a glass of water from a carafe. "And I think I had a leg up on you. I've been speaking French all my life. I also went to school in Paris from the ages of sixteen to twenty-four."

"Did you! Without your family?"

He nodded. "It's a normal custom here for well-to-do boys. My parents visited, once, maybe twice, to make sure I wasn't having too much fun, but they were mostly very busy here running our silk company."

"That's a terribly long time. Didn't you miss it here?" When I left my family, it was without a return date, something that gave me both the happiness I was desperate for and lingering guilt I'd never quite shaken.

"Yes and no. I knew I would return," he said. "And I liked my free-dom in Paris."

"Funny. That's what all the French say about here."

"Well, there's something about being *dépaysé*, isn't there? Maybe you care less when you're out of your native habitat. You know your imprint won't last forever."

"I still would try to act as though it might," I said, thinking how much I needed this experiment in Indochine to be successful.

"Then you are in the minority," he said. He stood and leaned against the boat's wooden railing, drink in hand, and didn't flinch when a spray of water caught his face, dampening the starched collar of his shirt but seeming to miss his jacket, which he hadn't changed.

"I would like to meet your husband," he said suddenly. "For business reasons, and to welcome him to this part of the world. Might you arrange it for me?"

"Of course," I said. Victor would happily meet a man as rich as Khoi. And he would be dreadfully jealous when he heard about the three Delahayes.

Looking out to sea, Khoi pointing out the more famous formations as the sinking sun hit the water, its glow spreading along the horizon like gold ink.

"I should go check on Marcelle," he said after a minute.

I nodded. "I like Marcelle very much."

"So do I," he said. "Women here, the Annamites, they aren't as free-spirited as Marcelle. As independent. She really lives by her own rules."

"She certainly does," I said. "But I think you'll find that many women are quite free-spirited; it's just that our societies—here or there," I said, pointing west, "don't want us to be."

"Maybe," he said politely, "but still, she's different. There's just something about her."

"Yes, there is," I said, and meant it.

When Khoi was gone, I watched the sun's rays of gold fade, the last gasp of light green yielding to darkness. Then, I made my way downstairs to join the others. I walked slowly, listening for voices, but heard only a slight murmur that might have been Marcelle.

When I reached the sitting room, I peered through the open door into the shadows, wanting to see if people were still smoking before I decided to enter or not.

I could see Marcelle and Khoi lying together, her head on his chest. He was tapping his fingers rhythmically to the piano music and playing with her hair. Next to them, but paying them no attention, were the journalist and Madame Claire Angevine. They were lying together. I looked for the journalist's *indigène* companion, but she was asleep, or nearly asleep, on a long, silk-covered mattress in the corner. The journalist's right hand was inside Claire's dress, which was unbuttoned low enough to show her slip. I watched as his hand moved slowly, fondling her breasts, his fingers lingering. Without thinking, I held my breath nervously. I looked for Claire's husband in the corner where he had been lounging when I left, but he was no longer there. Instead, he was in an armchair just across from his wife and the journalist, his eyes open, watching them. In the corner he had vacated, one of the Annamite attendants now sat, her legs folded under her, holding a pipe and other paraphernalia, looking at a spot on the wall as if her eyes didn't even register the scene in front of her.

I watched as the journalist's hand switched to Claire's other breast, this time moving in slow, hungry circles, and I leaned back against the wall. My head struck the plaster with an unexpected crack, a noise no one would have heard in any other setting but that reverberated here in this quiet room. I quickly stood upright, my heart pounding.

There was a rustle. Afraid to see who was stirring, I waited a few seconds, then turned and stole back upstairs to the deck. I sank into a chair facing the water and sat there, breathing quickly. What was this world I had walked into? A moment later, I heard someone approaching. Red. He was alone and ambling slowly my way. When he reached me, he put his hand on my shoulder and leaned heavily on it.

"Lie with me up here, pretty American girl. I can't sit up. Or is it that I don't want to sit up? Either way, I'd like to lie down, with you."

"You can't sit up, but you're standing?" I asked, feeling suddenly more drunk just by looking at him, as if his intoxication were rubbing off on me.

"Am I standing?" he said, grinning. "I suppose I am. There, let's relax over there," he added, pointing across the deck at six lounge chairs neatly arranged with small metal tables between them.

When we were positioned, he reached for my hand and said, "Did we spook you in there, American girl?"

"No," I lied. "I've just never done anything like opium. Any drugs. I don't know that I should start."

"That's not what I was referring to," he said, still holding my hand.

I didn't answer, casting my eyes to the deck floor and slowly pulling my hand away.

Red moved his head upright, reaching for my hand again, and gestured to one of the boys in the shadows. This time, I didn't pull it away. "Talk to me," he said. "It almost feels like our own private boat here."

"Shouldn't we join the others?" I said, looking at our intertwined fingers.

"Eventually. But first we should drink these," he said as the boy returned with two Pegu Club cocktails.

"That adult orange juice of yours," I said, taking one with my free hand. "It follows you just about everywhere, doesn't it?"

"More loyal than a dog, this alcohol." He handed me a glass, and we clinked. "Or a wife." He smiled languidly and said, "Here's to my favorite American." He leaned in close to me and I didn't pull back.

"You think without an audience you'd enjoy it more?" he said.

"Enjoy . . . ?" I asked.

"Smoking," he said, raising his eyebrows.

"Why do you enjoy it so much?" I deflected.

"This is Indochine. Opium is part of the country's soul. If you never look at it with smoke in your eyes, you'll never see all of its layers."

"Did you steal that line, too?" I asked.

"No, that one is authentic," he said, laughing. He finished his drink in two gulps and stood up, dropping my hand. "Come on. Something tells me that Victor Lesage's wife needs to live a little. With a face like yours, you were not meant to lurk in the shadows while the rest of us enjoy ourselves."

"Where are we going?" I asked.

"To get smoke in your eyes, and your lungs," he said.

We walked down the steps, Red having to hold on to the railing and the wall for support, and turned toward the cabins. I knew immediately that we were heading to his, but I didn't stop walking.

When we were just past my cabin, a boy came to see if we needed anything and Red told him to bring him a pipe. "To my cabin," he said, gesturing.

I held my breath and followed him into the room. It was a bit smaller than mine. I lingered in the door frame, wondering if I should sprint the other way. But I was too curious. I remembered the calm that overtook Red as soon as he'd inhaled. As scared as I was, that calm was too appealing. I had to try it.

I stepped inside, and we got comfortable, he on the bed, I not daring. A young man set the pipe up for us and handed it first to Red.

"Ladies first, I insist." He gestured to the man.

"Very well," I said, taking the heavy pipe in my hand and gripping it tightly.

"Jessie," said Red, laughing. "Just relax. Try not to look as if you have a broomstick down your shirt." He pressed down on my shoulders, the way Marcelle had when we'd first met.

"Will it make me feel—"

"It will make you feel nothing," he cut me off. "That's the beauty of it. Sometimes we just need to feel nothing. Especially Americans. You're a very high-strung people."

"But you must feel something," I said, flipping quickly from curious to terrified. "Feeling nothing sounds like death."

"You feel relaxed. As if you don't have a care in the world. You might just feel as if you're dreaming. You might even fall asleep. It will do you a world of good."

I breathed in some of the smoke, exhaled, happy to see that I was still upright, then inhaled again, three more times, each intake of breath longer and deeper. I lay back on the bed and closed my eyes, breathing much more slowly than usual.

"How do you feel?" he asked as I opened my eyes again.

"I feel . . . at ease," I said, surprised that I had been affected so quickly. "As you said, I feel relaxed. Perhaps too relaxed. I can barely move my lips to form sentences."

There is a moment before you kiss a man where your life seems to stand still. Your brain slows, then your heartbeat, which slows your pulse and relaxes your muscles. It's a rare, physical quietude. I knew Red was leaning in to kiss me just then. I saw his face inch closer and closer to mine, but I felt unable to stop him. I couldn't move. I ran my hand over my face. I hardly registered my own touch. My entire body felt soft, as if my muscles had snapped, and though I wanted to stop him, I also didn't want to ruin the feeling that had washed over me. The feeling of being free from my own body.

I closed my eyes and didn't push him off.

"I can't not kiss you," he said, leaning closer. "It's as simple as that. I can't not."

He leaned in and kissed me, somehow finding the strength to pull me into him.

"How is your marriage?" he murmured when we had pulled apart, our faces still close, almost touching.

"It's wonderful," I whispered, the words sounding strange, as if my voice wasn't my own.

He smiled, fatigue in his eyes, and kissed me again, harder this time. "I don't believe you," he replied.

———

I woke up the next morning bathed in dried sweat and guilt. The sweat was Red's; the guilt was mine. I turned to look at the chair in his room, and at the other side of his bed. Red wasn't there. I moved a few inches onto the drier part of the sheets, my stomach lurching as I moved. I put my hand on it and lay back, my head painfully heavy, my brain cloudy. I felt as if I'd drunk all the champagne in the world.

I closed my eyes but heard a knock that I couldn't get up to answer. The door creaked open, and I rolled over slightly to see who it was.

"Good morning," he said, striding in, an annoyingly casual movement, and gestured to the view out the window. "Fantastic, isn't it? Burma was scenic, but it didn't have anything like this."

"It is," I said. My stomach groaned again, and I pulled the covers over it to muffle the sound. I looked up at him. It had to be said. "Red, last night. It was a terrible decision on my part. Victor isn't perfect, but he's still my husband, and he's a good man. The best man I know, really. He doesn't deserve to have a wife who—"

"What do you know of your plantations?" Red asked, interrupting me.

"What do you mean?" I asked, confused. "I know quite a lot about the Michelin plantations."

"Do you?" said Red. He took an orange out of a bowl of fruit that was on the table near the window. He held it to his nose, the tip of it almost on the peel. "Like your watch," he said and pointed to my wrist. "It's a very nice watch."

"It was a gift," I murmured, flipping the face back around.

"Dau Tieng and Phu Rieng," he repeated. "Have you been there yet? Have you seen the plantations? Been on the ground? Seen the men who work there? Or the women? Eighteen percent of your coolies are women. Did you know that?"

"Yes," I said, though I hadn't.

"I thought so," he said. "It was in the newspaper a few weeks back. Still, I think you should visit in person. Smart woman like yourself. You've been here how long, a month or two?"

"Something like that."

"It's a world apart down there," he said, the tenor of his voice dropping. "That's what everyone says. Aren't you curious?"

"Not especially."

"Well, you should be. Maybe then you wouldn't feel so guilty about a small kiss."

"A small kiss?" I said, feeling sicker just hearing the word. "It didn't feel small. It felt like a big, Pegu-soaked kiss."

Red grinned, leaning back against the wall, watching me.

"I enjoyed it very much," he said as I forced myself to stand up and totter to the open window to get some air. "And you did, too. At least as much as you let yourself."

I put my hand on the screen a moment, blocking out the world in front of me. Indochine's restless dragon. I looked at my watch again, then at my hand. My body froze. I looked at it again, ran my left hand over my right, but it wasn't there. My emerald ring was gone.

"My ring," I said dully, in shock.

"This one?" Red asked as I turned around. He pointed at the night-stand. There was a small, folded handkerchief on it that I hadn't seen when I woke up. I rushed over. Inside it was my ring, the large emerald smashed to pieces.

TWENTY

Jessie

October 25, 1933

T rieu?" I called out. I'd rung for her a few minutes before, but she hadn't appeared yet. I squinted at the clock on my nightstand, its face barely visible in the shadowy bedroom. It was five minutes to six in the morning. I'd slept with the windows open and could see that outside the sky was still blue-black. It was late October, and somehow the early hour seemed darker than it had just the day before, when I'd also been awake before dawn. It was as if the earth had turned a bit too quickly away from the sun. Under the covers, I gripped the small silk bag containing my broken ring. When we were in the room together, I had knocked my hand on the wall and it had shattered, Red had said, surprised I didn't remember. I had been too shocked to cry when I found it, but now, holding its poor remnants, I wanted to scream. How could I have smoked that poison and let myself go? How could I have broken my ring? I knew that emeralds were far more prone to breaking than diamonds, one of the reasons I'd been more careful with it than I had my wedding ring. But how could I have shattered it? I had been so foolish.

"*Oui, madame, j'arrive,*" I heard Trieu call from down the hall as I flicked on my lamp, her voice muffled by the closed door. She opened it a few seconds later, leaving it ajar so the hallway light poured in. She was in a blue *ao* and black pants, but her hair was unbrushed, and she had sleep in her eyes.

"Trieu, I need to be on the morning train to Saigon. What time does it leave?"

"The train south leaves at nine o'clock, *madame*," she said. "But it does not go to Saigon. The railroad does not connect Hanoi and Saigon yet. It won't for many years still. You can take a train directly to Tourane, on the coast, but then you have to travel by car or boat to Nha Trang. From there, you can continue by train to Saigon."

"That's right. Victor mentioned that," I said. "Which is faster, car or boat?"

"Monsieur Lesage takes a car and spends one night along the route. There is a good European hotel in Quy Nhon, about halfway between the two rail stations. Le Grand Hôtel. There is running water, electric fans. It's very near to the beach. It's where your husband stays. I think this way is faster, or at least more comfortable."

"Yes, that sounds fine. Please arrange it," I said.

Trieu nodded and straightened the band-style collar of her *ao*. It was still open, and she quickly pushed the small gold button through its loop, murmuring an apology.

"Would you like to dress now?" she asked, stepping into the room.

"Not yet," I said. "I can dress myself for something as casual as a train ride."

"Of course," she said and backed quickly out the door.

I drained the cup of tea that had been placed by my bed the night before, not minding that it was cold. My heart was broken over my ring, but I was physically feeling like myself again and was glad I had my appetite back. Since returning from Ha Long Bay on Sunday, I had stayed in bed, barely leaving my room, trying to right my mind. For three days I had ricocheted between deep sleep and restive wakefulness. Lucie had come into my bedroom a few times, lying down with me, telling me stories about her days at school, as well as her time in the kitchen, which she seemed to enjoy more. But even with her animated face in front of me, I couldn't stop the images from those ten hours on the boat from flashing through my brain. I was unable to make sense of them, still feeling desperately unwell after the quantities of strong substances I'd consumed with Red. The champagne. The Pegu Clubs. The opium that had caused my nausea. That awful tar was still coating my lungs, I was sure of it. But one image that never appeared was my ring breaking. I had no recollection of it.

Trying to find peace in sleep, I'd close my eyes again and again, only for certain scenes to resurface: the guests pawing at one another, in the sway of desire and drugs; Marcelle in the arms of a man not her husband—and Red. Mostly I kept seeing my transgression with Red, the only misstep I'd made since meeting Victor. It felt as if that sin had broken my ring. Perhaps I had collided with the wall on purpose, knowing I didn't deserve it anymore. And I certainly didn't deserve to be Victor's right hand, tasked with confidential dealings.

When I'd woken this morning, I expected another such day but was surprised to feel as if I could breathe again. I was able to shut down the images from the strange interlude at Ha Long Bay. Instead, I concentrated on the trip I wanted to make. The trip south to our vast miles of gray and red earth.

Victor had called the plantations a man's world many times. He had never instructed me not to visit, but he hadn't invited me either, and I hadn't asked. But now I felt that I must go. Red was pushing for me to visit. Insisting. There had to be a reason why.

The way he had brought up the Michelin land the morning after our kiss, that stupid, reckless kiss. Why did he care if I'd seen it or not? It felt out of character. Red seemed like a man focused on living large without a care in the world. I supposed he had to dabble with the railroad expansion sometimes, but from what I could tell, his main priorities in life were getting highly intoxicated and making love to intoxicating women.

Lying between my sheets, which Trieu had been changing twice a day because of my cold sweats, I fingered the silk bag and thought about how I'd first met Red. He'd been one of the only men in the club when Marcelle and I had arrived for an early swim, an outing orchestrated by Marcelle. In hindsight, it was far too convenient.

I'd been wrong to stop worrying about her. I'd been too hungry to establish a life in Hanoi, and too desperate for friendship, especially with someone as vivacious and companionable as Marcelle. That childish longing, that need for intimacy, which I blamed on growing up with a horde of siblings, had made me silence my suspicions about her too quickly. I'd written off her mention of Switzerland as my tendency to overreact at times of change or upheaval. Victor knew that, too. But we'd made a mistake here.

I would explain to Victor my misgivings about Red, and he would understand why I needed to see the plantations.

I rang the bell that sounded in the servants' rooms again, and Trieu reappeared a few minutes later. Her hair was brushed now, her appearance much neater.

"I'd like to send a telegram to Victor," I said. I reached for the notepad and pen on my nightstand and scribbled a quick note. "Just in case I can't get him on the telephone in time," I said, handing it to her. "It's difficult to connect to the plantation. The service out there is dreadful."

"Of course," she said. "I'll send it at once."

In the note, I estimated I would arrive in three days' time, assuming the journey went smoothly. Victor would not be pleased that I was coming uninvited, but I told myself that when I explained about Red, he'd wonder why I hadn't come sooner.

Visit the Michelin plantations, Red had said. His voice had been light, yet there was an urgency in his words and in his expression.

I wondered if he thought I was the kind of woman who just sat idle and had no interest in how her husband made his money. I hoped he didn't. Regardless, he seemed determined to have me see more.

The door to Victor's closet was slightly ajar, and I could make out his rows of perfectly pressed suits, each spaced two inches from the next. Victor had only taken two with him to the south. He said it was different there. He didn't have to dress the way he had in Paris or even in Hanoi. Perhaps Red was right. Perhaps I didn't know enough about life on the plantations that helped keep the Michelin name so prominent.

I emerged from bed slowly and looked at myself in the mirror. I was wearing an old pair of Victor's pajamas instead of my nightgown. Trieu had helped me change when I'd sweated through it. I had eaten next to nothing for three days. My hair needed washing, my eyebrows shaping, my shoulders massaging so that their exhausted slump disappeared. I did not look like the elegant woman who had proven to be so confident, so capable in Haiphong. I looked like a stranger. I reached down and gripped my naked right hand. And now I had to make this journey without my ring.

TWENTY-ONE

Jessie

October 25, 1933

It was only the fourth time I'd been inside the Hanoi train station, yet it felt familiar. I was seated in the waiting area, on a wooden bench near the ladies' restroom, taking in my surroundings: the families rushing by with too many bags and not enough hands; the coolies with cargo wrapped in frayed cloth tied onto their backs, heading to the rear of the train; the well-dressed French travelers avoiding them as best they could; the more well-to-do Annamites chatting in unaccented French as they strolled from the ticket counter toward the tracks. I had pinned the bag with the ring inside my waistband. It was not the same as wearing it on my hand, but it was comforting to have it near me. It was smashed beyond repair; I knew that. This would have to do for now.

As I watched two native men disappear out the door to wait on the platform, I noticed a colorful poster on the wall near where they had just purchased their tickets. I hadn't spotted it before, as the stationmaster had bought my ticket for me while I rested. Now I went to stand in front of the poster. It was quite large, and I was surprised I'd missed it on my way in. It featured an imposing white train station, much like ours in Hanoi. But dominating the station was a giant sun with yellow rays so bright they seemed to extend past the edges of the poster, illuminating the wall around it. It was one of the houses of a hundred suns. I moved closer and read the words printed under the picture: "*Pour aller loin, pour payer moins, pour être bien, prenez le train.*" A push for the merits of train travel—affordable, comfortable, and able to take you far. I turned on my heel and rushed to the station's main door to see if Lanh was still there so I could show him that I'd found the poster he'd told me about. He'd want to know that another generation of children in Indochine was getting a chance to see the image that had so ignited his young imagination. But he and the Delahaye were gone.

The train was due in three minutes. Upon my return to Hanoi, I would ask the stationmaster if I could buy the poster. I wanted very much to give it to Lanh.

Boarding the train was a peaceful process for passengers in the front car, where I was seated, and utter chaos for those at the back, even more so than on my trip to Haiphong, since this train had many more cars. It was exhausting just watching the Annamites in third class shoving and jostling to board, but I found my way to my large plush seat with the help of an attendant, who opened my window wide for me. I hung my hat on the hook on the wall, the same hat I'd worn to Haiphong, and peeked in my traveling purse to make sure I hadn't forgotten anything. I'd been so concerned about my ring that I hadn't paid much attention to the rest of it. I had asked Trieu to put a small, framed picture of Lucie in the bag. This trip to Cochinchina would mean the longest separation for the two of us since Switzerland, seven years earlier. When I'd kissed her good-bye, I'd held her too tightly, and she had kissed both my hands.

"Don't worry, *maman*," she'd said as I wiped away tears. "A trip away is good for you, because you can be quite shy. That's what Papa says, isn't it."

"He does at times," I said. "But sometimes husbands don't know everything about their wives."

"I see," she'd said pensively. "I'll be here when you return."

I looked at the picture of Lucie and rubbed my index finger over it. Girls had been a burden in my family, but Lucie was a gift. That tiny seed, which I'd prayed would implant inside me, had brought me marriage, a ticket out of America, and now this life.

I placed the picture back in my bag, next to my engraved silver cigarette case. Having grown up covered in tobacco, I didn't find smoking the least bit appealing, but Trieu had packed it in my purse for the journey, saying that someone important might ask me for a cigarette, and it was only polite to be ready. You never knew who you might encounter on the journey south in the first-class car.

I took a cigarette out and spun it slowly between my fingers, thinking of my father, who rolled his own using the tobacco he grew on our farm. It was why I never smoked. The acrid smell always reminded me of him, of home. Still, I found myself pulling a cigarette out, lighting it, and placing it between my lips.

Inhaling just a tiny bit, I thought of my mother walking through my father's smoke rings, usually with a pregnant belly leading the way, muttering to herself in French. Seven thousand three hundred nautical miles. That's how far Hanoi was from Blacksburg, Virginia. It was one of the first things I'd calculated when Victor had told me we finally had the family's blessing to go. It was twice as far as Paris. I had thrown my arms around him and tried not to cry tears of joy. I'd saved myself in Paris, but with Hanoi, it felt as if he were saving me. I knew that living in Hanoi wouldn't prevent my being tracked down by Dorothy Davis. I wasn't on the moon. But the odds of my running into someone from Blacksburg, Virginia, in Hanoi were nil. There were fewer than a hundred Americans in the whole colony. It was yet another chance for reinvention.

As I took a real pull on the cigarette, the train started to move, accelerating as it left the city. Once Hanoi was far behind us, the train chugged toward the coast, hugging it like a frightened child. I watched rolling green hills slowly appearing as we rumbled through small villages and then flat vistas returning before we reached another part of the country that was cut into rice paddies.

After we left the town of Hue, nearly 350 miles from Hanoi, the rickety fishing boats bobbing a few feet from shore multiplied and the land grew hillier again, making it feel on many turns as if the train might pitch itself into the sea. The waves were small and soft, slapping rhythmically against the side of the boats below. Past Hue, the overgrown foliage alongside the tracks found its way in through the windows, to the delight of the only child in my car. I fell asleep to the sound of his mother scolding him. It had been hard to leave Lucie again after my days of oblivion, but hearing the voice of a child I didn't have to tend to reminded me that it was good for a woman to be alone sometimes.

I didn't wake up until we were traversing the Hai Van Pass, the high, scenic mountain pass that protrudes into the East Sea, Bien Dong, as the natives called it. The crossing meant that the end of the first train leg was near. The mist covering the pass dissipated quickly as we chugged out of it, and I soon saw small, white-sand beaches, deserted except for fishing boats. Then more miles of rice paddies, and soon after that, Tourane, where the track ended abruptly.

After the long train ride, I was happy to switch to a car for the next 335 miles. Perhaps because of my American heritage, long distances exhilarated me, even more so with a change of perspective.

My driver was a middle-aged man with prematurely white hair and a white driving suit to match who told me his name was Xuan. He said he'd driven Victor before but that he preferred not to converse on the journey because his French wasn't good enough. He made that declaration in perfect French, but I honored his request, saying almost nothing on the trip except to tell him when I needed a rest or glimpsed something I wanted to photograph with the Lumière Elax camera Victor had given me before we left Paris.

In the mud-splattered Hispano-Suiza, we made our way to the port town of Qui Nhon, where I spent a comfortable night in the

French-built hotel, a four-story white structure with a veranda on the first floor and a view of the beach that seemed to have been dipped in sunshine. In the morning, Xuan offered to drive me to the famous caves of the Marble Mountains or to the many large pagodas that the French cooed over, but I declined. Instead, we pushed on to the coastal city of Ninh Hoa for an early breakfast before reaching Nha Trang, just a few miles farther south. Not bothering to even glance at the city, I boarded a train nearly identical to the one from Hanoi, made sure I secured a window seat in the first-class car, and lost myself in the scenery of the remaining 250 miles to Saigon. I was scheduled to reach the southern city before nine the next morning, ending a seventy-five-hour journey. Trieu had said another driver would fetch me at the station and chauffeur me to Dau Tieng. At the hotel in Quy Nhon there had been a telephone, and I'd briefly considered calling Victor. But I'd decided the conversation we needed to have should be done in person.

When the train finally screeched to a halt at the Saigon station, everyone in the first-class car pushed their way to the exits as eagerly as if they were arriving in the heart of Manhattan. My body stiff from the journey, I waited for the throng to clear and disembarked last, meeting a porter with my suitcase on the platform. Outside the station, I heard a male voice call my name and spun around to see a young man of European appearance approaching.

"Madame Lesage, what a pleasure to have you with us," he said enthusiastically, extending his hand. "I'm Jacques Caron, one of the chief overseers at Dau Tieng. Victor asked me to meet your train."

"Oh, did he?" I managed to reply, taken aback that I was being met by a European and that he'd referred to Victor by his first name. "How kind of him. Are you . . . I hope this isn't putting you out in any way."

"You were expecting a native man to drive you," he said, grinning. Together we crossed the street, past the row of coolies competing for our fare just like those in Hanoi, shouting for our attention and flashing their nearly toothless grins.

"I suppose I was," I admitted. "My servant who arranged the journey told me to expect an *indigène* driver."

"You were going to have someone local," he said. "A driver named Nien was due to fetch you, but he was commandeered at the last moment by my wife, and Victor and I didn't want to leave you with a chauffeur we didn't know well. A woman in a car alone for hours with a stranger, it didn't sit well with me, or your husband."

"How kind of you to think of my safety," I said, although I didn't believe for a moment that this brash young man's actions were propelled by kindness. "But you shouldn't have come yourself," I went on. "You could have sent someone else."

"When I heard it was you arriving, I thought it would be the gentlemanly thing to do, particularly since we hadn't met yet. You have never graced us with your presence here in Saigon."

"No, this is my first trip," I said as Jacques took my suitcase from the porter who had been standing silently next to us. "I don't think I'll have time to see much of Saigon on this trip, unfortunately. It's just a visit to see my husband and the plantations."

"Of course. Your family's crown jewels in Indochine. I'm very lucky to work at Dau Tieng. And I know Victor is excited for you to be here, to finally see it all," he said as he started the car and pulled away from the station.

"Is he?" I asked, trying not to sound surprised.

"Very," said Jacques, making a right turn away from the station. "It's almost a four-hour drive to Dau Tieng, which is the largest of the plantations," he said when the yellow building was finally out of sight. "That's where you'll start your visit." He pointed to a glass bottle on the floor near my feet. "Cold water there. Should be nice and refreshing since it was on ice. Drink it when your stomach begins to feel even slightly sour, and try to look straight ahead when we are off the paved roads."

"I'm from the country," I said, looking out at the crowded road ahead of us.

"Not this country," he replied and sped up. "We are heading east of the city," he added, gesturing. "Would you like me to detour so you can see some of Saigon's jewels? Notre Dame Cathedral? The opera house?"

"No, just to Dau Tieng, please," I said, resting my head against the passenger window. I closed my eyes, putting my hand over my waistband so I could feel the little bag holding my ring. Assured of its presence, I let myself drift to sleep.

Three and a half hours later, I was roused by Jacques touching my arm. I opened my eyes, sat upright, and rolled down the window.

"We're just arriving," he said, pointing. "There, just beyond those trees, is Dau Tieng."

I blinked a few times to get the sleep out of my eyes and saw a barrier blocking the dirt road. On either side were squat watchtowers and men in uniform.

"Are those military guards?" I asked, looking at them more closely as we approached.

"Yes," he said, signaling to them out the window. "After what happened at Phu Rieng in '27, the murder of the overseer, they were stationed here at the gates and all around the periphery of the land. We do have men who try to escape, and so many acres are hard to monitor. Nothing to be alarmed by. Just a precaution."

"Why do men try to escape?" I asked as Jacques rolled his window back up.

"Oh, you know the nature of men. Some just don't like to work. Some are homesick, some want to run off and be revolutionaries. But those are fewer and fewer these days," he said. "It's not like it was in 1930, I'm told. Or even last year. Your husband, in just a few months' time, has things in firm control."

"I'm happy to hear it," I said, turning to get a better look at the military men after they'd waved us through.

We drove in on a wide dirt road, crossing an expanse far more open than I'd anticipated.

"All this is being replanted," he said, following my gaze, "which is why it's so bare right now. On the other side, there," he said, pointing to a mass of sprawling one-story buildings, "are the coolie villages, the hospital, the orphanage, the canteen. And beyond that is more land that we're clearing."

We passed rows of short rubber trees, all spaced with the precision of soldiers on parade, not daring to grow out of line.

"Your husband is in his house," Jacques said as the low buildings disappeared behind us. "I've worked on rubber plantations throughout my career, first in Brazil and now here, and this is the first time I've seen any family member from the company live on the plantation. He, and Michelin, should be applauded. It will make the difference in our success, I believe. In your success," he corrected himself. "You've already invested so much in research. New technologies for planting and tapping. That is already paying off. And with low labor costs, you are still making money in the depression. It's just the unrest that's been a problem, after last December, and Victor is prioritizing that."

"Yes, well, the Michelins are known for building loyalty in Clermont-Ferrand. It is time that they do the same here. I think Victor is quite capable—"

"I don't mean to be rude," he said, interrupting in a voice that indicated he didn't care at all about being rude, "but loyalty isn't the problem. It's communism. The men who find their way here and spread their lies to these uneducated men, advocating violence. That is the problem."

"Victor mentioned as much," I said, trying to remain pleasant. "But he already weeded one out, from what I hear. I'm sure he will have the problem under control soon, if he does not already."

"One can never have it fully under control," he said, turning the wheel sharply to avoid a dip in the dirt road. "But I think Victor can keep the spark from spreading into a blaze. The last thing we can do is let ideology burn this amazing place down."

"What are those buildings?" I asked, looking at a cluster of large, one-story structures in the distance, happy to change the subject. As we approached, I saw they were all connected by covered walkways.

"Hospital buildings," Jacques said, slowing the car.

"All of them?" I asked. "That seems like quite a lot."

"It's not easy work, planting. There are injuries, unfortunately. It simply can't be avoided. Having a modern hospital on the grounds is better for everyone. That's the French doctor's bungalow," he said, pointing to a building slightly set apart from the others. "The nurses' barracks are there, the indigenous workers' dormitory, the refectory and the kitchen just past it."

Beyond the buildings, the rows of rubber trees stretched away endlessly, vanishing into the horizon. Victor hadn't invited me to come to the plantations, but his judgment was off. Seeing the land transformed this way was extraordinary.

"He's a shrewd businessman, your husband," Jacques said. "No wonder the family selected him to come here."

I didn't bother to correct him about who had approached whom about Victor's new post.

"I've only worked here a year, but I've wanted to work for Michelin for a long time," Jacques continued. "France owes a great debt to the Michelin brothers for what they did for the country in the Great War. The planes they made, the factories they handed over to the army. They were a model for French industry."

"I'm glad you're here, then, working for them," I said, impressed by his knowledge of the Michelins' wartime contributions.

"All this was savage land," he said, driving now on a narrow but more manicured road. "*Les terres grises*," he said. The gray earth. "It was inhabited by natives and was producing nothing. Or very little. But now it's fruitful, after only a few years' investment. And we— the Michelins, I mean—have provided so many jobs to the coolies from the north. So many of them illiterate. Godless. Now they can support their families, even in a difficult economic time, with what we pay them."

I looked around for one of these illiterate, godless men but saw none.

"Is it strange that we haven't passed any people, any coolies?" I said. "I thought that nearly six thousand workers were employed between here and Phu Rieng."

"That's right," said Jacques. "And seventy more at Ben Cui. But we don't allow them to roam free. It's eleven o'clock, so they're working, of course. They work in large groups, in the fields, in the factories. At noon, they'll walk back to the canteen for lunch. A generous meal to get them through the day. Rice. Fresh fish. You'll see them then, if that interests you."

He pulled up in front of a handsome two-story white house and switched off the engine. He came around and opened my door.

"This is Victor's house, yes?" I said, looking at Jacques as he reached for my hand to help me out. Before he could answer, Victor appeared at the door, then hurried down the stairs, which were flanked by two large pots of flowers, and greeted me warmly.

"Thank you, Jacques. Most kind of you to fetch her," he said as we walked inside, ignoring his subordinate's attempt to start a conversation.

Victor kissed me, then reached for my bag and placed it by the door, motioning for us to go to the living room. "So," he said as we went inside, his voice curious. "Traveling down here practically un-announced. I only received your telegram yesterday. Is there something I should be worried about? I'm assuming you did not just feel a sudden passionate urge to visit Dau Tieng. Or am I wrong?"

"I have been interested in seeing the plantations, of course," I said, sitting down on one of the chairs in the small room. "But that's not why I rushed onto a train without discussing it with you first."

"Those are terribly uncomfortable," Victor said, pulling me back up and leading me to a large couch in the corner. "Let's sit here. Less-punishing furniture."

I looked around the quarters. They were pretty but sparse, with very little personal adornment besides a few family pictures on the mantel.

There was one of him and Lucie in a small frame and one of me that I didn't remember being taken. I was in the Luxembourg Gardens in Paris, and my hair was longer and loose on my shoulders, which were nearly bare. I looked at Victor after I'd registered it and saw a faint flush on his face, as if I'd caught him with something inappropriate.

"So, you do miss me a little when you're here," I said, smiling.

"I miss you very much," he said, smiling back. He picked up my hand, but I pulled it gently away from him when guilt started pricking at me.

"Do you know who Hugh Redvers is?" I asked, launching right into what had happened before I grew too scared to.

"I do," he said, dropping my hand. "British. Railroad man. Gives all the women syphilis. That's the one, yes?"

"The very one," I said, not mentioning how close I'd come to being one of those women. "I spent an evening in his company recently, along with Marcelle de Fabry, her Annamite lover, Nguyen Khoi, and a few other people. It's a long story, but I'll get to the point now and recount the rest later."

"Very well," said Victor, noticeably tensing.

"We were all on an excursion on Khoi's boat. During the trip, Red demanded to know why I hadn't been to visit our plantations. It wasn't just a simple question; he pushed the subject. He clearly wanted me to come here. So now I'm hoping you could explain why Hugh Redvers would insist that I visit? Is there something about Dau Tieng or Phu Rieng that I should know about? Or that your uncle and cousins should know?"

"No," said Victor, eyeing me a bit more warily. "Uncle Édouard and the rest of the managers know about everything that goes on here. The overseers keep them abreast of every detail, and now so do I." He leaned back. If he guessed that something untoward had happened between me and Red, he didn't say so.

"Marcelle de Fabry has an *indigène* lover she flaunts?" he asked instead. "That's very surprising. I wonder why Arnaud doesn't put a stop to that."

"Yes, she does. A very rich one," I said. "Although I think 'lover' isn't a strong enough word, actually. Love. He feels more like her love than her lover."

"How original of her. But it will end badly. Those types of relationships, unions, affairs, whatever you want to call it, always do."

"I don't really see an end in sight for them," I said.

"Yes, well, the world seems to right those sorts of things on its own. Or perhaps Arnaud will get some sense and put a stop to it."

"Perhaps," I said, not mentioning that Khoi seemed like a far more appealing choice than Arnaud.

"And Red being with Marcelle. Was that a coincidence or—"

"No. I don't think it was. She arranged the party. As I said, we were on her lover's boat."

Victor raised his eyebrows at me and reached for a cigarette from the case on the end table. "Where were you sailing?"

"Ha Long Bay," I said.

He looked at me for a long moment without replying. Finally, he lit the cigarette and said, "I hear it's very nice there."

"It is," I said, looking away from him.

"Maybe I was too quick to tell you I thought that woman's allusion to Switzerland was a coincidence," he said.

"Well, it still could have been," I replied. "But with all this nonsense with Red . . . it doesn't feel random, like an accident. His hope that I end up right here was not the least bit veiled."

"That's odd. Maybe he is involved with something untoward," said Victor, tapping his long fingers together.

"Like what?"

"A communist uprising? Or funding a communist uprising," said Victor.

"A communist uprising? Red can barely wake up before noon. Unless the uprising had to do with stealing whiskey or women, I doubt he'd be interested. And he's British, and a railroad man. An industrialist. Wouldn't that suggest he wants to stamp out communism, not throw wood onto the fire?"

"Not every European here is for industry, nor is every native a communist. It doesn't work that way. That would be too easy."

"I don't imagine it does, but even so, wouldn't Red want to reform his own industry first? How many coolies have died building the railway line south?" I asked.

"Twenty percent, on average," said Victor quickly. "And they're far less policed than we are. The work inspectors leave railroad construction alone because they want a train that goes straight down to Saigon even more than the rest of us, since they have to make the trip so often. Which means it's likely a higher percentage than that."

"Then why would a man like that have anything to do with our plantations?" I asked. "Or care about funding the communist workers?"

"I don't know," he said, his voice showing his frustration. "But if Red was involved with the communists, the railroad would give him very good cover," he continued. "Plus he's British. A dedicated rogue. The community in Hanoi seems so distracted by his womanizing, maybe it really is all just a successful ploy to disguise the truth."

"Seems a bit of a stretch."

"Maybe," said Victor, inhaling again. "Maybe he has some sort of alliance with the British rubber brokers. He was where before Hanoi? Java?"

"Burma."

"There's only minor production there," said Victor, putting out his cigarette firmly, "but production all the same. Maybe he has a man here for that reason. No one is investing more in research than we are. That could be what he's after. That makes quite a lot of sense, actually."

"But either way, why would he push me here? Wouldn't he want me to stay away, in that case, so that a conversation like this didn't occur?"

"Jessie, I wasn't there for this pleasure cruise you took. You should know better than I, shouldn't you?"

I didn't answer. If he only knew how much of a pleasure cruise it really was.

Victor ran his hands down his thighs, gathering himself. "If he's interested in our rubber research, I can't imagine why he'd want you to come here," he said at last. "If he's a communist sympathizer, or worse, then I can think of one reason."

"Which is?"

"You're my wife. A person who he assumes has influence over me. Which you do. A lot, as you can see," he said, gesturing to the house, the fact that we were in Indochine at all. "But one who he wrongly assumes scares easily."

After all these years, Victor still had no idea how easily I could be scared.

"He may think that. He probably does."

"Then come with me," Victor said. He grabbed my hand, and together we hurried down the stairs. Before we were out the door, Victor stopped. He looked at me, causing my heart to start racing. Then he lifted up my hand and held it.

"You're not wearing your ring," he said incredulously. "I don't think I've seen you without it a day since I gave it to you. Did you lose it?"

I pulled my hand away, letting it fall to my side. "I didn't lose it," I lied. "I just don't need to wear it anymore. I decided it was a bit of an unhealthy obsession, my spinning it all the time. I left it at home because I thought I could use a fresh start."

Victor nodded, then kissed me on the forehead. "I'm glad you're here," he whispered. "Here at Dau Tieng, and just with me. I'm glad you're my wife, and not having an affair with a rich native. And I'm glad you understand the intricacies of doing business in a place like this. It isn't easy, but I am trying my best."

"I know you are," I said, smiling. "And I'm glad, too," I said, taking a step closer to him, "that I'm your wife."

"Come," he said, sounding more animated.

We walked out the door and climbed into his black, open-top car, one much less polished and grand than the Delahaye.

He drove faster through the grounds than Jacques had, past a factory whose double door was wide open. Despite our speed, I caught a glimpse of the interior. I could see high wooden beams holding up the corrugated metal roof and a few men wearing thin shorts and nothing else, their bodies sinewy and dark.

"Not here," said Victor. "We're going to one of the coolie villages. There are several. But only one you'll care about right now."

After five more minutes on the dirt roads, we stopped at a small cabin about a hundred yards from the sleeping quarters. It was windowless and looked as if it might be a latrine or a bathhouse.

"Go ahead. Go inside," said Victor, pointing to the door but keeping the car engine running. He put a small silver key in my hand and nudged me to get out. "If he's so keen to have you here, and at this particular time, then he must want you to see this."

I gripped the key tightly, a surge of anxiety spreading through my body.

Victor could tell I was stalling and waved at the door again. "Go on," he instructed.

I put the key in the lock and turned it slowly. When it clicked, I leaned my weight against the door and pushed it open. As soon as I did, I clapped my hand over my nose and mouth, gagging from the overpowering stench of human feces. All I saw was blackness, but I opened the door wider, and in the shaft of daylight it let in, I could make out the shadowy forms of what was inside.

I stepped in, my face still covered. On the floor, without a wall to support them, was a row of five men. Their ankles were shackled to the same wooden bar, but two of them were lying down, not sitting up like the others. I stepped closer still and saw why. They were dead.

I took a deep breath, then lowered my hand from my face. As soon as I did, I jumped, losing one of my shoes. I moved frantically to put it back on, seeing a line of ants crossing my foot. They were all over the dirt floor. I stood up quickly and looked at one of the dead men. His skin had been partially eaten away. I turned away from him at once, nausea hitting me like a swell. I suddenly realized what I was looking at. I peered at the man closest to me and said, "*Ai trong mấy người này là Ly Duc Khai?*"

My Indochinese was still clumsy, but this they would understand: Is one of you Ly Duc Khai?

My heart began pounding the way it would in the seconds before my mother forced me to slaughter a chicken. The anticipation of the blood spattering from its neck, even if I had given it a blow to the skull before beheading it, the adrenaline surge that kept it moving even when headless, the tautness of its skin after I'd killed it. That was what I thought of as I looked at the emaciated, naked figures in front of me.

Two of the men who were still alive didn't look at me, their bodies bent over, their torsos nearly touching their legs, their ribs visible even in the dim light.

But the man closest to me, the one I had addressed, turned his head to see me. "I am Khai," he said.

His face didn't match his voice. He had somehow found the energy to smile. He had hope—I was a woman, after all, and women had softer hearts than men. Even Western women.

I took a step forward so he could see me better.

Ly Duc Khai was the first name on the list that I'd obtained for Victor in Haiphong.

I stared at him for a few seconds more, at his naked body, his fading smile.

I met his eyes and saw the soul of the man still there, despite his body giving out. I bit my lip as hard as I could. My tears were desperate to fall, but I could not let them. I did not deserve to cry.

I could not help him. I had created a life for myself where I was nearly as tied up as he was. I was powerless to release him.

"*Xin lỗi Anh.*" I'm sorry, I whispered in Annamese. "I'm so sorry."

I walked into the pungent room a few more steps until I knew I was far enough inside that Victor could not see me. I leaned down and touched his head, my hand on his hair, which was heavy with grease and the dirt he'd been lying on. And then I brought my lips down on it quickly. "I can't help you," I said in French. Then I stood straight up again and put my hand on his back. "Please forgive me," I said. "I am much weaker than you." I hadn't said those words since Virginia. Since the darkest day of my life.

A person could live for a week without water. But in that windowless room, in their coffin, it would be different. In three days at most, they would all be dead. I turned around, unable to bear the sight anymore. I shut the door behind me, locked it, and squeezed the doorknob, my heart hammering. Victor would be waiting for my reaction. What kind of a person was I, eight years into our marriage? Was I the kind of person who could support him as he carried out a plan that I had set into motion? As he made money that I needed more than he did? Was I the kind of woman who could forget such a sight and continue as a loyal wife no matter what? Or was I still the girl he'd forced on a train to be drugged in Switzerland? I felt much more like the girl on the train than I did a dutiful wife, but I knew that sentiment had to change. I slowly let go of the door frame, feeling my heart bleed. Even if I'd wanted to, I was powerless to save those men. Everyone's arms were linked together here: the government, the police, and businessmen like Victor. And those dying men were the enemy. They were trying to take what the French and so many Annamites had built and improved over the last nearly fifty years, the economic prosperity, and knock it down again.

But the real reason I was powerless was that I needed money, far more than Victor did. I needed a good life for my daughter. I needed the world I'd fought so hard to be a part of not to disappear. No matter what.

I closed my eyes a moment and exhaled what felt like the remains of my soul. Then I turned to Victor, sitting back comfortably in his open-top car, looking at me expectantly.

"They were just days away from starting a communist uprising here. They were hiding weapons. Daggers and knives that they made in the auto shop. And worse. Over a dozen guns that had been smuggled in. Burying them in the earth. They were stocking food, had been for months. But thanks to you, I beat them to it," he said, a glint of pride in his eyes. "I notified the police, who are as scared of another uprising as we are. It was decided that we should make an example out of these men instead. After this, things will be different. You'll see. There will never be another strike like 1930 here, not after these men meet this fate."

I lifted my right hand and threw the keys at him. "Then it's all for the better," I said, smiling.

again. But, realistically, that would be aided greatly by the cooperation of Sinh's father."

"He will never help us. And to what end, Marcelle? Paul Adrien still wouldn't be brought to justice. At most, he would be fined. Don't you remember in 1927 when that native overseer Nguyen Van Chanh was kicked to death by the French senior overseer at Phu Rieng? A man named Valentin. The other Annamite overseers reported it, the police all nodded and smiled, promising the workers justice. They launched an investigation that lasted several months and then a trial that went on for only a few days. The overseer Valentin admitted to kicking the man to death but said it was Chanh's fault. That the native man moved suddenly, and his spleen simply got in the way. Valentin was only trying to give him a small tap with his toe. Come to think of it, the story doesn't sound that different from what we were told."

"I remember it," I said. It was something that I had thought about often since I'd found out the Lesages were coming to the colony.

"Then you'll remember that the French overseer was found guilty of manslaughter and his only punishment was to pay the widow of the native overseer five piastres. Five! That is about sixty francs. So what would happen if we tried to get them to open a new inquiry into something they already investigated four years ago? Do you think they would really find a French policeman guilty of killing a communist? Even one with a father in the government? Sinh could have been walking down the street and Paul Adrien could have put a bullet in his head for no reason, and even if he were found guilty, his punishment would never match his crime." He put his head back, letting it almost bob, and closed his eyes. "European men are not punished here. Only Annamites are. In that same year, when the workers killed the European overseer of Phu Rieng, Monteil, the workers who orchestrated it were sentenced to death, two other men received life sentences, and dozens more were beaten within an inch of their lives to give up the names of other comrades. And that's just what the newspapers you and I read in Paris were able to dig out. Off the plantations, after the

TWENTY-TWO

Marcelle

November 2, 1933

I told Sinh's father," said Khoi, who had just returned to Hanoi from Hue.

"I'm so glad he saw you," I said, my anxiety over Khoi's trip subsiding. After our shock that Paul Adrien was in Indochine, Khoi had rightly decided that the first thing we should do was tell the Cao family. We had not had much communication with any of them in the last year. "How did he react?" I asked.

"He's not ready to call the firing squad on Haiphong, that's for certain. He just said, 'That's unfortunate.' I said, 'The man who shot your son is in Haiphong,' and he said those two words: 'That's unfortunate.' I used the word 'killed' instead and he repeated the same phrase."

"Well, it is unfortunate," I replied. "And fortunate."

"Fortunate because maybe we will find some closure. Other than that, what can we do? Murder him?"

"Potentially," I said, not entirely joking. I looked at Khoi's lacquered dining room table, the one that supposedly had blood in it. Far more valuable people had died in Indochine. "Or turn him in to the police," I suggested. "Have someone investigate the details of Sinh's death

Yen Bai mutiny when nationalists and soldiers revolted against the French, thirty-nine men were given death sentences. Trust me, no native man has ever been offered a five-piastre slap on the wrist for murder. Instead, we are guillotined."

"But we have to try something, Khoi," I said, unable to hide my frustration, my disappointment.

"What we have been trying," said Khoi as he paced the length of his living room, "is to help the men on these plantations live slightly better lives. We are carrying on Sinh's legacy without harming anyone except for Michelin. They harmed Sinh, we harm them by slowly taking their business in Indochine out of their hands. We ruin Victor's career and we send him and his helpful little wife back to France, disgraced."

"They don't seem anxious to sail," I said. "I think she had far too much fun on your boat."

"I thought she looked rather green and discouraged when she disembarked."

"We'll see," I said grumpily. "I think you need to remember that that family killed Sinh, Khoi. At the very least, they put him in a position to be killed. Victor included."

"I know, Marcelle. I know," said Khoi, collapsing next to me. "But we can't kill this man, too."

I didn't know that I could *not* kill Paul Adrien. Sitting there with him at the Sun Café in Haiphong, I'd believed that I could. I felt very capable of such a thing.

"I think," said Khoi slowly, "that what I want more than anything is to speak to him. I think I was so desperate to find him because I want to look at him. I want to talk to him. I want to see how he reacts when I mention Cao Sinh. I need to know if he delighted in shooting him or if he was just paid to do it."

"How do you know he would even speak to you? Maybe you're just another useless mite to him. Maybe the name Cao Sinh won't even mean anything to him," I countered.

"Maybe. But maybe not."

I thought of the man I'd drunk a whiskey with. I had no idea what he was and was not capable of. Men at rest were very different from men in the throes of chaos.

"You've never voiced this to me before—why?" I asked Khoi, reaching for a glass bottle of water that was nearby and drinking half of it down.

"Because I knew you wouldn't agree, Marcelle," said Khoi, exhaling loudly. He stood and moved away from me. "But I've realized that Sinh, being the consummate diplomat, the very good man that he was, with not one revengeful bone in his body, this is what he would want from me. He would want me to ask questions. He would want me to ask why."

"I don't agree. I think he would want us to try something official. Through the right channels," I said again, crossing my arms and lying on the couch the way Anne-Marie used to.

"Marcelle, think for a minute," Khoi said, watching me. "You know as well as I do that the French will do nothing. Especially not without Sinh's family involved. 'Who is he to you,' that's what they'll say. He wasn't even your lover. He was a friend. Your native acquaintance, they'll think."

"If Sinh's father would lead the charge . . ." I said, my words fading.

"But he won't, for the umpteenth time, Marcelle!" Khoi shouted. "It is frustrating, but he just won't do anything to jeopardize his position. He is more French, more assimilated, than many French-born. He is far worse than I ever was."

"You were never, despite what Anne-Marie and Sinh used to say to you, *assimilated*."

"Yes, I was! I still am. Don't you see it?" He trained his eyes on me. "Even you, in your way, want things to be wrapped in the same gloss as in France."

"*I* do not want you to be French. I barely want to be French."

"I know you don't want me to physically be French," he said, pensively.

"But the thing of it is, Marcelle," he continued as he paced, "would you be here, in my home, as my lover, if I didn't wear Western clothes? Would you even have spoken to me in Paris if I were wearing an *ao gam* instead of a suit? If I had a long goatee instead of having just had a shave? Or what if my French was heavily accented? Or if I didn't smell the way that is familiar to you, bathed in Acqua di Parma cologne? If I didn't have a Parisian tailor and money? What if I didn't have the kind of wealth that rivals any of the smug Europeans here? Would you still want me then?"

"Yes, I would," I spat out in frustration. "I don't care about your money. You know that. I care about you. And I care about what is fair. What is right. That's what we've been working toward since I first came here, haven't we? Finding justice for Sinh, for Anne-Marie. Trying to turn Michelin into something less terrible, keeping Lua Nguyen Thanh from being pulled away from your family. Khoi, I fell in love with the person that cared about doing these things. Who cared deeply about his family when I met him, and increasingly about his country."

He looked at me, his expression slightly calmer but his eyes full of grief. We had wandered into the backyard, too restless to stay indoors. "Sinh changed me, enormously. But now, I don't know. It feels strange to be pulling all these strings from this perch."

He looked up at his beautiful house, which rivaled a home in Versailles or Neuilly-sur-Seine. It was cream-colored, with rows of tall windows on each of the four floors, wrought iron balconies, and, on the top floor, rounded dormers puncturing the slate mansard roof. It was, by consensus, one of the prettiest homes in the north.

"Khoi, no one forced you into this giant house," I said wearily, turning away.

"I know. Look, I never declared myself a communist," he said. "I don't want to live in a hut and eschew all Western ideals. I still believe in capitalism, to an extent, just not colonialism. But these days, everything is different. After Yen Bai and the Nghe-Tinh uprisings three years ago, your delightful government decimated the communist and nationalist parties. The leadership went into hiding. I do think the communists will be the ones to eventually move us in the right direction. With complications to men like me, but most of the country is not men like me. As for the French," he said, looking at me meaningfully, "they did force me into this house. I would not be allowed to figure so prominently as a member of the chamber of commerce if I wasn't living like this, following their rules of so-called civility. Nor would I be allowed such economic freedom. That's the part I'm hung up on right now, for some reason. It's something you don't seem to understand."

"I'm trying," I said, biting back my annoyance.

"My father," said Khoi, pausing. "He, who thirty years ago managed to take his silk business beyond the borders of Indochine, providing to all of Southeast Asia, has somehow managed to keep the French out of our business. Until last year anyway. And that's in part because he's always done his best to assimilate. He's been breaking his back to be French enough since the day he was born."

"I have met your father many times," I said. "His back is just fine." I saw a servant walking toward us with fresh bottles of water and fell quiet. I had met Khoi's father many times, but I had never met his mother, Tham. I'd only laid eyes on her once. It was the week I'd arrived in Hanoi. I was desperately curious to see the woman who had borne and raised the man I was in love with, so I'd hidden in the shadows near his family's city house, a stately deco home far from the neighborhoods on the east side where the French lived. I saw her emerge just past dusk, dressed in a long, white, beaded gown, evidently heading to somewhere glamorous. No doubt it was a home or club that I would never see, someplace that the moneyed Annamites had managed to keep for themselves.

I could tell even from a distance that she was a beautiful woman, but I didn't want her to *have* to dress a certain way. I was starting to see Khoi's point. Would I have fallen in love with him if he wore traditional clothes, if he hadn't been trying to resemble a university student in Paris?

Khoi pursed his lips as his servant bowed and said, "Would you like to eat lunch outside, Monsieur Khoi?"

"*Non, merci*, Ngoc. We will come in and forage for food later."

She nodded and left, stepping quickly over the manicured grass.

"Even my servants speak French," he said, laughing. "Even though they are all Tonkin-born. How ridiculous is that?"

"Very," I agreed. "But I'm glad you're not yelling at me anymore. Are you convinced yet that I don't want you to powder your hair and sing 'La Marseillaise'?"

"I'm not," he said. "I think you would like that. But I am ready to start formulating a plan about how we confront Paul Adrien. You met him once, can you do it again? Can you somehow invite him here, without saying why?"

"Maybe. If I invite him to something he can't say no to."

"Like a party with a man playing the ukulele, another with a monkey on his shoulder, and a bathtub full of gin?" said Khoi, daring a smile.

"He doesn't deserve such a party. He deserves prison. But a party is a good idea. Yours are legendary. It would also be a very good way for you to finally meet Victor Lesage. It's odd that you still haven't."

"To be frank, I haven't wanted to. Perhaps the anger you hold for Paul Adrien, I hold for Victor. But I need to, so let's change that," said Khoi.

"And as for Paul Adrien, I'll find another way for you to meet him. For both of us to finally have that conversation."

Khoi opened his mouth to respond but closed it as we saw the same servant walking out again.

"There is a phone call for you," she said after she'd bowed in apology.

"I'll come in," Khoi said, starting to stand.

"It's not for you, sir," she said quickly. "It's for Madame de Fabry."

"Who is it, please?" I asked, surprised. No one had ever called me at Khoi's house.

"It is the concierge of the Hôtel Splendide," she said.

"Ah, yes, of course," I said, smiling, knowing immediately who it actually was.

I accompanied her inside, where Lap, the head butler, handed me the telephone. He stood next to me as I said hello.

"Le Chat d'Or. Thirty minutes," a man said and hung up.

"Thank you, that will be all," I replied to dead air.

When I walked back outside, Khoi had moved farther from the house.

"I forgot to tell you, regarding Anne-Marie . . ."

"Yes?" I said, my heart hurting at the sound of her name.

"In an odd twist of fate," said Khoi, "Sinh's father said he might know where she is."

"Oh, I hope so," I said quietly. I kissed Khoi on the cheek, thankful that through everything, even through our differences, we were still knotted around each other.

"Where are you going?" he called as I stood to leave.

"Le Chat d'Or."

"At this hour?"

"I have an errand to run," I said. "The phone call."

"Ah." Khoi nodded. "The money is in my dresser."

I had my chauffeur drop me by the opera house and then, when he was out of sight, climbed into a *pousse-pousse* and told the driver my destination.

Twenty minutes later, we were in the red-light district near Kam Thien Street at a large house known as Le Chat d'Or. Its plaster walls were washed a light pink, and its green wooden shutters were pulled closed. I climbed the stairs to the side entry on the second level and rang the bell. A pretty *indigène* who looked to be in her twenties opened it and told me to follow her up one more level. She left me in a sitting room where a woman in a billowing dress who was old enough to be her mother sat drinking tea, staring out the window. It was not shuttered and had a direct view of the staircase I'd just climbed.

"Where is Red?" I asked her, without bothering to extend a greeting. She looked me up and down and shrugged.

"Hugh Redvers. Red," I repeated. "I'm sure he's a regular here." I reached into my bag and put more piastres than she deserved on the table by her teacup.

"Come," she said, standing. Together, we walked down a window-less hallway and into a much larger room with a dining table where a stark naked Western girl was serving three Frenchmen their lunch. Another one was in a corner with a man and was doing a lot more than serving him lunch. Thankfully I didn't know any of the men, and they didn't look at me strangely, no doubt assuming I was another European whore about to shed her clothes. All the girls at Le Chat d'Or were from Central Europe. If the Frenchmen wanted local flesh, they went elsewhere.

"He's not here," I said to the woman. "Could you point me in the right direction before I become pregnant just by seeing all this?"

We walked back into the hall and turned right. "The women aren't getting pregnant," she said, her voice flat. "They're getting paid."

"I would hope so."

She peered into another room, gesturing for me to do the same. There was only one man inside, and I could tell just by glimpsing his bare bottom that he was not Red. "Listen, I'm not in the mood to see all you have on offer here," I said as we stepped away. "I'm just looking for Red." I reached into my bag and handed her more piastres.

She counted the money and said, "Top floor," before putting it in her dress pocket. She pointed to a staircase. "Best room in the house for Red. Always," she said before walking off.

How unsurprising.

I climbed the stairs to a landing and saw that there were four bed-rooms up there. Only one had the door open. It was the right room.

A thin blond woman, naked except for high-heeled pink leather shoes, was kneeling between Red's parted legs. His white dress shirt was still on, although unbuttoned completely, and he was wearing nothing else. He had one hand on her cheek, the other holding a cig-arette, and he was muttering something inaudible to her.

"Is this what you wanted me to observe?" I said loudly, taking a few steps into the room. "I've seen better."

"I don't doubt that you have," he said, smirking at me. He was definitely the kind of man who practiced that half smile in the mirror. "Cigarette?" he offered.

"I'll pass," I replied, keeping my eyes above his neck.

The girl who was hard at work pleasuring him paused, pulled her mouth off his erect penis, and looked at me, her lipstick slightly smeared, her irritation apparent.

"Don't pay attention to her, Katya. She's not staying long," said Red. "Unless she wants to join in?"

"She doesn't," I said, reaching into the bag hanging from the crook of my arm. I took out a bundle of piastres, which were wrapped in a thin piece of rice paper and tied with one of the Nguyens' green silk ribbons. I held it toward Red. "Would you like it, or shall I give it directly to her?"

"On the bed is fine," he said, motioning with his head.

"Done," I said, walking over and leaving it on the black cotton coverlet, careful not to touch the fabric.

"She went to the plantation, didn't she?" he said before letting out a low moan. The girl was back to work.

"Yes, she did." Pham Dat, the Hanoi stationmaster, had notified me when Jessie Lesage bought tickets all the way down to Saigon just days ago. I hadn't yet been notified of her return.

"And did she see anything shocking? Something that would make her abandon her loyalty to her husband and his unscrupulous family? Is she brandishing the red flag around town?"

"I don't know yet," I said honestly. It had been my idea to get Jessie to the plantations. One last attempt to let her prove she had a conscience. Perhaps if she experienced it firsthand, she would feel differently; she would see something that she couldn't write off as just furthering the family company. A beating by an overseer. A worker marked with scars from repeated caning. Something. I planned on probing the next time I saw her. If she was still singing the praises of capitalism, I'd know that she hadn't or, worse, that she had and just didn't care.

"I doubt she did," said Red. "I'm sure Victor hid all the misery away. But I do appreciate the money. Let me know what other asinine tasks I can do for you that pay this well. I'm open to—"

He stopped speaking, let out another groan, and placed his hand on the girl's face.

I headed for the door. "Don't make me come here again." It had probably been stupid to give Jessie one more chance. But she was a woman; a small part of me was still hoping she'd prove me wrong.

"Oh, it's not so bad, is it?" he replied, his tone urging me to look at him. I did. He put out his cigarette, then leaned forward and rubbed his hands over the girl's back and down over her large, hanging breasts. "Lovely," he said. "I'm sure you'd enjoy them, too, Marcelle. How did the newspaper describe a night here again? As a 'Sardanapalesque orgy,' I think it was."

I rolled my eyes and tried to ignore what was happening between his thighs, where that poor girl's head was bobbing faster. "How you haven't died of venereal disease yet is beyond me."

"The big boy's immune," he said, looking down at his erection.

"So long, Red," I said, stepping into the hall.

"So long, Marcelle. We'll always have Paris!" he called after me.

I froze, then turned on my heel and marched back into the room. "We never had Paris," I hissed.

"But we did," he said, all humor gone from his expression. "I had you in Paris, Marcelle de Fabry. Many, many times, I had you. They really don't make them any prettier than you, do they? I still remember every inch of that gorgeous body. I could probably draw a map of your freckles if I had enough to drink."

"As I said, I'm never coming here again," I said, feeling sick to my stomach.

"Marcelle," he said, his expression softening.

"What."

"One day, they'll be free," he said, nodding his head to the window, to the life on the street. "But until then, we might as well enjoy ourselves."

I slammed the door behind me and flew down two flights of stairs. As I navigated the iron steps outside, I passed a Frenchman who said something leeringly in Russian.

"I'm not a *valaque*," I barked, using the word the Frenchmen threw around for the white whores in Indochine. "So try to keep your zipper up."

I hurried down the street, crowded with locals, and found the same *pousse-pousse* driver I'd just had, all too happy to earn another fare. Red had maneuvered Jessie to the plantation, as I'd wanted. And I knew he'd done more than just that. Feel free to shake her, I'd said. I knew how well Red could shake. But now I wished I'd used someone other than him to do so. I'd only chosen him because he had a handsome face and no moral scruples and thus was perfect for such tasks.

Of course, he had to bring up Paris. I should have snatched the money right then and there.

Paris.

It was late January 1924, when I was only nineteen, and during an unusually warm winter. I'd been modeling in the Patou salon, a special presentation for our best clients, and Red had been there as a guest of a rich married woman he was sleeping with. But two days later, he was sleeping with me instead. We'd had a wild two-week love affair, but then he left for London, followed by Burma, and I never heard from him again. I realized what he really was when I started hearing stories about him in Burma. Years later, I heard that he'd made his way to Indochine. He would not be avoidable, that much I knew, but what I needed him to be was silent. I did not keep much from Khoi, but that, I would always have to.

TWENTY-THREE

Jessie

November 3, 1933

T hank you again for your kindness," I said smoothly to Jacques,
the Dau Tieng overseer, as he saw me to my seat on the train
back north. "Victor is lucky to have you working for him," I
added, trying to sound genuine.

I knew I had to smile at Jacques. I had to be the polite woman,
Victor's perfect, helpful wife. But I was shattered. I had no idea how
to be that woman anymore. My mind didn't feel connected to my body
at all. They were two separate entities, somehow traveling together.

"Innocent men used to die on these plantations in very high numbers, due to disease or negligent overseers," Victor had said during the
days I'd been with him. "I'm trying my best to see that that happens
much less. But men who are trying to incite revolution, especially violent revolution, we can't stand for that. We can't have a repeat of 1927
or 1930."

"Or 1932," I'd added.

"Exactly." He'd nodded as we walked up the stairs of the Phu Rieng
plantation manager's house for cocktails, both of us dressed like we
were dining at the Officers' Club instead.

"I'm the lucky one," Jacques said before he stepped off the train, moving aside for a passenger, a young man, who was climbing on. "I hope to work with the company, and your husband, for many years more," he said, smiling as he waved good-bye.

The train rumbled out of the station, and I sighed with relief, glad I would never have to see Dau Tieng or Phu Rieng again. I knew I could never go back.

I had been at the plantations for a week, keeping Victor company at night and spending my days mostly with the wives of the French overseers and managers. I was allowed a full tour of Dau Tieng and Phu Rieng only when accompanied by Victor. I'd fought my way through it all. But inside, I was completely empty—a hole where my heart used to be.

I had left a room of men in the stages of death with a smile on my face. Why? Because I believed that men ready to incite a communist revolution on the plantation deserved to be punished? I did believe that. I did. I had grown up poor; I knew that stripping away the dream of upward mobility, of future opportunities, did not work. Communism was a lovely-sounding concept that made no real-world sense. People needed to be able to better themselves if they were willing to try. To fight for a superior life. It was what I had done, always. So I agreed with Victor in theory, but did that mean handing down death sentences to those who believed differently? Who felt that communism offered a vehicle for freedom and a better future, one without colonial power? They were wrong, and their beliefs were dangerous. I knew that. Victor knew that. But did it mean that a man's life should be extinguished? Were we so committed to the success of Michelin that we would just lock men with communist leanings in a room until they breathed their last breaths? Could we really do that and be at peace with our own souls?

I thought of the woman I was when I first met Victor. I had used all my wits and resources to get to Paris, to bend my world in the exact right shape to fit into his. Where was that fiercely determined woman now? If I had witnessed something like that scene then, even though I was trying to be the perfect woman for Victor, I would have fought to convince him to act otherwise. I had a fire in me then and I would not have left that fetid death chamber with a placid smile on my face. But now?

I was his wife. I had asked him to leave Paris, his home, for my own selfish reasons. I was the mother of his child, whom he provided an exquisite life for. Everything I had asked Victor for over the years, he had given me, without question. And I had my siblings to think about. I still had to provide for them, too. I had to continue in this life I'd built. And so I had smiled.

Three hours later, I forced myself to eat a lunch of roast duck and potatoes in the dining car. I kept my head in a book, hoping no one would join me, so even the staff wouldn't speak to me. I ate and drank, but nothing had any flavor. It all tasted like dirt.

When I had stuffed myself, I threw some money on the table and stood uneasily, having finished four glasses of wine rather quickly. I felt the eyes of the staff on me and hurried out of the car before they offered to escort me back.

I walked through several wagons. I had one more to go until the first-class car. I pulled the door open quickly and was about to reach for the next one, but a sudden gust of wind rushed in and nearly knocked me down. I grabbed for the metal handles soldered onto the wall, meant to help with balance, and tried to find my footing again. When I regained it, I was staring out at a sliver of lush green countryside visible between the train cars.

What if we hadn't come to Indochine? What if I hadn't pushed Victor to invent a new post, all because one simple woman from Virginia had made her way to Paris, found me, and threatened to tell Victor everything I had not dared to all these years? If I hadn't let my fear control me, would those men have lived, or were they marked for death no matter what? Would the plantation manager have figured out their plan, too? Would he have killed them in the same vicious manner? Would the police, if I'd reported it to them? Or would they have sent them to a political prison where they would have met the same fate, or worse? I thought of the way Victor was with Lucie, the loving, doting father. How could that be the same man?

I gulped in the fresh air until I felt I was choking, sure that I could smell the scent of dying men. Ly Duc Khai was still with me, all of them were, and I was suddenly quite sure they'd never leave. I already knew the way nightmares became trapped inside a person. I was sure it was happening to me again.

I leaned forward toward the sunshine. I was not a large person. I could easily fall right off the small platform between the train cars. I looked at my right hand clutching the metal handle. My ringless hand. I let my fingers start slipping off, one by one, and when I let the final one go, my body lurched forward, I felt my face hit the metal door, then my torso, and then I felt a hand grab me.

"*Attention!*" I heard a man scream. He pulled me back with such force that we both hit the door I had just exited, on the other side of the small metal walkway.

"*Madame!* You nearly fell down!" he exclaimed. I turned and looked at him. It was one of the conductors, an Annamite man, perhaps in his forties, in a navy-blue uniform. "You could have fallen from the train. Are you all right? You must be careful here. It can be very dangerous," he said, leading me inside the next train car.

"Yes, thank you, I'm okay," I said, trying to collect myself. I stood upright, stepping back from him. I had nearly fallen out of the train.

"I'm very sorry," I mumbled. "I just had a bit too much to drink at lunch. I'm very embarrassed." I reached into my bag for some money.

"There's no need for that," he said, holding up his hands. "I'm glad I arrived in time."

"Please," I said, taking money out anyway. "I insist. You were so kind to help me. I don't know what would have happened if you hadn't been there."

He looked at me a moment. We both knew exactly what would have happened.

The conductor shook his head again and pointed to my bag.

"Please, you can put it back. I'm just happy I reached you. I'm glad you're still here with us."

If only he knew how little I deserved to be still there.

I slept for the rest of the journey to Nha Trang, and when I reached the station, the same chauffeur picked me up. This time, I was very glad for his silence.

"I need to make a stop before we get to the hotel," I said, the speed of my voice matching my racing heart. "I had a very arduous journey, and I need to calm my nerves. I need some help in doing so. I need to take something. I need to rest, I need help . . ."

"Opium will help, *madame*," he said, kindly interrupting my frantic talk so I didn't have to say it. "I know a local place near Qui Nhon that is very good. Everyone there will leave you in peace. And the opium they have is quite strong. It will help you rest awhile. I can see from your eyes that you need it."

I nodded, sure that my eyes were red and swollen. "That's just what I need, thank you for suggesting it," I said, rolling down the window, trying to lose myself in the country I'd been so desperate to come to.

The chauffeur was right. Everyone left me alone at the den in Qui Nhon. This time, I didn't hesitate at all when the girl brought the opium pipe to my lips. I inhaled and didn't stop breathing in deeply and exhaling out slowly until I felt my body drift away. When I woke up, I was in the hotel. I didn't remember getting there, but I was very happy that I was.

I stood up, took a bath, and then looked at my naked body in the mirror. Even that didn't look like mine. I was too thin and too bronzed. But I had to find a piece of myself or I would never make it home to Hanoi. When I had enough strength, I would tell Victor that seeing those men had marked me. Sickened me and made me deeply hate myself for doing nothing. I'd clawed through continents to create this life. But I couldn't keep living in it if I didn't say something.

A day later, I was back in Hanoi and felt a wash of relief when I saw the station. I felt that I'd been away for months instead of just twelve days.

Victor had sent a telegram to the house to say I would arrive the morning of November 6 so that Lanh could be waiting for me.

I was almost outside the station when I remembered the poster I'd seen on my journey out depicting the house of a hundred suns. I returned to the ticket counter, but it was no longer hanging by the timetables.

When I reached the wall where I'd seen it, I touched it but felt no pinholes. Perhaps it had been attached with adhesive. I badly wanted to give Lanh the poster, to show him that the government was still trying to enchant children and travelers with visions of the suns shining down on them. I needed to do something kind for someone.

I stopped a porter and asked for the stationmaster, but he shrugged. I waited five more minutes, keeping my eyes on the front door, where I knew he often escorted rich French travelers in, but there was no sign of him.

"Does *madame* need assistance?" a man behind the ticket counter asked, craning his neck to see me better. His hair was parted and slicked, and like all the other men, he was dressed in a dark uniform.

"Yes, I do," I said. "When I took the train to Tourane twelve days ago, there was a poster on the wall here." I pointed to my left. "It was an advertisement for train travel, showing a station with a big sun over it. I would like that poster. I will buy it, of course. If you have a moment, could you find it for me? And is twenty piastres enough?"

I reached into my bag, moving my hand through it quickly, searching for my money.

"Which poster was it, *madame*?" the man nearest to me asked, looking confused.

"It was an advertisement," I repeated. "An Indochine Railways advertisement. Just as I said, it was a print of a train station, with a sun above it, and the text read, '*Pour aller loin, pour payer moins, pour être bien, prenez le train.*'"

The man who had first spoken to me left his counter and came over to look at the wall where I was pointing.

"No, *madame*, I'm sorry. I don't remember it," he said, staring at the white wall, where only timetables were tacked up now.

He called out something in Annamese to the other ticket vendors, and they all shook their heads no, replying to him in their many tones.

"They don't know it, either," the man said. "There is never anything else hanging here. Only the train timetables."

I looked at the wall, stark white, unmarked, but the poster was so vivid in my mind I could have traced exactly where it was hanging. I was sure it had been there.

"I see. I apologize for taking up your time," I muttered, shuffling quickly away.

They were wrong—of course they were. They had to be. I ran out of the station, searching for Lanh, wanting nothing more than to hide with Lucie in the big yellow house.

TWENTY-FOUR

Marcelle

November 13, 1933

B e careful!" I exclaimed. I was used to the chaos of Dong Xuan market on the rue du Riz, but someone behind me had just slammed hard into my shoulder, making me stumble into a vegetable seller's wares. Pulling myself up from a pile of Chinese cabbages, I saw the shock in the vendor's eyes, only partly visible under her conical straw hat, and began to apologize, but I stopped when I heard a male voice also apologizing.

"I'm terribly sorry," the man said. "I don't know what happened." He turned to me. "Are you all right?" he asked as he held out his hand.

"You must be careful! Look what I've—" I exclaimed, then abruptly fell silent when I saw his face. It was Pham Dat, the stationmaster.

"Yes, yes, I'm fine," I said. "No apology needed. It can get so crowded here."

He nodded, still holding my hand. He was wearing a casual shirt and trousers, not his usual white uniform. He squeezed my hand tightly, and I felt him press a small piece of paper into my palm. I pulled my hand away discreetly, tucking it into my right trouser pocket.

"Let me pay this woman for the damage I caused," Dat said, indicating the vendor.

"There's no need," I said, pasting a polite smile on my face. "I will buy her produce. But it's kind of you to offer."

He nodded and walked quickly away. I had not thought that of all the people we paid off that Pham Dat would prove to be the most useful, but of late, he was worth far more than the fifty piastres we gave him at the start of each month.

I purchased all the vegetables the woman had spread out, stuffing them into my straw bag and a bundle of cloth she gave me. Then I toted them to the far end of the market, where beggars were waiting for the day to end so they could salvage the food that had been trampled or had spoiled in the sun. I dropped my vegetables with a woman cradling a young boy, slipping some piastres into her fist as well.

"Eighty," I whispered. "Don't let them steal from you."

Free of the heavy load, I hurried to the east side of the market, past the streetcar that ran through the middle of it, past coconut vendors with bright strips of blue and red cloth tied around their foreheads, toward a dozen young men wearing white sarongs. They were carrying boxes of live animals. I followed them to the cluster of meat sellers who came en masse on Sundays, past their rows of butchered and live animals to a man who was roasting a whole pig on a spit. The animal's mouth was wide open as if still in shock from its untimely death. The flames had seared half the poor beast and were burning brightly, the edges tinged blue as a crisp fall breeze fanned them. The market was not devoid of French women—some of us liked to shop this way, among the locals—but I still stood out from the crowd. Trying to look as inconspicuous as possible, I stood near the people observing the fire, many of them children, and took out Dat's note.

"Paul Adrien, the police officer, came in on the nine o'clock train," it read. I scanned it again, then crumpled it in my hand, my nails nearly puncturing my skin before I let my muscles relax. I walked past the fire and dropped the small piece of paper in the flames, watching it turn to ash. Paul was in Hanoi now. Khoi had said he wanted to speak to him. To see what his eyes looked like when he mentioned

Sinh. With the lure of a romantic engagement, and through a series of messengers, I had pulled Paul here.

Back at the perimeter of the market, my chauffeur was waiting. "The Aéro-club, please," I said. I saw him hesitate a moment before he started the engine and pulled out into the street without a word. Membership in the Aéro-club was restricted to men, but I couldn't let another moment pass before I told Khoi the news.

We pulled up to the handsome colonial-style building where men of Khoi's position met to discuss their passion for flying machines, and I searched for Khoi's black Bugatti.

"Circle around," I directed my driver. It took four trips through the neighborhood, but I finally spotted the Bugatti on a narrow street, nearly hidden behind a delivery truck.

"Pull up alongside, please," I said, lowering my window. Khoi's driver, Trung, recognizing my car, lowered his as well.

"I'm not feeling well," I told him. "I need Monsieur Khoi to return home. At once."

"*Oui, madame,*" he said, quickly opening his door.

We sped off, passing the adjacent French Aéro-club, a space where white men met to talk about exactly the same things as the locals—just not with them.

Thirty minutes later, we were at Khoi's house. I ignored the servants and headed straight to his bedroom, where I undressed, put on a silk dressing gown over my slip, and climbed between the covers.

Khoi would be worried about me, but that would make him move more quickly.

I shifted onto my left side and fluffed one of the green-silk-covered pillows. Above Khoi's zebrawood dresser hung a family portrait. It wasn't a formal gathering, just a group of Nguyens on a sojourn on one of the family's junks, but it was his favorite picture of all of them together, and mine, too. They were all dressed immaculately, in the slimmer silhouettes of the twenties, with their backs to the water. No land was visible behind them, no natural landmarks, nothing but the boat's railing separating them from the South China Sea. I liked it because it showed the Nguyens looking as if they still owned Indochine, despite the French overlordship. At least the water was still theirs, they seemed to say. *That* could never be taken away.

Luckily, the family was finally starting to understand that everything besides the water could be ripped out of their hands. Silk was not like rubber. It did not take years of investment and planting. It took dedicated wealth, which the French had not put into it until now, and experts on harvesting and spinning, whom they were finally hiring. It was time to panic.

Nothing could move slowly anymore, Khoi had stressed to his father, who had finally changed his mind about their business approach, who was finally giving his blessing as Khoi diversified their investments. His decades of obeisance to the French were starting to waver. He, it turned out, was not a perfect colonial-made copy of Sinh's father.

I was on Khoi's bed when I heard the door open. I looked up expectantly and saw him enter, appearing not the least bit concerned.

"Dying, are you?" he said, strolling over to his dresser. He placed his hat on it, right by the ukulele, then took his jacket off, hanging it neatly on the back of a chair on the other side of the room.

"Maybe," I said, motioning for him to close the door.

He walked over, then collapsed next to me. "You aren't. If you were, you would have just stormed the club, men be damned. I know you."

I smiled, because of course it was true.

"What is it, then?" he said loudly.

I cupped my hand over his ear. "Paul Adrien came up on the morning train. He's *here*. Paul is here."

"I don't want to know how you arranged it, do I?"

"You don't," I said, remembering Caroline's line at the club about the sexual arts. I had used a rather similar line in my note that I'd had delivered to Paul. I needed to do something to ensure his arrival.

"Then he needs to be here. When can you get him here?"

"I don't know," I said, having had no plan past getting Paul to Hanoi. "But I will. Soon."

TWENTY-FIVE

Jessie

November 14, 1933

I sat rigidly on the couch in my living room and picked up the black handle of our brass telephone with a shaky hand. I put my finger in the dial, pushed it in a slow circle, and placed my request with the *dame téléphoniste*. Two minutes later, I heard his voice on the phone.

"Red here," he said sleepily.

"Red," I echoed, caught off guard by the fact that he'd answered his own telephone. The French simply didn't do that. "This is Jessie Lesage," I said.

"I know," he replied. I could practically hear his smile. "The girl said as much. Nice of you to telephone me."

"I'd like to see you," I said, trying to make my voice sound easy, like his was. "Would you be able to meet me this afternoon for a bit?"

"Certainly," he said, without even a trace of surprise. "My place isn't too far from that row of palaces where you live. I'm on le rue Jacquin, across the lake. Why don't you have your driver deposit you here? I'll keep the bed warm."

"No," I said quickly. "How about La Taverne Royale?" It was one of the city's most popular bars.

"Not my style, *chérie*," he replied, yawning loudly. "Meet me at the hippodrome at four o'clock. There's a horse I'm going to bet on. You can be my good-luck charm."

Seven hours later, the Delahaye headed to the west side of the city. We roared past the narrow, closely packed streets where the locals lived, over the train tracks and toward the open spaces that began on the route du Champ de Course. After a bumpy twenty-minute drive, we turned sharply left and began to slow down. I rolled down my window for a better look. I could hear music playing faintly as the two-story pavilion where I was supposed to meet Red came into view. There were a few tented areas to the side of it, and in front was the racetrack, nothing more than cleared grass trimmed into an oval and surrounded by white wood-and-concrete barriers to keep the horses on course.

Lanh helped me out of the car, and I spotted Red in front of the pavilion, leaning against a slender column.

Feeling unsteady on my feet, I thanked Lanh and went up to Red, who kissed my cheeks familiarly.

"I didn't know there was horse racing here," I said, nodding at the track.

"There's everything here," he said, a half smile on his face. "Look up," he directed, pointing to the pavilion's second story. Dozens of Indochinese men were crowded together up there, facing the track.

"Want to join them? Live how the real people live?" he asked.

"You do not live how the real people live," I replied.

"Quite right," he said, laughing. "Come, let's sit here, in the shade."

We sat on the first level, our seats shielded from the sun by the roof's deep eaves.

"The racing is better in Saigon," said Red. "It's right at Le Cercle Sportif. But there's one horse here today, Midnight Blue, who is supposed to be a different sort of species. Part horse, part airplane."

He pulled a sheet of paper out of his pocket, and I watched him study the odds for each race. A job as a railroad man would be a perfect cover, Victor had said. I looked at Red, his shirt collar wide open, a worn wool blazer draped lazily over his shoulders. *Cover*, I scoffed. Red could barely cover his chest.

I wanted to ask him if he knew about those men at Dau Tieng. If he had wanted me to see them, wanted it to affect me. To hurt me. But first, I had to address what had happened on the boat.

"I'm mortified about Ha Long Bay," I said before the first race started, launching the conversation I'd been dreading for weeks. "Can we forget about it? And keep the details between us? I can't believe I allowed that to happen. It was completely out of character for me, if you can't already tell."

"You're going to have to adapt to this place one day, Jessie," he said, pointing to the horses being brought to the starting line by their jockeys. "*Chandoo* is a way of life. People aren't embarrassed by it here. It's as natural as smoking tobacco, although so much more enjoyable. In fact, your government would like you to keep smoking opium so they can profit off your future addiction."

"Red," I said, watching his horse, Midnight Blue, who did almost look blue, trot elegantly to the starting line. "That's not what I'm talking about."

"The Pegu cocktails, then?" he said, his attention elsewhere. "Look at that magnificent animal," he said. "I should have bet more money."

"Red, please," I said, my fears multiplying again. "Let's just have this conversation so that we can get back to normal." What would it take for me to feel normal again?

"Did I get you hooked?" he asked, still not looking at me.

"Red. I don't give a damn about your cocktails. What I'm talking about is the kiss."

"Whom did you kiss?" he asked, eyeing me mischievously.

"You! I kissed you," I said loudly. "*We* kissed."

"Jessie," he said, leaning away, just as the race began. "What are you talking about?"

"Our kiss," I said, louder than I meant to. "Our many kisses."

"We did not kiss." He placed his index finger on my lips for a few seconds, then removed it. "We have unfortunately never kissed. I know I was flirting with you, but it was all in fun. I am quite aware that you're married. I've made some foolish decisions during my time here, but I'm not that stupid. I'm not going to seduce some Michelin's wife."

"Stop being like this," I said angrily, my stomach queasy.

"Like what? Jessie, you and I never kissed," he said, vehemently now, his eyes locked on mine even as the horses leapt forward at the crack of the starting pistol.

"Yes, we did," I said, on the verge of shouting at him.

"Jessie," he said, putting his hand on mine. "If you think we kissed while we were indulging in a little tar, it must have been a lucid dream—which I've been told happens. But in real life, it did not."

"It did," I hissed. "It did."

Red jumped to his feet and cupped his hand over his mouth. "Run, you magnificent animal, run!" he yelled as Midnight Blue headed into the home stretch.

I held my breath as the pounding of the horses racing past us made our seats vibrate. I didn't exhale until they crossed the finish line. Midnight Blue came in second.

"Miserable idiot of a horse," said Red, kicking the empty seat in front of him. "I hope he's fed to the dogs later."

I stared at him silently.

"Jessie." His eyes had lost their usual gaiety, his mouth, which was barely holding his cigarette, turned down. "We didn't kiss. We most assuredly didn't. I'm sorry if you're remembering things differently, but I'm certain."

I was dangerously close to tears. "You kissed me, and then you insisted that I go to Dau Tieng. To visit Victor. And to see *them*, too. The dying communists. If you knew what was happening, why didn't you intervene? Call the police yourself instead of sending me?"

"What?" said Red. "I don't remember that, either. Who are 'the dying communists'?"

I didn't answer.

He looked back at his paper, then finally glanced at me again. "Haven't you been to the plantations anyway?"

"Yes," I said quietly. "Now I have."

I looked down at my hands, Red's eyes following mine.

"You haven't had your ring fixed yet," he said, touching my right hand with his. I pulled it away sharply. I knew that touch.

"The ring is irreparable," I said quietly.

The next group of horses was being walked toward the line, and I watched as the jockeys fought to rein in their energy until the critical moment.

"I should be off," I said, looking at Red. "I'm sorry to have bothered you."

"You're not a bother," he said, with a grin. I looked at his face, the curve of his lips. They were so familiar to me. He had to be lying.

"So long, Michelin," he said as I gathered my bag and stood up. "Don't worry, you'll soon get the hang of this place. Maybe opium just isn't the drug for you."

I ran out of the building, ready to fling open the car door, but Lanh saw me coming and opened it first.

I crawled in and started to weep into my palms.

"Are you all right? Is there anything I can do to help?" Lanh asked, turning around to look at me.

I shook my head no, my face getting wet.

"Shall I take you to a doctor, *madame*?"

"Please, no," I said, shaking my head again and pawing at my waistband, trying to find the bag with the shards of my ring in it. "I just want to go home."

I thought of my experiences these past few months in Indochine. The nerve-racking day at the café. Marcelle repeating that awful word. Kissing Red. Smoking tobacco, which I'd managed to avoid even while growing up on a tobacco farm, and then opium, even going to a den on my own. Seeing the caked blood on the back of the dead communist's head. Staring at the men shackled together at Dau Tieng, breathing in the nauseating scent of death. I thought I'd be able to handle anything, to be the helpmate Victor needed in this utterly foreign place. But I was failing. That was obvious to me now. I just couldn't allow it to become obvious to him. He'd think I wasn't being supportive, that I didn't care enough about his career. Maybe he'd think my nerves had gotten the better of me and bring me back to Europe. I imagined a stint in the institution in Switzerland, then back to Paris, where Dorothy would surely tell him my secrets with glee. Victor would never be allowed to manage any aspect of Clermont-Ferrand. And he'd try his best to divorce his crazy wife and keep Lucie away from me.

Overwhelmed again, I cried until I had no tears left. When I looked up, I realized that Lanh was driving us around in circles instead of taking me home. After I'd finally quieted myself, I told him I was ready to go.

It wasn't until our house was in view, our sunny home, that I spoke again. "Lanh," I asked, "do you remember those posters you were describing to me when I was on my way to Haiphong? The ones advertising train travel and the one hundred stations?"

"Yes, of course," he said, brightening.

"I know you saw them when you were a child, but have you seen any since? Around town or in the rail stations. Anywhere?"

"No, I haven't," he said after a short pause. "I don't think I've seen one in fifteen years."

I nodded again. Those men were wrong. Lanh had to be wrong, too. "Lanh," I said. "Please keep this episode between us. I don't want Monsieur Lesage to know. About anything."

"Of course, *madame*," he said, catching my eye in the rearview mirror. "Nothing that happens to you, in this car or out of it, is ever mentioned to Monsieur Lesage."

When we pulled up to the house, Lanh helped me out of the back seat. I leaned against him as we made our way up the slate walkway.

I needed to disappear for a few days. I needed my mind to go blank. But first, I needed my child.

"I would like to see Lucie," I whispered as we reached the door. "She'll make me feel better," I said, imagining the warmth of her hand in mine.

"Of course," he said as Trieu opened the door for us.

I tried to straighten when we walked in the foyer, to not make a spectacle in front of Trieu, but Lanh didn't let me.

"Allow me to help you upstairs," he said. "Then you can relax."

"Lucie," I whispered, looking in Trieu's direction.

"Madame Lesage would like her daughter brought to her room," said Lanh loudly as he helped me up the stairs.

"Miss Lucie is not home," said Trieu, looking at me with concern. "She walked to the lake with a friend after school to sail their toy boats. Cam is with her."

I looked at Trieu and then Lanh again and started to sob. Everything that I counted on to make me feel better was disappearing.

"Please," said Lanh, holding my arm tighter. "Bring Madame Lesage a glass of water. And hot tea. Very hot. And something to eat. Quickly," he added as he helped me upstairs.

When we got to the bedroom, he let my arm go and I shuffled inside my closet. I took off my clothes and then came out in my robe and slipped between the covers. I could feel Lanh's presence. He was outside the door, waiting for me to tell him I was fine, but I felt as if I might never be able to say those words again.

TWENTY-SIX

Marcelle

November 15, 1933

I t's very strange for me to hear that," Paul Adrien said, looking at me from across the small café table that I'd brought him to near the main gate of the Temple of Literature, the city's prettiest Confucian temple.

"I imagine it is," I said after I'd finished explaining to him that I had brought him to Hanoi under false pretenses.

"Because your letter was very . . . explicit."

"Yes, it was. But I had to make sure you came. And I thought perhaps something explicit might do the trick."

"It did," he said, leaning closer to me. "But that is not what you have in mind?"

"It is not," I replied sharply. "I'm afraid I deceived you."

"Well, even clothed, you're very pretty to look at," he said, moving his tall frame back in the metal chair. "Am I right in thinking that you and I only met that one time, yes? In Haiphong at the café. There was whiskey."

"That's right," I repeated. "And yes, there was much whiskey."

"But then you had a letter delivered to me. You said you wanted to see me. You paid for my journey here."

"I did."

"Because you have thought about me, nearly every day, for the last four years," he said, quoting the letter.

"That's right," I replied. Now that I had cleared up my false promises of a sexual relationship, I was enjoying his bewilderment.

"But you haven't known me for four years?" he asked.

"I have, in a sense," I said, looking at him. I had thought about this moment so many times, but now the words felt heavy on my tongue. "I've thought of you because you are the man who shot my friend Cao Sinh in the back. You are the man that killed him." I noticed Paul Adrien stop moving, his spine bent, his hands suddenly still. He knew who Sinh was. "What kind of man shoots an innocent person from behind? I wondered. Does a police officer in Indochine, especially one who works for the secret police, have a different type of mind than the rest of us? Is he just capable of more cruelty? And what kind of man can live with himself after doing that? What kind of man is Paul Adrien? That's what I've been thinking of for the last four years."

"I see," Paul said, closing his eyes for a moment. "If that's the case," he noted quietly, "then you have thought about me every day since the thirtieth of April 1929."

"That's right. As has he," I said, looking to my left. I stood up and gestured to Khoi to approach us. He had been sitting across the park, waiting for my indication.

I'd needed to be alone when Paul came since he was only expecting me. We could not do anything that would make him change his mind, to refuse to join me.

"Who is that?" Paul said, suddenly alert, as he watched Khoi walk over to us.

"That is Nguyen Khoi," I said.

"Sinh's family?" Paul asked.

"Yes," I replied without hesitation. "His brother."

When Khoi was next to us, Paul put out his hand in greeting, but Khoi just bowed his head and sat down. It was the first time I had ever seen Khoi let emotion reign over politesse.

"You'll talk, I'll listen," said Khoi. "And then if I think you merit it, I'll talk, and you'll listen, so you can get to know the man you killed."

"Yes . . . if that's what—"

"I need to know, in every detail, what happened on the last day of Sinh's life," Khoi said. "Perhaps that will help to stop the bleeding of our hearts."

"Or perhaps it will make it worse," I added. But to my surprise, I realized this was what I wanted, too. I needed to know as much as Khoi did.

"This may not make any sense, or any difference," Paul said after we were all quiet for a moment, "but I have thought of your brother Sinh every day since he died. Since I killed him. If there was one thing that I could change in my life, it would be that day. It would be that decision to pull the trigger."

Khoi looked my way and locked eyes with me for a moment, a small acknowledgment between us, that this man, as Khoi had guessed, was merely the executioner, not the one who decided the death sentence. That had been the Michelins.

"But why, then? Why would you do such a thing? Did he attack someone like we were told? It's just not possible," I said. "The investigation indicated that he had, that you shot him because of his aggression, but Sinh, he did not have aggression in him."

Paul nodded his head, but I couldn't tell if he was doing it out of respect or agreement. "After Monsieur Sinh was arrested," Paul said, moving his hands nervously on the table, "which happened as soon as he came off the boat, after his trunks and suitcases were inspected, he was detained in a holding cell alone for several hours, with me watching guard. Nothing went wrong then. He was very quiet. He sat on the ground, he tried to sleep. He was tired, frustrated perhaps, but not angry. But when he was released—and I only know this because I escorted him from the holding cell to an office—he was informed by my superior that the French government had banned him from ever returning to France because he was now accused of spreading communist

thought. And, they noted, his French 'friend' was never allowed to come to the colony. That friend was a woman, I imagined."

"Banned from ever seeing each other," I said quietly. "We were told that, too."

"It is not uncommon for political prisoners to be banned from returning to France," said Paul. "I saw it happen many times, for less than what your brother had done."

"But no one really cared about his political leanings," Khoi said quietly. "Not enough to grant that fate. What they cared about was that the man in question, Cao Sinh, was sleeping with a daughter of the Michelin family. *Un homme Asiatique*, a rich French girl, and a family reputation coupled with extreme racism—those were his crimes."

"I didn't know that," said Paul, his jaw tightening. "I didn't know that she was part of the Michelin family. The girl they banned from Indochine."

"And now you do," I said angrily. "Did you think it was just a lovely twist of fate that you were given this comfortable post by the Michelins? What they're doing is rewarding you for killing someone."

"I did think it was fate, yes," said Paul. "But I see that I was wrong."

"Where else did you go wrong?" asked Khoi, his voice rising. "Where else did you slip? Was killing Sinh an order or an accident?"

"It wasn't an accident," said Paul. "It was an order. But it was the wrong order. My superior, a man named Desroches, he was the one who told Cao Sinh that he could never go back to France. And that the girl could never come to the colony. After he spat those words, your brother lunged at him. He did, I suppose, attack him. But he was unarmed. And he was a smaller man. We could easily have pulled him off of Desroches, I see that now. But at the time, Desroches panicked. He ordered me to shoot. He screamed. He . . . he insisted. So I did. I shot. I had no intention of killing your brother. I don't think I even wanted to shoot him. It just all happened so quickly. But it came down to a young man, an ignorant young man, me, following an order. I regret it terribly. As I said, I have thought of your brother every day.

His death—or perhaps it would be less selfish to say my action, yes, my action—caused me to lose myself completely. I had trouble keeping a job in France. I was arrested for public drunkenness. For disorderly conduct. My wife left me."

"But then Michelin saved you," I said, feeling no sympathy for Paul Adrien, but perhaps less hatred.

"A colleague of mine, one who had been in the room the day your brother died, he knew what kind of shape I was in," said Paul, his hands moving again, nervously. "I didn't know it at the time, but I suppose it's clear now that he appealed to the Michelins and helped me here."

"How simple it all is. How simple they can make it," I spat out. "What you're earning here is blood money. It's because you saved the family from further embarrassment. You killed the yellow pest."

Paul paused and looked at Khoi, bowing his head apologetically. "I'm very sorry for what I did. I don't want any sort of payment for it from Michelin, that I'm certain of, so mine will be a short stay in the colony," he replied. "Very short."

I stood up, to let Khoi finish his conversation. I no longer wanted this man in front of me.

"You may be repentant now," I said, "but you are guilty of being woefully ignorant. For that, I'm very glad to hear you've suffered."

"I'd like to speak to his father, your father," he said to Khoi as I walked away, still believing Khoi was Sinh's brother. "I'd like to apologize."

"You would only be doing that to try to mend your own heart," I heard Khoi reply, "while ours remain broken. Do not look for anyone. Go back to France. This is not your country. It's mine."

———

I let Khoi's words fade away as I walked to my little red car and opened the door, feeling like I was entering a new phase of life. We knew how Sinh had died. A combination of his love for Anne-Marie, the weakness of men like Paul Adrien, and the hatred the Michelins carried for the very people they were colonizing had killed him.

I turned the handle of my car and climbed in, gasping as I realized there was someone already sitting inside. It was Red.

"Jumpy, Marcelle. So jumpy."

"What are you doing here, Red?" I asked, sitting down and leaning back against my closed car door as he grinned at me. He placed a finger against my lips to silence me.

"Today, I do the talking," he said. "Because you paid me so handsomely at Le Chat d'Or, and because your pretty face provided a little boost to the intense pleasure I was already receiving, I'm going to give you something for free."

"I do not need anything you're peddling," I said, turning back nervously to see if Khoi was heading to me. He wasn't.

"You'll want this," said Red. He leaned in close to my face and whispered, "I saw Jessie Lesage yesterday. We went to a horse race together, at her request."

"Did you?"

"Yes. See, sometimes you like what I peddle," he said, reaching out and touching my leg. I let his hand stay for a moment and then pushed it off my thigh. "At the race, she told me that she had gone down to Cochinchina, to their plantations. Then she asked if I knew about the dead communists. And if I did, why I didn't do anything to save them."

"Who are the dead communists?" I asked, taken aback.

"I have no idea."

"Did she say she tried to save them, whoever they are?"

"I don't know," said Red. "She was at a horse race wearing emerald earrings. I don't think she was busy being Florence Nightingale in Cochinchina."

"Right. It sounds like the only person she saved was herself, then."

He leaned back and reached for the car handle. "Usually people in this colony think it's me who needs saving. Not this time, though," he said, grinning. "Helpful?" he asked.

"Very."

"Good," he replied. "Then a kiss for old time's sake." He let go of the handle and leaned into me but pulled away right before our lips touched. "Don't worry, Marcelle," he whispered. "I'll never tell Khoi about Paris. Luckily for you, I like him too much. Him, and that boat."

TWENTY-SEVEN

Marcelle

November 16, 1933

B ird's nest soup?" I asked, picking up the beautiful handwritten menu from the dining room table, which was extended and set for twenty-six. "Impressive." I held up the thick sheet of rice paper, admiring the elegant image of a mulberry tree above the details of each course.

"Nothing but the best for our guests," said Khoi. "Now, how about you return to the living room before people think we've abandoned them?"

"They'd be thrilled if we did," I murmured. "Those who've never been to your house are itching to go upstairs. They all want to see how the Nguyens really live."

"Never," he said, bringing his lips to my neck. "I have to keep some secrets."

"I hope you at least locked up that photograph. If Victor wandered up to your room for some reason."

"I did," he said, kissing me quickly. "And you're still sure about the rest?"

"I'm still sure," I confirmed.

After I'd talked to Red, I'd run out of the car and spoken to Paul

Adrien again. I'd asked him if he knew what Red was referring to. Who were the dead communists on the Michelin plantation?

He'd told me about a list he'd given to Jessie in Haiphong, which in turn had been given to him by the chief Michelin recruiter in Tonkin at the request of Victor Lesage. It was a list of ten names. Men who were suspected of trying to incite a communist uprising.

"Did you tell her what to do with the names?" I'd asked Paul in a panic. "Did you suggest they kill them all?"

"No. No!" he'd replied. "I was told to give them to her and that she would deliver them safely to Victor. I didn't even know she was his wife when we met."

"It sounds like Victor Lesage then delivered those men a death sentence."

Paul had looked away from me and I'd felt very sorry for him in that moment, something I thought I would never be able to feel for Sinh's killer. This time it was he, not Victor, who had started the death march.

"I can find out more," he'd said. "I need to."

This morning it was Paul who contacted me.

"Ten known communists died. All from complications with malaria, Michelin is saying."

When I relayed what Paul had found out to Khoi, he'd slammed the window that he was closing in the living room so hard that he shattered the pane.

"Marcelle," he'd said, shaking the glass off his fingers. "I know you've been acting without me. Seeking your revenge in ways I would never agree to."

"Perhaps," I said cautiously, thinking of what I knew about Jessie that Khoi didn't.

"You'll get no more fights from me," he said, brushing the glass from the windowsill with his sleeve. "Do whatever you see fit. Push them both off a cliff at this point for all I care."

"Happily," I'd responded.

Khoi headed to the kitchen for the bird's nest soup, to taste the prized delicacy before it was served, and I walked to the living room door. I opened it and paused, breathing in the aroma of women's perfumes. I wanted to take a moment to watch the guests before toppling back into the evening.

On such occasions, the house seemed even more awe-inspiring than the everyday version I had come to know, because it was filled not just with life but also with palpable envy. How, all the French wondered—some of them audibly—could a mite have so much more than they did? Then, after consuming glass after glass of the mite's expensive champagne, they would have a change of heart and decide that instead of envying him, they should be applauding themselves, because obviously it was they, the French saviors, who had made this simple native man's success possible. I had heard this particular mental progression from many of Khoi's guests over the years. But they were wrong. It was *despite* the French that the Nguyens had succeeded. Everything they had was despite us.

I looked past the other guests in their colorful finery to where Jessie and Victor were seated on a deco couch recently shipped in from Paris. The upholstery was a deep blue cotton velvet, the cushions resting on glossy Macassar ebony wood. They had sunk comfortably into its depths and were busy sipping Veuve Clicquot and nibbling on the foie gras being passed to them every few minutes by Khoi's pretty female servants. This evening, each servant wore an *ao* of buttle green, the signature color of Lua Nguyen Thanh.

Khoi had once told me that the secret to the color was that everyone thought it was emerald green, but it was actually bottle green. "As in, the exact color of a bottle of rice wine," he'd said. "It's just on silk, so it looks a little darker, giving it the richness of emerald with the hint of something familiar. It's a secret mix of the elegant and the everyday." The result was the best color green ever produced.

With their hair uniformly cut in a bunt, chin-length bob, set off by a single waved lock, the servants looked nearly identical. The silk-factory dolls, Khoi had once called them. "It's ridiculous," he'd said the first time I attended one of his parties. "But my father likes them to be half servants, half models for Nguyen silk. And it works. Every female guest commissions something before she leaves. Even the French ones."

Khoi joined me a few minutes later, surprised to see me still by the door. I glanced at him but looked quickly back to the Lesages, sensing Victor's eyes on us. I hadn't seen him since the night we'd met in September, and in only two and a half months he seemed changed. His face still wore that imperious look, but also a shadow of fatigue. He looked older, not as fresh as he had that evening at the club. Perhaps ordering men's deaths was taking its toll.

Jessie was not seated near me for the meal, but after we'd finished and everyone was adjourning to the sitting rooms or the outdoor terrace, she rushed up to me and took my arm. I could tell she was drunk.

I lit myself a cigarette and handed her one, too. She hesitated a moment and then began to smoke.

"Marcelle," she cooed as we strolled outside. "This place. I assumed Khoi was well-off after seeing his boat, but this is something else altogether. It must be three times the size of our house."

"Oh, no," I said, inhaling deeply. "It can't be more than double the size." I looked at her, barely able to get the cigarette to her mouth. "I'm sorry I haven't seen you since that boat trip. I hope all the nonsense that went on that night didn't leave you disgusted with us." We sat in planter's chairs, and I inched mine closer to her, draping my arm behind her.

"Of course not," she said breezily. "I suppose that's just how things are here. In the Orient."

"Yes, I suppose you're right," I said.

"Red didn't come tonight," she said loudly, her words slurred.

"Red?" I replied, suppressing a grin. "Of course not. I thought it would be impertinent to invite him. What with your husband here and all. Would you like me to telephone him now? Shall I invite him to join us?"

"No, please don't," she said quickly. "I was just expecting him. You seem to always be with him."

"I'm seldom with him," I countered. "Where I always am is here."

"That's bold of you," she said, looking around at the mixed group. "To host a party with your lover." She rubbed her eyes, as if she couldn't quite believe what was in front of her.

"Is it?" I said, noting the mascara that she'd smudged. "I suppose. But life must be lived boldly in the colony if one is to survive. If I were to sit at home, lamenting Arnaud while he jumped in and out of other women's beds, I wouldn't make it here. Khoi is my life vest."

"And one with a palace," said Jessie. "That's convenient."

I looked back at the house. Every light was on, and against the night sky, it was at its most transfixing.

"I like it best like this," I said, admiring it for the thousandth time.

"So do I," she replied, "and I've only seen it this once."

I looked at her, her body sprawled awkwardly, her dress moving up her thighs. I had never seen her so intoxicated. "And I liked that bird-spit soup more than I thought I would," she added.

"Bird's nest," I said, unable to suppress a laugh. "But bird's spit is actually more accurate, since it's made from the saliva of swiftlets. Very good for your health."

She nodded, tried to sit up straighter, but fell off the end of the chair.

"Too much champagne," she said, closing her eyes as she lay where she'd fallen.

I stood and helped her up, leaning her back again.

"It's no wonder I don't see you at the club so much anymore," she said.

"I have been here quite a bit," I admitted.

"The Officers' Club," she said, slurring her words. "We women all go there on our first night in Indochine."

"Yes, we do," I said. I should have had a servant fetch her some water, but I was enjoying observing her loss of control too much.

"I'd like to spend time with you there again," she said. She opened her eyes and looked at me, her expression suddenly thoughtful. "You know what I've been thinking about? The day I met you. How we were scampering around behind the walls together at the club. To be honest, that was the most fun I've had in Hanoi."

I stared at her, her beautiful face tilted back at an unnatural angle. I thought of what I knew about her childhood. Of her parents, and how hard she'd had to work to rid herself of them. I hadn't grown up with much more than she had, but I'd had good, loving parents who were determined to give me a better life.

Perhaps I could say one truthful thing to her on a night that was devoted to secrets.

"It was fun, wasn't it?" I said. I reached out and touched her hand. "It's amazing we kept quiet after seeing that minister," I said, smiling at the memory.

"He was so fat," said Jessie. "And so naked."

We dissolved into laughter, and I poured us two more glasses of champagne.

"There's really a lot to amuse us spoiled French women in Indochine," I said. She was practically swaying when I handed her the glass. She certainly wouldn't remember this conversation the next day. "It's just that sometimes life gets in the way here." I watched her as I said it.

"Is that what you call it?" she said, her eyes trying to focus on my face in the dim lantern light.

"Yes. Life. Real life. Because even though Indochine can feel like one long vacation, it's not, is it? What happens here is just as important as what goes on in France or America."

"I think so, too," she said, closing her eyes. "But I like it here much more than in America."

"I'm sure you do," I said, exhaling my cigarette smoke into the black sky.

TWENTY-EIGHT

Jessie

November 16, 1933

D id you say something?" I said, turning to the young native woman sitting next to me. Her name was Binh Tieu and her husband had made money in rice, she'd mentioned earlier. Or maybe it was coal. She smiled at me, her mouth moving, but I couldn't hear her very well, so I leaned back and stared at her animated face. Khoi's native friends were so different from the locals I saw in the streets, through the Delahaye's windows. These people had lovely features and beautiful clothes and spoke unaccented French, unlike me. Eight years in France, and I still didn't sound like a Parisian.

I was still in the same chair where I'd been talking to Marcelle, but I couldn't remember whether that was just five minutes ago or an hour. The sky was still pitch black. It was hard to keep track of time when the sun disappeared. I remembered asking Marcelle about Red, but I couldn't remember if he was at Khoi's party or not. Perhaps that was why I was still sitting outside. To avoid him. I looked away from the pretty woman and saw a flash of light in the sky. It seemed too low to be lightning.

"I'm sorry," I said, leaning toward her. "What did you say?" Binh was wearing a short-haired fur jacket over her silver dress, even though it was a warm evening. I reached out to touch it but pulled my fingers away as soon as they brushed it. The pelt of the dead animal felt exactly like Lucie's hair when it needed to be combed. "I think I drank too much," I said, balling my hand up into a fist in my lap. "I need some air." I stood up to walk outside, then realized I was already there. "I'm sorry. How embarrassing," I said, falling back down on the chair.

"No need to be embarrassed, my dear," she said. "All we do in Indochine is drink too much. Keeps the malaria away."

"Does it? I haven't come down with malaria yet, so I suppose it works." I put my hands on my stomach, which felt like a churning car engine. "I feel utterly rotten," I said, the lightning flashing near us again. "I think I'm going to be sick. I need to move inside."

"Why don't you put your feet in the pool for a while?" she suggested. "The water is freezing. It will sober you right up."

She swirled her drink, which was dark and on ice, and pointed. Lanterns lined both sides of the long, rectangular pool, their tiny candles producing surprisingly large flames.

I contemplated the pool for a moment, but knew I was too drunk to walk over to it without stumbling.

"I can't—" I said, turning back to her and gasping when I saw a flash of exposed skin. "What are you doing?" I hissed, reaching for the woman's arm. She had taken off her coat and was unzipping the back of her dress. As she reached her right arm behind her, I saw blood dripping down her forearm. A stream of blood.

"You're bleeding!" I exclaimed, trying to get to her, to help her, but my body felt so heavy, I could hardly move. When I managed to stand, I collapsed onto her chair, but I immediately felt that my feet were bare.

I glanced down and saw I'd kicked off my shoes. I looked at the tops of my feet and screamed, leaping up with legs that felt detached from my body. My feet were covered in tiny black ants.

"We have to move from here," I shouted. The blood had dripped from the woman's arms to her dress, which was only half on.

She was crying. Her black hair, so elegantly styled when I'd sat down, was plastered to her cheeks with tears and sweat.

"I'll get my husband," I said, trying to put her dress back over her bare shoulders. "I'll find him!" I assured her as she pulled away from me.

"Jessie!" I heard her scream back at me, her arms around my shoulders. "Jessie!" she screamed again. She was shaking me and trying to detach me, begging me to stop.

"Jessie!" I heard a man's voice yell. I stopped moving and looked up. Behind me, grabbing for me, was Victor.

"Jessie," he repeated, more quietly. "What are you doing to this woman? Are you all right?"

"I am so terribly sorry, *madame*," I heard Victor say as his hand on my shoulder got firmer.

"Victor," I said, trying to make out his face in the dark. "You have to help her. Help Binh. She's bleeding!"

"What are you talking about?" He sounded terrified. "You're screaming. We could hear you in the house. And then I rush out to the terrace to see what is going on, and you're attacking this woman! What's wrong?" He gripped my arms. "Are you drunk? Are you sick?"

"I don't know," I said. I reached out for him, although I couldn't see him well. But I could feel his hands on my body and his anger rolling over me.

"We need to leave," he said. "Everyone is still there, staring at us." He looked toward the terrace, and I tried to follow his gaze, but all I saw was a sea of color.

"I'll say you're very ill," he said tightly. "We'll go around the side of the house, not through it. You can give your apologies another day." He let go of me a moment and turned to the Indochinese woman.

"Are you all right?" he asked. "Did she hurt you?"

"She's bleeding!" I called out. "And she was taking off her dress."

"I'm fine," I heard her say. "Just help your wife."

I felt Victor's hands go around my waist, hoisting me off the chair. Then I didn't feel anything else at all.

TWENTY-NINE

Jessie

November 17, 1933

"Victor, for the hundredth time, I am sure she needed help," I said, throwing myself back on my pillows. "I was trying to help her! I'm sorry I embarrassed you. I'm sorry I embarrassed myself. But I am sure she was bleeding. Not just a tiny cut, it was gushing down her arms."

"You're still not understanding," said Victor, his voice rising. "That's the problem. I don't care about the embarrassment, Jessie. We've lived through worse, haven't we?"

I looked at him and didn't answer.

"What I'm concerned about is you. This . . . psychotic episode that you had. And how you attacked that woman, just like—" He paused and looked at me very seriously. "Just like . . . before. It's as if you and the reality we are living in just splintered."

"I don't know. But I believed that she desperately needed my help. I remember seeing blood." I heard my voice cracking.

"I don't know what to think," he said. He sat slumped, as if exhausted. "You've been healthy for so long, and now this. I just don't understand it."

He would be far more terrified if he knew how many times I'd experienced gaps in my memory since we'd been in Indochine. My mind had felt unsteady almost since we'd arrived.

"I'm the one who's scared," I said, closing my eyes. I willed my brain to remember the events at Khoi's house. Attacking that woman, who in fact was not bleeding or half naked, according to Victor. Yet I knew what I'd seen.

I had a strong recollection of eating dinner at a massive, dark red lacquered table and talking to someone about bird's nest soup. Another Annamite woman, perhaps, but not Binh. I remembered the taste of the soup, like seawater. The slippery texture. How the liquid seemed to coat my tongue even after I'd swallowed it. Someone near me had explained that it took over a month to make that soup and that it included bird droppings as well as saliva. That I hadn't forgotten. And I could picture the large house illuminated like a palace floating in the countryside. But nothing was as vibrant as my conversation with Binh.

Past that, I had very little memory of coming home, or of the nightmares Victor claimed I'd had. I'd woken up four hours ago as my stomach lurched violently. I blamed the alcohol and the exotic soup. Victor blamed my mind.

My stomach was still in knots, and my skin was hot and prickling as Victor spoke. I picked at my itching hand, willing the skin to just fall off.

"I want to fix you, Jessie," he said, his usually impeccably coiffed hair falling in his face, his blue eyes looking lighter than usual, as if my behavior was causing his blood to drain. "I do not want you to suffer the same fate as others," he said. He meant his father. "But I don't know what to do."

"I'm sure I'll feel better soon," I said, trying to find some optimism.

"No," Victor said, shaking his head. "I'm sorry, but there's now a doctor downstairs to see you—"

"Victor, no!" I said, the tears immediately welling up in my eyes. "You know I—"

"I've waited hours to call her here," he said loudly. "She's been ready to see you since early this morning, but I wanted you calm before she did. This feels like the right time."

"I'm certainly not calm now!" I shouted back. I could not see a doctor. I knew what kind of doctor Victor had called. She would want to do a lot more than check my pulse and have me swallow an aspirin.

I sat up quickly and felt so light-headed that I had to lie down again. "I will not see her, Victor," I said.

"Look at you!" Victor said. "You're sick. You're very sick. I wanted to rush you to the hospital when we left the party, but I knew that might send you over the edge."

"No hospitals," I said, feeling my hands trembling. I balled them into fists to make it stop. "Never again."

When we had arrived in Hanoi, the French authorities had given us a list of French schools, French government offices, French hospitals. The first three on the list of hospitals were the Clinique Saint-Paul for pregnant women, the Hospice de Thai-Ha-Ap for incurables, and the asylum for the insane in Voi. The last was conveniently located just forty miles outside Hanoi, the pamphlet touted.

Victor walked over to the bed and reached for my hand, but I pushed him off. "I will crawl out of this room on my hands and knees if I don't have the energy to stand, but I will not see your doctor."

"Don't be like this, Jessie, please. See this woman. You need help. Let her help you in the comfort of your own home instead of in—"

"Instead of where? An asylum?" I shouted, a wave of anxiety crashing over me. I put my head in my hands and closed my eyes again.

"Instead of in her clinic," Victor replied quietly. He rang the bell for Trieu, who came quickly to the door.

"Yes, Monsieur Lesage?" she said as she pushed it open.

"Please bring the doctor up now, Trieu," Victor said with authority.

"I will jump off the balcony, Victor!" I shouted. I sprang out of bed, although barely able to stay upright, and made for the door that led outside. I flung it open harder than I thought I could, and it hit the

wall, one of the panes of glass shattering as it crashed into the plaster. "Do not bring that woman in here," I said slowly, ignoring the shards on the floor.

Victor caught me as I tried to step outside and wrestled me back into the room and onto the bed, elbowing me in the stomach, forcing me to lie down. I sucked in my breath sharply from the pain.

"Jessie." His voice was unyielding. "You have to get well. Please. I can't have you like this! I can't. I need you well again."

I looked up and saw the doctor, a white woman, standing in the door frame with Trieu. She had seen everything.

"You must not be feeling well," she said in French, coming into the room as Victor stepped away from me. She was perhaps in her fifties and wearing a simple blue cotton shirt and gray trousers. She was the kind of woman one would call handsome. Authoritative. She also looked like the kind of woman who would regard me as a fascinating specimen to test her pet theories on. Victor stood back to make room for her.

I watched her warily. She smiled at me as if she hadn't witnessed an unseemly scene between husband and wife. She plopped her black medical bag on the bed and opened it.

"I want to do a full physical check, but first, Madame Lesage, let me administer something to make you a bit drowsy. I think, more than anything, you need a good night's sleep."

She pulled out a small brown bottle shaped like a beaker, with a cork stopper and a brown-and-gold label. I recognized it at once. Somnifen. I sat up and knocked the bottle out of her hand with all the force I could still muster. It fell to the floor with a loud clink but did not break.

"Absolutely not," I barked, my eyes fixed on hers, my heart racing furiously. "I've had that before. I'll never take it again. You need to leave."

"Jessie!" Victor exclaimed, rushing back to the bed. "She is not going to leave." His shirt was stained with sweat under the arms and at

the collar. My heartbeat slowed as I looked at him. My husband who had left France because I'd wanted to, who had been faithful to me throughout our marriage. What had I done to him? But what had he done to me? He'd made me see those men, in various states of death. He'd made me complicit in the decisions he made on the plantation by inviting me into his work, but only partially. He'd said I had enormous influence over him, but he hadn't let me influence how he treated the insurgents he'd dug up. Michelin decisions were family decisions, he always said. His uncle knew about everything that happened on the plantation. But that moment had very much been his decision. He could have given those men jail sentences instead of death sentences. He hadn't.

This was not how it was supposed to be, I thought, tears streaming down my face. The colony was to be a fresh start, not a place to fall apart. I looked up at Victor, his sad, broken expression.

And yet—Victor would always win. He was rich and he was a man. In every instance, I was the one who depended on him, not the opposite. That was just the way it was in the world of women. Especially for poor women. Especially for mothers.

"Fine," I whispered to the doctor. "You can examine me. But don't bring that anywhere near me," I finished up, eyeing the bottle on the floor, thinking of all the barbiturates the Swiss had pushed in me. This woman surely wanted me in a corpse-like state, too.

Victor managed a half smile. "I'll be downstairs," he whispered and closed the door behind him.

The doctor took out a watch and checked my blood pressure with her contraption, staring at the second hand as she did. It was a cheap-looking watch that I wouldn't have trusted to time a pie in the oven with. Then she put a stethoscope around her neck and started listening to my heart.

"Your husband says you don't remember very much from the party last night," she said calmly. "And that the things that you do remember perhaps occurred slightly differently than the way you think they did."

"I don't remember much," I replied, shuddering at the stethoscope's cold, metallic touch. "But what I remember happened exactly as I think it did."

She went on to check my reflexes, looked into my ears and nose, then forced me to track a small light around the room with my eyes. She asked me if I could see certain things. The dresser. The lamp. The picture of Lucie that I loved so much. Then she asked me if I could see anything that perhaps wasn't real.

"How would I know if the things I see are real or not?" I snapped. "How do I know if you're even real?"

"I suppose you don't," she said, again in her overly calm voice.

I hated her voice. And I hated her. She was the last person I would tell about the strange scenes that had been rattling through my mind like a filmstrip since the previous evening. How I'd dreamt that my mother's stringy, oily hair, long and gray and tangled, was wrapping around my feet, between my toes, while I slept. No. This doctor would advise Victor to commit me for life if she knew.

"I just don't feel well," I said. "But I don't feel insane, if that's what you're dancing around."

"Your husband mentioned that you have a history of psychiatric hospitalization," she said, putting her instruments away and sitting on the edge of the bed. Her dark blond hair, I saw now, was pinned back with the metal pins favored by the Annamites. How long had she been in the country, I wondered, that she was using such cheap clips?

"What?" I asked, slowly registering what she'd just said.

"Your husband said you've had memory problems before, but also a history of psychotic episodes."

"I don't have a history of psychotic episodes," I retorted, my pulse taking off again.

"Your husband sees it differently. He said that you had trouble after your daughter was born. That you spent some time at the Prangins Clinic in Switzerland. That you lunged at a doctor there and had no recollection of doing so. And that the doctor ended up with two broken fingers and nearly went blind. He's worried that the way you lunged at the native woman at the party was similar to the way you attacked the doctor. Of course, Victor wasn't with you in Switzerland, but—"

"'Nearly went blind'?" I said, laughing. "That's quite the exaggeration." I spoke through clenched teeth, willing myself not to attack her similarly. "And that was many years ago."

"You've had no instances where you forgot things, or imagined things, since then? No hallucinations?" she asked.

I thought of my lips against Red's. How I could taste his saliva, feel his barely-there stubble against my face. I thought of the poster of the house of the hundred suns that the ticket agents claimed was never there. I shook my head stubbornly. "Nothing since Switzerland."

"I see," she said, reaching into her bag for a paper and pen. She paused for a moment, then looked at me again.

"You're still relatively new to the colony. Has the transition been difficult?" she asked brightly, feigned sympathy dripping from her voice.

"No," I said, staring at her. "I enjoy it here."

"Do you enjoy it a bit too much?" she asked, flipping the pages of her blank book. "How much have you been drinking?"

"No more than usual," I lied.

"Any drug use?" she asked.

"I suppose I've tried opium," I said, thinking of the first soothing lungful of smoke I'd inhaled on Khoi's beautiful boat.

"Did it have any adverse effects?" she asked.

"I don't think so," I said, staring down at my ringless right hand.

She looked at me levelly. "Very well. Look, Madame Lesage, as I said earlier, I think what you need more than anything is a good night's sleep." She stood up, excused herself, and came back a few minutes later with Victor. Her blue eyes were again appraising, clinical. I wanted her gone immediately.

"I've advised your husband to let you sleep for as long as possible.

To rest. Then we've decided that he'll take you away for a little trip with your daughter. A family vacation. He said that his cousin Roland and his family are planning to be at the beach in a week's time. That sounds like a perfect solution. It will get you out of the city, which really can be quite chaotic, and also have you around family. We both think that's the best short-term option."

I turned my head and looked over at the French doors. The shattered glass had been cleaned up. A servant must have done it while the doctor was tending to me. I hadn't even noticed.

"Fine," I said to Victor, turning my back to him. "We'll all go away."

THIRTY

Jessie

November 20, 1933

L et's just act normally, *please*," Victor said from where he'd
been watching me wake up. The morning light felt blinding,
though I could see that the bedroom curtains were half drawn.
I'd managed to sleep past sunrise. "For Lucie's sake," he added as I
squinted against the glare and turned away from the window. I blinked
a few times and peered down at the clock. It was 7:23. We were due
to leave for the station, to board the ten o'clock train to Vinh, in less
than two hours. I wasn't clearheaded, I could already tell that, and my
nerves had been set on edge by Victor's insistent expectations and
the looming reunion with his family, but I knew he was right. I did
want to act as normally as I could for Lucie's sake. I hadn't seen her
in four days, since the evening of Khoi's party, as Victor had told her
I was very ill with the flu, was contagious and couldn't be disturbed,
even for a quick hug. But I was sure she had heard me, not just when
that doctor had tried to drug me into a stupor but also, according to
Victor, shouting out in my sleep. As large as our house was, it seemed
designed to bounce voices, especially high-pitched, terrified ones, off
its thick walls.

I missed Lucie sorely, and I was afraid that if I acted anything but the ideal mother around her, Victor would panic. And in that frame of mind, he could do the unthinkable. He could keep me from her, and maybe for a very long time. ·

"Of course," I said, smiling at him, the corners of my mouth already belying my feigned confidence. He stood from the chair where he'd been sitting and came to the bed, lying down next to me. I leaned over and put my head on his bare chest, resting my weight on him, hoping that my touch might reassure him. Surprisingly, he put his arms around me, hugging me tightly.

"I don't know what happened at the Nguyen home," he said quietly. "I know what I saw, and you seem to know what you saw, but I want to forget all that. Because what I really know, what I'm sure of, is that I need you back, Jessie." His voice sounded suddenly tired. "I need you to return to me. The brave Jessie. The one who sailed to France by herself and drank at Maxim's and kissed a stranger in the Tuileries when she was only twenty-three years old. The one who committed her life to my career and our family and convinced me that it was my time to try to lead the family business abroad. You've been the driving force behind me as much as I have been behind you. What will happen to us if that disappears?"

I had always thought that Victor would be fine if I vanished. That because the world was so bent in his favor, he'd bounce right back up like a rubber ball and the memory of me would eventually fade. But maybe I was wrong. Maybe he did need me as much as I needed him, albeit in a different way. Because he loved me. Because I, a girl whose parents considered her a scrap of a person, a girl who was destined for a small, difficult life, had managed to change myself, and fate had agreed that I deserved something good. That I was loveable after all.

"That girl hasn't gone anywhere," I said, trying to sound like the person Victor remembered, the determined young American who'd shifted the universe on her own to make our meeting happen. I had thought that Lucie being taken away from me was the worst fate I could imagine, but losing Victor's love was just as terrifying a prospect. I had already had my family break apart once; I could never let it happen again. "She's still here," I declared. I placed my thumb on my ring finger, feeling the absence of my emerald ring. The little bag filled with its shards was now in the drawer of my nightstand. Parts of me were missing, but it didn't mean I couldn't piece myself back together again, almost as good as new. I could still live my life, even if my mind went its own way sometimes, at odds with the rest of the world. I could survive.

"Don't drink anymore," said Victor, letting me go. "And if you're taking other things, other intoxicants, don't take them. Please."

Other intoxicants. I thought of the way the smoke from the burning, sticky opium had felt in my lungs when I'd needed it the most, on my way home from Dau Tieng, distraught and unable to calm myself on my own. I looked into Victor's startling blue eyes, which glinted with the confidence built by generations of wealth and privilege. I wondered what it would be like to live the way Victor did. To have a good heart, a great heart, but one that only beat for certain people. Maybe my mind was somehow out of kilter, as he and doctors in two countries had claimed, but suddenly, that didn't bother me so much. I had lost a part of my soul at Dau Tieng that day, but I knew a wisp of it was still there. I hoped that one day Victor would realize that he'd lost a part of his soul to those men, too. Even if he'd been too proud to notice.

"It's nearly seven-thirty. We should be off soon," he said as he stood up. He straightened his pajama pants and looked at me, more seriously. "Don't make any apologies to the servants. They don't expect them, anyway. Just act as if nothing unusual has happened, and they will do the same. We'll all act the same. We will have our eggs and tea, dress, go to the station, and proceed as if the world has righted itself on its axis." He touched my head. "Even if it hasn't, exactly."

"Of course, Victor," I said, pushing back the covers and standing as well. "I think that's best."

He nodded and watched me as I put on a dressing gown and made for the door, eager to fetch Lucie.

"I'm feeling much better," I said brightly. "Really. I feel like my old self again." I walked out of the room and up the stairs, letting my put-on smile fade.

I was halfway up the stairs when Trieu stopped me.

"Madame," she said loudly. I turned to see her standing in the hallway, looking as polished as always. "Shall we dress you before you see Lucie?"

I stopped and was about to shake my head no, but then I realized that Lucie might be more convinced of my recovery if I looked the part. With my hair a mess, and in a wrinkled dressing gown, I was hardly the picture of well-being.

"That's a good idea," I said, turning around. "I need to look quite elegant, as we are meeting Victor's cousin, but also be fit for travel. We leave for Vinh shortly."

Trieu nodded understandingly and escorted me to my dressing room.

When I was presentable, Trieu placed my lucky red hat on my head, the only sign that she knew I needed the world to be on my side today. I thanked her, happy to have an ally, and hurried upstairs to Lucie's room. I couldn't wait to see her.

"Mama!" she exclaimed as soon as I burst through the door. I was too excited to open it quietly, feeling Lucie's absence like a hole in my heart. She was still in bed, flipping through a large picture book. When I approached her, I saw that it was written in Annamese. One of the servants must have bought it for her.

"I haven't heard you call me Mama in a long time," I said, sitting down and embracing her, careful not to crush her. "You sound like a little American. My little American."

I could tell I was holding her for too long, but I didn't want to let go. I waited until she wriggled out of my arms to sit back next to her.

"Are you not sick anymore?" she asked me quietly, looking down at her bedspread.

"I'm not sick anymore," I replied, with a big smile. I inched closer to her and leaned softly against her.

"Oh, good," she said, turning and hugging me back. "You've been sick so much, I worried you might not like Indochine. Maybe it makes you sad. Or allergic. Because you were less sick when we were at home."

"It doesn't make me allergic," I said, reaching for her hand. "I promise. And today we are going on a trip. All of us. Did Papa tell you? We're all taking a train together. Finally."

Lucie nodded excitedly. "Finally!" she echoed.

"But first, a bath," I said, helping her out of bed. When we were standing together, I heard the water running in the tub. Cam must have been listening and started it straightaway.

When Lucie was immersed in the warm water, her servant cleaning her, I switched to English to keep our conversation private. Intimate.

"We will be meeting your father's cousin Roland and his family in Vinh, so you will have to be very polite and well behaved. No shouting out in Annamese or talking about opium pipes. Okay?"

Lucie smiled at Cam as she scrubbed her arm with a thick pink bar of soap.

"Lucie, did you hear me?" I asked, trying to fight through the familiar pounding that had begun in my head. Lucie was not the problem in our family. I was, and my body seldom let me forget it.

She looked at me and nodded.

"Best behavior," I said.

"You're not allowed to speak English to me when we are on best behavior," she rightly pointed out.

"I'm well aware," I said, rubbing my eyes, which were still heavy.

I sat with Lucie as she finished her bath, letting her fill me in on the last four days. Perhaps I had made some wrong decisions in my life, but crashing into Victor's world was a brilliant one. Without it, I would never have had Lucie. Victor was right. The brave, decisive Jessie who kissed a perfect stranger in the Tuileries gardens needed to be found again.

An hour later, the whole family was dressed, starched, powdered, and settled in the car, Victor and I acting as if it were just another routine family trip.

When we arrived at the station, the stationmaster, a wiry, energetic man, greeted us, along with a porter, who took my bag from me. It was the one with the broken handle, which I'd grabbed in a hurry. I pointed it out quietly, not wanting to give Victor another reason to question my behavior, and Lucie quickly jumped in and explained to the porter in Indochinese that he had to be careful with it.

He nodded politely before the stationmaster barked at him and hurried off with all of our bags.

Once inside, Victor paid off the stationmaster so he would leave us alone; then we headed to the benches in the waiting area farthest from the entrance. The station was jammed with people.

"This is the busiest I've ever seen it," Victor murmured in annoyance. He turned sideways so a group of native men could pass.

Lucie hovered by the benches, not sitting down even as Victor and I did. I realized it was because she didn't want to wrinkle her dress.

"We have a very long train journey ahead of us," I reminded her, gesturing to the spot next to me. Lucie nodded and was about to sit when she was suddenly struck by a young boy who had rushed toward us. She tumbled back, her body slamming into the wooden bench. I reached out for her as Victor spun around.

"Careful, boy!" Victor yelled. The youngster was a shoeblack who had been coming after Victor's expensive brogues. Victor angrily swatted him on the back with his newspaper.

The boy grinned, ignoring Lucie and me, and suggested a shine, holding up his brush and pointing at Victor's shoes.

"After this!" Victor shouted, gesturing to frightened Lucie and adding a string of the few insults he knew in Annamese. "You're lucky I don't have you banned from the station."

I held Lucie by the shoulders. She was looking down at her dress in horror. On the upper part of her starched white skirt was a black, checkmark-shaped swoop of shoe polish.

"*Maman!*" she cried, staring at the stain. "He ruined my dress," she whispered, tears starting to flow.

"No, Lucie, no, don't cry," I said, hugging her, making sure to avoid the stain. "I'll take you to wash it. We can get it out, don't worry, *chérie.*" I patted her on the shoulder, but suddenly my nerves flared again in sympathy with hers. I had spent so much of my life comforting crying children, sibling after sibling, but when it was Lucie whose tears dampened my cheek, I usually shared them with her.

"Take her to the washroom," said Victor, stroking Lucie's head comfortingly while keeping his eyes on me. "I'll wait here." He gestured to the bench closest to the bathroom.

I nodded and pushed Lucie the few steps to the door.

When we were inside, and luckily alone, Lucie pulled her skirt up and looked at the mark, breathing deeply to try to stop her tears.

"Are you sure it will come out?" she asked.

"Of course," I said brightly, reaching for a hand towel. I wet it and soaped it up before starting to scrub.

We watched as my right hand moved back and forth and I tugged at the fabric with my left. But all that did was spread the black stain, so I crouched down on the floor to get a better angle.

I scrubbed as hard as I could and listened as her sobs quieted. If I could do anything right today, it would be this. To help my child. But as I looked up to smile at her, happy that the mark was starting to fade, black spots swam before my eyes and I had to bend my head quickly.

"*Maman?*" I heard her say, but her voice sounded small and far away.

"I'm just a bit faint," I said, standing up carefully. Feeling dizzy enough to fall, I gripped the sink and closed my eyes, letting my head drop heavily forward. The darkness felt welcome, and with my eyes still closed, I turned on the water. I opened them and watched the stream coming out of the metal tap. I placed one of my hands under it, keeping the other on the sink for balance.

When I felt a bit steadier, I bent down and drank from the sink, lapping the cool water in large gulps.

"I'm sorry, Lucie," I mumbled when I felt I could stand up again without help. I glanced in the mirror briefly, surprised by my pale reflection, then whipped my head to my left.

Lucie was no longer standing next to me.

"Lucie?" I exclaimed, turning around to the toilet stalls. Three were empty, but one had the door closed. I pulled it open, and it flew back, banging the wooden door of the next stall. Lucie wasn't inside. "Lucie!" I called out, running in a circle in the little room. She wasn't anywhere.

She was gone.

I ran out to the waiting room and checked the bench Victor had pointed to, but she wasn't there, either. Neither was Victor.

"Lucie!" I shouted, rushing between the benches, all jammed with travelers, and out to the central space. "Victor!"

The weather was the nicest it had been since we'd arrived, so it was no surprise that the station was packed, but suddenly I felt as if I were swimming in a sea of bodies, when I should have been able to spot them so easily.

"Victor!" I cried out again. I sprinted through the station, bumping people as I did, and out the front door. There were rows of vendors, some desultorily trying to make a sale, others asleep. At the end of one row, I saw a man selling sugarcane and ran to him. It was Lucie's favorite snack. I asked him if he'd seen a little French girl, accompanied by her father in a beige traveling suit, but he just smiled and held out a stalk of the sugarcane. I repeated the phrase in Annamese, but he just shook his head no. Lucie would have translated better than I did. Where was she?

Back inside the station, I looked up at the clock. The train for Vinh was due in two minutes. I ran out to the platform and studied the large group of travelers waiting. I even glanced down at the tracks, fearing the worst.

But Victor and Lucie were nowhere to be seen.

I rushed back inside to the bathroom where I'd washed Lucie's dress, but she was not there. She wasn't in the waiting area nearby. She wasn't anywhere. I sat down on the bench where Victor had said he would wait for us and started to sob.

"Madame Lesage!" the stationmaster exclaimed as he approached me, handing me his handkerchief. "What is the matter?"

He tried to guide me to a waiting area, but I balked. He handed me another starched handkerchief and sat next to me.

"Can I assist you in some way, Madame Lesage?" he asked as I cried.

"Yes. I hope you can," I managed to say, clenching his handkerchiefs in my fist. "Something just went terribly wrong."

"I'm sure I can help," he said soothingly. "That's why I'm here. Please tell me what's upsetting you."

My words poured out through sobs.

"Just a few minutes ago I went to the washroom to clean my daughter Lucie's dress," I said. "To get out a shoe-polish stain. A boy, a shoeblack soliciting my husband's business, had pushed up against her with his greasy brush, making a terrible mark on her white dress. But I couldn't wash it out. Then, I don't know what happened. I closed my eyes for a few seconds, perhaps a minute at most, and when I opened them, Lucie was gone. I ran out to find her, but she's not anywhere in the station—and I've looked everywhere—and neither is my husband, Victor, who was supposed to wait for us right here." I gestured toward the bench we were sitting on. "I've been running all over the station for fifteen minutes now, but I can't find them. I'm alone, and we are going to miss our train to Vinh. We have to meet Victor's cousin. It's a very important trip, and now he and Lucie have disappeared. They're gone." My voice cracked again.

The stationmaster looked at me intently. "You say that you are looking for your husband and daughter? Victor and Lucie Lesage?" he said slowly.

"Of course!" I said, exasperation getting the better of me. "You just greeted us outside a half hour ago! Who else would I be looking for?"

He shook his head and laced his hands together. "But *madame*, I'm afraid you're mistaken," he said, meeting my gaze. "I did greet you a half hour ago, as you said, but it was just you in the black car. Just you and your chauffeur. There was no husband and child. You were alone."

Alone.

There was no husband and child. I was alone.

"No, Monsieur Dat. You are mistaken," I said, shaking my head. "Of course they were with me. We are all journeying to Vinh together, as I said. To see Victor's Michelin cousin."

He looked at me with concern and repeated, "I am sure you were alone."

"That can't be," I insisted. "*You* are not remembering correctly."

I rested my heavy head in my hands, my vision blurring even more, and closed my eyes. "We traveled together to the station," I repeated, feeling queasy. "Victor, Lucie, and I."

I lifted my head with a jerk, propelled by a sudden idea. "Lanh will tell you!" I said loudly. "Please call my *tai xe* now. I insist. Phone our house. Lanh will have returned. And our servants saw us all off this morning. Please phone them," I begged. "Ask for Lanh, or Trieu. One of them should answer straightaway."

"Of course," he said, standing up.

The man had to be wrong. He had to be. But then I thought of the blood I had seen pouring down the Annamite woman's arms at the Nguyen house and Victor contesting my account. I thought of the poster I had seen displayed over the train timetables and glanced in that direction. The image of a hundred suns still wasn't there. Then there was Red. Red, whom I was absolutely sure I had kissed. Yet he'd assured me I was very wrong, and why would a man like that deny a conquest? I bit my lip, my tears welling up. This couldn't be happening again.

The stationmaster was walking back to me, and I could tell from his expression that he did not have good news.

"Did you phone, Monsieur Pham? Did you speak to Lanh? Or Trieu?" I asked anxiously when he was close.

"Yes, Madame Lesage," he replied, his voice even. "I made the call myself and spoke to Madame Trieu. I'm sorry, but she said that she saw you off this morning, alone. That your husband and daughter are in Trang An for the day. To see the caves."

"Caves! What are you talking about?" I cried out. "They are here, with me. Victor doesn't have time to take Lucie to inspect caves. Please help me look again," I said frantically. "Please."

"Of course we can look again, Madame Lesage," he said gently. "Perhaps they arrived in a separate car. Perhaps I just didn't see them."

I recognized the way he was staring at me, that look of feigned concern, when he was really trying to identify signs that I wasn't quite right. That I was crazy. It was how everyone in that psychiatric prison in Switzerland had looked at me.

I stood up and shook my head.

"You've been very kind. I'm sorry to have been such a bother, Monsieur Dat," I said, looking at his gold nameplate again. "You're right about everything, I'm sure. I must just be remembering incorrectly. Perhaps I'm unwell."

I turned around without thanking him and hurried out of the station. He didn't follow me.

I could still feel Lucie's touch and see the distress on her face when the shoeblack had collided with her. I wasn't unwell. I wasn't forgetting anything. My family had disappeared.

I sprinted down the street, a panicked surge of energy making me feel as if I were floating instead of running, but I stopped suddenly as I approached a large group of *indigène* children. They looked so similar, like siblings. They reminded me of the way people always said that my brothers and sisters looked alike.

Another one, that same Holland face, our teachers used to say at the start of every school year.

After I married Victor, I returned to America only once, traveling to New York and then on to Virginia. I knew it was the last time I would see my mother. With Victor's money, the generous allowance he gave me, I had moved every one of my siblings to upstate New York.

It had been my plan all along: As soon as I had the means, I would rip my siblings away from my mother and into the safety of a new, anonymous town. They wouldn't know what to do in a city, and it would be too expensive to support them there. But with Victor's funds, I bought a tobacco farm in Lindley, just west of Elmira, one of the few areas in New York known for the crop. Tobacco farming was the only work any of them had ever done. I could take them out of the South, but I only wanted to strip the bad from their lives, not the good.

To my brothers and sisters in Lindley, Virginia was just a distant spot on the map that they would probably never see again. When I told my mother she would be left to live out the rest of her life in Virginia alone, she hadn't even wept. She'd just looked at me coldly, as if she'd forgotten that I was her firstborn child, and said, "My family has disappeared."

But she had disappeared for me long before I did for her. The first time my father's fist hit my face and she did nothing to protect me, nothing to comfort me when the blows finally stopped—that's when she started to disappear. When my brother Peter, who was just three years younger than me, went blind in his right eye and partially in his left from a particularly vicious assault when he was only ten years old—that's when my parents turned into monsters. And when Peter's brain stopped working right—when he started suffering what the doctors called hallucinations, mania—that's when I knew I would never see my mother again.

Thousands of miles away, I shook my head, trying to fight the memories. In my worst moments, my mother always found a way to return to me, to seize my hand and try to wrench me down, just as she had done in life.

The words sounded in my head as I continued on down the street, whispers from voices I didn't recognize. I put my fingers in my ears, but still the sentence reverberated, circling me, strangling me. *My family has disappeared.* I looked over my shoulder, expecting to see my mother and her long gray hair, but all I saw was a sea of locals jostling one another as they navigated the crowded street.

At the end of the road, a house appeared to be in flames, but when I got near, I saw that it wasn't, just a vendor roasting nuts over a fire and the breeze carrying the smoke up. I sank to the ground, too tired, too confused, to go any farther.

Time seemed to stop, and my eyes grew heavier, but before they closed, I felt someone's breath on my forehead. A rickshaw coolie was bending over me.

"You need ride? Where you go, *madame*?" he said in a nasal voice.

I looked up at him and shook my head. I looked at his hands. They were dirty, with yellowed fingernails that were curling over. I looked more closely. The dirt on his fingers looked like opium tar.

I thought of the beds in Khoi's boat and then of the beds I knew were in all the opium dens in Hanoi. There, I could lie down. I could shake off the nightmare this day had become and give my mind space to right itself. I could try to piece together where my family had gone.

"Take me to Luong-Vuong," I said to the man. "I want to lie down at Luong-Vuong." I knew I didn't have to ask if he knew what it was.

He helped me into the back of his rickshaw, and I nodded off as we bounced through the streets. Then I felt us slowing, and someone carrying me inside, where I heard whispers, felt a woman's hand on my face, and then was lowered onto a wooden bed.

When I was horizontal, I let my hand go slack. "Take my money," I said into the air, letting my bag drop to the floor, desperate for past and present to just disappear in curls of smoke.

"Your pipe, *madame*," a woman said, holding up my head.

I took in the smoke deeply once, then a few times more in quick succession, before pushing her away with my limp hand. "No more," I said, rolling onto my side and trying to bring my knees to my chest. I wanted to shrink to nothing.

I was drifting in and out of sleep when I felt hands on me again. "I don't want any more," I said, trying to wave the woman away.

"It's Lanh," I heard a voice say. I managed to open my eyes. It was indeed Lanh. I held my arms out to him, not able to get up on my own.

Under Lanh's reassuring touch, I let my eyes close again and collapsed against him as he picked me up.

When I awoke, I couldn't tell if it had been minutes, hours, or days. I blinked and sat up slowly. I was in the back seat of the Delahaye with the doors open on either side, a cool breeze passing through. Outside the car, on a large rock, I saw Lanh sitting, though the edges of my vision were still frayed from sleep. We were on the bank of the Red River, in a spot he had driven me past before. A scenic detour, he'd called it. One of many he had taken, happy to meander and show me the city when Victor wasn't present. When he realized I was awake, he jumped up and came over to the car.

"Lanh," I said quietly, trying to focus on him. I stretched my hand out to him, and he helped me climb out of the car and steady myself on the dry reddish ground. He pointed to the rock and I shook my head, still feeling too unstable, so we both sat on the ground next to it instead, leaning against it for support.

I looked at him, hoping for answers.

"The woman who prepared your pipe at Luong-Vuong," he began. "She saw your identity card in your bag. She went to the hotel next door and telephoned the house. I answered. She robbed you, I think, but at least she telephoned." He gave me an anxious look. "Are you feeling like yourself now?"

"I don't even know what that means anymore," I replied. "But the world seems to be calmer. I think. And I feel less sick. The opium helped."

He nodded, his eyes still on me.

"What time is it?" I asked, looking up at the sun directly above us.

"It's almost noon," he replied.

It wasn't even midday and I felt like I'd already been to war.

"Lanh," I said, turning to him, suddenly remembering where I'd been before Luong-Vuong. "Did you take me, Lucie, and Victor to the station this morning?"

"Of course," he said without pause.

"Of course," I repeated, feeling the familiar, stinging sensation of tears ready to flow. I buried my face in my hands.

"I'm so utterly confused," I said through the sobs that needed to come.

"Do you not remember?" he said, inching away to give me some room.

"I do," I said, opening my eyes again. "I think that's why I'm crying. Because I do remember. Today, yesterday, all of it. I do remember, but everyone is telling me I'm wrong. That something is very wrong with me. But I don't think there is."

I glanced at him and he quietly said, "Who is telling you that you're wrong?"

I repeated the same story I had told the stationmaster. "But he told me I arrived alone. Without Victor and Lucie. And then he called the house and Trieu told him that they weren't in Hanoi at all. That they had gone to see the caves in Trang An together. Caves, of all things. I wasn't convinced by what he was saying, but I just don't trust myself lately, so I agreed and ran out of the station. As you can imagine, I was very distraught. All I could manage was to lose myself under a cloud of opium for a while. But then you found me, thank God. I knew I wasn't wrong. I don't know where they are, but I know they are not in Trang An and they did not disappear."

"Come," said Lanh, standing and helping me up. "I think I know what's wrong. We will find Lucie and Monsieur Lesage soon—I'm sure they are worried about where you are, too—and they may just be at the house. But there is something else that's even more important than the whereabouts of your family."

He helped me into the car, and we traveled in silence toward the house. I was still processing Lanh's words. The stationmaster had lied to me. But more importantly, my family had not disappeared.

Lanh turned toward our neighborhood, maneuvering the car around the usual potholes, but turned off before our street. He parked the car near the lake, in a quiet spot, and turned to me.

"Madame Lesage. Jessie," he said. It was the only time he'd ever said my first name.

"Lanh," I said softly, as if our relationship had somehow just shifted by him saying that one word.

"I know why you're feeling the way you are," he said, his hands in his lap, fidgeting. "And why you were too distraught to find your family."

"Victor would say it's because my mind is broken."

"Your mind is not broken," he said very quietly. He tilted his head up and looked at me, as if seeing me for the first time.

"What is it, then?" I asked, searching his dark eyes.

"You are a woman being preyed upon."

"By Victor?" I asked, my voice catching in my throat.

Lanh looked away but said nothing, letting the silence sit with us for a moment.

"Do you remember when we drove back to the yellow house after I took you to the hippodrome? After the horse race? You were very upset."

"I was," I said, thinking back to my conversation with Red. Of Marcelle.

"I asked Trieu to bring you something to eat and to make you very hot tea. Something to soothe you."

"I remember," I said, though it was blurry.

"I stayed near you that day because I was worried, and you've always been very kind to me. To us," he said, indicating his sister without saying her name. "When I wasn't by your side, I was in the shadows, not far away, making sure you were being taken care of. Trieu brought you what I asked, but you didn't drink all the tea she'd prepared, maybe only half, then you fell asleep. Trieu pulled all the curtains closed and then took the half-full cup downstairs with her when she was clearing your dishes, and I followed. When she was in the living room, on her way to the kitchen, she separated the cup from your plate and placed it aside. Lucie, who had been playing in the living room with her funny doll, that one with the pale face—"

"Odile," I whispered. I had bought it for Lucie before she was even born.

"Odile," he repeated. "Lucie left the doll and picked up the cup, smelling its contents and then lifted it up to drink from it. But before Lucie could drink the tea, Trieu, who was coming back from the kitchen, rushed over and knocked the cup out of her hands, causing it to shatter on the floor. I think she was as startled as Lucie was, in a way. It was forceful. She didn't think anyone saw it—I was in the shadows, like I said. She stared at the mess and then quickly apologized to Lucie. She said that her mother was quite sick and that if she used the same cup she could fall ill, too." He paused and looked at me. "I've seen you with your daughter. You share everything. You're a good mother. I knew you wouldn't have minded about the cup."

I looked at him, my layers of confusion multiplying.

"But Lucie never mentioned anything to me about that," I said, thinking back.

"I think she's very sensitive about your being sick," said Lanh.

I nodded, thinking of her words earlier that morning.

"With Lucie standing there, shocked, Trieu ran to the kitchen for a broom and rags to clean up the mess, and then Cam came and pulled Lucie away to wash her."

"But you were still there."

"I was, watching from the dining room. When they were gone, I quickly went over to the shattered cup, took some of the herbs out of the fragments, and wrapped them in a napkin."

"Why did you do that?" I asked, looking at him quizzically.

"I had a bad feeling. Trieu has never been anything but kind with Lucie. For her to push the cup like that was strange. It was out of character."

I nodded. It was true that Trieu was fond of Lucie. I had felt very lucky that they all pecked over her lovingly.

"That tea," Lanh said slowly, looking out at the river. "I had never seen those particular herbs before. Or I didn't think I had. So I took them to a doctor that many of the local people like me, servants, rely on. A Chinese herbalist. A highly regarded one."

"Out of concern for Lucie?" I said.

"No," said Lanh quietly. "Out of concern for you."

"What did he say?" I asked, searching Lanh's face.

"It didn't take him long at all," said Lanh. "He smelled the small bit I brought, then he ingested a little of it. A trace amount. As soon as he'd swallowed it, he said it was without any doubt an herb called *ky nham. Langdang* in his language, in Chinese."

"*Ky nham?*" I said numbly.

"*Ky nham,*" he repeated. "Henbane in French. *Hyoscyamus niger* is the medical name. It's a poisonous plant. And a very strong halluci-nogen."

"A hallucinogen?" I said, my stomach churning. "They've been giving me a hallucinogen?"

"I don't know who has. And I don't know if it was once or many times, but that day, when Trieu gave you that tea, that's what was in it."

"That can't be right," I said, thinking back to the tea I drank that day. It hadn't tasted strange. It tasted just like the tea I drank nearly every day. The one she had been serving me since my second day in Indochine—the day I'd seen the dead man. The king's herb, she called it. It had had no effect on me then. I'd been fine then. But when had I stopped being fine? It had all been so gradual. When was the line drawn dividing the Jessie Lesage who'd been able to handle her nervous energy into a woman who was consumed by worry, and much worse?

"Why would she give that to me?" I asked, my heart starting to pound.

"I don't know," said Lanh. "That's what I've been puzzling over."

"But when was that? The afternoon I spent at the horse race, that was six days ago."

"Yes," he said, apology in his voice. "I have known for a few days, but you were dealing with your own matters and I haven't been able to speak to you alone. But when I received this phone call today, I knew.

Something was terribly wrong, and it had to do with Trieu and that herb. I was sure of it."

Trieu. I thought of my relationship with Trieu. Don't try to befriend them, Victor had said. And I hadn't, but it didn't mean I hadn't grown fond of her. More than that, I had come to rely on her. She had seen me naked, bathed me, spoken to me at my most vulnerable. She must have been going up to her room every night and laughing at me. Me, the foolish woman, yet again.

"How long has Trieu worked in the house?" I asked.

"Not long. Madame van Dampierre hired her a few months before you arrived. That caused me to worry even more. Unlike Diep or Cam, she is still not very familiar to me."

"What else does this *ky nham* do?" I asked.

"It's a hallucinogen. That's what the herbalist said. A very strong one. The effects can last hours, he said, but can linger for days. In your case, I'm unsure. It depends how much she was administering. He also said that if ingested with alcohol, the effects could be worse. And drinking, it's something that all French women seem to do more in Indochine than they usually would," he said. "Alcohol aside, this herb, even in small doses, could cause confusion, problems with the memory, stomach illness. All things that perhaps you've been suffering from for some time?"

"Yes," I said, gripping my hands together. "But I thought it was just me. Just my mind refusing to cooperate with the rest of the world. A repeat of something that happened to me years ago. After Lucie was born."

"I don't know much about you, beyond what I see, but I don't think you're sick. Here or here," he said kindly, pointing to my heart and then my head.

I nodded, letting his disclosure sink in. In the past few months, what had been real and what hadn't been?

I was scared, and I was angry. My whole experience in Indochine felt stolen from me, as if I'd been living the way someone else had wanted me to. Ever since I'd left Virginia, I had done everything I could to have the freedom to choose my own path, to direct my life the way I wanted it to go. Trieu had taken that from me, just as my parents had when I was a child.

"I know I brought it up before. But those posters you described. The house of a hundred suns. You've really never seen them since you were a child?" I asked. More than anything, that's what I wanted to be true. To have seen the poster in the station.

He looked at me gravely and slowly shook his head no.

I bit my lip and thought about the words. If I had never seen them on a poster, how did I know them?

"When I traveled down to Saigon, just a few weeks ago, I thought I saw one of the posters you were describing hanging above the timetables. I have such a vivid memory of it. The image was of a station just like the one in Hanoi, and above it, it said, '*Pour aller loin, pour payer moins, pour être bien, prenez le train.*' But just my mind playing tricks on me, I suppose. Or Trieu playing tricks on me."

The instant I uttered her name, my sadness started to bleed into another rush of anger. Where were Victor and Lucie? We needed to return home and see if they were there. And if they weren't, we had to find them and, together, confront Trieu. They had not disappeared, and now we had to make sure that Trieu didn't, either.

THIRTY-ONE

Marcelle

November 20, 1933

A letter came this morning. It was brought by messenger
from Hue," said Khoi as I fell against him in the midday
sun that illuminated his backyard, making the grass look
electric.

"From Sinh's father?" I asked, looking at it in his hand.

"No. From Anne-Marie," he said, allowing himself to smile.

"From Anne-Marie?" I said, eagerly reaching for it. Khoi handed it
to me and I shivered, looking down at the ink on the envelope. Sinh's
father's address was in front of me, written in her beautiful, large looping hand. I gripped the page, bending my neck and placing my face
against it. "Across an ocean and more and I swear this envelope smells
like her, Khoi."

He smiled at me and nodded.

"Does she know we found Paul?" I asked.

"No, of course not," said Khoi, cocking his head. "How could she?
Did the angels bend down and whisper it to her?"

"Then what did she say? Why didn't she write before? It's been
years." I looked at the envelope again and started to cry.

"Maybe she could sense it," said Khoi. "That we needed to hear from her now. Maybe we are all still linked in that way, even without Sinh."

I nodded, not able to stop my tears from falling.

"Let's read it before we cry," said Khoi, running his hand across my cheek. "For so long we've been afraid that she was dead. That she was gone like Sinh. And now, look, we have this. So don't fall apart until we read it at least three times," he said, carefully opening the envelope and taking out the pages.

"You read the last letter that made me cry," I said, taking the paper from Khoi. "This time, I'll do it."

"I think it will be a happier letter," said Khoi.

I started it, hoping he was right.

My dearest friends,

It has been a week now that I've returned to Paris and I finally feel strong enough to write to you. I'm sorry it's been such a long while. I'm sure I made you think the worst with my silence, which I never intended. But in truth, I have been close to the edge many times since I last wrote. I've been in Italy, in Rome and Milan, which started out well, but this past year, I got quite caught up in some awful things. Violent protests, a few very dangerous decisions to try to push the fascists out of power. I had so much rage swimming through me, and it just refused to leave.

I had to flee Italy this year. I don't think I would have lived much longer if I hadn't. But I've found happiness since. I'm back in Paris, and I've taken up other interests. Now, I'm fighting to win the right to vote as much as I'm fighting for workers' rights, and the anti-colonial movement. I'm very involved with UFSF, the French branch of the international alliance for women's suffrage. I firmly believe that when women can vote, we can change the country, and the colonies. The women in UFSF are trying to convince me to be more reformist and less revolutionary, but don't worry, they haven't succeeded. I still wear a tuxedo most of the time, but they have in-

sisted that when I attend their meetings, I wear a shirt underneath. I've agreed, for now. But I did also convince the president to take up the ukulele. Charming instrument. I refuse to let its popularity die out with the jazz age.

Our plan is to get a woman into the government in the next few years. Some of us are convinced that it will happen sooner than that, and maybe it will. Maybe that woman could even be me. Now that would cause my father to have a stroke, wouldn't it?

I have not seen my family in two years. I wish things could be different, but there are some things which are not forgivable. What they did to Sinh is one of those things. If they ever want to try to right their wrongs, they can find me, but until then, I've decided to hold on to that part of my anger. But that's all I hold on to. I've forgiven the man who shot Sinh. I came to believe that while he played the role of executioner, that's all he was. I hope I'm right. Maybe one day, you will tell me you have the answer to that.

Sinh's father told me the last time we exchanged letters that you two were both in Indochine still. It made me very glad.

I hope you will stay there and live Sinh's life for him. But I also want you to come find me one day. My heart has been half empty for so long, but I know that when I see you again, it will feel less so. I have finally allowed myself peace. I hope you've done the same.

All my love,

AM

"Oh, Anne-Marie," I said, running my hand over her initials. "How I wish you were here."

"She's right. It's time for us to find peace, too," said Khoi, resting his head on my shoulder. "We won't stop trying to change things, but perhaps we can let ourselves breathe easier while we do."

I thought of the picture of Anne-Marie and Sinh hanging on the wall upstairs. We could perhaps have peace, but we could never again get back that joy.

"Yes, perhaps," I said softly. "But not quite yet."

We lay against each other then and stayed quiet for a time. I thought Khoi had drifted off to sleep, but when a cloud came through and covered the sun, creating momentary shade, he started speaking again.

"We are not perfect people, you and I," he said. "No one is. Even Anne-Marie and Sinh. I know we hold him up on a pedestal now, but he wasn't perfect. We all have moments of weakness, of strength, of stupidity. But if we're lucky, we have even more moments of love. We've had what feels like millions of those moments, and I know we have more ahead of us. We may not look it to outsiders, to your countrymen or mine, but we are, without a doubt, a perfect pair, despite our mistakes. We have been since the day we met. They were, too, but we are still together. Still alive. So we do deserve a little rest, Marcelle. Even you."

"Even me," I murmured.

Khoi did fall asleep then, but I was too restless to join him. Instead, I put Anne-Marie's letter in my pocket and had my driver take me home.

When I walked inside, the first thing I saw was a letter on the ground. I bent down and saw that it was from Pham Dat. The stationmaster. I ripped it open: "I took your friend on a wild ride at the station today. She was on her way to Vinh. She never made it. You'll be pleased by the outcome. PD."

I read the words again. "She never made it." What had he done to Jessie?

I had to get to the station.

I ran out of the house and got in my little car, ready to drive it myself.

I wasn't a block from the house when I saw someone running at me, sprinting. I gasped and stepped on the brakes. I had nearly hit a woman. When she turned, I saw that she'd stepped close to the car on purpose. She came up to my door, and I rolled down my window.

"We need to talk," she said. "Now. But not here."

I nodded and pointed to the seat beside me. Pham Dat would have to wait.

THIRTY-TWO

Jessie

November 20, 1933

"Where is she right now?" I asked Lanh, who was watching the river as it moved slowly toward the Gulf of Tonkin. "Trieu. Where is she?"

"At the house, I believe," he said. "Shall we go? I have a feeling we might just find Monsieur Lesage and Lucie there, too."

"Yes," I said, my voice finally sounding stronger.

Lanh stood up and helped me into the back seat. We drove in silence, my mind flooded with memories of everything that had happened since we'd arrived. I looked down at my hand, my right one still bare. That, sadly, was not a hallucination.

"When we arrive at the house, why don't I venture inside first and see who is home?" Lanh suggested. "If your husband and Lucie are in, or Trieu, I will come fetch you. But if they're not, there's no reason for you to have to move back and forth. You are still weak."

I nodded. "Thank you, that's a good idea," I said. I was desperate to see Victor and Lucie again, but Lanh was right. If they weren't there, I didn't want to leave the car.

When we reached the driveway, Lanh exited, closing the door

softly, and went inside. He was gone only a few moments and then came back outside at a run.

"Monsieur Lesage and Lucie are not there. Cam said that about a half hour ago, they came home from the station, very worried about you, but then left again."

"Left! Why would they leave?" I exclaimed. "Where did they go?" I was flooded with relief that they were together, and safe, but shaken that we had just missed them and now they were gone again.

"Cam said they returned to the station to see if you might have gone back there, and to get the bags, which thankfully didn't make it on the train without you. Cam will go there now and let them know that you're with me. And that you aren't ill anymore. Then you can all meet back at the house."

"That sounds fine," I said, leaning against the window. "I'm relieved they're all right. Though I still can't understand why they ran off."

Lucie had never run away from me before, even as a toddler. But there had been a time when one of my youngest sisters, Josephine, had run away under my charge. There were so many children to watch, and I had always been able to keep them together, but that summer day, Jo had managed to escape. It took me hours to find her, but I finally did, on the grounds of the agricultural institute. She was holding the hand of a woman who went to school there. One of the very few.

"I've found a new mother," she'd said when I'd run to her. There weren't tears in her eyes, just a look of determination plastered on her face.

"Do you need a new mother?" the young woman had said to her, looking at me with concern.

"I'm thirteen years old," I'd replied with disdain. "She's seven. She's my sister, not my child."

"Of course," she'd said, patting Jo on the head. "Why don't you go with your sister now?" she'd said, letting go of her hand.

Josephine had cried, had tried to hold on to the pretty woman, but she had scurried off, clearly not wanting to spend a moment more with us. We were dressed poorly. We weren't bathed. We were not the kind of children people were drawn to.

"I know it's awful at home," I'd said to Jo, hugging her tightly when we were alone again. "But I'll get you out one day. I swear to you. You just have to wait a little longer." I had wanted it to be sooner. I had tried to do it with my teacher's salary, but it wasn't enough. It had taken Victor and his money.

"Trieu," I heard Lanh say, bringing me back to the present. "She's not at home either," he said without turning around. "Diep, the cook, said she was at the market. The one near Truc Bach Lake."

"Let's go there then," I said as Lanh turned the car around quickly. "And Lanh?"

"Yes, Madame Lesage?" he said as he accelerated even more.

"I do know the name of our cook," I said, managing a smile.

"Of course," said Lanh, turning left from our street, accelerating on the wider avenue.

But I hadn't known the name of the stationmaster until today, the man who had lied to me with such a straight face.

Were Victor and Lucie going to speak to him when they returned to the station? I wondered. Had they spoken to him before they disappeared?

The stationmaster had never seemed like a cruel man, so for him to act in that manner meant he had to have been instructed to do so by Trieu. But why?

The only thing I could think of, the only link I could imagine between us, was the communists. The list of names. Maybe she knew that I had contributed to their deaths. Maybe one of them meant something to her.

I couldn't feel the joy I wanted to about Lucie and Victor being accounted for because everything else around me was still tainted by Victor's actions on the plantation. And my insufficient response since.

"Lanh, do you know the stationmaster here in Hanoi? Pham Van Dat is his name. Are you acquainted with him?" I asked as the market's fruit vendors came into view.

"Acquainted, no," said Lanh, slowing down. "But I do know that he's permanently available to the highest bidder. Why do you ask?"

"It doesn't matter," I replied, starting to understand.

When the car was parked, Lanh asked if I felt strong enough to walk. I nodded. My vision was still a bit blurred, and my body weak from panic, opium, and the cocktail of poison that I guessed Trieu had given me this morning and perhaps every morning for weeks, but I was no longer fearful. My head felt straight for the first time in months.

On foot, Lanh supporting my weight with his arm, we pushed through the jumble of shoppers and fruit and vegetable sellers.

"How will we find her?" I asked.

"We will just have to be observant," he said, gazing around. "Don't look only for her face. Focus on people who move like Trieu. Look for her rigid posture."

We stayed in that corner of the market for ten minutes, but as Lanh gestured for me to move on, I felt a sudden wave of nausea. I rushed to the edge of the crowd for more air, but quickly stopped in my tracks. Lanh grabbed me as I was starting to sway.

"I found her," I whispered.

We both looked where I pointed, Lanh still gripping my shoulders protectively. Trieu was there, in her beautiful blue *ao*, with a bag of leafy vegetables under her arm, speaking to Marcelle de Fabry.

THIRTY-THREE

Jessie

November 20, 1933

I had never been inside Trieu's bedroom. Almost two months in the house and I had never set foot in any of the servants' rooms except Cam's, since it adjoined Lucie's. It was very neat. Spotless. There was a small bed, the covers pulled tight, a table and a chair pushed in as far as it could go, and a dresser with a mirror above it. In the closet, Trieu's clothes hung neatly, her shoes spaced a few inches apart on the floor. Flinging open the closet door was the first thing I had done when I'd walked into her room.

I didn't know how long she would be at the market or if she would even come to her room when she returned. But I was not leaving it until she did. I looked at her small clock on her bedside table. It was nearly four.

Trieu knew Marcelle de Fabry. I was aware they had met before, the day I'd been in bed after seeing the dead man, my second day in Hanoi. But had they known each other before that? I looked at the dresser again. Trieu's hairbrush lay there, but nothing else. Not one photo, not one hairpin, nothing that revealed the true character of the woman I had trusted so implicitly. It occurred to me that though she had undressed me every day since I'd arrived, listened to my conversations, knew my food preferences, my sleeping patterns, my nervous tics, I had no idea who she was. I hadn't bothered to learn anything. Who had I become that I hadn't asked her a thing about herself besides her name? Had I lost my sense of humanity in the pecking order that the French imposed in Indochine? But even if I had, surely that wasn't enough to make Trieu want to poison me. Or kill me.

Why would she despise me that much? I kept coming back to the men at Dau Tieng.

When I heard footsteps on the stairs, I looked at my watch, quickly flipping it to see the face. I had been in her room for over an hour.

I watched as she opened the door. It was a very small room, she would see me in seconds, but for these few moments, I was watching her and not the other way around.

"*Madame!*" she screamed as soon as she looked up. "What are you doing here?"

It was the first time she had ever spoken out of turn to me, but I could already tell she knew exactly why I had come.

"Where were you?" I said, looking at her empty hands. She must have already dropped the vegetables off in the kitchen.

She entered without answering, pulling out the desk chair, stumbling over the legs as she did.

"Be careful," I said. "You wouldn't want to get hurt."

She looked at me again, unable to hide the fear on her face.

"I was at the market. Diep asked me to go."

"A simple errand, then, was it?"

She nodded, leaning on the chair. Her fingers gripped the back tightly.

"You're lying to me," I said, watching her posture change as I spoke. She had stiffened. Showing seeds of defiance. "I saw you with Marcelle de Fabry at the market today. And worse than that, I know about my special tea. A local recipe. Your traditional medicine. The king's herb. Isn't that what you called it? But I think you'd really only give such a thing to a king if you wanted him to start having visions.

Hallucinations. To make him think he had gone *insane.*" I went up to her. "Or if you wanted to kill him."

I pulled the chair from her hands and stared at her. "Why are you trying to kill me, Trieu? I am not a king. I'm just your employer's wife. So why have you been giving me poison since the moment I arrived?"

"It was not since you arrived," she spat back. "Perhaps you're going insane on your own."

My heart was racing. I had always resisted confrontation, but rage was propelling me forward.

Her face showed no sign of anguish or apology, no tears. I closed my eyes a moment, trying to regain my composure, then pushed her against the wall as hard as I could.

"Speak. Tell me everything, or I will call the police right now and have you jailed for the rest of your life. You'd probably be sentenced to just a few years for attempted murder, but with a large bribe, I'm sure the authorities would be happy to hand you a life sentence. This is Indochine, right? With the right-sized payment, anything can happen. Money is what makes the colony move."

"I don't care about your threats," said Trieu, pushing me away.

"You certainly don't care about any part of me," I said, "or else you wouldn't be poisoning me until I was on the brink of insanity."

"How did you find out?" she said, looking at me with disdain.

"No, I'm the one asking questions. Or shall we take a drive down to the police station?" I said, motioning to the door.

She looked at me but didn't say a word, walking over to her bed and sitting down.

"Fine," I said, going to her closet and starting to throw her clothes on the floor. "Where do you hide it? It must be in here." I looked in her shoes, and when I found nothing there, I went to her dresser and opened the top drawer, but she lunged at me, maneuvering her body in front of it.

"It wasn't my idea," she said, "though it was a good one."

"To try to kill someone you didn't know? That wasn't your idea?

Well, that's a relief," I said. I pushed her aside and reached for the drawer.

She pushed me back and sat directly in front of it. "Marcelle de Fabry asked me to do it."

I looked at Trieu, stunned silent by disbelief. She stared back at me with angry, wide-set eyes.

"What did you say?" I finally choked out. "Marcelle de Fabry had you poison me?"

I thought back to the night I first met her. To when she put her beautiful head on my shoulder, convulsing with laughter when we'd seen the naked minister. An instant friendship, I'd been sure. A spontaneous pull toward each other. How stupid I'd been.

"You're lying," I muttered.

"I'm not," Trieu answered defiantly. "Why bother to lie now? She asked me to do it, and she paid me. Very well."

"*We* pay you very well!" I countered, although in reality, I had no idea how much she was paid.

"I would have done it without payment," she murmured. "And you don't pay me well."

"How do you even know Madame de Fabry? Marcelle," I said, my voice dropping as reality continued to hit me.

"Don't tell the police, and I will tell you."

"You tried to kill me!" I said, choking back something between laughter and tears. "Why shouldn't I tell the police? About you and Marcelle!"

"I was making no attempt to kill you," she said. "I was trying to get you to leave."

"This house?"

"No. Indochine."

"To go back to France?" I asked.

She nodded.

"But why?"

"Say it first. Say that you will not tell the police," she said, crossing her thin arms defiantly.

"Fine," I said. If she could give me reason to go to the police about Marcelle, instead, that was enough. "But you will never work another day in this house. Or in Hanoi," I said. "Where are you from?"

"Nam Dinh."

"You'll be on the night train back there."

We looked at each other, I standing above her, she sitting on the bed. I moved to the chair so I could face her, eye-to-eye.

"Marcelle wants you to return to France. You and Monsieur Lesage."

"Yes, I gathered. Why?"

"Because you are making things worse than they were, and they were already awful."

"In Hanoi?"

She looked at me with disdain. "On the plantations. No one in your family has ever bothered to come here, but maybe that was a good thing because now that you're here, you've stripped the workers of even more, which I never imagined was possible. How can you take from people who have nothing? But you can, it turns out. You can take away their joy. Even their lives."

"How do you know so much about the plantations? You and I have never discussed them before," I said, not letting my mind go back to that room. To those men.

She looked at me defiantly. Her chin lifted proudly. "My brother worked on your plantations."

"He did?" I said incredulously. "Why didn't you tell me?"

"Tell you? That he didn't just work there, but *died* there? That he was kicked to death by his French overseer? That this Frenchman went to trial, one where your family brought the most expensive, aggressive lawyers from France? Even with those lawyers, he was still found guilty of manslaughter."

"And he was imprisoned?"

"Imprisoned?" Her eyes were two black storms in her beautiful face. "No. He was not imprisoned. The overseer's punishment, his only punishment, was a fine. He was ordered to pay my brother's wife, his widow, five piastres. Five!" she shouted. "What is that to your family? Even for a coolie that is only a week's pay. For you it is what? One or two of your double whiskeys?"

"Trieu. I don't remember hearing about this," I said, my voice falling from its fever pitch. "I'm very sorry for you. You should have told us."

"Do you presume to know about every death that occurs on your plantations?" she spat at me. "You? Who are you, anyway? You're just a pretty wife who thinks she's more important than she is. Who thinks she has influence over the Michelin empire. I can tell you from years of observation that you do not. You may have gotten your husband here, but you don't know anything about that company. There is no worse place than your plantations in Indochine. *Nowhere.* But you've already realized that. You and your husband saw it all. The rest of your family, they only hear about the terrible things that happen. The beatings, the hangings, but they can't see it. You, you do see it, and yet you still carry on."

"Yet you only wanted to kill me. Not Victor."

"I was not trying to kill you," she repeated. "I was trying to make you believe you were losing your mind again. Marcelle said that if we could do that, it would be enough to get your family to leave Indochine. That for you, for your health, Victor might leave. That little else would push him back to France. But that your well-being would."

I looked at her in disbelief.

"What do you mean 'losing your mind again'?"

"Marcelle has a dossier on you. Something she obtained in France. From a doctor."

"From the Prangins Clinic?"

"I don't think so," she said. "It had a man's name on it. I saw it once."

"Docteur Faucheux?" I asked incredulously.

"Yes, that's it," she said, triumphant. "A dossier from him."

"That's impossible," I said, thinking of the countless hours I had spent in that man's office.

"It's not impossible," she said. "As you said, money can make anything happen. She purchased it."

"When?" I croaked out.

"I don't know. Before you arrived. Before I started to work in this house."

"You only worked for Louise for a short time. Did you come just for this? Just to poison me and get me to return to France?"

"Something like that," she said, keeping her eyes averted. "It's what my brother would have wanted."

She looked out at the lake, and I followed her gaze.

"You have the best view of it from here," I said after a moment's silence.

"One of the perks of living in the attic," she said. "The only one."

"How long have you lived here, Trieu?" I asked. "In the yellow house."

"Four months before you arrived," she said without looking at me.

"So Marcelle was plotting all this for that long?"

"I don't know," she said, still speaking at the wall.

"Trieu, you do know."

"It's been far more than four months," she said finally.

"But we only had six months' notice that we were coming to the colony."

"You do understand that Michelin is more than you and your heartless husband, right? You are just little spokes that make the tires spin. Marcelle has hated Michelin long before she ever heard you were coming to the colony. She's hated you since Cao Van Sinh died. Since your family ordered his death."

"Who is Sinh Cao?" I said, growing more confused.

"Why don't you ask your husband," she said, her chin raised again. "He knows. His cousin Anne-Marie de la Chaume was in love with him. And she was Marcelle's very best friend. Marcelle and Khoi, everything they have done in Indochine, all of it has been for them."

Anne-Marie de la Chaume and Cao Van Sinh. I had never heard those names before.

"I'll ask Victor," I said earnestly. "I will. But what I don't understand, and need you, not Victor, to answer, is how Marcelle tricked Louise van Dampierre into hiring you?"

"Tricked!" she exclaimed, turning to me with an incredulous look on her face. "Louise van Dampierre was Marcelle's closest friend in the colony. It was easy to get me into this house."

"That poison. That *ky nham*. Is it also in Marcelle's house?" I asked.

"I doubt it."

"Put it there," I said, pointing to her dresser. "Now."

She opened the bottom drawer and took out a small cotton bag.

"I thought it would be silk," I said, grabbing it from her hand. I moved it between my fingers and then handed it back to her. "Marcelle's. Now," I ordered. "If she's home, find a way to get her out."

"She's not home," said Trieu.

"Where is she, then?" I said.

"Where she always is."

"At Khoi's palace."

Trieu nodded and put the cotton bag in her pocket.

"Did she break my ring?" I said, the bag jogging my memory and pitching me back to my nightmare on the boat. "Did she smash my emerald ring when I was on the Nguyens' boat?"

"I don't know," said Trieu.

"Well, I do," I said, making for the door.

"She knows about the men," Trieu called after me as my hand turned the doorknob. "On the list in Haiphong. She knows you killed them, and so do I."

"I didn't kill them," I said without looking at her.

"But you didn't save them, either. That's the same thing."

I turned toward her slowly.

"You don't know what happens on those plantations," she said.

"I do. Like you said, I was there. I spent several days," I countered.

She shook her head and laughed, clearly laughing at me.

"You saw what you imagine is the worst of it, but death is not the cruelest fate. It's the daily abuse, physical and psychological, that kills most of the men—and women. You glimpsed the face of death, but you didn't see the everyday sins."

I thought of my own family, the piling on of constant abuse that was far more damaging than the more occasional blow to the head, and didn't reply.

"Before he died, my brother told me everything. In the fields, in the hospitals, in their dormitories, women are touched constantly. Defiled. Their children don't go to school. They can't read. They never see their parents. The ones who are Lucie's age speak like babies. As for the men, they're nothing but mules for you, for the Michelins. They die like rodents, but with less mercy than a trap. Maybe you didn't bother to look past what your husband showed you, but you should have. I've observed you closely these past months, even if you didn't bother to look at me. You're not one of these French idiots. You have intuition. You could have seen what was right in front of you. You just didn't care to look."

"Trieu, I'm sorry. I understand your hatred for that overseer. For the whole Michelin family. If I were—"

"For Michelin! How self-centered can you possibly be?" she said, stepping closer to me. "Actually, don't bother with an answer. I've seen it for myself."

It was awful to think about having been watched with such judgment all these months. It was almost as nauseating as the rest of her actions. Suddenly, the beautiful yellow house that I so adored felt like it was a glass house, completely transparent.

"That man, that company, killed my brother," she spat out. "But my world has been much bigger than that for years. I don't just hide inside like you and think about myself all day. I think about my people, my country. Because this is my country. Not yours."

"Trieu, I'm not even—"

"Yes, I know. You're not even French. You can be whatever it is that you are, but I am Annamite. I am Northern. And I am going to help lead this country when we finally rid it of the foreign pest. Rid it of you."

"You and the communist party."

"Yes," she said with pride. "It is a place for women. And I suppose the party really has your family to thank for my loyalty. You all brutally killed my brother and I learned to control my anger through political agitation."

"And aren't you lucky to have Marcelle's money to pay your dues," I countered, leaning back on the wall.

"I am lucky," she said quietly. "And as she is far more generous than your husband, I'm doing much more than paying my dues. You believed my life was a simple one. I was just a peasant sweeping your floors and powdering your nose. But I am so much more. Our cells are multiplying, and some of that is thanks to me. Your simple servant girl."

I looked at her beautiful face, and suddenly felt a strange pang that I would never see it again.

"Trieu. Is that your real name?" I asked.

"No," she said, glaring at me.

"What is it, then?"

"It's Hoa," she said proudly. "Like the flower."

I nodded, closing the door quietly behind me.

THIRTY-FOUR

Jessie

November 20, 1933

I looked up at Khoi's dazzling white house and blinked. It was truly a storybook place, especially in the late-afternoon light. Lanh had driven off, as I'd asked him to. When I felt brave enough, I started to knock on the front door. Loudly.

No one came, but Trieu had said she was sure Marcelle was there. She had to be watching me.

I went around the side of the house, remembering the large doors in the back.

I stopped when I saw the chair where I'd been sitting with the *indigène* woman the night of Khoi's party. The blood on her arms, her bare skin, it had all seemed so real to me. But it wasn't.

The back doors weren't open, but they were made of glass. I would be impossible to ignore.

Suddenly, I thought about how many opportunities there had been to poison me. Trieu, of course, had access to me every day, and I'd grown very fond of the morning tea she served me, but there was also Marcelle. I thought of the cigarettes she had handed me when we'd been together, the opium we'd smoked prepared by Khoi's servants. Trieu certainly had not acted alone.

I heard a sound that broke my reverie. Marcelle was at the glass doors, looking out at me. She slowly opened them and stepped out but didn't approach me. I ran to her before she could go back inside.

"I'm sorry to come here," I said, panting, my eyes moving rapidly back and forth. "I'm just so sick. I'm . . . I didn't know where else to go."

"Come," she said, gesturing to the pool, which was still uncovered despite the recent cooler temperatures. "Lie back here," she said, sitting down on one of the chaise longues. "You'll feel better."

I shook my head, kicked off my shoes, and sat by the pool, putting my bare feet in the water.

She looked at me oddly, then sat next to me, keeping her body away from the edge. She leaned back on her arms and watched me. I wish I knew the last things she'd said to me as a friend. But I never would. After today, I would never see her again.

"I was out of town, and I, I'm not sure why but I started to feel so ill. I didn't know where to go." I threw myself to the ground and swatted at the sky.

"Are you feeling any better?" she said, eyeing me cautiously. "This isn't the same illness that you had at Khoi's little get-together, is it?"

How rich. A party with hundreds of dollars' worth of champagne and piles of steamed lobsters and imported caviar was a "little get-together." Some communist sympathizer she was.

"I don't feel any better," I said, putting my hands on either side of my head. I pushed them against my skull and then started hitting my head, hard. "It's here. It's all here. It's a mess. And I just don't know why." I started to shake.

"Do you need a doctor?" she said as I met her gaze. Her voice was full of concern, but her eyes were laughing at me. I could finally see it. All this time, what I'd taken for joy, for mirth, for a sparkling personality, was actually muffled laughter, at my expense.

No longer.

"No," I said, my expression abruptly hardening, my voice suddenly clear. "You know, I do feel better. I actually feel fine." I placed my hands in my lap and smiled.

She startled, trying and failing to hide her surprise at my quick turn for the better.

"You look rather shocked, Marcelle. Does my sudden burst of good health surprise you?"

"Well, you seemed so sick," she sputtered, trying to stand. I reached out, put my hand on her shoulder, and pushed her back down forcefully.

"I have seemed sick, haven't I?" I said, moving closer to her, so that our legs were almost touching. "Practically the whole time we've known each other. I sure have felt sick. Why do you think that is?"

"I don't know," she said coolly, reaching for my hand on her shoulder and lifting it off. I let her. She was starting to understand. "Some people just don't take to Indochine. The heat, the food, the lifestyle, or lack of lifestyle, it's just not for everyone."

"But especially not for me," I hissed. "Because before you even met us, you hated me and Victor. And you were plotting my demise with confidential medical files. Because you are crafty and devious and rotten to the core." I got even closer to her. "You're an utter bitch, Marcelle," I whispered.

"I have no idea what you're talking about," she said, staring straight in front of her. "You really seem quite ill. Perhaps I should call a doctor. You have a history of outbursts, after all. Why, just a few days ago dozens of people saw you ranting and raving about a bleeding woman. Maybe it's reason enough to send you back to Switzerland. The Prangins Clinic, wasn't it? Though we do have our own facilities for that sort of thing here. Insanity, that is. I'm sure you'll find them very comfortable."

"I never said Prangins," I replied, glaring at her.

"Of course you didn't," she said lightly. "And neither did I. All it took was the mere mention of Switzerland, but my goodness, didn't you squirm. It was wonderful to watch you, Jessie, it really was. I wish

I'd been there when Red smashed your ring on the boat, just like I asked him to. Good old Red, a faithful dog that one. He said you squirmed then, too, despite being out of your mind. I'm sorry I missed it, but I've played the scene over in my mind many times, as I'm sure you've played over in yours the scene of those dead men at Dau Tieng."

"You're right," I said, my anger with myself competing with my anger toward her. "I have."

"You're a broken person, Jessie," she said, shaking her head at me. "I don't know how you can just sit by and sip champagne married to that devil of a man. It's no wonder you're going crazy."

"I'm not crazy," I said, staring at her. "You and Trieu—I'm sorry, *Hoa*. You and Hoa have tried to convince me otherwise, but I'm not. My mother-in-law tried to make me think so in Paris, even convinced her son to support her, but that didn't work, either."

"You were mad enough—or perhaps just stupid enough—not to see that you had a communist leader in your own home."

"You put her in my home!"

"No," she said firmly. "*You* put her there. Your little company, that family, the one you so desperately wanted to be a part of. Besides, you were broken years ago, weren't you? By your parents. Your father. How often were the beatings again? Near daily, once you were older? He only hit the babies about once a week, is that right? Is your brother Peter still blind from it? Half mad, too, yes?"

I stared at Marcelle, my mind white with anger. I had never talked about my childhood with anyone but my siblings and that doctor. Each time I shared those pieces of my past, I had to fight to remember I was safe now, that I had escaped. And now Marcelle knew. Probably Trieu. Certainly Khoi. I hated her. I hated her with more passion than I'd felt for any human besides my parents.

"But the worst of it," she said, leaning in and whispering, "was the baby. What was she called, again? Oh, never mind, I remember. Eleanor. Baby Eleanor. She wasn't quite right at birth, was she? Mongolism? Was that why your father drowned her in the lake? I can't imagine what it was like for you to watch her die. You were the one who telephoned the police, right? And testified against your own father. I was able to find a little newspaper clipping from that, too. From your hometown periodical, of all things. As I said, I was in America years ago. I still have many friends there. But you never had many friends, did you? Who would want to be friends with such a damaged little girl? With a Holland? Even her own mother never loved her. But maybe that was due to madness, too. There's mental illness around every corner with you."

I felt the tears forming, but I would not let them fall.

"'Complicit.' Isn't that what you said on the stand?" she said softly. "She never hugged you. Never comforted you. Encouraged him, you said."

I stared at her hateful face. Like Trieu—Hoa. A woman I once found so beautiful, turned hideous.

"But then that woman found her way to Paris. Dorothy, wasn't it?" she spat out. "Like a little country chicken swimming over to France to deliver Victor the news. The truth about the trash he'd married. How much does he know, Jessie? Does he know that your parents are alive? You told that doctor that he doesn't. He doesn't know your mother is a muttering lunatic, a pariah in your hometown, and he can't possibly know about your father. I'd keep that a secret, too. Does he know how much of his money you send to that gaggle of siblings?"

"Who are Sinh and Anne-Marie?" I asked, pinching my eyes closed again.

"Just two more people whose lives the Michelins ruined. That's what it seems like you were put on earth to do, doesn't it? Ruin lives and deceive people. Build a life based on lies. You know, Caroline was right. To achieve all this," she said, smirking, "you really must be quite gifted in the sexual arts."

She paused, then lifted her hand as if to slap me in the face. When I flinched, she started to laugh. And at that moment, I cracked.

I lunged at her and grabbed her by her neck, as forcefully as I could, squeezed with all the muscle I had, and pulled her with me into the swimming pool, holding her head underwater.

Marcelle was much taller than me, and certainly stronger, but I had the element of surprise on my side.

She thrashed her arms and legs, trying to find her footing, trying to grab my arms to free herself, but she was already getting weak from the lack of oxygen. The next thing to go was the muscles in her neck. She had tried to push her head out, to break through my hands, but that bobbing motion was weakening.

I watched as her thrashing died down, as her movements started to slow. No one would blame me for her death. It was the easiest crime a person could commit. All I had to say was that I was hallucinating, under the influence of a psychotic that Marcelle herself had administered to me. When the police checked, it would be all over her home.

After a few minutes, Marcelle's legs were no longer moving, and her dark hair was floating out around her head, which had become quite easy to hold now that it was barely moving. Her hair looked like a beautiful black halo, swaying in the water like algae.

How long had I been holding her down? Five minutes? Longer? I instinctively looked down at my watch, but my arms were still submerged in water. A person could stay underwater for quite a long time and still live. Fifteen minutes. But after ten minutes, brain damage was very likely. It was something I'd thought about for years—ever since Eleanor had died. I watched as Marcelle's arms went limp, barely able to move. And then a strand of her hair came apart from the mass, stroking the side of my hand. I jumped. The thick strands, the dark color, it felt just like Lucie's. And even more like Eleanor's. I immediately let go, lifted her head out of the water, and pulled her partway up the concrete pool steps. When she was securely above water, I looked at her, her beautiful face still. I shook her shoulders, and she gasped for air and started to cough violently.

I stared at her for a few moments, then bent down and whispered in her ear. "Go back to France, or I really will kill you. Or better yet, I'll make sure you rot in a jail cell, just like I made sure my father would. Turns out I have a knack for putting people behind bars."

Marcelle did nothing to acknowledge what I'd said, coughing harder and wheezing, water still in her lungs. It was enough. I started to rise but stood quickly when I heard a bang. The back door had flown open, and Khoi was running our way. What he wanted was Marcelle, not me. I started to sprint in the other direction as fast as I could, away from the house.

Lanh was idling just around the corner, as promised.

Wordlessly, he handed me a large pinch of the *ky nham* I'd asked him to buy. I ingested it, then drank from the glass bottle of water he handed me.

"Are you sure it's not too much?" I asked. Just as it had in the tea, the herb had a pleasant, earthy taste to it. There was no indication it was going to make me half crazy.

"I'm sure," he said. "Enough so you will be sick again, but this time, not too sick."

"Walk with me a few blocks and then leave me," I said. "Then go back to the house and telephone the police. Tell them where they can find me. The rest will work itself out."

"*Oui, madame*," he said, taking my arm. He helped me lie on the ground, then walked to the car, opened the door, and looked back at me to make sure I was all right.

I smiled at him and pointed at the sky. The sun was bright and comforting.

"For you, it will always shine like that," he said, getting in the car.

I lay back on the stretch of grass, looking up at the sky, waiting to feel sick again. I now knew all the symptoms, physical reactions I had mistaken for frayed nerves.

Marcelle was probably inside the house by now. Khoi would have called a doctor, and she would be filling his head with lies. She thought she knew everything about me, that smug, awful woman. But there was one thing she didn't know. One thing I had never uttered aloud, even to the doctor.

My sister Eleanor was dead because of me.

Eleanor was my mother's last baby. After she was born in my parents' bed on the first Saturday in June 1918, with only the help of a midwife, my mother swore she would never have another one. Especially after she saw Eleanor's face, which she and my father immediately called "simple."

"There's something wrong with her," my father said, handing her back to my mother after holding her for only a minute or two.

"Your father's never touching me again," my mother said to me, exhausted from the birth. She was hugging the tiny baby, but just twelve hours after she was born, she came to me with her and said, "Jessie, you take her." She had done the same thing with the two girls born before Eleanor. I was sixteen. I was used to being my siblings' mother and the only source of adult love in the house.

Eleanor was a terrible sleeper. Maybe if she'd been a good baby, things would have ended differently, but she wasn't. I tried to quiet her as best I could at night, taking her out of the house into the sticky summer air when she woke up, but sometimes nothing I did would soothe her.

My father had kept from backhanding us—or, worse, beating us senseless—until we were old enough to at least cover our faces with our hands. But with Eleanor, he didn't wait. One night after drinking himself into a stupor on homemade alcohol, he hit her across the face when she was wailing. She fell unconscious.

She came back to life somehow after that and slept in my arms, but she had stopped crying. Her screams had turned to barely audible whimpers. She might have been different from the rest of us when she was born, but my father had handicapped her for life with one blow to the head.

I didn't want to leave her side after that, not trusting anyone else with her, but when school resumed in September, I had no choice. I was aware by that point that my only paths out of Blacksburg were education or marriage to someone on the outside. Someone who had no idea who the Holland family was.

I walked home from the first day of school the long way, as I had in previous years, enjoying my thirty minutes alone, the only time I ever had away from my siblings or schoolmates. Sometimes students from the technical institute came to that corner of the woods in the afternoons, as there was a pretty pond there, but mostly there were only deer. On that hot day, I didn't see another living soul.

I walked past the pond into another clearing in the woods but stopped when I heard a noise. I thought it was an animal, but I turned to see that it was a man. My father. He was standing by the pond, swaying drunk. In his arms, he had the baby. In one motion, before I could open my mouth, he took her tiny body and pushed her under the water. Even from afar, I saw a ripple as he held her down. She was moving something, a tiny arm, a leg, as she struggled to survive, even at three months old.

I wanted to run to her, to save her. My father was drunk, I could have knocked him down, but I stood paralyzed. In those few seconds my mind dictated that I should stay still. More than I wanted to save the baby, I wanted to save myself and the rest of my siblings, who had already endured so much from him. That desire overwhelmed my instincts to rescue Eleanor.

When my father stood up, there was no baby in his arms. Before he could see me, I turned and sprinted away. I ran all the way into town, to the police station, without a glance over my shoulder. I told them what I'd just seen, not adding that I could have reached the baby in time if I'd tried. The officers sped in their cars to the pond, and in the oppressive summer air, they fished out the dead child and went to find my father.

I could have saved her, I told myself, looking out at the water after they'd gone. But what kind of life would she have had? She would be happier in death, I was sure. And with her death, I would be happier in life.

My father was sentenced to life in prison. My mother was distraught, not because her baby was dead, it seemed, but because she was left to run the farm alone, left with all her children, whom she didn't love and had never once tried to protect from her husband.

Years later, when I became a mother, I realized that I probably could have done both. I could have found a way to save the baby and save myself. But at sixteen, I'd been too terrified to try.

I looked at the sky, which was starting to wave in front of me, and thought of Marcelle floating facedown in the water, just as Eleanor had.

It was strange to realize how much Marcelle had known of my life before we met. How much she hated me because of the man I'd married. If she'd only known that she could never hate me as much as I hated myself for Eleanor's death, maybe things would have ended differently. I looked down at my watch. It was faceup and still ticking perfectly. Victor was right; it was a very good watch.

My stomach started to lurch, and I closed my eyes, waiting for the police to find me.

THIRTY-FIVE

Jessie

November 21, 1933

The chickens on the Holland farm. The only animals among the tobacco. I dreamt that I had to collect one for the slaughter, in the dead of winter. I only needed one at a time, usually. But how did a person decide whose time it was to die? Even a chicken? Just as I always did, in my dream I chose one that was looking away so I didn't have to see its eyes.

I had almost murdered Marcelle exactly the same way, without seeing her eyes.

"Madame Lesage," I heard a voice say over and over as I started to wake up. It wasn't until I dared to open my eyes that I saw I'd been dreaming. I wasn't back on my parents' farm. I was still in Indochine. In a hospital bed. The voice I was hearing was a doctor's. But next to him was Victor.

"Oh, thank God," Victor said, hurrying to my side and putting his arms around me.

"Where did you go?" I said, weeping and holding him, not even acknowledging that I was in a hospital. I knew why, even if he didn't. "At the station. Where did you go? You and Lucie just disappeared.

I was terrified," I said, my voice muffled as I buried my face into his shoulder.

"Lucie rushed out of the bathroom," said Victor, releasing me. "She said you were sick and needed help. We went to ask the stationmaster if there was a doctor nearby, as Lucie was very upset, and he said there was, just a block from the station. I went running off to find him, and Lucie came with me. I didn't realize until I reached the doctor's office that she was right behind me. She should have gone back to you, but she followed me. When we returned to the station with the doctor, you were gone. Up and vanished. We were looking for you everywhere, all over the city. We were traveling by taxi and *pousse-pousse* because Lanh was gone, too. Lucie was extremely upset. But then, luckily, we were at the station again, fetching our bags, when Cam came to explain. We've been at the hospital now for hours. All day."

"All day?" I repeated. "How long have I been here?"

"About eight hours," said the doctor, pushing his glasses up his long, thin nose. "It's nearly midnight and you came in a bit after four. You were awake for some of it, but I don't think you'll remember."

I shook my head. I remembered nothing. I looked at his dark brown hair, his tired blue eyes. He did not look the least bit familiar to me.

"I'd like to examine you again now that you are awake, Madame Lesage, but there is a police officer here who would like to speak to you first," said the doctor. "May I show him in?"

"Of course," I said weakly. When the doctor left, Victor reached for my hand and whispered, "Lanh told me everything."

I nodded, gripping his hand harder.

"But don't tell this policeman a thing," he added, before greeting the uniformed man as if they were old friends. "Better if we take control of the situation ourselves," he whispered. "My uncle, I'm sure, would prefer it."

When the policeman had gone, I turned to Victor and for the first time noticed that he'd grown older. He did not look like the carefree boy whom I'd met at Maxim's; he looked like a man who had seen quite a bit of the world, not all of it good. He had slight lines at his eyes, and his lips seemed thinner, less inclined to smile.

"Victor," I said, turning to my side. "Who are Anne-Marie de la Chaume and Cao Van Sinh?"

He thought for a minute and then sat on the side of my bed in his wrinkled clothes.

"Anne-Marie de la Chaume? I haven't thought about her in years. She's a cousin of mine, distant, on the Michelin side. I believe she went crazy a few years ago. And the other name? What was it?"

"Cao Van Sinh," I repeated.

"A native man? Did he work for us? I don't know. I don't recognize that one."

"Marcelle said you would know it. She said that the Michelins ruined their lives. Trieu said that it happened several years ago, perhaps before Marcelle and Arnaud came here."

"I know who he must be then," said Victor after a pause. "I had forgotten about this family stain but you saying her name has jarred it back. Anne-Marie fell in love with a native man. Cao Van Sinh must be him."

"You have a cousin who fell in love with a native man? A Michelin cousin?"

"I do," he said. "I'd forgotten, but at the time it did cause quite a stir."

"Where is she now?"

"I have no idea. France, I imagine. Though she could be anywhere. From what I heard, she lived a life devoid of boundaries."

I stared at him, waiting for him to continue.

"Anne-Marie was a student in Paris when I worked for André. That much I know. And she fell in love with this man, who must be Sinh Cao. He was a communist and she became a communist, too. She even wrote for *L'Humanité*, if you can believe that." He looked at my face. "Yes, I suppose we can believe anything at this point," he continued. "Her parents found out and were very upset. Her mother is the Michelin, her father is a minister. Or a senator? Something important, and very conservative. They learned that Sinh was traveling back to Indochine, and they asked André to intervene on their behalf. They wanted to make sure that this boy, this communist, could never set foot in France again. I think I helped André with it all, actually. We dealt with the secret police all the time then. We still do. André wrote to someone in Annam, that's where this boy was from, I believe, and it was done."

"And that caused Marcelle and Khoi to hate Michelin? And to hate us by association?"

"Maybe," said Victor reflectively. "Who are they to her?" he asked, his eyes red and exhausted.

"I believe they are Anne-Marie's best friends," I said after a moment. "Family, to her."

"I remember now," said Victor, standing up suddenly. "That boy, he died. In Haiphong. Something went wrong when he was detained at the port, and I think by no fault of ours, except maybe tangentially, he was shot. He died in Haiphong."

"He died?" I exclaimed.

"Yes," said Victor. "I'm only remembering it now because we just again employed the man who shot him. A few days after we arrived, Édouard sent a note saying that we were indebted to him—that he'd helped solve a problem for us—but that he'd fallen on a bit of a hard time and that we should hire him. He was a policeman before, but now he's in Haiphong. You met him, actually," he said, pausing, as if starting to see the way the web was weaved. "In Haiphong. His name is Paul Adrien."

THIRTY-SIX

Jessie

January 7, 1934

I turned in the Delahaye and looked out the back window at the yellow house as it faded into the distance, its beloved shape receding behind us. It wasn't Lanh who was taking us to the train station; it was a hired man. Lanh was on vacation. Victor had wanted to do something kind for him, a gesture to show how thankful we were that he had saved me. A trip, I had suggested. A long rail journey so he could see every train station in the country if he wanted to.

Next to me was Lucie, in pants instead of a starched dress. She looked like a different child, as we had cut her long hair to her chin the week after I'd left the hospital. We had all needed a fresh start, but thankfully, she still felt like my Lucie. I put my right hand on hers but gripped the gift that Lanh had given me before he left with my other. He had told me not to open it until we were out of Hanoi, and somehow I'd managed to obey his wishes.

After weeks of chaos, calm was starting to return to our lives.

After a second night in the hospital, the doctor told me that he suspected poisoning. I had been fearful that I would have to lead the horse to water concerning the diagnosis, but the French doctor was thankfully intelligent enough to recognize how my symptoms fit together.

When the policeman got involved, I told him that I strongly suspected Marcelle de Fabry was behind my poisoning. She had illegally obtained my medical files from France. She was plotting my return trip before I even arrived in Hanoi. Her cigarettes, I told them. That was how she poisoned me. And through my drinks, too. Through a strong tea. The policeman went to the de Fabry home, where he and another officer found a large amount of *ky nham*, as they later described it to us, in her dresser and, as I had suspected, rolled into cigarettes. Arnaud was home at the time, an unfortunate turn of events. He said it was all a great misunderstanding, that they used the herb in small quantities themselves as a relaxing agent, and accompanied the police to Khoi's palatial home, where Marcelle was.

I was later told by Lanh, who obtained the full story from Khoi's surprisingly bribable servants, that Marcelle flew into a rage, claiming I had tried to murder her and she had never administered poison to me. She repeated exactly what her husband had said. They used the herb for themselves. She was the one who was being targeted, she claimed. She showed the police the marks on her neck. She said it was a miracle she was alive. That if Khoi had not spotted her, she would be dead by my hand.

The police had countered her. They said they had more than enough to arrest her and mentioned the name of my doctor in France whom she had bribed. She didn't admit anything to them, but the servants told Lanh that her guilt was obvious.

When the police came to the yellow house a day later, they told us that they planned to arrest Madame de Fabry, but Arnaud was attempting to bribe them out of it. He had put up quite a sum of money to keep his wife out of prison, even a courtroom.

"I don't care how much he's given you," Victor had shouted. "She has been steadily poisoning my wife for two months! The fact that she lived is by the grace of God alone and her good American stock. You have to—"

"Force them to leave Indochine for good. Exile or prison. Offer that to Marcelle and see what she decides," I'd said. I knew that Marcelle would choose a jail cell in Indochine over an apartment in Paris, just so she could be near Khoi, but Arnaud, I was sure, would not allow it.

And he didn't. He arranged for a position back in France, we were told. The police assured us that they would sail soon and never set foot in Indochine again. And at my behest, they ensured Khoi could not go with her.

"See that they leave very quickly, please," I'd asked the police officer when Victor left the room. "I can't stand the idea of having to see her again. And also"—I handed the man a large stack of crisp piastres—"see that she is under your watch between now and the day she boards the boat. I want to make sure she never sees Nguyen Khoi again. I'm sure that even one conversation between them will be to further plot my demise."

"Of course, Madame Lesage," he had said, taking the money. "Your leniency with her is to be admired."

He had no idea that even a few years away from Khoi could smash her heart for good.

I looked down as the car jolted forward, our temporary driver not as experienced as Lanh. A new ring was on my finger. It was a light blue stone, not worth anything. Glass, most likely. Cam had said that it had been sent to me by Lanh's sister after Lanh told her that I'd been in the hospital. The Michelin money was so often used for good. That's what Khoi and Marcelle didn't understand. That girl was receiving a great French education, and her life would be forever changed because of it. I would certainly see personally to that.

Soon, the beautiful yellow house was out of sight. I was sure I would return, as Victor didn't intend to sell it, so we could use it when we were ready to visit Hanoi, but I was happy to leave for a while. We were all moving to Saigon. Lucie would enter a new school there, one of the only ones in the country that hired native teachers as well as European to teach the French children. Her day would be longer, they told us, but it was for the best. I would be busy opening real schools on the Michelin plantations, for the children, and for the coolies to learn French, a project Victor had promised me I could undertake when we had been in bed one night after I'd left the hospital. Trieu had once told me that less than one-fifth of native boys went to school. And that for girls the numbers were far less. She'd said it during one of her false odes to the French way of life, but I'd remembered the abysmal statistics. On our plantations, every child would attend school, and the laborers would be given time to study, too. Victor would see that they were given more time off to do so, for no one on a Michelin plantation should leave illiterate. Though still deeply committed to maximum efficiency and profit for the plantations, he'd sold the idea to his family by guaranteeing it would improve worker retention rates. I prayed that he would be able to keep his word.

When I'd shared my idea with Lanh, he'd suggested that education was not just needed for the natives. That if the Europeans on the plantation were to learn Annamese, that perhaps the historically tense relationship between workers and managers might change. He suggested that it would be a good way to build loyalty to the company and to show Michelin's investment in the colony. Victor, after looking at the relatively low financial cost of it all, had agreed.

"Lucky for Victor to have a clever wife," he'd whispered in my ear, recalling our first night in Indochine, and Marcelle's declaration.

I let his praise ring out in my mind, but I couldn't let it sit without finally telling him the truth.

When it was just the two of us alone, and I was at last feeling stronger in body and mind, I told him about Eleanor. I explained the way she'd died, those few seconds where I had chosen to act with myself in mind instead of her. It had led to crushing guilt that I knew would never leave me. Victor wrapped his arms around me as I cried. Then, at last, I told him about my parents. They were not dead. My father was in prison, and while my mother was free, she had lost her sanity long ago. I told him about my brother Peter, about how much of my allowance was sent off to him and my other siblings every month. I admitted that it was my intense fear of his finding me out, my fear of my daughter then being taken away from me, of a repeat of Switzerland, that had caused me to keep lying. And I told him about Dorothy—it was not because I was a clever wife that we had come to Indochine. It was because my growing pile of lies had finally caught up with me. They were the noose around my neck.

I expected anger and a feeling of betrayal, but Victor was steady and calm. He finally spoke at length about his own father. About his mental demise and how he'd let his fear of his father's state guide too many of his decisions. We realized, together, that we did not have to shoulder our burdens alone.

But there was still the burden of what I'd seen. Of what Victor had orchestrated. The ten names on the list. The dead communists.

"They were inciting rebellion," Victor said wearily, without conviction. "It was the right thing to do. It was the police that suggested it."

"But they died, Victor," I said. "They were someone's children, too."

"They were no longer children," he shot back.

"There must be another way," I'd pressed.

"Yes, there is," he'd said confidently. "We will weed out those men before they ever get that far with such plans. They'll go to prison, and not ones of our making," he'd assured me. "We can't just let them roam free—our success has to come first. For Michelin, and the colony," he'd added.

Maybe someone like Marcelle wouldn't have been able to stomach such a bargain, where self-interest was clearly still king, but I could.

My family came first. Always. Even if I had to make difficult decisions for the right outcome.

"Did you see this?" Victor said to me as our car rumbled over the bridge out of Hanoi. I looked at the newspaper in his hand.

"Khoi is to be married. It was even in the French paper. A girl from an indigo-producing family. They own many plantations. See, there are natives who own plantations, too. We don't have a monopoly on everything," Victor said.

I raised my eyebrows and took the paper from him. There was no picture of her, but I didn't have to see her to know she was not as beautiful as Marcelle. And that Khoi would never love her. I also knew that this marriage would be as much of a sham as Marcelle and Arnaud's, and that one day, despite my best efforts, Khoi would find a way back to her. They were impossible to tear apart.

I looked over the bridge at the water below. Marcelle was looking at water, too. And in a few days, her view would be of the Seine. She had said many times how at home she was in Indochine. But it was my turn. It was my time to make it home.

I finished reading the article.

The Nguyen family had started to expand their silk empire, the writer detailed. They were building a large factory in the north thanks to their recent acquisition of the Compagnie Générale des Soies in Lyon, a company that was previously seen as a rival. It had had large textile holdings in Nam Dinh, and had the potential to compete with native companies, with Nguyen silk, if the colonial government backed it. Instead, the Compagnie Générale des Soies had just sold its holdings to the Nguyens.

Hanoi was a very small town. Marcelle and Trieu I had managed to exile, but Khoi remained on top. The Nguyens could have their silk, but the natives could never have our rubber.

That train ride with my family was much more enjoyable than any moment I'd spent traveling alone. And when we reached the hotel in Tourane, Victor suggested that I sleep in the same bed as Lucie. She cuddled next to me, falling asleep under my armpit with the light next to us still on. It was the first night since we'd arrived that we hadn't needed a fan, so I just listened to her breathe, reaching down and touching her perfect face. Lucie Eleanor Michelin Lesage.

I kissed Lucie again, then rose out of bed and found Lanh's gift, which Lucie had placed on my suitcase, a new one with an intact handle.

I undid the ribbon that was tied around the gift and smiled as I realized it was one of Lucie's white hair ribbons. It was silk, likely Nguyen silk. I laid it flat on the suitcase and unwrapped the box. Inside was a large, thick sheet of paper that was rolled up tight. I slowly unfurled it, my smile growing as I did. It was the train timetable from the Hanoi rail station.

I looked at the first line. The train to Haiphong left Hanoi twice a day, once at nine a.m., then again at six p.m. I ran my fingers gently over the schedule from left to right, then up and down. At the very top of it, Lucie had drawn a large, yellow sun.

·✦·

Epilogue

Lucie Lesage
Paris, France
September 24, 1956

"Shall I try to drop you closer to the entrance, *madame*?" the taxi driver asked as we pulled up to the Gare Saint-Lazare, the classical façade darkened by heavy rains. "Do you have an umbrella? I can escort you in if not, though short of forging a tunnel to the entrance, we will not stay dry. Look," he said, gesturing outside. "This weather reminds me of the early hours of *la crue de la Seine*, the great flood of 1910," he went on, his eyes darting up to the rearview mirror to see me. "I was just a boy then, but I remember it so well. Saint-Lazare, it was like a castle floating on the sea—"

"I do have an umbrella, yes, thank you," I said, interrupting him and reaching down to pick it up from the damp taxi floor.

"Good," he said, eyes back on the road. "It will help. A little," he added, trying to maneuver the black Citroën taxi between the rows of cars all trying to inch closer to the station. I looked at the Citroën's familiar dashboard as he stepped quickly on the gas to squeeze between two more taxis that had just turned in opposite directions. My family's company, Michelin, had become the majority shareholder of Citroën at the end of 1934. That celebratory day in December was the first time I'd ever tasted champagne. My parents had consumed at least a dozen glasses between them and were not the least bit bothered when I simply picked up a bottle and gulped straight from it.

After the driver slowed to a stop near the main entrance, I reached in my bag and paid the fare. In front of us, men and women ran quickly, holding all sorts of things over their heads to fend off the rain—umbrellas, newspapers, small traveling bags, heavy suitcases, a towel, even a leafy branch that was doing nothing to keep the inventive young man's head dry.

"You weren't alive in 1910," the driver continued, "but you must have seen photographs of that day. The heavy rainfall. The aftermath. We Parisians are used to a drizzle, but nothing like that. Or this."

I nodded and pulled the belt of my beige raincoat a little tighter. "I've experienced rain like the day of the great flood," I said, placing a silk scarf over my head and tying it tightly around my neck. "But it wasn't in Paris. It was in Indochine. Many years ago, in Indochine."

He turned around in his seat. "Now we say *le Viet Nam. L'Indochine, c'est fini.*"

"Yes," I acknowledged, "I know." Two years ago, Indochine finally became *le Viet Nam,* after nearly a decade of war with France. It was still divided between the communist north and anticommunist south, but it was its own now, no longer a French colony. "When I was there," I said firmly, "it was Indochine."

I opened the door and ran to the station, feeling like a well-outfitted duck. Inside, I joined hundreds of others who also looked like they'd arrived via bathtub. All around me coats were being removed and shaken out, hair patted dry, laments muttered about ruined shoes and delayed trains.

I took off my own coat and scarf and then joined the line at the ticket counter, requesting a first-class seat for the three p.m. train to Deauville.

"The train is delayed one hour," the seller said. "And then, it will only leave if the rain lets up. It doesn't look like it will, but take a chance if you'd like."

"I will," I said, handing him the fare. "And you may be surprised. Sometimes the heaviest rains are the shortest."

He nodded politely and motioned to the man behind me to step forward.

I took my bag and walked to the restaurants near the shopping arcade. The smell of damp clothes permeated the air along with a feeling of agitation, of having to travel with wet stockings. I entered the first café I saw, sat under a large advertisement for Rouyer cognac, and ordered a coffee. In the corner, Charles Aznavour's "Sur Ma Vie" was playing on a record player, a song that was being hummed in every corner of France. I sipped the coffee and smiled at the waiter. "Do you have anything else?" I asked.

"Besides coffee?"

"No, besides this song," I said, nodding toward the corner.

"Of course, *madame*. If you think you're tired of hearing it, imagine how I feel." He let the song finish and then changed the record. A few seconds later Jo Stafford's "You Belong to Me," an American hit from a few years before, filled the room and I nodded in appreciation.

I ordered a croissant, ate it slowly, and had started to signal to the waiter for another coffee when I glimpsed something through the café's glass door that made my heart catch. I stood up immediately, nearly knocking over the table with my knees.

"Are you all right, *madame*?" the waiter asked as he approached.

"I'm fine. I'm sorry," I said, reaching into my bag. "I must go." I dropped coins on the table, too many coins, and pushed the chair back in a hurry.

"You saw a ghost?" he asked.

"No," I said, without looking at him. "I saw a color."

I rushed back into the humming crowds. Among the dark pantlegs and damp skirts, I was sure I'd seen a flash of green silk covering a woman's legs. But not any green. Nguyen green. A dress in the most beautiful hue caught between the practical grays and lifeless blues of the other travelers.

I walked out to the Salle des Pas Perdus, the waiting hall, tempted to crouch onto the floor to have a better look. I was quite sure that there was only one woman in the world who would wear green silk of that particular shade in a rainstorm. Marcelle de Fabry.

I darted from corner to corner as quickly as I could despite my traveling bag starting to feel like a sack of cement hanging on my arm. I looked everywhere, but I didn't see Marcelle, or any woman in green silk.

I had lived in the same city as Marcelle de Fabry for seventeen years, that much I knew, and I had never seen her. Looking for her had become a habit, especially when I was in the Fourth Arrondissement, as I'd heard she lived on the Quai de Bethune, yet until today I hadn't even glimpsed her shadow.

Marcelle de Fabry. The woman my mother hated. The woman who had tried to poison her, or kill her, depending on who was telling the story. My father leaned toward kill. My mother had settled on poison. Maybe it was because of these stories, or through my understanding of Indochine as I grew up, of the growing number of people, French and Vietnamese, who believed what Marcelle did, but she had become mythical to me.

I had only met her once, but that moment had sewn itself into my memory. We had spoken in Hanoi shortly after my family arrived on a day when my mother was ill. Marcelle had come into our yellow house, conversed with my mother's servant Trieu for quite some time, and then talked to me in a way that made me feel very grown up. She'd been wearing green silk that day. A color that I eventually learned was known in Indochine as Nguyen green.

Perhaps I hadn't seen what I thought I had. Perhaps it was just speaking about Indochine with the taxi driver that made my imagination conjure Marcelle, the old memories flooding me like the rain outside. I'd only spent six years in Indochine, but they were formative years. I arrived at age seven, and when we left in July 1939, just two months before France declared war on Germany, I was thirteen, and a very different child. I suppose I wasn't a child at all.

My parents didn't want to leave, even with the war looming, and neither did I, but my father's family, my grandmother in particular, insisted. The world was descending into madness, she'd said. It was safer for us to be home at such a time. Especially since my mother had just had a baby, my brother Charles.

I had told my mother then that we were already home and she'd nodded and said, "I know. We will come back when the dust settles." We had never returned. Since 1939, we'd all lived in Paris. Never— much to my parents' grave disappointment—in Clermont-Ferrand.

The extended Michelin family had made promises to my father, that much I was aware of. I knew that going to Clermont, the fulfill-ment of those promises, was contingent on peace and prosperity on our plantations. We had prosperity while my father was at the helm, good schools and a nicer orphanage thanks to my mother's efforts, but we never had peace. He hadn't been able to get the plantations to settle, as he used to call it. Even when he started spending weeks at a time at Dau Tieng and Phu Rieng when we moved to Saigon, the un-rest never stopped. The family in Clermont-Ferrand was disappointed by the ongoing turmoil, the dismal mortality rates, the continued rise in communist activity. They were particularly sensitive to the unrest because from 1936 on, Clermont was no longer immune from it. In June of that year there were twelve thousand strikes in France and Mi-chelin was included. Thousands of workers at our factories hoisted up a red flag and screamed their support for France's largest labor union. In 1937 it was again my father's turn to deal with uprisings, a massive strike at Dau Tieng. We sent many men to prison after military inter-vention, and as my father said, "It didn't make Michelin look good."

But since Michelin was still financially prosperous, there were no plans to sell the land. We had held on during the Second World War and during the French Indochina War, even though parts of our plantations had been destroyed and European overseers killed. "Michelin rubber will always come from Indochine," my father declared.

But Victor Lesage was no longer the one to guarantee that. After we returned, he was placed in charge of the Michelin guides in Paris, which had ceased being printed during the war. But in 1944 the guide was requested by the Allied forces and my father took charge of re-printing our 1939 edition. Within weeks, they were in the hands of all the American soldiers, the maps of utmost importance, and even had translations done by my mother added to the back.

My parents had money and the right name, they'd contributed to the war effort, but they were never let inside the machine at Clermont, even when so many of the Michelins died fighting, a reality that only made the company seem more French, more important, more patri-otic. That a decade later they were still making books instead of tires had taken a terrible beating on their pride. They carried that burden, but they carried it together. Through everything, my parents had held on to each other.

Soon after we'd moved back to Paris, I found a picture in the back of an old Michelin guide, made when the covers were blue. The photo-graph was taken on a beautiful boat in Ha Long Bay and Marcelle and my mother were next to each other, all smiles and lightness, along with the most attractive set of people I'd ever seen. My father was not there.

I loved that my mother looked happy, as it was taken during a period during which I remembered her as anything but. I now un-derstood why. After Indochine, my mother was very frank with me. The early days in Hanoi had been a difficult time in her marriage, but not the hardest time in her life. That had been her childhood. I knew about Eleanor, my namesake. I'd still never been to America and my mother had only returned once, to attend the funeral of her brother Peter, who had hanged himself from an oak tree. She'd explained why he had, and said that if I ever wanted to travel to America, she'd allow it. Even to Virginia. I told her that I had no desire to. Where I wanted to go was back to Indochine. "When the dust settles," she repeated.

We both knew that it was a place where the dust had a lot of trouble settling.

Wandering back to the Salle des Pas Perdues, the room of lost steps, I looked at my mother's watch, flipping it around to the face, and realized it was time to make my way to the trains. I entered the Salle d'Échanges and was suddenly flooded by sunlight streaming in from the pointed glass canopies. It was still raining, but the drops were falling much softer now. When I reached the middle of the platform, I surveyed the tracks, remembering a story my mother had once told me about one of the strangest days we spent in Indochine. I wondered which one of the tracks I was looking at now would take me to Normandy, to Deauville, where my husband and children were waiting for me to begin our holiday. I had stayed back to finish our first Michelin guide to Italy and had closed it with the decision to award no stars. Italian cuisine was all one flavor, I'd determined: tomato.

Then, in the noise of the station, I heard something. A name called out, the name of a man I had never met.

Across the platform was Marcelle de Fabry, in a green silk dress. Walking toward her was Nguyen Khoi.

I moved a few steps back, not wanting to be seen. I was thirty years old now, and Marcelle surely wouldn't be able to place me as the seven-year-old girl she'd made such an impression on, but I didn't want to take the risk.

I had never seen Khoi before. I had stared at his picture many times in the newspapers, and had followed his movements over the years because of Lanh. Once my family sailed back to France, Lanh returned to Hanoi to be closer to his sister and started working as the driver for the governor-general, thanks to a good word from my father. Despite the miles between us, we exchanged letters often. It was he who told me that during the war for independence Khoi's beautiful house, one filled with a wife and four children, had been taken over by the government and turned into a boarding school.

Lanh and I also wrote about the train stations. We still called

Hanoi's the House of a Hundred Suns and Saigon's the Second Sun. Saint Lazare, we decided, was the Waiting Sun. One awaiting his arrival. And we wrote about the people we had shared our lives with. He told me about Trieu and her role in the rise of the Communist Party. About how she had traveled to China and had led an underground cell in Tonkin upon her return. She'd married a fellow leader and had been in prison herself when he was shot by a French firing squad in 1940. Now she worked for the party in the north, no longer hiding her political identity.

Khoi had his arm around Marcelle now, who was as elegant as I remembered. She looked as if she'd been born in that color green, and he was as striking as in the picture on the boat, even though his hair way starting to gray.

It was Lanh who had told me of Marcelle de Fabry's divorce after the Second World War. Almost a decade later, in 1954, he wrote to say Khoi had moved with his wife and children to Paris, as they had lost everything in the revolution. Nguyen silk had been nationalized, all the family's private property seized by the government. He had come to Paris and was living as other moneyed Vietnamese were, as an émigré. In 1955 he had been granted a divorce and two months later had married Marcelle, the woman who haunted me, and my family; the woman who'd always had his heart.

Lanh once said that all roads led to train stations, and as I had learned in my childhood, Lanh was seldom wrong. I looked around me, at the station that Claude Monet had painted eleven times, at the people waiting for their trains. There were no shoeblacks desperate for customers, no bags so worn at the edges that the clothes were falling out at the seams. The porters didn't have glassy eyes, the sugarcane had been replaced with chocolates and roasted hazelnuts. And almost everyone looked cut from the same cloth. Except for Marcelle and Khoi.

To some, I imagined, they were just two elegant people well into middle age. To others they were an upsetting sight—a pair who shouldn't be together. But they were proof that the outside world didn't matter, all you needed was two—coupled with a youthful daring that for them was proving to be ageless. In France the color green meant money, envy, new beginnings. In Viet Nam it meant Nguyen *lua*. And for those few souls who didn't know the silk company, the color green meant lust. That's what they were to me. The passion of a nation desperate to be its own, the desire of two people trying to live differently. I looked again at the woman who was still audacious enough to wear three yards of green silk in a rainstorm and then closed my eyes, listening to the light tap of the raindrops. It now sounded like applause.

Acknowledgments

Many thanks to:

My brilliant, lovely, and amazing-in-every-way editor, Sarah Cantin at St. Martin's Press. Sarah, can you believe this is book five together? What an honor to have worked on every one of my novels with you. Thank you for championing this story and making it sing like only you can.

Bridget Matzie, my wonderful agent, who guides each project with an expert hand.

The brilliant team at St. Martin's, especially Sally Richardson, Jennifer Enderlin, George Witte, Andrew Martin, Lisa Senz, Katie Bassel, Michael Storrings, Rachel Diebel, Sallie Lotz, Brant Janeway, and Jordan Hanley.

Eagle-eyed copy editor Mary Beth Constant.

Liz Ward, who yet again served as my first reader and editor. Liz, I stand in awe of your way with words.

Professor Martina T. Nguyen, who so generously gave her time and expertise to this project and helped me make sure that I was honoring a country, its history, and its people to the best of my abilities.

Yolande Vu for her invaluable help translating phrases from English to Vietnamese.

Rachel and Jim Dougan, who have championed me and my work since my first book and were especially helpful with this one. I hope to one day be as creative as the both of you.

My squad in Washington, D.C., and beyond who kept me sane and motivated every step of the way, especially Raia Margo and Aliénor van den Bosch.

D. Neary, forever an inspiration.

Georgia Bobley, my favorite early reader.

Kari-Lynn Rockefeller for cheering me on and constantly dropping knowledge.

Professor Kathleen Hart and the Vassar College French Department for feeding my love of French and teaching the works of brilliant francophone writers from all over the world.

The staff of the Washington, D.C., Wing who supported me, and made me laugh even when I was crashing on deadline. I'm so lucky to have written this book in such a gorgeous space and with so many talented women by my side.

My brother Ken, a force of positivity.

My incredibly patient husband, Craig. Always the anchor, allowing me to be the sail. You are in a class apart.

My parents. In so many ways, this book is for you. A brilliant, wonderful Asian man and a beautiful European French-speaking woman still in love fifty-plus years later.

I am so appreciative that I had the following resources to turn to as I wrote:

Les plantations Michelin au Viêt-Nam by Eric Panthou; *The Red Earth: A Vietnamese Memoir of Life on a Colonial Rubber Plantation* by Trần Tử Bình; *French Women and the Empire: The Case of Indochine* by Marie-Paule Ha; *Dumb Luck* by Vũ Trọng Phụng; *Before the Revolution: The Vietnamese Peasants Under the French* by Ngo Vinh Long; *Métisse Blanche* by Kim Lefèvre; *The Devil's Milk: A Social History of Rubber* by John A. Tully; *On and Off Duty in Annam* by Gabrielle von Hoenstadt; *Indochina: An Ambiguous Colonization, 1858–1954* by Pierre Brocheux and Daniel Hémery; the Bates College honors thesis "Private Union, Public Conflict: Life and Labor at Michelin in the Twentieth Century" by Madeleine Curtis McCabe; "The Scientist, the Governor, and the Planter: The Political Economy of Agricultural Knowledge in Indochina During the Creation of a 'Science of Rubber,' 1900–1940" by Michitake Aso, and the websites entreprises-coloniales.fr, belleindochine.free.fr, saigoneer.com, and historicvietnam.com.

To see a list of all the Vietnamese words and phrases used in this book with full diacritical marks, please visit my website, at www.karintanabe.com.